THE WHISPER

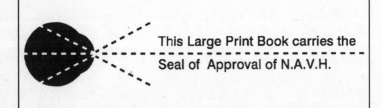

This Large Print Book carries the
Seal of Approval of N.A.V.H.

THE WHISPER

CARLA NEGGERS

THORNDIKE PRESS
A part of Gale, Cengage Learning

GALE
CENGAGE Learning™

Detroit • New York • San Francisco • New Haven, Conn • Waterville, Maine • London

GALE
CENGAGE Learning

Copyright © 2010 by Carla Neggers.
Thorndike Press, a part of Gale, Cengage Learning.

Thorndike Press® Large Print Basic.
The text of this Large Print edition is unabridged.
Other aspects of the book may vary from the original edition.
Set in 16 pt. Plantin.

LIBRARY OF CONGRESS CATALOGING-IN-PUBLICATION DATA

Neggers, Carla.
  The whisper / by Carla Neggers.
    p. cm.
  Originally published: New York : Mira, 2010.
  ISBN-13: 978-1-4104-2706-9
  ISBN-10: 1-4104-2706-4
    1. Women archaeologists—Fiction. 2. Murder—Investigation—Fiction.
  3. Boston (Mass.)—Fiction. 4. Large type books. I. Title.
  PS3564.E2628W47 2010
  813'.54—dc22   2010017464

Published in 2010 in arrangement with Harlequin Books S.A.

Printed in the United States of America
1 2 3 4 5 6 7 14 13 12 11 10

For Leo

1

Beara Peninsula, Southwest Ireland — late September

Scoop Wisdom opened his daypack, got out his water bottle and took a drink. He sat on a cold, damp rock inside the remains of the isolated Irish stone cottage where the long summer had started with a beautiful woman, a tale of magic and fairies — and a killer obsessed with his own ideas of good and evil.

The autumn equinox had passed. Summer was over. Scoop told himself it was a new beginning, but he had unfinished business. It'd been gnawing at him ever since he'd regained consciousness in his Boston hospital room a month ago, after a bomb blast had almost killed him.

He was healed. It was time to go home and get back to work. Be a cop again.

He set his water bottle back in his pack and zipped up the outer compartment. A solitary ray of sunshine penetrated the tangle of vines above him where once there'd been a thatched roof. He could hear the rush of the stream just outside the ruin.

And water splashing. Scoop shifted position on the rock, listening, but there was no doubt. Someone — or something — was tramping in the stream that wound down from the rocky, barren hills above Kenmare Bay. He hadn't seen anyone on his walk up from the cottage where he was staying on a quiet country lane.

He stood up. He could hear laughter now.

A woman's laughter.

Irish fairies, maybe? Out here on the southwest Irish coast, on the rugged Beara Peninsula, he could easily believe fairies were hiding in the greenery that grew thick on the banks of the stream.

He stepped over fallen rocks to the opening that had served as the only entrance to what once had been someone's home. He could feel a twinge of pain in his hip where shrapnel had cut deep when the bomb went off at the triple-decker he owned with Bob O'Reilly and Abigail Browning, two other Boston detectives. He had taken most of the blistering shards of metal and wood in the meatier parts of his back, shoulders, arms and legs, but one chunk had lodged in the base of his skull, making everyone nervous for a day or so. A millimeter this way or that, and he'd be dead instead of wondering if fairies were about to arrive at his Irish ruin for a visit.

He heard more water splashing and more female laughter.

"I know, I know." It was a woman, her tone amused, her accent American. "Of *course* I'd run into a big black dog up here in these particular hills."

In his two weeks in Ireland, Scoop had heard whispers about a large, fierce black dog occasionally turning up in the pastures above the small fishing and farming village. He'd seen only sheep and cows himself.

He peered into the gray mist. The morning sun was gone, at least for the moment. He'd learned to expect changeable weather. Brushed by the Gulf Stream, the climate of the Southwest was mild and wet, but he'd noticed on his walks that the flowers of summer were fading and the heather on the hills was turning brown.

"Ah." The woman again, still out of sight around a sharp bend in the stream. "You're coming with me, are you? I must be very close, then. Lead the way, my new friend."

The ruin was easy to miss amid the dense trees and undergrowth on the banks of the

9

stream. If he hadn't known where to look, Scoop would have gone right past it his first time out here.

A woman with wild, dark red hair ducked under the low-hanging branches of a gnarly tree. Ambling next to her in the shallow water was, indeed, a big black dog.

The woman looked straight at Scoop, and even in the gray light, he saw that she had bright blue eyes and freckles — a lot of freckles. She was slim and angular, her hair down to her shoulders, damp and tangled. She continued toward him, the dog staying close to her. She didn't seem particularly taken aback by finding a man standing in the doorway of the remote ruin. Scoop wouldn't blame her if she did. Even before the bomb blast, he had looked, according to friends and enemies alike, ferocious with his thick build, shaved head and general take-no-prisoners demeanor.

For sure, no one would mistake him for a leprechaun or a fairy prince.

Her left foot sank into a soft spot and almost ended up in the water. Mud stains came to the top of her wellies. "I saw footprints back there," she said cheerfully, pointing a slender hand in the direction she'd just come. "Since I've never run into a cow or a sheep that wears size-twelve

10

shoes, I figured someone else was out here. A fine day for a walk, isn't it?"

"It is," Scoop said.

"I don't mind the outbreaks of rain." She tilted her head back, letting the mist collect on her face a moment, then smiled at him. "I don't do well in the sun."

Scoop stepped down from the threshold and nodded to the dog, still panting at her side. "Yours?"

"No, but he's a sweetheart. I suppose he could be aggressive if he or someone he cared about felt threatened."

A warning? Scoop noticed she wore a rain jacket the same shade of blue as her eyes and held an iPhone in one hand, perhaps keeping it available in case she needed to call for help. It would be easy to think it was still 1900 in this part of Ireland, but that would be a mistake. For one thing, the area had decent cell phone coverage.

"Looks as if you two have bonded."

"I think we have, indeed." She slipped the iPhone into a jacket pocket. "You're the detective who saved that girl's life when the bomb went off at your house in Boston last month — Wisdom, right? Detective Cyrus Wisdom?"

He was instantly on alert, but he kept his voice even. "Most people call me Scoop.

11

And you would be?"

"Sophie — Sophie Malone. We have friends in common," she said, easing past him to the ruin. The dog stayed by the stream. "I'm from Boston originally. I'm an archaeologist."

"What kind of archaeologist?"

She smiled. "The barely employed kind. You're in Ireland to recuperate? I heard you were hurt pretty badly."

"I ended up here after attending a friend's wedding in Scotland a few weeks ago."

"Abigail Browning's wedding. She's the detective who was kidnapped when the bomb went off."

"I know who she is."

Sophie Malone seemed unfazed by his response. Abigail was still on her extended honeymoon with Owen Garrison, an international search-and-rescue expert with roots in Boston, Texas and Maine. Will Davenport had offered them his house in the Scottish Highlands for their long-awaited wedding, and they'd accepted, quickly gathering family and friends together in early September. Scoop, just out of the hospital, had had no intention of missing the ceremony.

"Wasn't it too soon for you to fly given your injuries?" Sophie asked.

12

"I got through it."

She studied him, her expression suggesting a focused, intelligent mind. He had on a sweatshirt and jeans, but she'd be able to see one of his uglier scars, a purple gash that started under his right ear and snaked around the back of his head. Finally she said, "It must be hard not to be in Boston with the various ongoing investigations. You have all the bad guys, though, right? They're either dead or under arrest —"

"I thought you said you were an archaeologist. How do you know all this?"

"I keep up with the news."

That, Scoop decided, wasn't the entire truth. He was very good — one of the best in the Boston Police Department — at detecting lies and deception, and if Sophie Malone wasn't exactly lying, she wasn't exactly telling the truth, either.

She placed her hand on the rough, gray stone of the ruin. "You know Keira Sullivan, don't you?"

Keira was the folklorist and artist who had discovered the ruin three months ago, on the night of the summer solstice. She was also Lieutenant Bob O'Reilly's niece. "I do, yes," Scoop said. "Is Keira one of the friends we have in common?"

"We've never met, actually." Sophie

13

stepped up onto the crumbling threshold of the ruin. "This place has been abandoned for a long time."

"According to local villagers, the original occupants either died or emigrated during the Great Famine of the 1840s."

"That would make sense. This part of Ireland was hit hard by the famine and subsequent mass emigration. That's how my family ended up in the U.S. The Malone side." She glanced back at Scoop, a spark in her blue eyes. "Tell me, Detective Wisdom, do you believe fairies were here that night with Keira?"

Scoop didn't answer. Standing in front of an Irish ruin with a scary black dog and a smart, pretty redhead, he could believe just about anything. He took in his surroundings — the fine mist, the multiple shades of green, the rocks, the rush of the stream. His senses were heightened, as if Irish fairies had put a spell on him.

He had never been so in danger of falling in love at first sight.

He gave himself a mental shake. Was he out of his mind? He grinned at Sophie as she stepped down from the ruin. "You're not a fairy princess yourself, are you?"

She laughed. "That would be Keira. Artist, folklorist and fairy princess."

14

Sophie's expression turned more serious. "She wasn't reckless coming out here alone, you know."

"Any more than you are being reckless now?"

"Or you," she countered, then nodded to the dog, who had flopped in the wet grass. "Besides, I have my new friend here. He doesn't appear to have any quarrel with you. He joined me when I got to the stream. He must be the same dog who helped Keira the night she was trapped here."

"You didn't read that in the papers," Scoop said.

"I live in Ireland," she said vaguely. She seemed more tentative now. "The man who was also here that night . . . the serial killer. Jay Augustine. He won't ever be in a position to hurt anyone else, will he?"

Scoop didn't answer at once. Just what was he to make of his visitor? Finally he said, "Augustine's in jail awaiting trial for first-degree murder. He has a good lawyer and he's not talking, but he's not going anywhere. He'll stay behind bars for the rest of his life."

Sophie's gaze settled on an uprooted tree off to one side of the ruin. "That's where he smeared the sheep's blood, isn't it?"

Scoop stiffened. "Okay, Sophie Malone.

15

You know a few too many details. Who are you?"

"Sorry." She pushed her hands through her damp hair. "Being here makes what happened feel real and immediate. I didn't expect this intense a reaction. Keira and I both know Colm Dermott, the anthropologist organizing the conference on Irish folklore in April. It's in two parts, one in Cork and one in Boston."

"I know Colm. Is he the one who told you about the black dog?"

She nodded. "I ran into him last week in Cork. I've just completed a postdoctoral fellowship at the university there. I hadn't paid much attention to what all went on out here and in Boston." She took a breath. "I'm glad Keira wasn't hurt."

"So am I."

Sophie looked up sharply, as if his tone had given away some unexpected, hidden feeling — which for all he knew it had — but she quickly turned back toward the cottage, mist glistening on her rain jacket and deep red hair. "Do you believe Keira really did see the stone angel that night?"

"Doesn't matter what I believe."

"You're very concrete, aren't you?" She didn't wait for an answer. "The story she was researching is so charming — three

16

Irish brothers in a never-ending struggle with fairies over a stone angel. The brothers believe it'll bring them luck. The fairies believe it's one of their own turned to stone. Every three months, on the night of the solstice or the equinox, the angel appears on the hearth of a remote cottage in the hills above Kenmare Bay."

"The old woman who told the story to Keira in Boston —"

"Also told it to Jay Augustine, and he killed her," Sophie said, finishing for him. "Colm says when Keira came out here in search of this place she thought she might encounter a bit of fairy mischief. Maybe she even hoped she would. But a killer? It's too horrible to think about."

Scoop stood back, feeling the isolation of the old ruin. Except for the dog and the sheep up in the pastures above the stream, it was just him and the woman in front of him. How did he even know she was an archaeologist? Why should he believe a word she said?

"As many tombs and ruins as I've crawled through in my work, I'm not much on small spaces." She seemed to shrug off thoughts of blood and violence as she tugged her hood over her hair. "You can imagine contentious Irish brothers and trooping fair-

17

ies out here, can't you? Keira's story is very special. I love tales of the wee folk."

"Believe in fairies, do you?"

"Some days more than others."

"So, Sophie Malone," Scoop said, "why are you here?"

"Fairies, a black dog and an ancient stone angel aren't reason enough?"

"Maybe, but they're not the whole story."

"Ah. We archaeologists can be very mysterious. We're also curious. I wanted to see the ruin for myself. You're a detective, Scoop. Okay if I call you Scoop?"

"Sure."

"You can understand curiosity, can't you?"

He shrugged. "Sometimes."

Her sudden, infectious smile reached to her eyes. "Ah. I can see you don't like coincidences. You want to know how we both decided to come here this morning. I didn't follow you, if that helps. I've never been subtle enough to follow people."

"But you weren't surprised to find me here," Scoop said.

"I wasn't, especially not after seeing those size-twelve footprints in the mud." She eased in next to the dog. "I'll be on my way."

"Are you heading straight back to the village?"

"Maybe." She patted the dog as he rose

18

next to her. "I'll have to see where my new friend here leads me. Good to meet you, Detective." She smiled again. "Scoop. Maybe I'll see you in Boston sometime."

Scoop watched her and the big black dog duck back under the gnarly tree. She had a positive, energetic air about her. Nothing suggested she wasn't an archaeologist. Whoever she was, he'd bet she was the type who wouldn't let go once she got the bit in her teeth.

What bit did Sophie Malone have in her teeth? What, exactly, had brought her out here?

He slipped back into the ruin, smelling the damp stone and dirt. He reached for his backpack. This time he didn't notice any pain in his hip. As he slung his pack onto his shoulder, he peered through the gray, dim light at the hearth where Keira claimed to have seen the ancient stone angel as the ruin partially collapsed around her. When she finally climbed out the following morning, the angel was gone. Whatever the case, no one else had ever actually seen it.

Keira would only say she believed the angel was where it was meant to be.

Scoop pictured Sophie walking upstream with the black dog next to her, her red hair flying, her bright blue eyes, her slim hips —

her smile.

Yep. Love at first sight.

"Damn," he muttered, adjusting the pack on his shoulder, feeling only a dull ache where once there'd been fiery pain.

Being in this place was definitely getting to him.

He headed back outside. The mist had subsided, and the sun was angling through the wet trees. He noticed Sophie's and the dog's footprints in the mud. She was right about the ongoing investigations in Boston, but she was wrong about one thing. They didn't have all the bad guys. The major players in the violence of the past three months were dead or under arrest, but there were still unanswered questions. In particular, Scoop wanted to know who had placed a crude explosive device under the gas grill on Abigail's first-floor back porch.

Even if it was a cop.

Even, he thought, if it was a friend.

He was an internal affairs detective, and two months ago, he'd launched a special investigation into the possible involvement of a member of the department with local thugs. His bomber?

Maybe, maybe not, but Scoop didn't much like the idea that another cop had almost blown him up.

He started back along the stream, Sophie's and the dog's footprints disappearing as the ground became drier, grassier. When the stream curved sharply downhill, he emerged from the trees into the open, rock-strewn green pasture high above the bay. A stiff, sudden breeze blew a few lingering raindrops into his face as he continued across the sheep-clipped grass. He came to a barbed-wire fence and climbed over it, jumping down onto the soft, moist ground. On his first hike up here two weeks ago, tackling the fence had caused significant pain, and he'd caught a still-healing wound on a barb, drawing blood. Now he was moving well and seldom felt any pain, and his scars were tougher.

A fat, woolly sheep appeared on the steep hillside above him. Scoop grinned. "Yeah, pal, it's me again."

The sheep stayed put. Scoop looked out across Kenmare Bay to the jagged outline of the Macgillicuddy Reeks on the much larger Iveragh Peninsula. He'd driven its famous Ring of Kerry and done a few hikes over there, but he'd spent most of his time in Ireland on the Beara.

He continued across the steep pasture to another fence. He climbed over it onto a dirt track that led straight downhill to the village. As he passed a Beware Of Bull sign tacked to a fence post, a movement caught his eye. He paused, squinting through the gray mist. Across the pasture, he saw a large black dog lope through the middle of an ancient stone circle and disappear into a stand of trees.

It had to be the same dog he'd seen with Sophie Malone.

The mysterious redheaded archaeologist was nowhere in sight, but Scoop knew — he couldn't explain how but he knew — he'd be seeing her again.

He smiled to himself. Maybe fairies *had* put a spell on him.

2

Sophie didn't let down her guard until she reached Kenmare.

She drove straight to the town pier, parked and pried her fingers off the steering wheel. As if the black dog hadn't been enough to remind her she was out of her element on the Beara, she'd had to run into a suspicious, absolute stud of a Boston detective.

She exhaled, calming herself. Going out to Keira Sullivan's ruin would have been enough of a heart-pounding experience all by itself, without Scoop Wisdom. He was as tough, straightforward and no-nonsense as she'd expected from the accounts of the violence in Boston over the summer, but he'd looked as if he'd been awaiting the arrival of ghosts or fairies.

He'd gotten her instead.

And what was she?

She hadn't lied. She *was* an archaeologist.

23

But she hadn't told him everything — not by far — and obviously he knew it.

Sophie got out of her little car and paused to watch a rainbow arc across the sky high above the bay. The yellow, orange, red and lavender-blue streaks deepened and brightened, tugging at her emotions. She'd miss Irish rainbows when she was back in Boston.

She shook off her sudden melancholy. She was leaving tomorrow, and her parents and twin sister were arriving in Kenmare later that afternoon for a send-off dinner. In the meantime, getting weepy over Irish rainbows wasn't on her ever-expanding to-do list.

She squinted out at the boats in the harbor. The Irish name for the village was *Neidín,* which translated as "little nest," an apt description for its location at the base of the Cork and Kerry mountains.

"Aha," she said aloud when she recognized Tim O'Donovan's rugged commercial fishing boat tied to the pier. The old boat looked as if it would sink before it got halfway out of the harbor, but she knew from experience that it could handle rough seas.

She spotted Tim by a post and waved to him. He was a tall, burly, Irish fisherman with a bushy, sand-colored beard and emerald-green eyes. He glanced in her

24

direction, and even at a distance, she heard him groan. She could hardly blame him, given his unwitting involvement in her own strange experience on the Irish coast a year ago — months before Keira Sullivan's encounter with a serial killer.

Whispers in the dark. Blood-soaked branches. Celtic artifacts gone missing.

A woman — me, Sophie thought — left for dead in a cold, dank cave.

Suppressing a shudder, she made her way onto the concrete pier. Tim had managed to avoid her for months, but he wouldn't today. She moved fast, determined to get to him before he could jump into his boat and be off.

When she reached him, she made a stab at being conversational. "Hey, Tim, it's good to see you." She pointed up at the fading rainbow. "Did you notice the rainbow just now?"

"If you want me to take you to chase a pot of gold, the answer is no."

"I'm not chasing anything."

"You're always chasing something." He yanked on a thick rope with his callused hands and didn't look at her as he spoke in his heavy Kerry accent. "How are you, Sophie?"

"Doing great." It was close enough to the

truth. "I gave up my apartment in Cork and moved into our family house in Kenmare. My parents and sister will be here later today. I've been here two weeks. I thought I'd run into you by now."

"Ah-huh."

"Have you been seeing to it I didn't?"

"Just doing my work."

"I've been back and forth to Cork and Dublin a fair amount. My father's family is originally from Kenmare. I've told you that, haven't I?"

"Along the way, yes." His tone suggested that playing on their common Irish roots would have no effect on him.

"Taryn's only staying for a night or two, but my folks will be here for at least a month."

"You're going back to Boston," Tim said.

"Ah, so you *have* been keeping tabs on me."

He glanced up at her. "Always."

She grinned at him. "You could at least try to look disappointed. We're friends, right?"

He let the thick rope go slack. "You're a dangerous friend to have, Sophie."

With the resurgent sunshine, she unzipped her jacket. "Yeah, well, you weren't the one who spent a frightening night in an Irish cave."

"Oh, no — no, I was the one who didn't talk you out of spending a night alone on an island no bigger than my boat. I was the one who left you there."

"The island is a lot bigger than your boat. Otherwise," she added, trying to sound lighthearted, "you'd have found me faster than you did."

"I was lucky to find you at all, never mind before you took your last breath." He gripped the rope tight again but made no move to untie it and get out of there. Still, he regarded her with open suspicion. "I'm not taking you back there. Don't ask me to."

"I'm not asking. That's not why I'm here. I don't want to go back." She fought off another involuntary shudder. "Not yet, anyway. Maybe one day."

Or maybe not ever, but she wasn't telling Tim that. Whether she was being stubborn or just had her pride, she didn't want him to think she was afraid to return to the tiny island off the Iveragh coast where she'd encountered . . . she wasn't sure what. She knew she'd almost died there.

"Do you still have nightmares?" he asked, less combative.

"Not as many. Do you?"

He grunted. "I never did have nightmares, but as you say, I wasn't the one —"

"That's right, you weren't, and I'm glad of that."

"I hear you finished your dissertation."

She nodded. "It's been signed, sealed, delivered, defended and approved."

"So it's Dr. Malone now, is it?" He seemed more relaxed, although still wary. "What will you be doing in Boston?"

"Mostly looking for a full-time job. I have a few things lined up that'll help pay the rent in the meantime."

Tim's skepticism was almost palpable. "What else?" he asked.

Sophie looked out at the water, dark blue under the clearing early-afternoon sky. Tim O'Donovan was no fool. "Did you know a Boston police detective's staying out on the Beara?"

"Sophie." Tim gave a resigned sigh. "You went to see Keira Sullivan's ruin, didn't you?"

"It makes sense. I'm an archaeologist. I've crawled through literally hundreds of ruins over the past ten years."

"This isn't just another ruin. It's where that Yank serial killer —" He stopped abruptly. "Ah, no. Sophie. Sophie, Sophie.

28

You're not thinking he was responsible for what happened to you. Don't tell me that."

"Okay, I won't."

"Sophie."

"It doesn't matter what I think. He's in jail. He can't hurt me or anyone else."

"I never should have told you that story," Tim said quietly.

Sophie understood. Over Guinness and Irish music one evening a year ago, he had transfixed her with a tale he'd heard from a long-dead uncle who had served as a priest in a small village on the Iveragh Peninsula across Kenmare Bay. A coastal monastery, Viking raids, a secret hoard of pagan Celtic artifacts — how could she have resisted? For centuries — at least according to Tim — the story had been closely held by the priests in the village. It was a tangle of fancy, history, mythology and tradition — with, she'd suspected, a large dose of Tim's Guinness-buzzed Irish blarney.

"I was procrastinating," she said to him now. "That's why I started going out there. I was mentally exhausted, and I just wanted to go on a lark."

"A shopping spree in Dublin wouldn't have done the trick?"

"I never expected to find anything, or end up in a dark cave with spooky stuff happening around me. It wasn't a dream, Tim. It wasn't a hallucination."

"You were knocked on the head."

She sighed. She didn't remember how she'd been rendered unconscious — whether she'd accidentally hit her head scrambling to hide, or whether whoever had been on the island with her had smacked her with a rock. When she'd come to, it was pitch dark, cold and silent in the cave.

Tim unknotted the rope automatically, as he had since he'd been a boy. There were seven O'Donovans. He was the third eldest. "My mother prays for you every night," he said. "She's afraid it was black magic at work, or dark fairies — nothing of this world, that's for certain."

"Thank your mother for me."

"I try not to mention your name to her. I should never have told her what happened. She's the only one who knows —"

"It's okay, Tim."

They'd set off a year ago on a warm, clear late-September morning — Sophie remembered how calm the bay was, how excited she was. She'd had her iPhone and everything she needed for less than twenty-four hours on her own. Tim had returned to pick her up the following morning. When she wasn't at their rendezvous point, he'd set out on foot to look for her. At first he'd assumed she'd got herself sidetracked and was annoyed with her for delaying him. Then he'd found her backpack in a crevice near the cave. She remembered the panic in his voice when she'd heard him calling her, and the relief she'd felt knowing he was there and she would survive her ordeal.

Of course, he'd wanted to kill her himself when she'd crawled out of the cave.

He'd called the guards. By then, there was nothing for them to find. They believed, in spite of Sophie's academic credentials, that what she claimed to have seen and heard was the product of a concussion, dehydration, adrenaline, a touch of hypothermia and no small amount of imagination. They'd made it clear they thought both she *and* Tim were nuts. She for going out there, no matter how experienced and well prepared, he for letting her talk him into leaving her alone overnight on the thimble of an island.

"How long are you going to stay mad at me?" Sophie asked Tim now.

"Until I'm explaining myself before St. Peter, should he have me."

She smiled. "He'll have you because the devil won't."

He grinned back at her, a glint of humor in his green eyes. "True enough. Don't think I don't know why you're here, Sophie Malone. You want to know if anyone's asked me about you, and the answer is no."

"You're sure?"

"Oh, trust me, I'd remember."

"Keira Sullivan is romantically involved with an FBI agent — Simon Cahill — and her uncle's a Boston homicide detective."

"Bob O'Reilly," Tim said. "Yes, I know."

Sophie wasn't surprised. "They've both been out here this summer. There's the Boston detective out on the Beara now. Scoop Wisdom."

"None of them have looked me up. I fish, Sophie, and I play a little music. I stay away from trouble."

"I don't want to cause you any more problems."

Tim stood up straight and looked out at the sparkling harbor. "I believe you, Sophie. I do. I don't know how you hit your head, but I believe you found Celtic treasure. I believe you heard whispers, and I believe you saw hawthorn branches dipped in blood." He turned to her, as serious as she'd ever seen him. "I wish I could tell you who or what it was in that cave with you."

"I wish you could, too, Tim."

"They say the woman who hid the treasure died on the island."

If there ever were such a woman. No historical record existed of her that Sophie had been able to locate. Tim's story told of a woman fleeing to the island with her pagan treasure to escape Viking raids in the eighth century. Then again, he'd said, maybe it had been English raids in the seventeenth century, or maybe to trade for food for the starving in the famine years.

Hard facts were a little tough to pin down.

Sophie had no intention of arguing Irish tales with an Irishman, especially one who was still irritated with her for putting him through hell. She shivered in a sudden gust of wind, but she knew it wasn't the cold she was feeling. It was the lingering effects of that night a year ago.

Tim put a big hand on her shoulder. "Let go of what happened to you." His voice was quiet now. "Get on with your life."

"I am. Don't worry about me, okay?"

"Worry about you?" He laughed, hugging her to him. "I want to drown you in the bay. Dragging me to that barren rock. No sign of you when I came after you. There I was with you gone and nothing but the wind, the waves, the crying birds. I get chilled to the bone thinking about it."

Sophie couldn't help but smile. Tim was dramatic. She glanced up at the brightening sky, no hint left of the rainbow. "I wonder if it was sheep's blood on the branches I saw."

Tim was thoughtful. "It was sheep's blood at the Beara ruin."

"Yes, but Jay Augustine left that blood for Keira Sullivan to find, assuming she lived through the night. The blood and branches I saw disappeared. If I'd managed to get a few drops on me, it would have corroborated my story. The guards could have tested it —"

"Don't, Sophie. What's done is done."

She looked down at Tim's battered boat, bobbing in the rising tide. "We could put all this out of our minds for a while and go sightseeing for seals and puffins."

Tim obviously knew she wasn't serious. "You're playing with fire, Sophie," he said heavily. "You know you are."

"The guards must have a report in their files on what happened a year ago, and obviously they know about Keira's experience on the Beara. They haven't come to reinterview me. I just keep wondering if I missed something. . . ." She didn't finish and instead shook off her questions and smiled at Tim. "Stay in touch, okay?"

"Sophie —"

"All will be well."

"Yes, it will be, please God," he said,

watching her as she headed back down the pier.

"Oh, and Tim," she called cheerfully, turning back to him, "if you want to get anywhere with my sister, trim your beard and bone up on your Yeats."

He jumped into his boat, as comfortable at sea as he was on land. *" 'Tread softly because you tread on my dreams,' "* he recited, crossing his hands over his heart. *" 'A pity beyond all telling is hid in the heart of love.' "*

Sophie laughed, enjoying the moment. She saw he was laughing now, too, and she felt better as she walked to her car.

After their look around the island produced nothing — not even a drop of blood on the gray rock much less a bit of Celtic gold — the guards had asked her and Tim not to discuss the incident in the cave with anyone else, in order to avoid a rush of treasure hunters. She'd tried to put her experience behind her, even to the point of wondering if she, too, should just blame a concussion, dehydration, fatigue, isolation, overwork and imagination — if not ghosts and fairies, which, she suspected, deep down Tim believed were responsible for her ordeal.

Then last week, she'd pulled her head up

from her work and had lunch with Colm Dermott, back in Cork on behalf of the folklore conference, and he'd told her about the violence in Boston over the summer. She'd been vaguely aware that Jay Augustine, a fine art and antiques dealer who had turned out to be a serial killer, had latched on to Keira's Irish story in June and finally was arrested, after trying to kill Keira and her mother. His violence and fascination with the devil and evil had inspired Norman Estabrook, a corrupt, ruthless billionaire, to act on his own violent impulses, which had led to the bomb blast in late August that had injured Scoop Wisdom and culminated in Estabrook's death on the coast of Maine.

Sophie couldn't shake the similarities of Keira's experience on the Beara to her own on the island. She had to know. Had Jay Augustine followed her a year ago and left her for dead? Had he made off with the artifacts — whatever their origin or authenticity — she'd seen in the cave? Without proper examination, she couldn't say for sure what they were, but she had a solid recollection of the pieces — a spun-bronze cauldron, gold brooches, torcs and bracelets, glass beads and bangles. She hadn't imagined them, even if Irish and American authorities had already reviewed her account of her night in the cave and decided it wasn't worth pursuing further.

She climbed into her car. She was tempted to head to the village and settle in her favorite pub for the rest of the day, but instead she got out her iPhone and dialed her brother Damian, an FBI agent in Washington, D.C.

"Hey, Damian," she said. "I was just watching an Irish rainbow and thought I'd call. Taryn's on her way, and Mom and Dad will be here in time for dinner and Irish music. We'll miss you."

"I'll be in Ireland in two weeks."

"I'll be in Boston then. I leave tomorrow. It's not as spur-of-the-moment as it sounds. I'm staying in Taryn's apartment on Beacon Hill. Doesn't that sound cozy?"

"What's going on, Sophie?"

"They teach you that in FBI school — how to turn someone saying 'cozy' into something suspicious? Never mind. I was just out on the Beara Peninsula where that serial killer struck. Would you know if he was involved in smuggling and selling stolen artifacts?"

Silence.

Sophie knew she'd struck a nerve but pretended to be oblivious. "Damian? Are you there? Are we still connected?"

"We're still connected. Any kind of stolen artifacts in mind?"

"Pagan Celtic."

"Why?"

"Because it's my area of expertise. Keira Sullivan's stone angel was Early Medieval Celtic from the sounds of it. I'm just curious if this Augustine character was into Celtic works in general."

"He was interested in killing people, Sophie."

She looked out at the pier, tourists gathering for a boat tour of the coast. "I get your point, Damian, but you know what I mean."

"You're the archaeologist. I'm the FBI agent. You tell me. Do you know anything about Celtic artifacts showing up on the black market?"

This time, she was the one who didn't answer.

"Sophie?"

"My battery's dying. I'll call you later."

She disconnected and dropped her phone back in her jacket pocket. As if putting herself on the radar of one law enforcement officer today wasn't good enough, she'd had to call her FBI agent brother. She started her car and let herself off the hook. Calling Damian made sense. He was assigned to FBI headquarters in Washington. He could

38

find out just about anything.

She wondered if she'd have a better chance if she told him about her experience last year.

"Probably not," she whispered as she drove back down the quiet street. The Irish authorities already knew about the incident. If she told Damian, he'd look into it, and she didn't want to send him and the FBI off on some wild-goose chase if she were totally off target.

More to the point, he'd tell their parents, and why get them all worked up over what could be nothing?

She had a few hours before they arrived. Her sister would get there sooner. Sophie decided to forget missing Celtic artifacts and jailed serial killers for the moment and head to the house and cook, clean and do what she could to make her life look as if her family didn't need to worry about her.

3

Beara Peninsula, Southwest Ireland

A wild hurling match was on the small television in the sole village pub. Scoop sat on a stool at the five-foot polished wood bar. He'd had soup and brown bread, then settled in with a Guinness during an afternoon shower. The peat fire was lit. The bartender's brown-and-white springer spaniel was asleep on the hearth.

Life could be worse.

"I miss my garden," he said to Eddie O'Shea, the wiry, energetic barman. In late June, Eddie had helped identify Jay Augustine as the man responsible for the sheep's blood up at Keira's ruin.

Eddie busied himself at the sink behind the bar. "Time to go home, is it?"

"Past time, probably. I might have some butternut squash I can save. The firefighters and paramedics trampled the hell out of my tomatoes and cauliflower. Of course," Scoop added with a grin, "they also saved my sorry life."

"And you saved Bob's daughter," Eddie said. He'd met Bob O'Reilly on Bob's trip to Ireland earlier in the summer. Bob'd had to see Keira's ruin, too. "A few tomatoes are a small price, don't you think?"

"No price at all." Scoop stared into his Guinness, but he was back in Boston on that hot summer afternoon, minutes before the bomb went off. Fiona O'Reilly, Bob's nineteen-year-old daughter, had dropped by to see her father. She was a harp player, as smart and as pretty as her cousin Keira and as stubborn as her father. "This wasn't Fiona's fight. She was an innocent by-stander."

"Was it your fight?"

"Doesn't matter. It's my fight now." He thought of the special investigation back in Boston. Had his bomber been staring him in the face? Had he missed something? "I want to know who planted that bomb, Eddie. It could have been anyone. The meter-reader, the plumber, the mailman, a cab driver. Pigeons. Who knows?"

Eddie reached for Scoop's empty glass. "You go after police officers suspected of wrongdoing. Do you suspect it's a cop you're after?"

41

Scoop didn't respond, and Eddie didn't push him for an answer. Few of the handful of people in the pub seemed to be paying attention to the game on the television. Most were locals, but Scoop picked out a young couple who undoubtedly had come in on the bicycles he'd seen outside the pub. He could hear the pair chatting in German. They looked happy and carefree, but probably they weren't. There'd be issues back home — jobs, relatives, health issues. Something.

No one's life was simple.

Definitely time to go home. Maybe being back in Boston would jog his memory about the minutes, hours and even days before the bomb blast. After three weeks recuperating on the other side of the Atlantic, he hadn't produced a face, a name, an incident — a shred of a memory that would take him from the shadows of uncertainty to the identity of the person who had assembled the bomb and delivered it to the home of three detectives.

He'd have to face finding temporary housing when he returned to Boston. The triple-decker was badly burned and under repair. Bob O'Reilly was from Southie and knew carpenters, electricians and plumbers and was overseeing the work, but it'd be a while before any of them could move back in.

Scoop eased off the stool, left enough euros to cover the tab and headed back outside. The village was quiet, the sun shining again, glistening on the rain-soaked sidewalk. Brightly painted houses lined both sides of the street. He half expected Sophie Malone to walk up from the harbor.

It was eerie, that certainty that he hadn't seen the last of her.

He shook off his strange mood and turned onto a narrow lane that ran parallel to the bay, at the foot of the steep hills that formed the spine of the peninsula. A half-dozen brown cows meandered down the middle of the lane toward him. City cop though he was, Scoop had grown up in the country and didn't mind cows. He stepped close to an ancient stonewall and let them pass. As he continued down the lane, he tried to pay attention to the details around him and not get lost in his own thoughts. He noticed a half-dozen sheep in a pen and heard more sheep *baaing* up in the hills.

He came to the traditional stone cottage Keira had rented back in June and let him use the past two weeks. She'd come to Ireland to paint, walk, research her old story and delve into her Irish roots, but her summer hadn't worked out the way she'd meant it to. The cottage was just the sort of place he'd have expected her to stay. Getting blown against his compost bin and almost bleeding to death had helped him realize he could have fallen in love with her, but being here in Ireland had convinced him that he hadn't — that it wasn't meant to be.

Keira was meant for Simon Cahill, the bull of an FBI agent who'd come here to search for her when she'd gone missing in the Irish hills.

It'd been a hell of a summer, Scoop thought.

A massive rosebush dominated the otherwise prosaic front yard, its pink blossoms perking up in the sunshine. He noticed the kitchen door was partially open and immediately tensed, although more out of force of habit than any real alarm. He wasn't expecting company, and his rental car was the only vehicle in the gravel driveway. Most likely he simply hadn't shut the door properly when he'd left for the ruin that morning.

Wrong on all accounts, he observed as a man with medium brown hair eyed him from the small pine table where Keira had left an array of art supplies. He had several days' growth of beard and looked exhausted, if also intense and alert. He wore canvas

44

pants and a lightweight leather jacket. "I never could draw worth a bloody damn." He spoke with a British accent. He leaned back in his chair and held up a sheet of paper with a crude pencil drawing. "What do you think?"

"Is it a sheep?"

"There you go. No. It's an Irish wolfhound."

"I was just kidding. I knew it was a dog." Scoop pulled off his jacket and set his backpack on the floor. "Myles Fletcher, right?"

"Right you are," Fletcher said matter-of-factly, setting his sketch back on the table. "Did you ever want to be an artist when you were a boy, Detective Wisdom?"

"Nope. Always wanted to be a cop. I bet you always wanted to be a spy."

The Brit grinned. "Simon Cahill warned me you were no-nonsense."

"You're SAS and British SIS. Secret Intelligence Service — MI6. James Bond's outfit."

"All right, then." Fletcher yawned, his gray eyes red-rimmed. Wherever he'd come from, he hadn't had much sleep. "You'll want to know why I'm here. I'll get straight to the point. I have information that a Boston police officer was involved in making and planting the explosive device that gave you those scars."

Scoop remained on his feet, silent, still.

"This police officer worked with the men who engineered the kidnapping of Abigail Browning. Smart businessman that he was, Norman Estabrook delegated the job. He wanted Abigail. He didn't care how he got her."

Scoop leaned against a counter. During Abigail's three-day ordeal, he had been in the hospital, out of commission. Fletcher's role in helping her wasn't common knowledge even in the police department, but Scoop had managed to piece together various tidbits and drag more out of his friends and colleagues in law enforcement. The Brit had latched on to a connection between drug traffickers and a terrorist cell and following their trail had taken him to American billionaire Norman Estabrook. For at least two years, no one, including Fletcher's own people back in London, knew Fletcher was even alive.

In the meantime, the FBI was onto Estabrook's association with the drug traffickers and had him under surveillance in the form of Simon Cahill. They arrested the hedge-fund billionaire in June. By late August, he was free again. He disappeared, and Myles Fletcher, still deep undercover, still on the trail of his terrorists, found himself in the middle of the angry, entitled billionaire's elaborate scheme to exact revenge on the FBI for his downfall. Estabrook's scheme included setting off a bomb as a diversion to kidnap Abigail, FBI Director John March's daughter, a Boston homicide detective and Scoop's friend.

Caught between a rock and a hard place, Fletcher had done what he could to help Abigail. Once she was safe, he took off again.

Now he was sitting in an Irish cottage kitchen drawing pictures of dogs.

What a day, Scoop thought. First Sophie Malone, now Myles Fletcher.

A coincidence? Not a chance. "You wouldn't be here if the main thrust of your mission wasn't completed," Scoop said.

Fletcher shrugged. "I suspect your bad cop is someone you know," he said. "Someone you wouldn't think twice to have over for a pint or two."

"Any names?"

"No. Sorry." Fletcher stretched out his legs, looking, if possible, even more tired. "I've done no research on my own. My focus has been on other matters. This is your fight. You were injured in the blast, and you work in internal affairs. Even if you don't know this particular officer yourself, you'll have instincts about those who go bad."

"Where did you get this information?"

"Here and there," Fletcher said vaguely as he rose, visibly stiff. "It's my guess that these thugs, including your bad cop, were involved in other illegal activities in Boston, and that's how they hooked up with Norman Estabrook."

Scoop stood up from the counter but said nothing. The Brit was the one doing the talking.

Fletcher picked up a rust-colored pencil from the table. "But you were onto a connection between these thugs and a member of the department before Estabrook snatched Abigail, weren't you, Detective?"

Scoop thought a moment before he responded. "I had a few whispers. Nothing more."

"I imagine that's the truth, as far as it goes. Frustrating, when you know some but not enough . . ." Fletcher let it go at that. "I expect that you're very good at your job."

"So are you. You're more adept than most at lies and deception."

"That's why I'm alive, here, trying my hand at a sketch. Let's spare each other,

48

then, shall we?" He ran his thumb over the sharp tip of the pencil. "I'm impressed with what Keira can do with colored pencils. I'd always thought they were for children, not working artists." He set the pencil back on the table and flipped through a stack of sketches Keira had started of various bucolic Irish scenes, pausing at one of a shovel laid across an old, muddy wheelbarrow in a garden. "I wouldn't mind living inside one of these pictures. A green pasture, a stream, prancing lambs. A beautiful fairy princess. What about you, Detective?"

"I grew up on a farm. I liked it, but I'm not nostalgic about that life. What else can you tell me?"

"There's a woman. An American archaeologist. She's been doing scholarly work in Ireland and Great Britain for the past several years."

"Sophie Malone," Scoop said.

Fletcher glanced at him, then continued, "You ran into her when she was here in the village earlier today, didn't you?"

"Yep. I did. Red hair, blue jacket. Had a big black dog with her and talked about the wee folk." Scoop picked up the pencil Fletcher had used and realized it was nearly the same shade as Sophie's hair. A deliberate choice on the Brit's part? "The dog

49

wasn't hers. Want to tell me what's going on, Fletcher?"

"I wish I knew. I strongly suspect the men our dead billionaire hired were also involved with Jay Augustine. I don't know in what capacity."

Nothing legal, Scoop thought, but he said, "Augustine's a serial killer. Serial killers tend to be solitary."

"I'm not talking about his violence. Augustine was also a respected dealer in fine art and antiques."

"What's that got to do with Sophie Malone?"

Fletcher grinned suddenly. "I've no idea. As I said, I haven't done any research of my own. I suppose Augustine could have consulted her as an expert in his role as a legitimate dealer."

"Are you linking her to this bad cop?"

"I'm saying her name came up at the same time as the likelihood that a police officer constructed and planted the bomb that exploded at your house last month." Fletcher walked over to the front window, determined and focused but also obviously past being dead tired. "I wish I could be more helpful."

"Funny, you and Sophie Malone turning up here within a few hours of each other."

"Isn't it, though?" He nodded out the window. "Here we go. Just what we need."

For all Scoop knew, the big black dog was back with a troop of fairies.

Instead, FBI Special Agent Simon Cahill and Will Davenport — a British lord and another James Bond type — entered through the kitchen door. Casual, irreverent, black-haired Simon and wealthy, regal, fair-haired Will, both around Scoop's age, in their mid-thirties, were as different in appearance as they were in temperament and background, but they were close friends.

Right behind them was Josie Goodwin. She had on a sleek belted raincoat, her chin-length brown hair pulled back and her mouth set firmly as she shut the door behind her. She pretended to be Will's able assistant but was undoubtedly SIS herself. Scoop had met Josie and Will at Abigail's wedding at Davenport's country house in the Scottish Highlands. Josie, who was in her late thirties, had muttered over hors d'oeuvres at the reception that if she ever saw Myles Fletcher again, she would smother him with a pillow.

As far as Scoop knew, this was their first meeting since Fletcher had slipped undercover two years ago, leaving everyone he knew — including Josie Goodwin and Will

Davenport — to think he was dead.

She entered the kitchen without a word and leaned against a counter. Strongly built and obviously well trained, she looked as if she'd have no problem dispatching even a hard-assed spy like Myles Fletcher.

Fletcher ignored her and directed his attention at the two men. "Simon. Will. It's good to see you." Finally he turned to Josie and winked at her. "Hello, love."

"Bastard," she said, then beamed a friendly smile at Scoop. "You're looking well, Detective. Much better than at Abigail's wedding. Some of your scars seem to be fading already."

"I feel fine," Scoop said. "I'm ready to get back to work."

Simon stood by the kitchen door, near Josie's position at the counter. "Moneypenny here wouldn't listen to good advice and stay in London. She had to follow us to Ireland."

She gave Simon a good-natured roll of her eyes.

Across the tiny cottage, Fletcher was at the front window again. "More company."

Scoop noticed Simon's expectant, troubled expression, but Will Davenport was more difficult to read. The kitchen door opened on a gust of wind, and flaxen-haired

Keira Sullivan entered the cottage, followed in another half second by black-haired Lizzie Rush. They were both thirty, both coming to terms with the dramatic changes in their lives over the past summer. Lizzie was Will Davenport's new love, and however she and Keira had gotten to the little Irish village, it hadn't, obviously, been with either him or Simon. Scoop was trained in reading body language, but it didn't take an expert to detect the tension between the two pairs of lovers.

With a curt nod at Davenport, Keira swept past Simon and greeted Scoop with a kiss on the cheek. "This place agrees with you," she said, then, without waiting for an answer, turned to Josie. "Lizzie and I were in Dublin. It took a bit of doing on our part to figure out what was going on. I'm glad you could get here."

"Wouldn't have missed it for the world," Josie said dryly.

Fletcher returned to the table of art supplies. He looked less tired as he smiled at Keira. "Your charming cottage suddenly seems very small, indeed, doesn't it?"

"I have a feeling not for long," she said, no curtness to her now. Her breathing was shallow, her cornflower-blue eyes filled with fear and anticipation.

Something was up, Scoop thought, observing his half-dozen visitors.

Fletcher picked up the sketch he'd done and handed it to Keira, her hands trembling visibly as she took it. "Here you go," he said. "It's an Irish wolfhound. I think of him as a shape-shifter in the midst of going from man to dog. That explains the quirks in my rendition, don't you think?"

Josie Goodwin snorted from the kitchen. "So does being a bad artist."

"It's wonderful," Keira said, gracious as always.

Lizzie Rush walked over to the unlit stone fireplace and stood with her back to it. She was the director of concierge services for her family's fifteen boutique hotels, including in Dublin and Boston. She was small and black-haired, with light green eyes and an alertness about her that supported the rumors Scoop had heard that her father wasn't just a hotelier but also a spy who had taught his only child his tradecraft.

She was the one who'd called Bob O'Reilly with the split-second warning that a bomb was about to go off on Abigail's back porch.

Davenport, clad in an open trench coat, kept his focus on Fletcher, who had quietly moved away from to the front door. Without raising his voice, Will said, "Simon and I are going with you, Myles."

Fletcher pulled open the door and left without responding. The door shut with a thud behind him. Unless the departing Brit could shape-shift himself into a bird, Scoop figured Fletcher had a vehicle stashed nearby.

Davenport — well educated, well trained and very experienced — looked over at Lizzie, but he didn't smile or go to her, didn't speak, just tapped one finger to his lips and blew her a kiss, then turned and headed out after Fletcher.

"Damn Brits," Simon muttered, then shrugged at Josie. "Sorry, Moneypenny."

"I had much the same thought." She stood up from the counter and inhaled sharply as she nodded toward the front door. "You're going after them, aren't you?"

"Yes." There was no irreverence in Simon's manner now. He was deadly serious. He walked over to Keira by the table of art supplies and half-finished sketches and touched her long, pale hair. "Keira . . ."

"You have a job to do. Go do it. Stay safe. Keep your friends safe." She placed Fletcher's sketch back on the table and caught Simon's big hand in hers, no sign she was trembling now. "Come back to me soon."

55

Simon kissed her but said nothing more as he went after the two British spies.

Once the door shut behind him, Josie let her arms fall to her sides. "All right, then. They're off, and now it's just us girls again."

Scoop raised his eyebrows.

Her strain was evident even as she smiled at him. "Sorry, Detective."

"Honestly, Scoop," Keira said, attempting a laugh, "you look even more ferocious these days. Who'd ever know you adopted two stray cats?"

"The cats know," he said.

Tears shone in her eyes. "They must miss you."

"They're in good hands. Your cousins are taking care of them." Not Fiona but her two younger sisters, who lived with their mother — Bob O'Reilly's first wife. Scoop tried to keep his tone light. "Your uncle's having fits. Now Maddie and Jayne want him to adopt cats."

"I'm just glad yours survived the fire," Keira said quietly. "When are you going back to Boston?"

"Tomorrow," he said, deciding on the spot. First the mysterious archaeologist, now British spies and the FBI. Too much was going on for him to justify even one more day in Ireland. Answers weren't here,

56

in Keira's idyllic cottage.

Lizzie sank onto the sofa where, in his first days at the cottage, Scoop had lain on his stomach for hours at a stretch, easing himself off medication and trying to remember anything that could help with the investigations back in Boston. She kicked out her legs and propped her feet up on a small coffee table. Although she was a hotel heiress accustomed to five-star surroundings, she didn't look out of place in the simple cottage. From what Scoop had seen of them, Lizzie Rush and Lord Davenport — who was accustomed to castles — were at home wherever they happened to find themselves.

"I have a room all set for you at our hotel in Boston anytime you want it," she told Scoop.

"That's very kind of you, Lizzie, but another detective's offered me his sleeper sofa."

"Who?" Keira asked, skeptical.

"Tom Yarborough."

She sputtered into incredulous laughter. "You two would kill each other."

Probably true. Yarborough was a homicide detective — Abigail's partner — and not an easy person on a good day. He hadn't had a good day in months.

"My family would love to have you at the Whitcomb," Lizzie said. "Consider it done, Scoop. I'll text Jeremiah and let him know."

Jeremiah Rush was the third eldest of Lizzie's four male Rush cousins. With her father frequently gone and her mother dead since she was an infant, she had practically grown up with them north of Boston.

"What about you three?" Scoop asked, taking in all three women with one look.

"We'll keep ourselves busy," Josie said. She opened up the refrigerator, giving an exaggerated shudder of disgust as she shut it again. "Rutabagas and beer do not a meal make."

"I've been eating mostly at the pub," Scoop said.

"Yes, well, one would hope."

He went over to the front window and looked out into the fading daylight. The weeks of healing — of being on medical leave, away from his job — finally were getting to him. He turned back to the women. "When did you all get here?"

"Just now," Keira said. "Lizzie and I came on our own."

"Chasing Will and Simon?"

Her cheeks turned a deep shade of pink, but Lizzie was the one who spoke. "Not chasing. Following. They tried to divert us with a few days of shopping in Dublin."

"Guess they had to give it a shot," Scoop said with a smile.

"I flew from London," Josie said. "I hired my own car at the airport."

"Were you following Will and Simon — or Myles?"

She walked briskly to the table Fletcher had vacated and gazed down at his drawing. "I don't know what you mean. I'm the trusted assistant of Will Davenport, the second son of a beloved marquess. Whatever else you're thinking is pure fancy."

Scoop didn't argue. What Josie Goodwin knew and how she knew it was a matter he preferred to leave to speculation. He shifted to Keira, staring blankly at a sketch she'd started of the tranquil village harbor.

"Do you know an archaeologist named Sophie Malone?" he asked abruptly.

"I've heard of her, yes," Keira said, perking up. "Absolutely. She's a very well respected archaeologist. She's volunteered to chair a panel on the Irish Iron Age at the folklore conference in April. The conference is shaping up to be quite an event. It's good to have something fun to focus on after this summer." She abandoned her sketch. "Was Dr. Malone here?"

Scoop nodded. "We ran into each other

up at the ruin where you found your stone angel. She mentioned she'd talked to Professor Dermott. She didn't stay long. I could have scared her off."

"Not you, Scoop," Keira said, a welcome spark of humor in her eyes.

Lizzie lowered her feet to the floor and sat up straight, frowning at Keira and Scoop. "Did you say Sophie Malone?"

"What," Scoop said, "am I the last person to know who she is?"

"She worked at the pub at our Boston hotel when she was in college," Lizzie said, rising. "We're about the same age. I was in and out of town a lot at the time, but I remember her. We were both interested in all things Irish."

"Have you seen her since?"

"Not that I recall. She and her twin sister and their older brother were born here in Ireland. Their parents worked in Cork. I took special note, I suppose, because of my mother, who was Irish." Her tone softened. Shauna Morrigan Rush had died in Dublin under mysterious circumstances when Lizzie was a baby. "Strange, isn't it? The ripple effects of life."

Josie, who hadn't stirred during the exchange, picked up the electric kettle on the counter and lifted the lid as she shoved it under the faucet. "Sophie Malone's not another of John March's informal spies, is she?"

"Not that I know of," Lizzie said. For the better part of a year, she herself had anonymously provided the FBI director with information on Norman Estabrook, who had been a frequent guest at various Rush hotels.

Josie filled the kettle, then plugged it in and switched it on, her movements brisk, efficient. "You *do* have tea, don't you, Detective?"

"On the shelf above you."

She reached up and got down a tin of loose-leaf tea and set it on the counter, her casualness studied, as if she didn't dare go where her mind wanted to take her. "Did Myles happen to run into this Sophie Malone?" she asked without looking at Scoop.

"I don't think so, no."

She turned to him, her gaze direct and unflinching. "But he mentioned her, didn't he?"

"He had his reasons for coming here."

Josie opened the tin of tea. Scoop figured that even someone who wasn't trained in detecting lies and deception — which surely Josie Goodwin was — would guess he

61

hadn't told all he knew. She didn't push him further. Keira and Lizzie eyed him but said nothing.

He retreated to the small bedroom and got his suitcase out of the closet. He had the bones of a plan. He'd head to the airport in Shannon and book the first flight he could get to Boston tomorrow.

He was packed in less than ten minutes. When he returned to the main room, Keira had torn off a fresh sheet of sketch paper and placed it in front of her on the pine table. She was staring at it as if she were trying to envision a pretty, happy scene — as if she'd had enough of violence, mystery and adventure and just wanted to hole up with her paints and colored pencils.

Lizzie Rush was back on the sofa, frowning, the spy in the making.

Josie lifted the lid on an old teapot and peered inside. "The tea's ready, but I gather you're not staying."

"No," Scoop said.

Her deep blue eyes narrowed slightly as she answered. "Safe travels, then."

"Jeremiah will be expecting you at the Whitcomb," Lizzie said.

Keira looked up from her blank page. "Tell my uncle not to worry about me."

Scoop smiled at her. "That's like telling

the rain to stop falling in Ireland. It's just not going to happen."

As he headed out the side door, the three women didn't interrogate him or try to stop him. He didn't know whether they could guess what he was doing and approved, or if they just were resigned that he'd made up his mind and there'd be no stopping him.

Unlike Simon Cahill and Will Davenport, he had no one to kiss goodbye.

And no one waiting for his return to Boston.

Except his cats, unless they'd decided they preferred the company of Keira's young cousins.

4

Kenmare, Southwest Ireland

Sophie walked next to her twin sister, Taryn, enjoying the sounds of traditional Irish music drifting from Kenmare pubs on what had turned into a perfect September evening. One last downpour seemed to have done the trick. Fresh from London, Taryn wore slim jeans with flat-heeled black boots and a black sweater that came down to her knees. Although they were fraternal, not identical twins, Taryn also had red hair, but hers was two tones darker and wavier — and easier to manage, Sophie had decided when they were six, because Taryn always seemed to manage it. A few pins and clips, and she looked gorgeous. She had the lead in a new romantic comedy, but her first break had come performing Shakespeare in Boston. She was as dedicated to her acting career as Sophie had ever been to earning her doctorate, or Damian to becoming a federal agent.

With her afternoon of cleaning, cooking and thinking, Sophie had been in her hiking clothes, still encrusted with mud from her trek on the Beara Peninsula, when Taryn arrived. Taryn, however, had seemed unsurprised and hadn't asked what her sister had been up to. Sophie had quickly changed into jeans, a sweater and walking shoes. They'd set out on foot from their house to the lively village of bars, restaurants and shops.

Sophie paused at a hole-in-the-wall pub on a narrow side street. "Tim O'Donovan and his friends are playing here tonight," she said.

Taryn's expression didn't change. "How nice."

"Do you want to go in, or shall we choose another pub?"

"This one's fine."

Her sister's nonchalance was totally feigned, Sophie concluded as they entered the warm, noisy pub. A waiter led them to a table against the old brick wall. She and Taryn had done a Kenmare weekend in the spring, indulging themselves at an incredible bayside hotel spa and listening to traditional Irish music every night. Tim had swept them off for a boat ride — one that didn't go near the tiny island of Sophie's misadventure. He'd fallen hard for Taryn, and she for him, except she'd never admit as much, even to Sophie. An Irish fisherman didn't fit into Taryn's already complicated life.

Just a touch of spring fever, she'd said, flushed as she'd headed to London.

Tim had grumbled that he should have known better than to swoon over a woman who was an actress, an American and Sophie's twin. Sophie had met him two years ago when she'd spent part of the winter in Kenmare, working on her dissertation. Right from the start, she and Tim had been more like brother and sister. Not the case, she thought, with him and her twin sister.

Taryn peeled off her teal wool scarf; she'd wound it around her neck, making it look easy, sophisticated and sexy all at the same time. She had an unobstructed view of the small stage where Tim and his friends, who looked as if they'd just come from catching dinner, were setting up, but she carefully pretended not to notice them as she and Sophie each ordered a glass of Guinness.

"I spoke to Damian just before I arrived in Kenmare," Taryn said.

"I'm sure he wishes he could be here."

"You're not a credible liar, Sophie. I'm

only slightly better because I'm an actor, but lying doesn't come easily to either of us. Damian said he talked to you earlier today. He sounded put out with you. Are you mixed up in some top-secret FBI investigation?" Even as Sophie thought she was suppressing any visible reaction, her sister gasped. "Sophie! I was just kidding, but you *are* mixed up in something."

"No, I'm not. I asked Damian about what's gone on in Boston this summer. That's all. It's natural I'd be curious."

Sophie had no intention of getting into her experience in the island cave a year ago. Taryn didn't know — unless Damian had decided to call the guards himself and had found out about it and told Taryn. Which Sophie doubted. She didn't like keeping secrets from her family, but they'd only worry if they knew, never mind that she'd promised the guards she wouldn't tell anyone.

"What did Damian tell you about Boston?"

"Nothing much."

"Sophie —"

Fortunately, their parents entered the pub and joined them at their table. They'd come straight from Dublin. James and Antonia Malone, Sophie thought with affection, were relishing their early retirement, diving into their love of storytelling, music, drama, art and exploring. Their twin daughters' red hair came from their mother, although the shade was unreliable since she'd started using a near-orange dye now to cover any gray. She was as tall as Taryn but had Sophie's sense of adventure. A lifelong New Englander, she'd met their father, the son of Irish immigrants, hiking on the Dingle Peninsula in college.

They'd been home in western Massachusetts during her brush with death last year. There was nothing they could do if she'd told them but worry. She'd returned to her work on her dissertation and tried to put the incident behind her.

Tim looked straight at Taryn and gave her a sexy smile as he put his fiddle to his chin. Then he and his friends launched into a rousing, pulse-pounding rendition of "Johnny I Hardly Knew Ye." Their music was lively and authentic, the perfect counter to a stress-filled day.

Taryn sipped her Guinness, her attention riveted on the musicians. "They're really good, aren't they, Sophie?"

"Fantastic."

The compliment was sincere, but she hoped Tim wouldn't decide to join them on his break given their earlier talk on the pier. Of course he did, pulling over a low stool and plopping down. Sophie knew that was the risk she'd taken in choosing this particular pub. She trusted him not to tell her family about the island, but that didn't mean he wouldn't blab about her excursion to the Beara Peninsula that morning.

"The Malones return to our wee village," he said, grinning.

He obviously wasn't going to bring up anything awkward. Sophie tried not to look too relieved. Taryn smiled, but she was unusually quiet, letting her sister and parents carry on the conversation with Tim. Their parents had met him on a visit to Kenmare months before he'd fallen hard for Taryn — before he'd let Sophie talk him into dropping her off on the island.

They talked about music and hiking and weather, and he finally got up for his next set. His gaze settled briefly on Sophie, but it was enough. She got the message. He hated withholding information from her family, and he knew she was up to something.

"I head to Boston tomorrow," she said, pretending she hadn't already told him. "I'm staying at Taryn's apartment there."

He shifted to Taryn. "What about you?

When do you go back to Boston?"

"For good? Not for a while. My play in London runs through October. After that, who knows? I'm waiting for word about a trip to New York. It could come anytime. I'll just be there for a few days, though."

"Do you have an audition?" he asked.

She lowered her eyes. "Something like that."

"I've a distant cousin in Boston." Tim gave Sophie a pointed look. "A firefighter."

His tone suggested he'd been doing some research of his own on the goings-on in Boston over the summer and the injured police detective staying on the Beara. Given their earlier conversation, Sophie wasn't surprised or irritated. If she could do it all over again, she'd never have gone out to the island a year ago. She wasn't even sure she'd have had lunch with Colm Dermott last week and listened to him relate what he knew about Keira Sullivan's unsettling night alone in the Irish wilds.

When Tim returned to the stage, James Malone eyed his two daughters with open skepticism. "When I was a working stiff in corporate America," he said, "I learned about subtext. I would say there was an encyclopedia of subtext in that exchange. Either of you want to tell me what just went on?"

Taryn, good actress though she was, floundered, but Sophie grinned at her father and held up her glass of Guinness. "You know these Irish men, Dad."

"That's my point," he muttered.

His wife elbowed him before he could say more and raised her own glass. "And to us poor women who love them."

Sophie laughed, relishing her time with her family. Her parents were having a ball with their retirement. Let it be that way for a long time, she thought, just as, out of the corner of her eye, she noticed a lone man enter the pub. As a waiter led him to a small table, she was surprised to recognize Percy Carlisle, a wealthy Bostonian she hadn't seen in a year.

Taryn leaned close to Sophie. "What's he doing here?"

"I have no idea," Sophie said half under her breath. She left her drink on the table and quickly stood up, heading to his table. She dropped onto the chair across from him without waiting to be invited. "Hey, Percy. I didn't know you were in Ireland."

"I only arrived last night. Helen and I were in London."

"Is she here with you?"

He shook his head. "She's gone back to

Boston."

A waiter appeared, and Percy ordered coffee, nothing else. He was in his early forties, dressed in a heavy wool cardigan and wide-wale corduroys that bagged on his lanky frame. He had inherited a family fortune and spent most of his time pursuing his interests in travel, art, music, history and genealogy. Sophie had run into him on occasion when she was a student in Boston and had done research at the Carlisle Museum. They'd gotten along without becoming real friends or, certainly, romantically involved. She hadn't seen him since she'd moved to Ireland to continue her studies — except briefly late last summer when he'd looked her up while he was visiting friends in Killarney.

"I was in the area and remembered your family has a house here," Percy said now. "I was on my way there when I saw you and your sister head in here. I was in the car — it took some time to park. I just came from Killarney National Park. For some reason, I'd never been. It's stunning, isn't it?"

"Sure is." Situated among clear lakes and forested hills, the park was as beautiful and inviting a setting as she could imagine. "I hiked the old Killarney road to Kenmare the other day."

"I wish Helen had been with me. She'd have loved it, but she has business in New York to clear up. She's giving up her job at the auction house there. It's a big change, but she's excited about it. We're moving in to my family's house in Boston, did you know?"

"I hadn't heard, no."

"Helen's handling the transition. I've maintained the house since my father died, but I never thought I'd live there again." Percy's dark eyes lit up. "Helen is a ball of energy. I'm lucky to have her in my life."

"I look forward to meeting her."

Sophie smiled at his obvious happiness. He and Helen had been married only two months — the first marriage for both. His father — Percy Carlisle Sr. — had been an amateur archaeologist famous for taking off in search of lost treasure. Sophie remembered when he'd invited her into his office in the museum shortly before his death. He'd stood with her at a wall of photographs of his exploits and gone over each one, describing memories, enjoying himself. He'd acknowledged to Sophie that his only son wasn't nearly as adventurous. "Perhaps it's just as well," the old man had said.

She pulled herself out of her thoughts. Her Guinness was making her head spin.

73

Trekking out to the ruin on the Beara and meeting Scoop Wisdom — scarred, suspicious — had launched her back to her own trauma a year ago with an intensity that had left her off balance, on edge.

The waiter delivered Percy's coffee. He took a small sip, keeping the mug in one hand as he nodded to her parents and sister. "I saw Taryn when she played Ophelia in Boston a few years ago. She's quite amazing."

"That she is. She loves her work."

"Always a plus." He set his coffee on the scarred table. "Do you love your work, Sophie?"

"I do, yes."

"I've heard you're involved in the upcoming Boston-Cork conference on Irish folklore. Will that look good on your CV?"

"Sure, and it'll be interesting as well as fun."

"But it's unpaid," he said. "How are you managing these days?"

"Same as I did throughout graduate school."

"Tutoring, fellowships, teaching a class here and there?"

"Every job's a real job."

"I admire your attitude." He picked up his mug of coffee. "If there's ever anything I

74

can do for you, Sophie, you've only to ask."

"Thanks. I appreciate it," she said. "I'm heading back to Boston tomorrow. I have a few leads on full-time work."

"Best of luck to you." Percy watched the musicians chat among themselves for a few moments. "I considered driving down to the village where Keira Sullivan says she found that stone angel."

His comment caught Sophie by surprise. "Do you know Keira?"

"Only by reputation. Everyone's still very shaken that Jay Augustine proved to be a killer." He seemed to wait for Sophie's reaction. She sat forward, but before she could say anything, he continued, "I wasn't friends with the Augustines or even close to it. I'd see them socially from time to time at various functions in New York and Boston. Charlotte Augustine's moved to Hawaii, did you know?"

"No," Sophie said.

"She's seeking a divorce. I can't even imagine what it must have been like for her to discover she was married to a murderer." Percy stared into his coffee. "The Boston police and the FBI interviewed me in July, not long after Augustine's arrest. I wanted you to know so that you don't get the wrong idea. It was routine. I'd done a few perfectly

75

legitimate deals with him. The police talked to everyone who'd done business with him."

"That makes sense, don't you think?"

"Of course. I understood completely." Percy faced her again, his expression cool now, slightly supercilious. "What about you, Sophie? Did you have any dealings with Jay Augustine?"

"No, none." She tried to lighten her tone. "No money, remember?"

But he continued to look troubled and annoyed. "I'm a very careful, experienced collector, Sophie. Very few pieces available on the market today would interest me. My family . . . my father . . ." He broke off, sitting back. "Never mind. You probably know as much about my family's art collection as I do."

"I've never crawled through your attic —"

"We don't keep anything of value in the attic. We are familiar with the protocols for storing and preserving works of art."

Sophie sighed. "It was a joke, Percy." She noticed with relief that the musicians were about to get started again. "Did you buy from the Augustines or sell to them?"

"Both."

"What kind of —"

"Nothing that would interest you. Nothing Irish. Nothing Celtic."

"Percy," she said, ignoring his sarcasm, "why did you look me up last September?"

He frowned at her. "Last September? What are you talking about?"

She repeated her question.

"Just what I told you at the time," he said. "I knew you were studying in Ireland and had a house here in Kenmare. I was here playing golf with friends and decided to find you and say hello."

"No one put you up to it?"

"What? No. Believe it or not, Sophie, I'm perfectly capable of thinking for myself."

"That's not what I meant, and I think you know it. Percy, when you were here last year, did you find out that I was exploring — having myself a bit of an adventure between chapters of my dissertation?"

"Following in my father's footsteps?"

"Making my own."

"He never liked Ireland. He was far more interested in archaeological sites on the European mainland, in South America, Australia. However, to answer your question — I heard that you were chasing ghost and fairy stories with an Irish fisherman out here somewhere."

"Did you tell Jay Augustine?"

The color immediately drained from his face at her blunt question. "I didn't even see Jay Augustine." Percy stood up, his coffee barely touched. "I have to go. I just wanted to stop in and say hello. Enjoy your visit with your family, Sophie, and good luck finding full-time work. Don't forget to let me know if I can help."

"I'm sorry, Percy. I didn't mean to offend you."

"We should both forget this killer."

Sophie thought she heard genuine concern and regret in his voice, but she didn't know him well enough to be sure. "I've seen pictures of him. He looks so normal. I wonder what he's thinking now, locked up in his Boston jail cell. This has upset you, too, Percy. It would be weird if it didn't."

"Of course it's upset me."

She noticed Tim glowering at her. He wasn't aware that Percy Carlisle had looked her up out of the blue a year ago. She glanced at her family. Her father looked as if he were about to make up a reason to come over to Percy's table.

Tim and his friends started to play again, jumping right into their own mad rendition of "Irish Rover."

"You should get back to enjoying the evening." Percy withdrew his wallet and pulled out a few euros. "Stop by the house and meet Helen when you get back to

Boston. We've hired a retired Boston police officer as our private security guard. I'll make sure he knows to expect you. I never would have considered such a move, but after this summer . . ."

"I understand," Sophie said.

He placed the euros on the table. "I know you do, Sophie. It's good to see you."

As he made his way through the crowd, he didn't seem to hear the music, and he left without a word to anyone. Sophie returned to her family. Her father frowned at her, but she picked up her Guinness and offered a toast, dodging his curiosity as they clapped and tapped their feet to the music. They finished their round of drinks and headed out together, Taryn blushing when Tim shouted out to her and blew them all a kiss. His friends hooted, diving into their next song.

Out on the street, the evening air was cool and clear, perfect for the walk back through the village. Sophie asked her parents about their plans for the next month — anything, she thought, to keep the conversation away from her visit with Percy Carlisle and her impending return to Boston. By the time they crossed the stone bridge above the falls, stars sparkled in the night sky. Sophie lingered, listening to the flow of the water over the rocks, pushing back her analytical side and letting herself feel the presence of her ancestors.

After a few moments, she and her sister and parents continued down the road to their house, situated on a hillside above an old stone wall and painted bright yellow. The interior was open and comfortable, decorated with colorful furnishings and art they'd all collected over the years. Sophie pleaded fatigue and an early start and bolted straight for the bedroom she and Taryn shared. It had twin beds, skylights and a small window with a view of the starlit bay. She undressed quickly and climbed into bed, fighting back tears at the prospect of leaving Ireland tomorrow.

Taryn sat on the edge of the bed across from her. "Sophie, are you okay?"

She pulled her duvet up to her chin. "Just a little distracted."

"There's something going on with you. I know there is." Taryn peeled off her scarf, the moonlight on her face as she studied her sister. "You haven't been yourself for weeks. Months, really."

"Taryn . . . don't go there. Please."

She kicked off her shoes. "Whatever's bothering you has to do with what's gone on in Boston, doesn't it? I swear I can feel you being pulled in that direction."

Sophie rolled onto her back and stared up at the skylight. "That's because you've had too much Guinness."

"Maybe." Taryn leaned back onto her elbows and sighed. "Do you ever think about chucking your career and opening an Irish inn?"

"And marrying an Irish fisherman who plays the fiddle?"

They both laughed. "Oh, Sophie. What a couple of romantics we are under our tough-redhead exteriors." But Taryn's light tone didn't last, and she sat up straight. "You'll be careful in Boston, won't you?"

For no reason at all, Sophie thought of solid, scarred Scoop Wisdom as he'd watched her at Keira Sullivan's ruin. Had the violence of the past summer started there, on the night of the summer solstice — or had it started a year ago, on a thimble of an island off the Iveragh Peninsula?

"Sophie?"

"Yes, Taryn," she whispered. "I'll be very careful."

5

Beara Peninsula, Southwest Ireland

Nights on the Beara Peninsula were quiet but also incredibly dark, and Josie Goodwin found herself restless, frustrated and decidedly annoyed with her lot. As much as she liked Keira and Lizzie and enjoyed their company, she hated being left behind, stuck in a cottage in the Irish hills while Will, Simon and Myles were off doing . . . well, whatever they were doing.

She had few details. She'd learned early that morning that Myles was en route to Ireland and had alerted Will, who in turn had alerted Simon. In the month since Myles had again disappeared after helping to free Abigail Browning, he had continued to avoid communications with anyone in London. For the past two years, he'd sacrificed much to establish his cover as a rogue SAS officer and penetrate a deadly association between drug traffickers and a terrorist cell.

His cover was so deep, so impenetrable, that no one — not even Will Davenport — had known what Myles was up to. Josie and Will had believed Myles had been dragged off in a firefight in Afghanistan and killed — and not heroically at that. Killed by his terrorist friends after he had betrayed his colleagues to them.

But he hadn't been killed, and he hadn't betrayed anyone.

Now it was time he had help.

Josie resisted the temptation to pace. What she wanted to do was to return to London. But what could she do there?

Nothing more, she thought bitterly, than she could do right here.

With a heavy sigh, she surveyed the tidy room. Keira had lit a wood fire. Lizzie was washing up in the kitchen. Scoop Wisdom had left little evidence that he'd been here at all, never mind for two weeks. Josie walked over to the front window and looked out at the stars and half moon. She wondered if Myles would have let Norman Estabrook and his thugs kill Abigail before he risked compromising his own mission. He would never have considered such a dire option. He tackled problems head-on and went after the outcome he wanted — in that case, Abigail Browning free and safe, Norman Estabrook and his thugs dead or captured and he, a British agent, with the key information he needed to carry on his mission.

Josie could see Myles giving her one of his crooked, cocky grins. "No worries, love," he'd say.

She'd never met a man so certain he could achieve whatever he was after.

She raked a hand through her hair. How could she blame Myles for the risks he'd taken — for his courage, his sacrifices?

Because she bloody well could, she thought, forcing herself to smile at her two housemates — Lizzie in the kitchen, Keira heading for the bedroom. "You'd never know Scoop had ever been here, would you?"

"That's typical Scoop," Keira said. "You should see his apartment. He had to get rid of everything after the fire, but he likes living a stripped-down life. He doesn't need much more than a good colander for his garden harvest."

"I like how you say 'fire,' " Lizzie interjected. "It was a bomb."

Despite her blunt comment, Lizzie was an optimist by both nature and conviction and every bit Will Davenport's match. Josie had begun to doubt if he'd ever find the woman who was. Lizzie Rush not only knew her way around five-star hotels — she had taken on a billionaire and his professional thugs, and she'd held her own with Myles, Will, the FBI and the Boston police.

Lizzie was joining Keira and her young cousins and their detective father for tea on Christmas Eve at the Rush hotel in Dublin. They'd invited Josie. She just might chuck London for a few days and go at that.

Assuming she wasn't in prison for killing Myles Fletcher in his sleep.

Of course, that would require he avoid getting himself killed on his own first. Will and Simon had gone after him in part because they were convinced — as Josie was — that Myles was on the verge of getting himself killed. It had been a long, difficult, treacherous two years. He had done his share. Would he ever be able to return to a normal life? Would he even want to?

Josie refused to go down that particular road. For a time, she'd thought Myles was, finally, a man who understood her, and she'd thought she understood him — including the challenges of being involved with him.

Of loving him.

She smirked to herself. That had been

madness, hadn't it? Fortunately, she had her son, Adrian. She'd gone outside before dark and called him. He'd had schoolwork to do. He was with his father, an accountant who hadn't been pleased at all when he'd seen through Josie's charade of a life. He hadn't wanted a wife who was an intelligence officer in any capacity, even if it was largely behind a desk. He wanted a normal life. Who could blame him?

Adrian adored Myles and had asked about him frequently in the initial months after his presumed death and betrayal. Josie had been prohibited from saying anything — that Myles was alive, dead, missing. And what had she known? Nothing, as it turned out. Just as well she'd stayed mum. Adrian had finally stopped asking, but only after telling Josie that he knew Myles would be back.

Keira carried an armload of blankets and sheets from the bedroom. "It'll be like a sleepover. Girls' night. We can have a pillow fight."

Lizzie paused at the sink, and she and Josie both gaped at Keira as if she'd lost her mind. Girls' night? A sleepover? A pillow fight?

"Don't look so shocked," Keira said with a laugh, dumping the linens in a heap on the sofa, her pale hair hanging in her face. "I've never been one for troops of girl-friends, I admit, but I do like having you both here. Two of us can share the bed and one can sleep on the sofa, or one in the bed, one on the sofa and one on a mat on the floor. It'll work."

"Of course it will," Lizzie said, smiling.

Josie angled Lizzie a sharp look. "If you polish that kettle for one more second, you'll rub a hole in it. What is it, Lizzie? What's on your mind?"

Lizzie dropped her cloth and abandoned the kettle. She stared out the dark window above the sink. "I was just thinking about Sophie Malone." She sighed and faced Josie again. "I'm forgetting something. I know I am, but I can't think what it is."

"Something important?" Josie asked.

"I hope not."

Keira sank onto the sofa next to her heap of linens. "Sophie's a Celtic archaeologist originally from Boston, and she's participating in the folklore conference. I can understand that she'd want to see the ruin. She just happened to pick a morning Scoop was there."

"Yes," Lizzie said, "but that doesn't mean that's all there is to it."

Josie stood by the fire, welcomed its

warmth on her back. "These days, nothing is ever quite as it seems, is it?"

Keira fingered the hem of an inexpensive sheet. "Sophie got to Scoop, don't you think?"

"Is our Dr. Malone attractive?" Josie asked.

Keira blushed. "It's not *that*."

"Nonsense. It's always *'that.'*"

Obviously preoccupied, Lizzie walked over to the pine table. "I didn't know Sophie that well when she worked at our hotel in Boston." She picked up a charcoal pencil from Keira's array of art supplies, then immediately set it down again. "I *know* I'm missing something. I'll remember, though."

Of that, Josie had no doubt. Both Lizzie and Keira had faced considerable danger and violence since June and had come out on the other side in good shape.

Josie hadn't faced anything more dangerous or violent than her e-mail In-box.

"Are you going back to London tomorrow?" Keira asked her.

"I've no idea what I'm doing tomorrow," Josie said, keeping any trace of bitterness out of her tone. "Today didn't go as I expected. Why should tomorrow?"

Lizzie, obviously as restless as Josie was, pushed aside Myles's pathetic Irish wolfhound drawing. "We can all drive to Dublin in the morning and have tea and scones at my family's hotel there," she said.

"You mean you want to talk to your cousin the doorman," Keira said. "See if he can help you remember whatever it is about Sophie Malone you think is escaping you."

Lizzie stood up straight. "We need to know exactly what her interest in your stone angel is."

"It's not my stone angel," Keira said quietly. "It belongs to Irish legend now."

Josie had noticed Keira struggle with her emotions since Simon's departure. The upheavals of the past three months had to be finally catching up with her. She'd encountered a brutal killer, fallen in love with an FBI agent and learned of family secrets — the mysterious circumstances of her own conception here on the Beara Peninsula, a terrible murder thirty years ago that had haunted her mother and uncle. Before she'd had a chance to absorb all that, her life was again disrupted when Norman Estabrook decided to exact revenge. He'd trusted Simon, never once thinking he was an undercover FBI agent. As payback for what Estabrook regarded as Simon's betrayal, he'd sent a killer after Keira. She and Lizzie had stopped him in the ancient stone

89

circle just down the lane.

And now here we are again, Josie thought. Lizzie, hotelier and daughter of a spy. Keira, artist and folklorist. The two women were in love with dangerous men, and not a little dangerous themselves.

And me?

She was the enigmatic British spy, she thought with amusement and just a touch of bitterness. After Myles, she'd given up hope of having a normal relationship with a man.

Any relationship at the rate she'd been going for the past two years.

Now what? Myles was alive and he wasn't a traitor, but nothing would ever be the same between them. There was no going back to their lives prior to his supposed death and treachery. He'd made his choices.

Lizzie sighed, shaking her head. "Stop kidding yourself, Josie."

"What?"

"You're as in love with Myles Fletcher as ever."

"As ever? I've never been in love with him —"

Lizzie and even Keira burst into laughter. Josie suppressed a flicker of impatience. What did these two women know about her life? But she knew her mood had nothing to

90

do with them and everything to do with those few minutes with Myles that afternoon. Being near him again after two years hadn't been what she'd expected. She could almost feel his mouth on hers, his hands on her — the path to ruin, that sort of thinking.

"All right, then," she said briskly. "It's late and I'm hungry. What shall we fix for supper?"

Lizzie raised her eyebrows. "You're blushing. A stiff-upper-lip MI6 agent —"

"I keep Will Davenport's calendar," she said with a mock sniff, "nothing more."

"Myles will come back to you," Keira said softly.

Josie snorted. First the bloody bastard had to live through the week. But she smiled and reached for her coat. "Shall we just head to the pub before Eddie O'Shea closes up for the night?"

Keira slipped on a long, thick sweater. "You're not going to tell us where Myles, Simon and Will have gone, are you, Josie?"

"You're assuming I know."

"They're not fishing in Scotland, that's for sure," Lizzie muttered.

She led the way out into the night. She looked as if she could have slept on bare rock in a gale and awakened fresh and ready to go. Josie found herself wanting to tell her new friends more about herself, but she knew she wouldn't. Let them wonder about the true nature of her work without any confirmation or elaboration from her. That she wanted to chat with them just proved how comfortable she was with these two women.

Quite scary, actually.

Discovering Myles wasn't dead or a traitor had thrown her off completely. She'd become so accustomed to shutting off any thought of him — any feeling. She couldn't bear thinking about him. Then all of a sudden . . . there he was, mixed up with a dangerous American billionaire and chasing terrorists.

He'd never expected to survive this mission. She'd seen that in his gray eyes just a few hours ago.

Couldn't she have found an easier man to love?

It was almost ten o'clock when they arrived at the pub. Eddie O'Shea was closing up, but he let them in and served them fish soup and warm brown bread that he said his no-account brother Patrick had made. Josie sat with Keira and Lizzie at a table by the peat fire, Eddie's springer spaniel sleeping soundly on the hearth.

"You look worried," Lizzie said.

Josie nibbled on one last bite of bread, liberally spread with Irish butter. "I have this terrible sense of foreboding." She realized what a ridiculous and unhelpful thing that was to say and attempted a smile to cover for herself. "Perhaps it's just due to an impending bad night on the sofa."

"Don't worry about Keira and me, all right? Do what you have to do." Lizzie leaned back, as at ease in the simple Irish pub as she was in one of her family's hotels — or Will Davenport's mansion in the Scottish Highlands. "Keira and I can check with Colm Dermott in Cork on our way to Dublin and ask him about Sophie. We'll be fine."

Josie had no doubt about their abilities, but they would also follow a lead if one came to them. They were curious about Scoop Wisdom's archaeologist. Just because he was a police officer who'd just recovered from serious injuries sustained in a bomb blast and just because Myles had been at Keira's cottage didn't mean there was any danger in asking questions about Sophie Malone.

Didn't mean there wasn't, either, Josie thought, tempted to order Irish whiskey to go with her soup and bread.

Keira twisted her hands together, as if

they'd gone too long already without holding brushes and pencils. "It's not as if I don't have time to kill," she said wistfully. "I haven't a single image in my head to draw or paint."

Josie recognized her new friend's malaise for what it was — painter's block. Perhaps a trip to Cork and Dublin would be a good distraction. It certainly wasn't on the face of it unsafe, but as they headed out onto the dark, quiet lane, Josie couldn't suppress what she could only describe as a chill up her spine.

She blamed Myles Fletcher and wished she'd ordered that whiskey after all.

6

Shannon, Ireland

Scoop eased into the security line at Shannon Airport before the long flight back across the Atlantic. He'd stayed in a lousy hotel a few miles from the airport, its saving grace a full Irish breakfast that had helped chase off his bad dreams about scary dogs and mean fairies.

Definitely good to be heading home.

He spotted red hair about ten people ahead of him and immediately thought of Sophie Malone — not a reassuring sign of his state of mind before a seven-hour flight. He took another look, figuring he *had* to be wrong, but there she was — the red-headed archaeologist he'd met yesterday morning and a British spy had warned him about yesterday afternoon.

She grabbed a bin, turned and waved, smiling as if she'd expected to find him behind her in a line at the airport.

Scoop got through security and caught up with her in the busy duty-free shop. She wore slim black pants and a long dark gray sweater, a contrast to her muddy hiking clothes and bright blue rain jacket of yesterday. Her hair was pulled back but still had a wild look to it. He'd showered, shaved and put on his most comfortable khakis and lightweight sweater.

"We must be on the same flight," he said.

"Lucky us." She opened the glass door of a cooler and reached inside. "Water?"

"Yeah, thanks. Did you drive in this morning?"

She nodded. "My folks are staying in Kenmare. I took their rental car back, and they kept my car. They're taking off for a few days to hike the Kerry Way. Doesn't that sound idyllic?"

"You mean more idyllic than spending the day on a crowded flight across the Atlantic?"

"You have a wry sense of humor, Scoop," Sophie said, leading the way to the cash registers with two bottles of water. She'd bought the biggest size. "The headwinds add time to flying west. It's so much easier flying to Ireland than flying home from Ireland."

"You seem like an experienced traveler."

"I guess so. In some ways it feels as if I'm

96

leaving home rather than going home."

Scoop reached for his wallet, but she shook her head, insisting on paying for both bottles of water herself. As she fished out euros, his cell phone vibrated in the front pocket of his carry-on pack. He stepped out of the line and took the call.

"According to one of Will's friends in London," Josie Goodwin said, "Sophie Malone is booked on the same flight to Boston as you are."

"So she is," Scoop said.

"Standing right there, is she?"

"Yep. What friend in London?"

"Lord Davenport knows all kinds. I also learned that Dr. Malone met just last week with an octogenarian expert in art theft."

"Is he another of Davenport's London friends?"

"Not exactly. Our octogenarian's name is Wendell Sharpe. He frequently consults with INTERPOL. He and Dr. Malone had tea at the Rush Hotel off St. Stephen's Green in Dublin. Odd coincidence, don't you think?"

"Not after yesterday. What did they discuss?"

"I don't know yet. She's a legitimate academic. Quite well respected. She recently completed her dissertation and a postdoctoral fellowship here in Ireland. Her field is the Celtic Iron Age, particularly in Ireland and Great Britain. She's an expert in Celtic visual arts."

"Does she like sugar in her tea?"

"Lemon," Josie said.

Scoop had no idea if she were kidding. "Who does she know in Ireland? Who are her friends here?"

"We're working on that."

"We?"

Josie sighed. "Keira has painter's block, and Lizzie's bored."

"They aren't law enforcement," Scoop said. "Or spies."

"Neither am I. I work for a British aristocrat. I plan his fishing and golf trips."

"Where are you three now?"

"Keira and Lizzie are en route to Dublin via Cork. I'm still at Keira's cottage."

Collecting reports from her spy friends, no doubt. Scoop noticed Sophie had finished paying for the water and was heading toward him. He had a sudden bad feeling about her — Myles's visit, what she was holding back. "Stay put," he told Josie. "Get Lizzie and Keira back there. You can all chase rainbows and drink Guinness."

"You can be quite annoying, can't you, Detective Wisdom?"

"What? I wouldn't mind chasing rainbows and drinking Guinness."

But Josie Goodwin had hung up.

Sophie joined him and handed him his bottle of water. "Try to drink every drop on the flight," she said, shoving her own bottle into an outer compartment of her shoulder bag. "It'll help."

"Mostly I was passed out on pain meds on my flight from Boston to Scotland." Except when he and Bob O'Reilly, who was in the seat next to him, had discussed how a bomb had ended up on Abigail's back porch. Scoop slid his phone back in his carry-on. "Guess who that call was about?"

"No idea."

Her body language indicated she knew exactly who. He tucked the huge water bottle into his pack. "It was about a certain Sophie Malone, Ph.D."

"Who would be calling about me?"

"A friend here in Ireland." Not a lie, technically, although he'd only met Josie Goodwin three weeks ago at Abigail's wedding. "I'm cautious these days."

"So you're checking me out?" She paused, narrowing those bright blue eyes on him. Her freckles didn't stand out as much in the artificial airport light. After a couple beats, she nodded thoughtfully. "All right.

That makes sense. You're a detective who just went through an awful experience. I'm from Boston, I'm an archaeologist and I interrupted your visit to the ruin where a serial killer terrorized a friend of yours."

"Plus you're hiding something."

"Aren't we all?" She seemed unperturbed by his skepticism as she hoisted her bag back onto a slender shoulder, strands of red hair dropping into her face. "Where are you sitting?"

"Row 40."

"I'm way up front. Just as well, don't you think?" She smiled at him. "I have a feeling if I were any closer, I'd be a distraction."

Looking at her, all Scoop could think was that he had to get out of Ireland and back to his home turf. He let his gaze linger on her longer than was necessary, or wise, but she didn't seem to notice. It had to be the fairies. He was attracted to cops, prosecutors, the occasional crime lab technician. Not red-headed experts on the Iron Age.

"This friend who called," she said. "Is it Keira Sullivan?"

"Doesn't matter, does it?"

"Keira and I are going to be working together on the Boston-Cork conference, and Colm Dermott and I are colleagues. If you've planted ideas in their heads about

100

my hiding something, I probably should know."

"Hell of a small world, isn't it? I didn't plant ideas in anyone's heads. I'm not here to screw things up for you. You seem like the type who needs to stay busy."

"I suppose I am. I suspect you are, too."

He grinned at her. "See? Something in common." They passed a rack of Irish souvenirs on their way out of the duty-free shop. "You didn't show up at that ruin yesterday just out of professional curiosity."

"And you know this how?"

"Instinct."

Her eyes sparked with challenge. "Ah."

He set his pack on an empty chair and didn't let her doubt faze him. "You have some kind of personal stake in what happened there. You volunteered for the conference. Why? Something to do with Jay Augustine? Did you do business with our jailed serial killer?"

"You've been away from your job a long time. I'm sure it'll be good to get back to work and have real cases to focus on."

"I have real cases now."

She didn't falter for even half a second. "Even better. It'll be good to get back to them full-time." She headed for the ladies' room and tossed him another smile as she pushed open the door. "See you at customs."

He sat down, but Sophie wandered off when she came out of the ladies' room and managed to avoid him until they boarded the plane. He had an aisle seat. She did, too. She wasn't way up front. She was seven rows ahead of him. Either she couldn't add, or lying was her way of telling him not to bug her on the flight.

He didn't bug her, but he kept an eye on her while he read a book and drank the water she'd bought him. It was a long, skin-crawling seven hours across the Atlantic. He had smart, pretty Sophie Malone a few rows in front of him, a four-year-old kicking his seat behind him and, directly across the aisle, two old women who talked for all but about six seconds of the flight. Sitting still had never been his long suit, and almost getting blown up in his own backyard hadn't helped his patience.

His conversations with Myles Fletcher and Josie Goodwin hadn't helped, either. Was Sophie onto something — deliberately or inadvertently — that would interest British intelligence? A professional, or even a personal, interest in Keira's ruin was one thing. Keeping secrets was another.

When the plane landed, Sophie jumped

up and squeezed past a young couple with a toddler. If Scoop tried the same maneuver, he'd knock someone over, but she was slim, agile and much faster than anyone would expect just looking at her. She also had a big, friendly smile. Scoop was faster than he looked, but that was it. He wasn't slim or agile, and he certainly didn't have a big, friendly smile.

He wondered if being back on American soil would help him lose that fairy-spell, love-at-first-sight feeling. So far, not so good.

He caught up with her again at baggage claim. "Share a cab?" he asked as she lifted a backpack off the belt.

She hooked its strap onto one shoulder. "Oh — no, thanks." She motioned vaguely toward the exit. "Someone's picking me up."

Scoop didn't even have to be good at detecting lies to see through that one. Not that she was trying hard to hide that she wasn't telling the truth.

He could have taken the subway, too, but he went ahead and grabbed a cab.

He'd be seeing Sophie Malone again. It wasn't a question of if. It was a question of when and under what circumstances.

Scoop had the cab drop him off in Jamaica

Plain. He stood in front of the triple-decker he owned with Bob O'Reilly and Abigail Browning. It was a freestanding, solid house, one of thousands of triple-deckers built in the early 1900s for immigrant workers. It had character. Abigail and Owen were due back soon from their honeymoon. Bob was working. He and some of the guys from the department had boarded up the windows with fresh plywood and strung yellow caution tape across the front porch.

Scoop had never figured his second-floor apartment would be the last place he owned, but he'd had no immediate plans to move. He, Bob and Abigail all hated that three police detectives had brought violence to their own neighborhood. Their street was semi-gentrified, with mature trees and well-kept gardens. There were young families with kids on bicycles, teenagers playing street hockey, professionals, old people.

Scoop unlocked the side gate, left his carry-on and duffel bag on the walk and headed to the postage-stamp of a backyard. The bomb had set off a fire on Abigail's first-floor back porch that burned straight through to her dining room. His porch, directly above hers, had also burned. The firefighters had gotten there fast and stopped the fire from spreading, but with the extensive smoke and water damage, the entire three-story house had to be gutted. Bob was in charge of figuring out what came next. It'd be a while before they could move back in.

Abigail planned to sell her place and move with Owen into a loft in the renovated waterfront building where the new headquarters of Fast Rescue, Owen's international search-and-rescue outfit, were being relocated from Austin. Bob had mentioned maybe he could take the top two floors and Scoop could move to Abigail's place. Sounded good to Scoop, but it'd involve redesigning and probably more money.

He squinted up at his boarded-up apartment. He'd done his mourning for any stuff he'd miss. Photographs, mostly, but his family had copies of a lot of them — nieces, nephews, birthday parties, holidays.

The air still tasted and smelled of charred wood and metal. He walked over to the edge of his vegetable garden. He'd been weeding when Fiona O'Reilly had arrived that day and offered to help him pick tomatoes.

That was what they'd been doing when the bomb went off. Picking tomatoes.

"Hell," he breathed, remembering.

The bomb had to have already been in place under Abigail's grill when they'd all

105

gotten up that morning.

It was constructed with C4. Nasty stuff.

He, Bob, Abigail, Owen and Fiona had made lists of people they'd seen at the house in the days before the bomb. Everyone. Cops included.

Maybe especially cops, Scoop thought, sighing at the weeds that had taken over his garden. He could still see where firefighters and paramedics had trampled his neat rows in the rush to save his life and keep the fire from spreading to neighboring homes. He'd trampled a few gardens in his years as a police officer. He noticed a couple of ripe tomatoes and squatted down, pulling back the vines, but the tomatoes had sat in the dirt too long. The bottoms were rotted.

"What the hell," he said, "they'll make good compost."

He yanked up a few weeds, aware of the scars on his back, his shoulders, his arms. He'd grabbed Fiona, protecting her as best he could from the shards of metal and wood as he'd leaped with her for cover — the compost bin Bob and Abigail had moaned and groaned about when Scoop had been building it.

He got to his feet and looked up at the sky, as gray and drizzly as any he'd seen in Scotland and Ireland. He had no regrets about being back home.

He had a lot of work to do.

He headed back out to the gate, picked up his stuff and unlocked his car, sinking into the driver's seat. He'd have no problem readjusting to driving on the right. He glanced at himself in the rearview mirror. He looked as if he'd flown on the wing of the plane instead of in an aisle seat. He needed a good night's sleep.

Where? Should he take Lizzie Rush up on her offer to put him up at her family's five-star Boston hotel — the one where Sophie Malone used to work?

"Might as well," he said aloud, and started the car.

7

Boston, Massachusetts

Sophie's iPhone jingled, signaling an incoming text message. She'd texted Damian when she'd landed in Boston. She checked her screen as she emerged from her subway stop onto Boston Common. Her brother's response was about what she'd expected: Nothing new. Go dig in the dirt.

She smiled. The Malones were known for not mincing words, Damian especially.

After the long flight, she welcomed the walk up to Beacon Hill. The narrow, familiar streets and black-shuttered town houses helped her to shake off the odd feeling that she was out of her element, on strange and unpredictable ground. She'd gone to college in Boston. She had friends there. It wasn't as if she'd just landed in a foreign country or a city where she didn't know anyone.

She descended steep, uneven stone steps

to a black iron gate between two town houses. Since giving up her apartment in Cork, she'd felt uprooted, but unlike Scoop Wisdom and his detective friends, her homelessness was by choice and finances.

No one had blown up her house.

Using the keys Taryn had given her, Sophie unlocked the gate and went through a tunnel-like archway that opened into a small, secluded brick courtyard, one of Beacon Hill's many nooks and crannies. Passersby would never guess it was there. The owners of a graceful brick town house had converted part of their walkout basement into an apartment, with its own entrance onto the courtyard. Taryn had rented it when she was performing Shakespeare in Boston and hadn't let go of it.

Sophie unlocked the door, painted a rich, dark green, and set her backpack on the floor of the small entry. The tiny apartment, with its cozy Beacon Hill atmosphere, suited Taryn's personality and unpredictable life-style. She'd sublet it to an actress friend for the summer, but she'd departed in early September for a role in Chattanooga.

Taryn had placed a round table by the full-size paned windows that looked onto the charming courtyard, where neighbors had set out pots of flowers. A perfunctory kitchen, with downsized appliances, occupied one windowless wall. On the opposite wall a low sectional anchored the seating area in front of a nonworking fireplace.

No cockroaches scurried on the hardwood floor, which Sophie took as a hopeful sign. She'd forgotten just how low the ceilings were. She wasn't claustrophobic, but she hadn't been wild about small, cramped spaces even before her brush with death in an Irish cave. Her experience at archaeological sites had forced her to learn how to deal with them.

She dragged her backpack into the bedroom, its sole window level with the street. She unpacked and, restless after her hours with a suspicious Boston detective behind her, dived into cleaning the apartment from top to bottom. She mopped, scrubbed, vacuumed, put fresh sheets on the bed, dug out clean towels and debated walking to the grocery for a few provisions. Taryn's actress friend had left mustard, salsa and carrots in the fridge and an unopened pint of vanilla ice cream in the freezer. Not terribly promising.

Sophie abandoned thoughts of food and instead changed into leggings and an oversize T-shirt and set out on a run, winding her way over to the Charles River Esplanade. It was early evening, gray but not raining. She didn't push hard. After three miles, she felt less jet-lagged, less a stranger in a strange land and slowed to an easy jog back up Beacon Hill.

She took a shower, slipped into a skirt, a sweater and flats and headed out again. She didn't feel like cooking. She wasn't even sure she felt like eating, but she walked down to Charles Street to the Whitcomb, the Rush family's Boston hotel.

Good-looking, tawny-haired Jeremiah Rush stood up from the antique reception desk in the lobby. "Sophie Malone!"

"Hey, Jeremiah. Long time."

He stepped out from behind the desk, his dark gray suit clearly expensive and fitting his lean frame perfectly. "I thought you might turn up. Lizzie called this morning and said you were on your way back to Boston."

"Lizzie? How did she know?"

"A Boston cop she ran into in Ireland," Jeremiah said, no sign he considered the call from his cousin odd. "She didn't go into detail."

"What's Lizzie doing in Ireland anyway?"

He grinned. "Who knows?"

"Did she ask you to report back should I

turn up?"

"She did, indeed."

Sophie supposed she shouldn't be surprised to undergo a certain amount of scrutiny after she'd encountered Scoop Wisdom yesterday, but she hadn't expected Lizzie Rush to be on her case. Had the call he'd taken at the airport that morning been from her?

"It's great to see you, Sophie," Jeremiah said. "I hear it's Dr. Malone now. Congratulations."

"Thanks." She relaxed some. "It's good to see you, Jeremiah. I just got in."

"Guinness beckons, does it? It's on the house. I remember when you'd be doing homework on your break. You had more drive than I ever did in school. Have to celebrate your milestone, right?"

"Definitely. Thank you. Join me if you can get away from the desk."

"I will. Oh, and I should warn you." He lowered his voice, as if he were telling her something he shouldn't. "The cop who told Lizzie about you is staying here. Detective Wisdom. I just checked him in."

Sophie glanced at the stairs down to Morrigan's, the hotel's upscale Irish bar named for Lizzie's Irish mother. "Is he down there now?"

"Not at the moment. I thought since you're both just back from Ireland . . ." Jeremiah didn't finish. "I should know better than to try to figure out what all Lizzie's up to. Enjoy your drink."

Sophie thanked him again and trotted down the stairs. She sat at a high stool at the bar and ordered a glass of Guinness, watching the bartender, new since she'd worked there, go through the proper two-part process to pour it.

She'd taken just two sips when Scoop Wisdom descended the stairs, eased over to her and pointed to a table. He had on a dark sweater and dark khakis and looked as if he weren't struggling with jet lag at all. "Come sit with me."

Sophie set down her glass. "As in, you'll arrest me if I don't?"

"As in, we need to talk."

She wondered if Jeremiah had tipped Scoop off that she was on the premises, or if the man's cop instincts were just on overdrive where she was concerned. He walked over to a small table under a window that looked out on Charles Street, quiet on the dreary late-September night. Sophie took another quick sip of her Guinness, welcoming its strong, distinctive flavor. She left her glass behind when she went over to

113

Scoop's table.

"Amazing," she said, sitting across from him. "Yesterday we met unexpectedly in an Irish ruin, this morning we run into each other at the airport and now here we are in a Boston pub. What're the odds?"

"Pretty good, I'd say."

She ignored his dry sarcasm. "It's after midnight in Ireland. Can you feel the time change?"

Scoop settled back in his chair. "What's your game, Sophie?"

He knew something. She could see it in his dark eyes as she decided on a response. He was an internal affairs detective, presumably especially good at telling when someone was dissembling. She wasn't good at spotting liars. She was good at doing the painstaking, detailed work of an archaeologist and curious by nature, but, as Damian had reminded her, a good education and a curious nature didn't make her a detective.

Which at least gave her an angle to try on Scoop. "No game," she said. "I'm just a curious person with a love for Ireland, archaeology and history. I'm borrowing my sister's apartment. I have a few odds and ends lined up to put food on the table, and I'm teaching a couple of college classes next semester while I set up interviews for a tenure-track position. I have a good lead on one here in Boston."

"Will your work with the Boston-Cork folklore help?"

"Sure. I'm looking forward to it. I have several people in mind already for my panel, but I'll be putting out a call for papers in the next day or two. It's an honor to work with Colm Dermott. He's brilliant. Everyone I know loves him." Sophie paused as a waiter placed what appeared to be a frosty glass of soda in front of Scoop. "Smart man, Detective Wisdom, staying away from alcohol in the middle of an interrogation."

"It's not an interrogation. If it were, you'd know."

"Hot lights? Thumbscrews?"

He gave her just the glimmer of a smile. "Tape recorder." He didn't touch his drink. "What else, Sophie?"

"A friend here in Boston offered me a job tutoring student athletes a few hours a week. Hockey players, mostly. Ever play hockey, Detective?"

"Yeah, I played hockey. Still do. You take the job?"

"I did. I can start as soon as I'm able."

"Good. Start tomorrow."

"You know, Scoop," Sophie said, "I don't take to being bossed around. Even my

115

parents had a hard time telling me what to do when I was a kid. My sister, too. We're twins."

"Noncompliant personalities?"

"I think of us as independent. When we were kids, we'd go off on our own and explore the little Irish village outside Cork where we lived."

"Sounds to me as if your folks didn't watch you. Why were you living in Ireland?"

"My father was sent there by his company. My mother taught school."

He raised his glass. "You used to work here at Morrigan's as a student."

Sophie resisted the temptation to jump up and run. His scrutiny — his knowledge of her — was unsettling. "You've been checking me out. Has Lizzie Rush been helping? I'd run into her from time to time when I worked here. She was always very nice. All the Rushes are."

"She was a part of what went on in Boston this summer."

"That's what I hear."

He sipped his drink and set the glass back down, his gaze leveled on her. "A lot's gone on lately that involves Ireland and Boston."

Sophie nodded, trying not to stare at a thick, obviously fresh scar that started just above his collarbone and continued around

116

to the back of his neck. She'd noticed it yesterday at the ruin. As scarred as he was, Scoop struck her as solid and competent — and impossible to kill. Yet if he'd been standing in the wrong place or hadn't reacted as he had, the bomb could have killed him instantly. The shrapnel that no doubt had caused the scar she saw now could have nicked an artery instead. He could have bled to death in his own backyard.

She didn't have visible scars from her night in the cave. She remembered Tim O'Donovan waving to her as he sailed off, leaving her on the island for the sixth time in as many weeks. This time, she wasn't just there for a day hike. She was staying overnight.

It hadn't occurred to her anyone would follow her out there.

She became aware that Scoop was watching her closely. "What's on your mind, Sophie?"

She made herself smile. "Dinner, actually. I didn't eat a bite on the plane."

"I cleaned my plate." She noticed a flicker of amusement in his eyes, but it didn't last. "You might just ease back from whatever you're up to and stick to your job hunting."

"You look for bad cops. Do you think one was involved in what happened to you?"

"Anyone in mind?"

"I don't know any police officers. Other than you." Technically, her statement was true. Her brother was an FBI agent, not a police officer. She leaned back in her chair and did her best to come across as casual, friendly and open, with nothing to hide. Telling him about the cave would only invite even more suspicion and difficult questions. "I figure we've bonded now that we've both encountered a mysterious big black dog in the Irish hills."

"Sophie, if you're meddling in a police investigation —"

"I'm not."

"If you have your own agenda, it amounts to the same thing."

"I don't have an agenda. At the moment I'm thinking I should have known better than to have alcohol when I'm jet-lagged and hungry."

"Drink's on me."

"Actually, it's on Jeremiah Rush. He was still in high school when I worked here. He and his three brothers and Lizzie all have had to learn the family business from the ground up. They're all hard workers."

"Okay, I get it," Scoop said. "You have good reason to be here. No axes to grind. Where can I find you, besides tutoring hockey players?"

"My sister's apartment is on Pinckney Street."

He withdrew his wallet, pulled out a business card and handed it to her. "Call me anytime, day or night, if you decide you want to tell me the rest."

"There is no —"

He held up a hand, stopping her. "Don't even try it with me. There's more, Sophie. There's a lot more."

She kept her mouth shut this time and got out of there.

When she reached the street, she knew she couldn't go back to the apartment right away. Her internal clock might still be set to Irish time, where it was after midnight, but she was too restless yet to sleep, read or work.

She walked past Morrigan's and felt Scoop Wisdom's eyes on her but refused to look down and see if he was, indeed, watching her.

Percy Carlisle's house was a few blocks away in Back Bay.

She'd head over there.

8

Scoop figured he could kill his jet lag by having a beer and a nice dinner or by taking a walk and following Sophie. When he saw her in the window, heading in the opposite direction from her sister's apartment, he decided on the walk.

He paid for his soda and received another call from Josie Goodwin as he started out. "Talk to me, Josie," he said. "What do you know? How's Ireland?"

"Lovely. I'm alone in a cottage in the dead of night with nothing but cows, sheep and the wind for company. I'm thinking of becoming a farmer."

"I have a single brother who's a farmer."

"Give him my number." She cleared her throat and continued briskly. "I have a tidbit of information that could prove useful . . . or not. We've discovered a cryptic report of a call to the Irish Garda by our archaeologist friend last September."

"How cryptic?"

"I have no details yet whatsoever. Apparently there wasn't a crime. For all I know, Dr. Malone asked the guards to clear a bat out of her bedroom."

"You can find out more?"

"Of course," she said airily. "In the meantime, Taryn Malone, Sophie's twin sister, is presently starring in a popular romantic comedy in London. She's an accomplished Shakespearean actress." Josie yawned, then added, "That's not terribly helpful, is it?"

"Everything's helpful at this point. Anything from Lizzie and Keira?"

"They've arrived safely in Dublin. They missed Colm Dermott in Cork."

"I'm glad you listened to my advice," Scoop said dryly.

"Did you think I would? Of course you didn't. You know, Scoop, our Dr. Malone could simply be a wildly curious academic with ties to Boston."

"These days, that by itself could get her into trouble." He turned down Beacon Street, spotting Sophie up ahead. "Anything more on the octogenarian expert in art theft?"

"Still working on that one."

Scoop sighed. He wasn't sure he should encourage Josie Goodwin — not that he

121

needed to. "Thanks. Find out why Sophie called the guards last year. If you need any official help on your end —"

"With what? Looking into a woman because she ventured into an Irish pasture?"

"Put that way," Scoop said, "this all does sound crazy."

"But it's not, is it? Oh, listen to me. Next I'll be seeing fairies trooping in the hills." Josie sighed heavily. "As lovely as it is here, I'm not one for the countryside."

"Sweet dreams," Scoop said with a grin.

Josie muttered under her breath. He couldn't quite make out her words but they sounded impolite. When she disconnected, he picked up his pace, closing the gap between him and Sophie. He expected her to turn around and chew him out for following her, but she seemed unaware of his presence.

She approached an elegant Back Bay mansion that he recognized as the Boston home of Percy Carlisle. Carlisle's name had surfaced over the summer as one of Jay Augustine's wealthy customers in his role as a respected dealer in high-end antiques and works of art. As far as Scoop knew, none of Augustine's clients were under suspicion of any involvement with the man's violence.

A thin man in a baseball cap walked out

to the street and greeted her.

It wasn't Percy Carlisle.

Scoop recognized Cliff Rafferty, a newly retired police officer, and, suddenly feeling protective of Sophie, fell in next to her. Rafferty dropped a cigarette onto the sidewalk and rubbed it out with the toe of his shoe. His last assignment with the department had been working security at the Augustine showroom in the South End in the weeks after Jay Augustine's arrest.

"Hey, Scoop," Rafferty said, "I didn't know you were back in town."

"I got in this afternoon. You're working for the Carlisles?"

Rafferty shrugged. He was in his mid-fifties, with leathery skin from his four-pack-a-day smoking habit. "It's a cushy private security gig. Who's your friend here?" He held up a hand and grinned at Sophie. "Wait. Let me guess. You're Sophie Malone, Mr. Carlisle's archaeologist friend. He left a message last night to expect you. Cliff Rafferty. Nice to meet you."

Sophie gave Scoop a sideways glance but made no move to step away from him. She smiled at Rafferty. "Nice to meet you, too. How did you recognize me?"

He pointed at her head. "Red hair." He grinned again, the corners of his eyes

123

crinkling under the streetlight. "Plus I looked you up on the Internet. You're listed as a postdoctoral fellow on your university Web site. Your picture's right there." He nodded toward Scoop. "You know Detective Wisdom?"

"We were on the same flight from Ireland today."

Rafferty didn't look satisfied with her answer, but he turned to Scoop. "I went by your place after the bomb. It's a mess. Where you staying?"

"Hotel for now," Scoop said.

"At least that nutball billionaire can't try again. How's Abigail?"

"She and Owen are still on their honeymoon."

"That'll help her put this thing behind her. She's tough. She'll get right back on the job." He shifted his attention back to Sophie. "What can I do for you, Dr. Malone?"

"I was just getting some air after my flight," she said.

Rafferty made a face. "I hate flying."

"Have you ever been to Ireland?"

"Yeah, sure. I had to see the ancestral homeland, you know?"

"Is Helen Carlisle home?"

"She's inside," he said.

As he spoke, a tall, slender woman came out of the house, shutting the solid, black-painted door behind her and descending the steps to a brick walk. She joined them on the street. She wore a knee-length red sweater but she looked chilled. Scoop put her at around forty. She had pale blue eyes and thick dark hair that hung loose to her shoulders. If she had on any makeup, he couldn't tell. She was very attractive, but he liked standing close to disheveled Sophie. Across from him at Morrigan's, he'd noticed that she had a dimple in her left cheek when she smiled — not that he'd given her much reason to smile, coming down hard on her the way he had.

Being out of Ireland wasn't helping him with the fairy spell. He was as attracted to her now, even after Josie Goodwin's report, as when he'd first spotted her in the Irish greenery.

Rafferty made the introductions. "Mrs. Carlisle, Detective Cyrus Wisdom — Scoop to most of us — and Sophie Malone, the friend Mr. Carlisle mentioned would stop by. Scoop, Sophie, this is Helen Carlisle."

"What a pleasure to meet you both," Helen said. "Sophie, it's so good to finally meet you. Detective Wisdom, I'm honored to meet you. You're a hero. All of us in

125

Boston are fortunate to have brave police officers such as yourself looking after us." She didn't pause long enough for Scoop to respond. "Cliff, I didn't realize you knew any of the officers involved in that awful explosion."

"I know them all," Rafferty said.

Helen Carlisle turned her attention to Sophie. "How was Percy last night?"

Sophie ran her fingertips along a black iron fence, her sweater and skirt askew at her hip. "Fine. I only saw him for a few minutes."

"I hated to leave him," Helen said. "I had business in New York — I just got back a little while ago — and I'm overseeing the renovations here at the house."

"Your husband's still in Ireland?" Scoop asked.

"I'm not sure where he is. He's off on one of his personal retreats. He warned me about them when we first got together. We're newlyweds, but we both had full lives before we were married. We try to respect that." She smiled pleasantly and wrapped her sweater more tightly around her. "I have plenty to do here. I keep hoping to discover a 'find' tucked away in a far corner of the attic or cellar. It'd be such fun to happen onto some long-forgotten artwork of real

126

value. You must know that feeling, Sophie, as an archaeologist."

"I do," she said, shivering in a sudden spit of rain. "I shouldn't keep you, and jet lag's really hitting me all of a sudden."

"Thank you for stopping by. Come again. I imagine Percy will be back before too long." Helen turned to Scoop, raindrops glistening on the bright red wool of her sweater. "You, too, Detective — come again anytime."

She retreated back up the walk to the house. Rafferty watched her a moment before turning back to Scoop. "Augustine's arrest has made a lot of rich folks nervous. What an animal he turned out to be. The Carlisles had nothing to do with his violence. His dealings with them were strictly professional."

Scoop almost welcomed the cold drizzle. "You met the Carlisles when you worked security at the Augustine showroom?"

"Yeah. Cushy job, guarding paintings and statues. This new job's pretty cushy, too." He withdrew a pack of cigarettes and tapped out one. "See you when they hand out your commendation for bravery. Enjoy the limelight while you can." He stuck the cigarette in his mouth and nodded to Sophie. "Dr. Malone."

He went back up the walk. Sophie shivered again. "It's colder out than I expected. I can feel fall in the air."

Scoop resisted an impulse to slip an arm around her. "You must be about dead on your feet."

"You, too," she said, almost smiling.

"We're still on Irish time. I'll walk you back to your place."

"As far as the Whitcomb is fine."

"You're not very trusting, are you?"

She laughed, tucking her hands into her sweater pockets. "I got on the same plane with you, didn't I?" She glanced back at the Carlisle house, the front door shut, lights shining in the tall windows. "A bit different from Keira's Irish ruin, isn't it?"

Scoop shrugged. "Right now I'll settle for a bed and a blanket."

"Me, too," she said, then caught herself. "I mean —"

"It's okay. You're jet-lagged."

"Very jet-lagged," she said, almost falling against him as she started down the street.

Scoop walked alongside her to Charles Street. The rain stopped, but the wind picked up. She looked cold and tired, but she had the presence of mind not to go back into the hotel with him and instead continued on to her sister's apartment on her own.

A good thing, Scoop thought when he headed downstairs for a drink and a sandwich and found Bob O'Reilly at the bar.

"When I was in Ireland and couldn't sleep," Scoop said as he eased onto a high stool next to Bob, "I'd sit up with a book and listen to the sheep and cows in the hills. In another twenty years, maybe I'll retire there."

"In another twenty years," Bob said, "you'll be running the department."

"Nah. I'm no good at the politics."

Bob O'Reilly was a big, burly fifty-year-old divorced father of three daughters. The son of a cop, he'd wanted to be a homicide detective even before a young woman two doors down from where he grew up in South Boston was kidnapped, sexually abused and murdered. That was thirty years ago. He still carried a picture of Deirdre McCarthy in his wallet.

Deirdre's mother had told Keira the story about the three Irish brothers, the fairies and the stone angel that had taken her to the Beara Peninsula. But Patsy McCarthy had also told the story to Jay Augustine, believing he was a respected dealer interested in her collection of angel figurines — and he'd killed her. Keira and Simon had found her body.

Bob drank some of his beer. His curly red hair was a tone lighter and brighter than Sophie Malone's and touched with gray. Not good, Scoop told himself, that he was thinking about the shade of Sophie's hair.

He ordered a club sandwich and, following Sophie's lead, added a Guinness to go with it. "Lizzie Rush booked me a room here," he said. "She insisted."

"I'm in Keira's place up the street," Bob said. "I took the lace out of the windows, but it still feels like I'm a creep or something, sleeping in my niece's apartment."

Scoop's beer arrived. "Do you know Cliff Rafferty's working security for a rich couple in Back Bay?"

"Yeah," Bob said, "I do."

"The Carlisles. Know them?"

"Old-money Boston. I think it's just the son left now. He did some business with Augustine. The wife — I forget her name . . ."

"Helen," Scoop supplied.

Bob lifted his glass. "Yeah. Helen. She worked at an auction house in New York before she married Percy. There are no missing Carlisles or auction house workers or anyone else to tie Augustine to them."

"As a killer," Scoop said.

"As opposed to what?"

130

"What if he was involved in pushing stolen art?"

Bob set his glass down and sighed. "Don't complicate my life more than it already is, Scoop, all right?"

"Cliff Rafferty's been out to our place."

Bob didn't respond right away. Finally he pushed aside his glass as if Scoop had just ruined his evening. "Hell, Scoop, what are you doing? You'll make yourself crazy. You'll make *me* crazy. Anyone could have planted that bomb. You said it yourself. Norman Estabrook could have slipped a few bucks to the meter reader to stick it under Abigail's grill. Said it was a present. A surprise. Who knows?"

"Estabrook was caught up in Jay Augustine's obsession with evil. There could be a stronger connection between those two than we realize."

Bob's eyes — the same shade of blue as those of his three daughters and niece — narrowed on Scoop. "What's going on? What do you have?"

Scoop drank more of his Guinness, remembering evenings alone on the Beara Peninsula when he'd force himself not to speculate, not to lose himself in the possible scenarios and suspects. He and Bob weren't on the investigation. They couldn't be. They

131

were personally involved.

Victims.

He hated that word.

"Nothing," he said finally. "Grasping at thin air. You ever run into an archaeologist named Sophie Malone? She used to work here."

Bob sighed. "Archaeologist, Scoop? What the hell?"

"We met in Ireland yesterday and ended up on the same plane back to Boston today. Just one of those things."

"Yeah. Imagine. That's the short version?"

Scoop nodded and looked at the sandwich placed in front of him. He'd lost his appetite.

"You need sleep," Bob said. "Jet lag makes me feel like I have dryer lint in my head. Keira had me try some scheme she read about on the Internet. Basically you don't eat for about twelve hours on the day you travel. You just drink a lot of water."

"Did it work?"

"I don't know. I didn't make it past four hours. Did you run into Keira in Ireland?"

It was a blatant ploy for more information, not that Scoop blamed him. "I saw her and Simon yesterday before I headed to the airport." He decided not to mention the Brits. "They're good."

"The fairy prince and princess," Bob said, only half joking.

"I could believe in fairies after going out to Keira's ruin."

"Cathartic being there, wasn't it?"

"Yeah." He almost could hear the dog splashing in the stream, Sophie's laughter. "Yeah, it was."

Bob scratched one side of his mouth, looking the experienced homicide detective he was. "I'm not an enemy, Scoop. What else happened in Ireland?"

"It rained a lot my last week there."

Bob stood up. "Go to bed."

"Your beer's on me."

"Yeah. Good. We'll talk tomorrow."

He thumped up the stairs. Morrigan's had emptied out. Scoop ate a few bites of his sandwich and drank more of his Guinness. It was true that anyone could have planted the bomb. The triple-decker had no alarm system. There wasn't much of a lock on the gate. There was often no one at home, although he, Bob and Abigail had unpredictable schedules — which could be a deterrent to some stranger walking out back with a pipe-bomb stuck under his shirt or hidden in a backpack.

Another cop could have found out their schedules.

133

Scoop gave up on his sandwich and took his beer upstairs with him. His room was on the third floor, small, understated, with upscale towels and bath products and a fussy little table that he could use as a desk. He didn't care. The water was hot and the bed had clean sheets. The rest didn't matter.

No question it beat Tom Yarborough's sofa bed.

Yarborough had been out to Jamaica Plain countless times as Abigail's partner, but Scoop couldn't see him planting the bomb. Too ambitious. Too by-the-book. If Yarborough had an axe to grind or was after some extra cash, he'd go all out — he wouldn't do one small job for a billionaire like Norman Estabrook.

Given the increasingly late hour in Ireland, Scoop texted Josie Goodwin instead of calling: Ask your friends about Percy Carlisle.

He didn't waste time typing more of an explanation. Josie would have no problem figuring out who Percy Carlisle was. Maybe she already knew.

As Scoop washed up, he got an answer from Ireland: Will do.

Obviously his new British friend wasn't sleeping, which didn't bode well for his own night. He returned to the bedroom and

134

finally noticed the Whitcomb had a turn-down service. The drapes were pulled, soft music was playing and chocolates were on his pillow.

Definitely better than Yarborough's sofa bed.

9

Sophie woke up to not so much as a coffee ground in the cupboards and decided she should have gone to the grocery last night instead of getting herself further under the suspicion of a Boston police officer. Never mind how sexy Scoop was, she thought as she headed through the archway and out to the street. She couldn't just blame jet lag for her reaction to him — she hadn't been jet-lagged on the Beara Peninsula.

The wee folk, then. She'd blame them.

She smiled, debating her immediate options. Breakfast on Charles Street and chance she'd run into Scoop? *Hope* she would? The sky had cleared overnight, and it was a bright, pleasant late-September morning, a perfect day to help her kick any lingering jet lag and adjust to being back in Boston.

"Hey, Sophie — Dr. Malone." Cliff Rafferty got out of a car just up her quiet, narrow street and shut the door. "I hope I didn't startle you. Mr. Carlisle — Percy — mentioned your sister has an apartment up here. It wasn't hard to get the address. You two look a lot alike." He gave Sophie an easy grin as he tossed a cigarette onto the street and approached her. "I looked her up on the Internet, too."

Sophie relaxed slightly. She'd slipped into jeans and a dark green long-sleeve top, not bothering with a sweater. "I'm borrowing her place until I figure out what comes next. What can I do for you, Mr. Rafferty?"

He looked up at a windowbox dripping with ivy on the town house behind them, then at her again. "Like being back in Boston?"

"So far, so good. It hasn't been a full day yet."

"Feels great being done with school, doesn't it? All those years of classes, papers, research, and now you finally have those initials after your name."

He had an engaging manner, but Sophie assumed he'd looked her up for a reason beyond cheerful chitchat. "It does feel great, but there are more classes, papers, and research ahead. If I'm lucky."

"At least you'll be paid more as a professor than as a student." He shoved his hands into the pockets of his lightweight jacket. He had on baggy jeans that were an inch too short and running shoes. "You and Scoop Wisdom last night. That took me by surprise. I gather you didn't just meet on your flight back to Ireland yesterday."

"Just about. I ran into him on the Beara Peninsula the day before."

Rafferty's gaze was distant now, reminding her that he'd been a police officer. "Scoop's quite the ladies' man. He seems taken with you."

"I wouldn't know about that," Sophie said, heat rushing to her cheeks.

"Bet you'll find out." Rafferty winked at her unexpectedly, then withdrew a slip of paper from his pocket and handed it to her. "I need to talk to you. Not here. My place. I wrote down the address. Give me an hour."

Sophie folded up the paper. "I haven't had breakfast. Why don't we go for coffee? You can talk to me now."

"Nah. You come to me."

"What's this all about?"

"You're an expert in Celtic archaeology," he said. "I have something I want to show you. Get your opinion."

"Is it Celtic?"

"I don't know. If I knew . . ." He didn't finish, looking awkward now, even defensive.

138

"I was a cop for thirty years. I might not have played things as straight and narrow as Scoop Wisdom would want, but I never hurt anyone."

"Can I bring someone with me?"

"Yeah, why not? Go find Scoop and ask him if he wants to go with you. See how far you get." He grinned at her, then raised his thin shoulders in an exaggerated shrug. "Show up or don't. Your call. Just make it this morning. I'm working this afternoon."

He walked back to his car, got in and waved as he drove past her on the one-way street. Sophie watched him, trying to make sense of their conversation. Did he want to talk to her about stolen Celtic artifacts? His last assignment as a police officer had been working security at the Augustine showroom after Jay Augustine's arrest. He'd gone right from there to his job with the Carlisles.

Sophie headed back down the steps and through the gate and the archway into the secluded courtyard, dialing Taryn's number on her iPhone. Taryn picked up on the second ring, just as Sophie unlocked the apartment door. "Hey, Taryn," she said, "where's your car?"

"It's probably on Anderson or Myrtle, but it could be anywhere. I have a friend who moves it every ten days. Sophie, what's going on? You sound out of breath."

"That's because I'm walking fast."

"All right." Taryn didn't sound reassured. "I'm on my way back to London. If you need me, I'll be there."

"Thanks. What color's your car? I can't remember."

"Dark blue. It's a Mini —"

"That I remember," Sophie said with a smile, trying to sound less agitated. "All's well, Taryn. I'll be in touch."

Sophie disconnected and grabbed Taryn's car keys out of a drawer in the kitchen, then ducked back out to the street. She located the Mini in front of a small market on the next block. She still had time before meeting Rafferty and walked down to Cambridge Street — deliberately avoiding Charles Street and the Whitcomb Hotel — and got a coffee and a bagel. She ate the bagel on her way back up Beacon Hill and sipped her coffee as she unlocked the Mini and slid behind the wheel. It started right up.

Luckily she'd already set her coffee in the holder when Scoop Wisdom materialized by the passenger door. She hit a button to automatically roll down the window. "Good morning," she said. "Are you looking for me?"

"Uh-huh. Where are you off to?"

She didn't want to tell him, but she didn't want to lie, either. "Cliff Rafferty asked me to stop by his place."

Scoop opened the passenger door and got inside. "Talk."

"I don't want to be late."

"Then drive and talk. Or I'll drive and you can talk."

"It's my sister's car." Sophie noticed how close he was in the seat next to her. He had on a dark tan windbreaker, khakis and a chocolate-colored shirt that made his eyes seem deeper, richer. "Do you know where Rafferty lives?"

Scoop shook his head. "No."

She handed him the address. "I think I can figure out how to get there, but since you're a police officer —"

"I know the street."

She smiled. "Thought you might."

As she drove slowly down to Cambridge Street, Sophie told him about Rafferty's visit.

"You don't know what he has in mind," Scoop said.

"Neither do you. If he'd meant me any harm, he could have run me over going for coffee."

Scoop frowned at her, then shook his head. "I guess you can't be a shrinking violet digging up old bones."

"I generally don't dig up bones. My field is the Celtic Iron Age with a focus on Irish and British Celtic art."

"Such as?"

"Not necessarily 'art' as we think of it today."

"No sofa paintings?"

"No sofa paintings." She made her way to Commonwealth Avenue. Driving on the left had become natural for her in Ireland, but she readjusted quickly. "Think in terms of the art of everyday items — cauldrons, weapons, tools, jewelry."

"Is there a market for this stuff?"

"For the right collector, definitely, but there are rules for anything that's found during an excavation. I can't just pocket an Iron Age gold brooch and put it up on eBay."

"I read about that gold found in England by a guy with a metal detector."

"Yes, that's an amazing discovery. He unearthed a major hoard of early Anglo-Saxon gold and silver buried in a farmer's field in Staffordshire. It'll take years for archaeologists and historians to assess the objects. Most are articles of warfare. A true treasure."

"Who gets it?"

"Since it's over three hundred years old, it's been declared the property of the Crown."

"It'd be stealing if you tried to sneak artifacts out of Ireland?"

She wasn't sure he was asking a question, but said, "Undoubtedly, yes."

Scoop eased back in his seat as she drove past the sprawling campus of Boston University. "What happened to you in Ireland last year, Sophie?"

"You mean —"

"You called the Irish police."

She tightened her grip on the steering wheel. "What did you do, call the guards yourself over a Guinness last night? Why? What did I do to pop onto your radar?"

"I mentioned your name to friends in Ireland," he said.

She glanced over at him. "That's an incomplete answer."

"I'd get an F if you were grading me?"

"I'd hand your paper back and ask you to finish your answer," she said.

"That's because you would be the professor and I would be the student and therefore at your mercy. Right now —"

"It's the other way around. I'm at your mercy."

"We're just two friends talking in a very

little car." He pointed at a throng of students about to cross from a Green Line MBTA stop on the track in the middle of Commonwealth Avenue. "Careful."

"I won't run anyone over," Sophie said, "and last year I got in over my head on an adventure."

"Treasure hunting?"

She shook her head. "I just told you that I don't treasure hunt."

"You didn't go off with a metal detector yourself?"

"Ireland has the strictest laws in the EU against metal detecting at possible archaeological sites. To answer your question, no, I did not go off with a metal detector."

She was aware of his dark eyes on her as they came to Allston. He directed her to Cliff Rafferty's street. She parked in front of a two-family brown-shingled house with a giant oak shading a small front yard, its roots breaking apart the sidewalk.

Scoop unfastened his seat belt. "Do you think Cliff wants to see you because you're an archaeologist or because you're friends with Percy Carlisle?"

" 'Friends' is too strong."

"Were you two —"

"No," Sophie said quickly.

They got out of the car. "You and I aren't

finished," Scoop said, going ahead of her to the front door.

Sophie mounted the steps behind him, checking the address Rafferty had scrawled on the slip of paper. "He's on the upper floor." She reached past Scoop's broad shoulders for the doorbell but noticed the door was slightly ajar. "He's expecting me. He probably doesn't want to come down to open up."

Scoop pushed the door open and called up the stairs. "Cliff? Scoop here with Sophie Malone. We're on our way up."

There was no answer. Sophie started up the steps, but Scoop put a hand on her hip and eased past her. She stayed behind him, observing that the injuries he'd sustained in the bomb blast didn't impede his ability to climb a flight of stairs.

When they came to the second-floor landing, Sophie took a sharp breath and grabbed Scoop by the upper arm, her gaze riveted on the French door. Three realistic-looking replicas of human skulls had been tacked to the frame, one on each side and one directly in the middle of the lintel.

"Scoop . . ."

He glanced at her. "Stay close to me."

She dropped her hand from his arm. "The ancient Celts revered the human head."

Scoop grimaced. "Yeah. Great." He tapped open the door and called into the apartment. "Hey, Cliff. I jumped in the car with our Dr. Malone here."

Again there was no answer.

They entered a narrow living room that ran across the front of the house. A sentimental Irish tune was playing softly in the background. Sophie realized it was coming from the flat-screen television. A DVD was running, displaying familiar scenes of Ireland — the Cliffs of Moher, the Healy Pass, a rainbow over a lush, green Irish pasture.

"Something bad has happened," Sophie said.

Scoop withdrew his weapon. She hadn't even noticed the holster under his jacket. He touched her hand. "Just stay close." He squeezed her fingers. "Real close. Got it?"

She nodded.

Staying in the middle of the room, they stepped onto a worn rug and walked past the coffee table. It was piled with rolls of coated wire, wire cutters, plastic-coated blasting caps and a block of what looked like wrapped clay but Sophie assumed was probably C4 or another type of explosive.

Bomb-making materials.

Just beyond the coffee table, yellow and red glass beads were scattered on the hard-

146

wood floor at the edge of the rugs. "Scoop, glass beads are often found in Celtic graves."

But she didn't go on. More skulls were arranged on the woodwork of the double-doorway between the living room and the adjoining dining room.

Scoop stopped in the doorway and turned to her, grim, controlled. "Don't look," he said.

It was too late. She could see Cliff Rafferty hanging from an exposed beam in the dining room. She recognized his too-short jeans, his scuffed running shoes, his jacket. She didn't want to look at his face but did. From his coloring, the position of his neck, his twisted features — there was no question he was dead.

The rope had been tied to a heavy-duty eye hook screwed into the beam.

Her breathing shallow, her heart racing, Sophie edged next to Scoop. A small, round dining room table had been pushed against the wall. More glass beads were scattered on the bare floor between the table and the hanging scene.

A cast-iron pot was positioned directly under Rafferty's feet. He could have used it to stand on — or had been forced to stand on it. Sophie leaned forward and saw the pot was filled with parts of a disassembled gun, each part damaged, as if the weapon had been systematically hammered and destroyed piece by piece. A police badge, also dented and distorted, had been placed on top of the gun parts.

Next to the pot, on the floor, were two halves of a crude torc fashioned out of twisted gold wire, obviously deliberately cut in half.

Sophie made herself exhale slowly through her mouth. "Scoop, these are ritualistic symbols —"

"I see. You can tell me what they mean later." His dark eyes held hers for an instant. "Don't touch anything and stay right with me. Got that, sweetheart? Right with me."

They checked the rest of the apartment — the kitchen, bedroom and bathroom — and headed out to the back porch, a robin perched on a nearby maple branch. Scoop dialed his BlackBerry. Sophie noticed even his hands weren't shaking. While he identified himself and gave his report, she watched the robin fly away and contemplated the grisly scene in the apartment behind her.

"Backup's on the way," Scoop said as he disconnected.

She stepped back into the kitchen. She was shaking now. She tried to stop but bit her lip, drawing blood. Rafferty's body was just out of view in the dining room. She controlled her emotion and said quietly, "He didn't kill himself."

"Why do you say that?"

She faced Scoop, his expression unchanged, nothing about him suggesting he was affected by the past few minutes — by the terrible death of a fellow police officer. "The pagan Celtic practices reenacted in the dining room and living room suggest ritual sacrifice, not suicide." She crossed her arms on her chest, trying to keep herself from shivering. She wasn't cold. In fact, quite the opposite. It was warm in the apartment. She saw that no windows were open. Had the killer shut them before setting to work? "Before you ask, no, I don't know anything for certain. This isn't an archaeological site. It's . . ." She didn't finish.

"Sophie, easy — you okay?"

"I didn't expect this."

"Try to remember everything Cliff said to you. Don't try to draw conclusions on your own. Just remember."

She forced herself to remain steady on her feet and focused on Scoop, his jaw set hard, nothing about him even close to relaxed. He was intense but under control. "I assume you saw the bomb-making materials on the coffee table," she said. "What if Rafferty asked me here to confess his involvement with the bomb at your house?"

"Trust me, Sophie. It won't help to speculate."

"Maybe his guilt was weighing on him, and he arranged a suicide that made sense to him." She felt a sting of pain on her mouth and realized she'd bit her lip. "Except I don't believe that, based on what I see and what he told me. He said he wanted my opinion on something."

"Something to do with archaeology or with the Carlisles?"

"I don't know. He wouldn't say. The glass beads, the skulls, the pot filled with smashed parts of a gun — the hanging itself — all could fit into some garbled, twisted notion of pagan Celtic rituals. I'm not talking about modern paganism —"

"It's okay, Sophie. This scene means whatever the person who arranged it wanted it to mean, whether it was Cliff or someone else."

Her gaze rested on toast crumbs on a plate in the stainless steel sink.

Scoop touched her arm. "Don't try to make sense of things right now. You're an archaeologist. You're used to looking at evidence. You know how to be objective. You know you can't just assume a piece of glass you find in the dirt is some ancient artifact. It could be part of a beer bottle some drunk tossed."

"I get your point." She pulled her gaze from the sink. "You're right. I shouldn't let myself be driven by assumptions and get tunnel vision. Do I stay here or —"

She broke off, suddenly overwhelmed by the stifling heat in the apartment, by the proximity of death.

She was gone, running out the back door, down the balcony steps. She didn't breathe until she was out on the street, just as she heard sirens and the first cruiser arrived.

10

Kenmare, Southwest Ireland

Josie paused to admire the view of Kenmare Bay from the front steps of the Malones' Irish holiday house and found herself yearning for a few weeks on her own, with nothing more pressing to think about than whether to spend the afternoon on a long walk in the hills or curled up with a book.

She'd missed Antonia and James Malone and Sophie's twin sister, Taryn.

Not a total waste of a trip, Josie thought, but it was close.

Keira and Lizzie had finally caught up with Colm Dermott in Dublin that morning. He'd told them he'd talked to Sophie recently. They'd discussed the panel she was doing at the folklore conference and a bit about the violence that had touched Keira and Lizzie — even him — over the summer. He hadn't taken Sophie's interest as anything but natural curiosity and her role as an archaeologist.

Otherwise, he was clueless about what she might be up to.

"Perhaps nothing," Josie said aloud, hopping off the steps.

She started down the steep hill to her car. She noticed a man standing on the edge of the quiet road and faltered, hoping her sleepless night had got the better of her and she'd conjured him up.

She wasn't that lucky.

The man in front of her car was, indeed, long-lost, treacherous, sexy-as-hell-itself Myles Fletcher.

Josie didn't say a word as she navigated a series of small puddles from an early-morning shower and collected her thoughts. When she came to the road, she stuffed her hands into her coat pockets and suppressed, at least for the moment, any emotional reaction to his presence. "Will and Simon?" she asked crisply.

Myles opened the car door and dumped his rucksack in the back as if he had every right to do so. "They caught up with me and dinged me back here."

"Did they, now?"

He shrugged. "They're pursuing a different angle."

"A dangerous one?"

He grinned at her. "No more dangerous than me turning up here."

"You're compromised," she said, ignoring his irreverent humor. "Whoever you all are after now knows you're a British intelligence officer. That's why Will and Simon sent you away."

"I'm here because there's nothing more I can do. The next steps aren't up to me anymore." He stood in front of the open car door. "I arrived back in Ireland this morning and took the bus to Kenmare looking for you. I thought you could use my help."

"How did you know to find me here?"

"A fair guess."

Josie wasn't convinced. Myles would tell her what suited him. She went around and yanked open the driver's door with a bit more force than was necessary. "Is anyone after you?"

"Other than you, you mean?"

Whatever his particular way of going about things, she had no doubt Myles wouldn't be here now were he not confident he hadn't been followed. She didn't need to waste her breath telling him what they both already knew: His dangerous, solitary work over the past two years had secured critical information that Will and Simon — British intelligence and American FBI — could now use to finish the job.

In one brusque move, Josie climbed into the car and let Myles do whatever he meant to do.

He got in beside her. "It's just you and me, love."

"I have no illusions, Myles." She thrust the key into the ignition. "You're not here for me. Fasten your seat belt. I won't have you bloodied should I ram us into a tree."

He pulled his door shut and clicked on his seat belt, settling back comfortably in his seat. "Where are we going?"

"Doesn't matter, does it? I've already been to hell and back these past two years."

She could feel his gray eyes on her as she started the car. He hadn't shaved. He looked exhausted, irresistible and perfectly capable of slitting an odd throat or two if necessary. Why, she thought, hadn't she simply stayed in London? She had a great deal of freedom with her job, and certainly no one had sent her to Ireland to chase after an American archaeologist.

"Let me guess, then, love." Myles watched casually out his window as she pulled onto the road, maneuvering through a large puddle. "You're looking into the Irish life and times of Sophie Malone."

Josie groaned, nearly choking the engine.

"There. I was right. You *did* provide Scoop Wisdom with information about her."

"Only her name."

"In what context? Not a good one, I imagine. And here he'd just seen her at Keira's ruin. No wonder Scoop wants to know all he can about her. It's not as easy as I'd hoped to find decent intel on her. Her sister's gone back to London. Her parents have trekked into the Irish hills with tents and rucksacks." Josie gave a mock shudder. "Will appreciates the charms of camping, but I do not. You, Myles?"

"I could do with a real bed," he said, just a bit of huskiness to his voice.

Well-trained intelligence officer that she was, Josie saw to it no color rose in her cheeks. "I met this morning with an Irish detective I know. Seamus Harrigan. Is he the one who told you I was in Kenmare?"

Myles closed his eyes and didn't answer.

"He's aware that the Malones own this house but only because he lives in Kenmare — not because of anything Sophie or her family has done."

"Did Seamus direct you here?"

"That's a bit too strong but I was able to fill in the blanks." She noticed Myles hadn't opened his eyes. "He wasn't pleased to hear from me, I have to say. Perfectly understandable. Three months ago we had Seamus crawling through a ruin in search of a serial killer. Last month we had him questioning a hired thug about a bombing and kidnapping in Boston."

"He was doing his job," Myles said with a yawn.

"Yes, that explains it, doesn't it?" Josie trod too hard on the gas and took a turn far more sharply and speedily than was necessary or safe, but she'd passed various defensive driving courses. Not that the Irish guards would accept that as a reason not to ticket her. She came to a stop and glanced over at Myles. He at least had his eyes half open now. "Sophie Malone was involved in some sort of incident a year ago. Seamus wasn't on the case but told me what he could."

"What sort of incident?"

"The bizarre sort with no evidence. Seamus gave me the name of a local fisherman. I'm off to find him now." She turned onto the main road back toward the village. "Does that sound too deadly dull for you, Myles?"

"A chat with an Irish fisherman would be a nice change of pace," he said, making himself comfortable. "You look tired. Would you like for me to drive?"

"No." She was immediately annoyed that he thought she looked tired when, of course, he was the reason for her bad night and he himself was clearly much worse off. "Are you even legal to drive these days?"

He yawned again, pushing back his seat to accommodate his long legs. He had dark shadows under his eyes, but she found him as rugged and sexy as ever. He gave her a quick smile. "You're a madwoman behind the wheel, love. Always have been."

"Would you like me to put you on a flight to London?"

"What would I do in London?"

"Go visit your mother. Two years, Myles. She hasn't known if you were alive or dead."

"No, she has. She's known."

"How? Carrier pigeon?"

He ignored her, and she continued over a small suspension bridge, then turned onto a side road just before the village center. Myles had always had an uncanny ability to push right past anything he didn't want to discuss.

She had no trouble finding parking by the town pier. As she got out of the car, a strong gust of wind buffeted her, but she found it refreshing. Just a few minutes in close proximity to Myles had her feeling hot and out of sorts. She struck off across the road without a word or a glance in her passenger's direction. She didn't want to think about him — where he'd come from, how long he planned to stay, *where* he planned to stay.

"I had a nice, calm life before you turned up again, Myles," she muttered, not sure he could hear her — not caring, either. She stepped onto the concrete pier, the wind worse there, and sighed. "A very nice, calm life."

He fell in easily next to her. "If you'd wanted a nice, calm life, you wouldn't have gone for a career in British intelligence."

"I must've landed in the wrong queue somehow. I thought I was signing up for church choir."

She saw the glimmer of a smile beneath his beard stubble and fatigue. He moved with no apparent concern that they might run into snipers, thugs, terrorists or madmen in quiet Kenmare. Of course if he were concerned, he would move with the same nonchalance.

Josie approached an old fisherman in a traditional Irish knit sweater that had seen years — decades, probably — of wear and asked him where she might find Tim O'Donovan. The fisherman gave her a suspicious look and pretended not to understand the question. She said, "We're friends with Sophie Malone."

The old man's suspicion eased. "Tim's due anytime, please God," he said in a heavy West Cork accent and headed down the pier toward the road.

"Let's wait here," Myles said, the sky and bay making his eyes seem a bluer gray. "The air feels good."

Josie took in a sharp breath. "You didn't expect to be alive today, did you?"

"Nor yesterday, either." He crooked his arm toward her and smiled. "Shall we watch the tide and pretend we're a pair of holiday lovers?"

"Damn you, Myles." She slipped her arm into his, welcoming his warmth. She leaned against him, just for a split second. "I hate you, you know."

He winked at her. "That's my girl."

Suddenly she wished they *were* tourists without a care beyond which lace shops to visit and which pub to pop into for a bite. He maintained an outward air that his two years undercover — alone, in constant danger — hadn't affected him, but Josie knew they had. She noticed a scar on his jaw under his right ear that hadn't been there when he'd gone off to Afghanistan.

"Did you tell yourself you'd died in that

firefight?" she asked quietly. "Is that how you managed?"

"I focused on the job I was in a unique position to do."

"Should you have been killed, did you have a plan to get word to Will, at least, that you weren't a traitor?"

"All this talk of my demise, love." He grinned at her. "Should I be near deep water with you?"

His humor, she knew, was his way of deflecting her questions. He wasn't introspective. He was a man who lived in the present. "You could have let us help —"

"It was too big a risk. The people I was chasing would have won."

"Will they win yet, Myles?"

The wind caught the ends of his dark hair. "Not the ones I was chasing."

"Because they're dead," Josie said bluntly.

"There you go again."

But his lack of a denial meant she was right. "Will and Simon are after their friends and associates, aren't they?" she asked softly.

He brushed her fingertips with his and let that be his answer.

She could hardly breathe. "Are you free now? Safe?"

"I don't know, love." He angled her a wry look. "Will I be sleeping near you and a pillow tonight?"

She was tempted to elbow him off the pier, but a bearded man decades younger than the old fisherman ambled toward them. "I understand you're looking for me. What can I do for you?"

"You're Tim O'Donovan?" Josie asked with a smile.

No smile back. "I am."

"I'm Josie Goodwin. This is my friend Myles. We'd like to talk to you about a friend of yours."

"Sophie Malone," he said. "Seamus Harrigan told me you'd be looking for me. Sophie's gone back to Boston."

"What happened last year, Tim?" Myles asked.

Josie winced at his blunt question. Leave it to Myles to dive in before they'd reassured the Irishman. He'd never been one for subtlety. The wind blew hard, and she thought she felt raindrops but supposed it could have been saltwater. She shook off a sudden chill as O'Donovan crossed his muscled arms over his broad chest. He stood at the edge of the pier, his back to the water as if he had no worries about taking a wrong step. "Sophie's a restless soul, and she has a natural curiosity and an investigative mind. Put all that together . . ." He

162

dropped his arms to his sides. "I suppose that's why she's an archaeologist and not a fisherman."

Myles leaned casually against a post. He had no apparent worries, either, about falling into the water. "What caught the attention of her restless soul, natural curiosity and investigative mind a year ago?"

The Irishman squinted out toward the mouth of the harbor. "A tale of invaders and treasure."

Josie gritted her teeth. "Well, that narrows things down nicely, doesn't it?"

O'Donovan rubbed the toe of his scuffed boot across a thick rope tied to a fishing boat that presumably belonged to him. Myles nodded at the battered boat. "Looks as if she's seen a gale or two. Did you take Sophie somewhere in her?"

"Many times. She's a serious scholar and game for anything. Have you met her?"

Myles shook his head, and Josie said, "What about you? How well do you know Dr. Malone?"

O'Donovan leveled emerald-green eyes on her. "What business is that of yours?"

"None," Josie said, and gave him a cheerful smile. "You seem protective of her. I can understand. Here's a woman far from home —"

"She was born in Cork. Her family owns a house here in Kenmare."

"All right, then. She's Irish born but her parents are American. She attended college in Boston and did graduate work in Ireland. Now she's returned to Boston. She's rather rootless, wouldn't you say?"

O'Donovan took in a breath and held it as if he didn't want to answer Josie's question but knew he would. Finally he exhaled and said, "I would, indeed."

"Is she reckless?" Myles asked.

"We say a person's reckless when things don't work out. When they do, we say that same person is brave."

"One can be both reckless and brave." Josie managed not to look at Myles, although she expected he knew she was talking about him, too. "I'd like to win your trust, Tim. Whatever happened to Sophie last year involved you and obviously troubles you."

Myles edged closer to Josie, for no apparent reason that she could discern. "Did Sophie talk you into searching for Celtic treasure?" he asked.

"No. She talked me into taking her to a small island down the bay so she could look into a story I'd told her."

Josie bit her lower lip. This was how Keira

164

Sullivan's ordeal had started three months ago — with an old story. She'd been researching a book she was writing and illustrating, as well as dipping into her own complicated past.

"Would finding lost treasure help Sophie land a job?" Myles asked.

O'Donovan squatted down and started unlooping a thick rope from metal cleats, his fingers callused, his hands obviously very strong. "She says it's the opposite. She's a serious scholar. She's no treasure hunter. If she'd believed she'd find anything, she'd have called for a proper excavation."

"How often did you take her out to this island?"

"Five or six times. The last time, she discovered a cave and nearly didn't come out again."

He didn't elaborate, but Josie could see the regret in how he tore at the rope, how he'd bit off each word. "What happened, Tim?"

He shook his head. "Who's to say?"

"Why did she go out to this particular island?"

"She was writing her dissertation. She said exploring the island got her away from her work and helped clear her head." The muscles in his arms were visibly tensed, and he stood up again, the rope in hand. "On that last trip, she talked me into leaving her overnight. She'd never done such a thing. She had me believing she'd have a good time camping. She'd be safe. I left her there."

Myles had taken a few steps toward the middle of the wide pier, keeping quiet as he watched the fisherman. Josie didn't move. "Did she get hurt?" she asked softly. "Did someone follow her out there —"

"Talk to her." The fisherman tossed the rope down into his boat and moved to tackle the next line. Dark clouds had moved in overhead, the spits of raining turning to a steadier drizzle. He didn't seem to notice. "I wasn't there."

"Sophie could have wandered into a dangerous situation through no fault of her own," Josie said. "Or yours."

Myles narrowed his gray eyes on O'Donovan but made no move toward him. "You're worried that whatever happened to her isn't over."

"Maybe," he said, squatting down, pulling on a thick knot. "Again, I wasn't with her on the island. I only know what she's told me."

"And what's that?" Josie asked.

"She says she came across a cauldron of

gold artifacts in the cave. She didn't have a chance to examine them before she heard whispers. At first she thought it was me — that I'd decided not to leave her out there after all and had come back."

"But it wasn't you," Myles said.

O'Donovan sighed heavily. "No, it wasn't. She saw branches smeared with blood — or what looked like blood — and she hid deeper in the cave. She hit her head somehow and lost consciousness. When she came to, there were no more whispers. I came for her the next day, as agreed. I had to look for her. By the time I found her, there was no sign anyone else had been on the island."

Josie shuddered. "Frightening. Was Sophie in the cave all night?"

"She was," Tim O'Donovan said tightly. "She believes whoever stole the cauldron left her for dead."

"Do you think she made up this story?" Myles asked.

"No, but that doesn't mean it happened the way she believes it did."

Myles frowned, the gray of his eyes now a deep slate. "Fairies? Ghosts? What are you suggesting?"

"As a boy, I heard tales the island's haunted. Sophie could have been pulled there by dark forces." Tim rose, shrugging his big shoulders. "The island's very small. It took me less than an hour to find her. She was hurt, cold, angry, afraid. She doesn't remember how she got her concussion. More than likely she experienced something she couldn't explain and hid for her life in that cave, and she's tried to make sense of what happened ever since."

"What about you?" Myles kept his gaze steady on the fisherman. "Did you sneak back to the island and steal this cauldron filled with gold? Fake the blood to frighten her, then take it with you to make her look less credible?"

Josie could have pushed Myles off the pier herself, but O'Donovan didn't seem to take offense. "I did not."

"You believed Sophie's story enough to call the guards," Josie said. "Did they look into boats that might have passed the island while Dr. Malone was there, anyone who might have heard her discuss her trips there, or this particular trip, or might have seen her —"

"Ask Seamus."

"Seamus said Sophie wasn't seriously hurt and there was no evidence a crime had been committed. Unintelligible whispers, blood and gold only she saw — the guards had nothing to go on."

"She survived, thanks be." O'Donovan abandoned the rope and rose again, his movements smooth for such a large man. "I don't even know you and here I've told you more than anyone else since that day. Do people always voluntarily tell you things, Josie Goodwin?"

She smiled. "Not always voluntarily."

He didn't smile back. "I wish I knew more." When Josie started to thank him, he cut her off. "Just see to it no harm comes to Sophie."

"We'll do our best."

Josie didn't know why she included Myles in her statement, but Tim O'Donovan nodded and said, "If there's anything I can do to help . . ."

"Call Seamus if you remember anything else about Sophie's experience on the island," Josie said.

He jumped down into his boat. The worsening conditions didn't seem to faze him. Myles started toward the road, and Josie lingered a moment, watching the fisherman go about his routines to set off down the bay, hoping she hadn't missed anything — even just a question that could help jog his memory.

She joined Myles at her car. She glanced back at the harbor, O'Donovan's boat chugging along in the wind and rain. "I've not the smallest urge to go to a tiny Irish island on my own."

"Would you go with someone else?" Myles asked as he climbed into the car.

Josie got behind the wheel again. "Not with you, Myles. The two of us alone in a car is enough tension for me, thank you."

"You're going to torture me forever, are you?"

"I haven't decided." She pulled off her damp coat, struggling with it, but he didn't offer his help. She must have looked as if she'd elbow him in the head if he did. She might, anyway. She balled up the coat and shoved it in back with his rucksack. "You could have trusted us, Myles. Will and me. If not me, then Will. If not Will, then me."

"It wasn't a question of trust," Myles said quietly, with none of his usual cockiness, "and to tell one of you what I was into was to tell the other. You both were emotionally compromised by our friendship. I couldn't take the chance."

Josie started the car. "Whether you could or couldn't, you didn't. Lizzie and Keira wouldn't wait two years for word on the fates of the men they care about."

"Do you think so, Josie?"

No, she thought. They'd wait forever.

170

They'd wait until they knew for certain.

"Did you believe I was dead?"

"I'd hoped you'd lost your memory and opened a bake shop in Liverpool."

He laughed suddenly, unexpectedly, and at first she wanted to stop the car and kick him out the door, but she found herself laughing, too.

"Damn you, Myles. I suppose if you hadn't gone off —" She shook her head, abandoning her thought. "Never mind. I was going to say Will wouldn't have found Lizzie, but I don't believe that. I believe they were destined for each other."

"Josie Goodwin, the romantic?"

"Don't choke on your tongue, Myles. I'm a human being. A *woman,* believe it or not. Lizzie's the woman for Will. You've seen that for yourself, haven't you?"

"I have, indeed."

Josie felt a stiff wind buffet the small car. "Keira and Simon were destined for each other, too. You should see them together. He's an utter charmer — he does an amazing fake Irish accent and will argue with anyone over anything, and everyone still loves him." She turned on the windscreen wipers, the rain coming down hard now. "They'll both come back, won't they?"

"I'm sure of it."

171

"You're always sure. It's your nature."

"What Simon and Will are about needs to finish this way."

"Their way, you mean."

"And yours, Josie. Don't tell me you're not staying out of London for a reason. You don't want to have to answer a lot of questions about what Will and Simon are up to yourself." Myles leaned back in his seat. "Now we have this Sophie Malone and her mad island adventure."

"Nothing is ever simple with Will and Simon and their friends, is it?"

"As if it is with us?"

She came to a stop at the end of the road out to the pier and gave him a sideways glance. Those dove-gray eyes. The lines etched in his face. The hard edges that were Myles Fletcher. Of course she'd had to fall for him. How could she not have? But her life would have been so much less complicated these past few years if she hadn't.

He touched a finger to her lips. "Don't say anything more, love. Let's just keep sparring a while longer, shall we? I can't go where you want to go."

"Repressed bloody bastard," she said.

He looked relieved. "Where to next?"

"Dublin," Josie said without hesitation. "Sophie met with an art theft expert there.

172

I'm developing a theory."

"She's after her missing artifacts."

"The whispers, the blood — she must be wondering if Jay Augustine was responsible for what happened to her in that cave. At least he's where he can't harm her or anyone else."

"Suppose he had help," Myles said quietly.

Josie gave him a sharp look, the chill back in her spine. "Myles — what do you know?"

"Drive on, love. It's a long way to Dublin."

11

Boston, Massachusetts

Bob O'Reilly shoved a hand through his hair as he stood on the cracked sidewalk in front of Cliff Rafferty's house and glared at Scoop. "You and your archaeologist haven't been back in town twenty-four hours, and you find a cop swinging from a beam in his dining room. Hell of a homecoming."

Scoop didn't blame him for being annoyed and frustrated, but his focus was on Sophie. She'd finished talking with two homicide detectives — who hadn't known Rafferty — and was in the shade of the oak tree at the edge of the walk. She'd stood up well to the pressures of the past couple hours. He had secured the scene before the first cruiser had arrived, but with the bomb-making materials in Rafferty's dining room, the FBI and ATF had rolled in right behind the BPD. The medical examiner was there. The crime lab. The district attorney's office.

174

Onlookers from the neighborhood were behind yellow tape.

It was a mess.

"I could have stopped her from coming over here," Scoop said half to himself.

"How?" Bob asked, skeptical.

"I could have cited police business."

"She's a Ph.D. She'd have seen right through you and come anyway."

"I could have taken her car keys and flung them down a drain."

Bob rubbed the back of his neck, looking less irritated and agitated. "You didn't let her come out here alone. That's one thing, anyway."

"Yeah, Bob. Sure."

"So, Scoop," he said, "was Rafferty on your radar? You've been working on something. You were before this. Before the bomb."

"If I'd had anything on Rafferty, I'd have arrested him. He wouldn't be dead."

Bob had been a police officer for a very long time, and his eyes showed his experience as he narrowed them on Scoop. "You were onto a cop connection to local thugs before Norman Estabrook set his sights on Abigail. Those bastards who grabbed her had someone on the inside. You had that in mind when you looked at the lists we compiled of people who'd been to the house in the days before the bomb went off."

"Any ongoing special investigation changed the minute that bomb exploded and we became personally involved."

Bob ignored him. "Cliff's name get your attention?"

"There were a lot of names on those lists. There was no evidence."

"There's evidence now."

Scoop felt the warmth of the sun on his bare head. His exposed scars might as well have been on fire. "Unless it was planted."

"Another cop, Scoop?"

"I've been walking the Scottish and Irish hills for the past month. You tell me."

Sophie turned, her skin grayish as her bright blue eyes focused on him and Bob. Scoop wondered how much she'd over-heard. As obviously shaken and disturbed by Rafferty's death as she was, she'd main-tained her composure, answering questions, keeping any theories to herself unless asked.

Bob crooked a finger at her, and she came over to them. Strands of her dark red hair fell in her face, but she didn't seem to notice. He said, "Tell me how you ended up here."

She motioned toward Rafferty's front door. "I told the detectives —"

"Tell me."

She debated a moment, then nodded. "All right."

Scoop kept quiet, watching and listening as she spoke. She was precise, detailed and objective in her description of events. He could picture her in front of a university classroom or at an archaeological excavation — smart, professional — but he could sense her underlying emotions. Shock, revulsion, fear — and just the slightest hint, again, not so much of lies and deception but of incompleteness.

She was leaving out something.

"The skulls," Bob said. "What do they mean?"

"I can only tell you what I know, in general, about their significance to prehistoric Celts. They believed the head was the source of a person's strength and power. Warriors would decapitate enemies in battle and string the heads on their belts and around the necks of their horses."

"Okay. What about nailing skulls to a door?"

"The same. Heads tacked to the entry of homes were a status symbol. There was probably a ritualistic, magical purpose. The scene upstairs seems to be an attempt to create a sacred space, with the skulls marking the border between the physical and the spiritual world."

"Why?"

She shook her head. "I don't know what whoever tacked up those skulls had in mind. The supernatural was an ever-present force in the lives of the Celts. They made little distinction between gods and ordinary humans, the living and the dead. Gods could become men and men become gods."

Bob scratched the side of his mouth for a second, digesting Sophie's explanation. "What about the disassembled gun in the pot?"

"The broken weapon of the warrior."

"A police officer," Scoop interjected.

Sophie glanced at him, and he saw the strain in her eyes. But she stayed focused as she turned back to Bob. "Placing the pieces of the gun in the pot could be the killer's way of symbolically appropriating the power of the owner."

"We don't know yet Cliff was killed," Bob said. "He was retired. He didn't have any power."

"He had a gun. He had decades of experience as a police officer. He was a private security guard for a wealthy couple."

"Fair enough. The glass beads?"

"Glass beads are often found in Celtic

graves. Torcs are, too, but in this case, the broken torc could identify a vanquished enemy. Then there's the manner of death." She took a breath and looked out at the street, as if just needing to see something normal. "Hanging and strangulation were used in conducting ritualistic human sacrifice."

Bob glanced at Scoop, then back at Sophie. "Great," he said without enthusiasm.

"Human remains aren't my area of expertise, but remarkably intact corpses have been discovered in the bogs of Europe. The anaerobic conditions preserve organic material. As it happens, the Celts often made votive offerings in wet places. I have colleagues who specialize in peatland archaeology."

"So bogs were a natural choice to dump a body?" Bob made a face. "What, you've examined murder victims from 300 B.C.?"

She gave him a small smile. "Not me personally. We now know there was never a pan-European Celtic culture with a central government. The Celts were a collection of warring tribes who shared a similar culture and language. We have only limited understanding of the practices I'm describing. The Celts didn't leave us with a written record. Theirs was an oral tradition."

"What do you go on, then?"

"The archaeological record and descriptions of contemporary Classical writers."

"The Romans?"

She nodded. "Ireland was never conquered by Rome, but the Celts of mainland Europe and Great Britain were. Obviously they were enemies, which undoubtedly colors Roman perceptions of the Celts. We also have ancient epic pagan tales written down by Early Medieval Irish monks. They're an important source, but, of course, they're a mix of fantasy, mythology, legend —"

"And a lot of BS, too, probably. I get it," Bob said. "One of the crime lab technicians is a pagan. Nicest, happiest person you'd ever want to meet."

"What I just witnessed has nothing to do with modern pagans or Celtic revivalists."

Bob nodded. "I get your point."

"Am I free to leave?" Sophie asked.

"Yeah, go on. We'll find you if we have more questions."

She glanced at Scoop, then headed straight for her car.

"Hell, Scoop," Bob said on a breath. "That's one creepy scene up there. So what *were* you thinking, coming out here with her?"

"I wasn't thinking I'd find Rafferty dead."

Just as Sophie reached the street, a car screeched to a stop. Frank Acosta, a robbery detective and Rafferty's former partner, jumped out, ducked under the crime-scene tape and charged in front of her, blocking her path to her sister's Mini.

"I figured he'd show up," Bob muttered next to Scoop.

In his late thirties, Acosta was known as one of the better-looking detectives in the department with his dark hair, dark eyes and what Abigail, an otherwise hard-driving, sensible woman, had tried to explain to both Bob and Scoop was a crooked, sexy smile. She'd never had any interest in Acosta, she'd said. She was just explaining.

That was last spring, when Frank Acosta had come to the attention of internal affairs for sexual indiscretions. He had treaded the line but hadn't crossed it, and he'd been warned to clean up his act. But he was no fan of internal affairs.

He was clearly emotional as he inserted himself between Sophie and her car. "You're the archaeologist who found Cliff?" He choked out the words. "What happened? I just saw him yesterday afternoon. We had coffee. He was fine."

"Hold on, Frank," Bob called to him.

181

Acosta pretended not to hear him. "Then you show up, and now he's dead."

"I saw him this morning," Sophie said softly, "and he was fine then, too. I'm so sorry. I can see he was —"

"We worked together for two years. I've known him since I was a rookie." Acosta glared at Rafferty's house as if somehow it had betrayed him. He was grim, covering his grief with anger and aggression "I hear you're just in from Ireland. You're an expert in Celtic Iron Age art."

"That's right."

"You can recognize real artifacts from fakes?"

Scoop resisted any urge to jump in. Acosta was deliberately trying to catch Sophie off guard. "It depends," she said, cool and controlled — more the academic at work than someone who'd just walked in on her first hanging victim. "What kind of artifacts are we talking about?"

"I don't know. Hypothetical artifacts. Celtic, say."

" 'Celtic' is a general term. Even scholars argue about its meaning. Celtic can describe an Iron Age brooch from France, or an Early Medieval Christian chalice from Ireland — or a shawl in a Harvard Square gift shop."

It was just the sort of response that Acosta would take as smart-ass. He inhaled sharply, and Scoop found himself moving toward Sophie. Bob stayed back and watched, undoubtedly missing nothing.

Acosta didn't let up. "Let's say we're talking about hypothetical Irish Celtic Iron Age artifacts. Would you know if they were authentic?"

"It depends," she said, guarded. "I certainly can recognize an authentic Celtic design, but unprovenanced pieces can be difficult to date with any certainty. It's problematic when archaeological evidence has been moved from its original site — whether it happened a hundred years ago or a few months ago."

"Same in our line of work," Acosta said, less combative.

Bob unwrapped a stick of gum. "What's going on, Frank?"

Acosta kept his gaze on Sophie as he answered. "We discovered missing inventory in the Augustine showroom — you know Cliff worked security there until he officially retired three weeks ago. We brought in a kid last week who worked there part-time before Augustine's arrest. He said he saw gold Celtic artifacts in the climate-controlled vault. They're not there now. No record of them. Nothing."

"How did he know these pieces were Celtic?" Sophie asked.

Acosta made a spiral motion with one finger. "The swirls."

She nodded. "The curvilinear motif is a signature feature of Celtic design — spirals, circles, knots, tendrils, the play of symmetry and asymmetry. It's a truly great artistic legacy. Do you have photographs of these pieces? A specific description, their provenance —"

"I just got this kid's word. They weren't logged in properly. He saw them in late May — well before anyone knew Augustine wasn't just a respected art dealer — and didn't think about them again until we went through the vault with him. Charlotte Augustine says she never saw them and knows nothing about them."

Sophie was very still, pale and visibly shaken but no longer shivering. "Does this kid know when these pieces first came into the Augustines' possession?"

"No idea. Strange, though. Here's this kid pointing out missing inventory, and now here you are, an expert in Celtic archaeology fresh from Ireland." Acosta pointed up to the second floor of the house. "And here's Cliff dead."

She stared at him a moment, as if debating how to respond, then turned to Bob. "Am I still free to leave?"

"Hold on," Acosta said, obviously ready to jump on Bob if he interfered. "How do we know you're not a collector who'll do anything to get your hands on Celtic artifacts? How do we know you're not representing a collector — someone who wants the real thing and doesn't care about legal niceties?"

Sophie tilted her head back. "Are you asking me?"

Acosta acted as if he didn't hear her. "How do we know you didn't sneak over here this morning, kill Cliff and stage the scene?"

"I gave the investigating detectives the paper he handed to me this morning with his address —"

"He could have given it to you last night when you stopped by the Carlisle house. Yeah. I can see you're surprised. Cliff e-mailed me after you left." Acosta crossed his arms on his chest, staying between Sophie and her car. He looked hot, irritated. "How would you be able to tell our hypothetical Celtic Iron Age artifacts weren't something you could pick up at Pier 1 or a Celtic revival fair?"

"As I said, by various means."

"Would you bring in an expert like your-self?"

"I wouldn't. I'm not a dealer or a collec-tor —"

"Ever advise dealers or collectors?"

She shook her head. "No."

"Friends?"

"No."

"Anyone dealing in stolen or illegally obtained artifacts would have to know what to look for, that it's valuable, who to sell to. Are authentic Celtic Iron Age gold artifacts in high demand?"

"It wouldn't matter if they're considered national treasure —"

"Forget that part."

"I can't give you a definitive answer. It's not my area of expertise."

Acosta wasn't ready to quit, and Bob, as a senior officer, wasn't ready to shut him up. Neither was Sophie, who could have walked away. Scoop wasn't sure why she didn't. He suspected it had to do with whatever she was holding back.

His dark eyes steady on her, Acosta kept going. "Did you slip something out of a dig to make a profit, then get cold feet when Augustine turned up as a killer?"

"No, I did not," Sophie said.

"Did you come here to cover your tracks and keep Cliff from turning you in?"

"I came here because he invited me."

"Percy Carlisle did business with the Augustines. His wife worked at a New York auction house up until recently. They both know how to avoid getting mixed up in buying stolen works, fakes, stuff that's not legally on the market." Acosta paused, studying Sophie, who didn't appear to be letting his aggressive, suspicious attitude get to her. "How well do you know the Carlisles?"

"Not well," she said. "I should go. I'm sorry for your loss, Detective."

Scoop tried to tune into her nonverbal cues, the way she held herself, the set of her jaw, the tension in her shoulders — any nuance, any hint, that would tell him what she was thinking. She seemed unaware of his scrutiny, her attention on Frank Acosta. When he didn't respond, she headed around him to her car. He didn't stop her.

Scoop walked past Acosta and out to the street as Sophie yanked open the little driver's side door. "I haven't lied to you," she said without looking at him.

"You just haven't told me everything. Where are you headed?"

"I'm checking in at the offices of the

Boston-Cork conference. They're on —"

"I know where they are. I'll talk to you later. Stick to your work, Sophie. Leave Rafferty's death to us."

"I intend to," she said, sliding in behind the wheel.

In two seconds, she was gone, and Acosta stuck a finger in Scoop's face. "That woman is trouble. She didn't come back to Boston just to go job-hunting. She's up to something. Mark my words."

"I'm sorry about Cliff," Scoop said. "I know you two were friends."

"Spare me, Wisdom. You're the biggest son of a bitch in the department. If Cliff screwed up, you'd have hanged him yourself."

12

Sophie jumped at the blare of a siren, then at a barking dog as she fed the meter where she'd parked a half block up from the Carlisle house. Her fingers were cold, despite temperatures near seventy degrees, but she knew it was nerves. She quickly talked herself out of ringing Helen Carlisle's doorbell. The police were there. No need to risk prompting more questions about her own behavior. Instead she decided to head straight to the Back Bay offices of the Boston-Cork folklore conference, just a few blocks away.

As she headed down the busy street, she checked her iPhone and saw that Tim O'Donovan had tried her several times. She called him back in Ireland. Before she could get out a greeting, he said, "Two Brits were here asking questions about last year. What's going on, Sophie?"

"Go hide, Tim."

189

"I'm not one for hiding."

She was aware of cars crowding the busy street, car doors shutting, a young woman — obviously a student — walking four small dogs, panting as they strained on their leashes. It was a gorgeous early autumn day. She noticed a touch of red and bright orange in the leaves of a shade tree, even as she fought back images of walking into Cliff Rafferty's apartment — of his body hanging from the beam, of Scoop's dark eyes as he'd turned to her.

Tim broke into her thoughts. "Sophie? What's wrong?"

"You saw me with Percy Carlisle the other night, right?"

"I've not met him myself, but I know who you're talking about."

"He told me he'd hired a retired police officer — Cliff Rafferty — as a sort of security guard or advisor. I'm not sure exactly what his job description was."

"He's been fired?"

"No — no, it's not that. I'll find a photo of him and e-mail it to you. Tell me if you've ever seen him before, if he came around asking about me, or if you saw him at the pier or in town."

"You mean last year," Tim said.

"Anytime, anywhere."

"Sophie, what's happened?"

She stepped out of the way of three men in suits who didn't seem to notice her at all. She hoped that meant she didn't look as if she'd just come from a murder scene — didn't look shaken and sick, worried about what Detective Acosta had told her about missing Celtic artifacts.

As objectively and succinctly as she could, she told Tim about finding Rafferty. "I don't believe it was a suicide. I don't think the police do, either. There's no way to know at this point if his death's connected to what happened to me —"

"No, Sophie. Don't. Not with me. You believe this police officer's death is connected to what you went through on that island."

She didn't argue with him. "Are the two Brits who came to see you friends of Will Davenport? When I saw Colm Dermott last week, he told me that Lord Davenport helped with the investigation into Keira Sullivan's ordeal on the Beara. He played a role in Jay Augustine's arrest."

"I'm having a drink with a friend in the guards and will see what he can tell me."

Will Davenport was also romantically involved with Lizzie Rush, who had alerted her cousin Jeremiah that Sophie was on her way back to Boston. "Be careful, won't you?"

"Ah, that's funny," Tim said. "Sophie Malone telling me to be careful."

She appreciated his humor but noticed her hands were shaking. "I don't want you to suffer for something you had nothing to do with."

"I had everything to do with what happened to you on that island," he said, serious again. "I left you there."

"There's no point rehashing the past."

"I trust you, Sophie, but if you're hiding anything at all, I'd give it up now."

"I might have an unpaid Irish speeding ticket. Not that the guards are known for handing out speeding tickets."

Tim sighed. "Sophie."

She came to the ivy-covered converted town house where the conference offices were located. "It's my turn to try to inject a note of humor into a grim day."

"Go for a Guinness, then."

"I'm dropping in on the Irish folklore conference offices."

"Ask if they need fishermen musicians. Ah, Sophie. What a day. Be well. This police officer's gone to God."

"I suspect that was the idea," she said.

"Does your family know any of this?"

"No, Tim, they know nothing. I prefer to keep it that way."

"I would, too," he said as he disconnected.

Sophie mounted the steps to a polished oak door and announced herself through an intercom system. A buzzer unlocked the door, and she went into a small entry and up two flights of narrow stairs to the third floor, where she introduced herself to a heavyset, middle-aged woman, who rose from behind a glass-topped desk.

"It's a pleasure to meet you, Sophie. I'm Eileen Sullivan. I'm Keira's mother." She had her daughter's blue eyes and fair coloring, and her hair was cut very short, her clothes plain and loose-fitting. "I just spoke to my brother. Bob O'Reilly."

"Then you know —"

"Yes, he told me what happened this morning. It must be a terrible shock for you. Can I get you anything?"

Sophie shook her head. "I just wanted to stop in and introduce myself."

"I'm the only one here at the moment. Colm's in Ireland, but I assume you know that. We're excited to have you organizing a panel for the conference." Eileen frowned, obviously concerned. "What about a cup of tea and a bite to eat?"

Between waiting for the detectives and going through the questioning, it was well past lunchtime, but Sophie didn't feel hungry. The thought of food nauseated her.

"At least tea," Eileen said.

Sophie relented with a smile. "That'd be lovely."

Eileen went down the hall, and Sophie sank onto a cushioned chair in a corner, next to a table piled with books on Ireland. A poster of the upcoming conference was on the wall. Keira Sullivan had clearly done the watercolor illustration of an Irish cottage, with sheep and a stone circle in the background. It was beautifully done, cheerful and inviting. Sophie picked up a book of photographs of Ireland and found one of Kenmare. She pretended she was there, walking its pretty streets with nothing more pressing on her mind than which restaurant to choose for dinner.

As if her life wasn't screwed up enough, her brother, the FBI agent, texted her: All is calm, all is bright in Boston?

What would she tell him? *Dear Damian, I just found a dead police officer?*

She texted him a vague answer. I'll call you later.

Let him find out on his own about her morning. She didn't want to be the one to tell him.

Eileen Sullivan returned with a mug and one-cup teapot on a small tray. "I wasn't sure if you took cream and sugar, but I can go back for them."

"This is great, thanks."

She smiled, setting the tray on the side table. "You must be tempted to jump on the next flight back to Ireland."

"I am," Sophie said truthfully. She thought of Scoop and his intensity and focus when he'd realized they'd walked into a potentially dangerous situation. Running back to Ireland would mean leaving him behind, and she didn't want to do that. Finding Cliff Rafferty together had forged a bond between them — she couldn't explain it. Besides, she'd only make him more suspicious if she left. She smiled back at Eileen. "Thanks for the tea. I'm thrilled to be involved in the conference."

"Everyone's eager to see what you come up with. I know very little about pre-Christian Ireland, but I'm fascinated by the various ways the early church incorporated pagan traditions." Eileen stood up straight, her concern unabated. "You're pale, and for good reason. You're not a law enforcement officer trained to walk in on the type of scene you just left. Is there someone I can call for you? Do you have any friends in town?"

Sophie poured the steaming tea into the pottery mug. "I'm just getting my bearings. The tea will help." She noticed it was Irish Breakfast as she curled her stiff fingers around the very warm mug. "Thank you."

Not looking particularly reassured, Eileen returned to her desk. This was a woman, Sophie knew, who had left behind her life as she'd known it to become a religious ascetic in a cabin she'd built herself deep in the New Hampshire woods. Jay Augustine had come close to killing her and Keira there. He hadn't counted on the two women being able to defend themselves against him.

Eileen eyed Sophie for a moment. "I can see you're preoccupied," she said with understanding. "You're trying to make sense of Cliff's death. Bob would just say to leave the investigation to the detectives, as if that solves everything."

Sophie managed a smile. "He already did say that." She drank some of her tea. "You knew Cliff Rafferty?"

"Yes. Yes, I knew him. He started out in the police department a year or two after my brother. I was still living in Boston. Keira was just a baby, so this goes back a few years. We weren't close — Cliff, Bob and I. I ran into Cliff earlier this summer, before he retired. His death . . ." Eileen stared up at the poster of the conference as if to draw solace from the scene, just as Sophie had. "I'd hoped the violence had finally ended."

Eileen Sullivan seemed open and interested, not unaffected by her encounter with a serial killer but not haunted, either.

Sophie forced herself to drink more tea, but her fear was clear and sharp and had been from the moment she'd seen the fake skulls tacked to Rafferty's apartment door. Her encounter with Detective Acosta had only further crystallized what she'd already been thinking. What if her experience in a cave across the Atlantic a year ago had helped trigger the violence in Boston over the past three months?

What if it had helped trigger the violence Cliff Rafferty had encountered today?

With Jay Augustine in prison and Norman Estabrook dead, who had created the bizarre scene at Rafferty's apartment?

Who'd killed him?

Sophie simply couldn't believe he'd committed suicide.

She tried more of the tea, her head spinning with jet lag and the aftereffects of her adrenaline surge. "I don't know if you're aware that Percy Carlisle and his wife had

197

hired Officer Rafferty to help them with security." She looked up from her mug. "Do you know the Carlisles?"

"By reputation only," Eileen said. "They're not involved with the conference if that's what you're asking. Do you know them?"

"I know Percy a little. I did research at the Carlisle Museum when I was in school here. I only met Helen Carlisle last night."

"You're trembling," Eileen Sullivan said quietly, rising.

"I probably should get something to eat." Sophie tried to ignore her spinning head, a wave of nausea. "I'm eager to hear more about how the conference is shaping up. Colm's a ball of fire, isn't he?"

"Tireless. Sophie —"

She was on her feet, unsteady, ragged. "I think I'll go ahead and grab lunch before I keel over. Another time?"

Eileen seemed to understand that Sophie needed to get out of there. "Of course. Anytime."

"Thanks. It's great to meet you."

Sophie bolted out of the office and down the two flights of stairs, bursting into the bright afternoon. She took the steps two at a time. She hadn't thrown up when she and Scoop had found Cliff Rafferty, or in front of him and half the law enforcement personnel in Boston when they'd descended onto the scene, but now she felt her stomach lurching.

She stopped in the middle of the shaded sidewalk and put her hands on her knees, taking a few deep, calming breaths. She knew she had to eat something before she passed out. She stood up straight, careful not to move too fast, and there was Scoop, three feet in front of her, unsmiling. She hadn't heard him. She hadn't so much as seen his shadow.

"You need smelling salts?" he asked.

"Not anymore. You're a jolt to the system all by yourself."

"Good." He didn't seem particularly concerned that she might pass out. He had a sandwich in a wrapper and handed her half. "It's cheese."

The smell of the cheese managed not to turn her stomach. "Thanks." She didn't take a bite of the sandwich. "I left you stranded. How did you get here?"

"Another detective dropped me off. Be glad you were trying to keep yourself from fainting. He's not someone you want to meet on a bad day."

"I wasn't trying to keep myself from fainting."

"Pitching your cookies?"

"You know," she said, "it's entirely possible I'm feeling vulnerable after what we just went through. It was a shock to my system. I'm still getting my bearings. Plus my body's still on Irish time."

"You're hungry." Scoop pointed at her with his half of the sandwich. "Eat up. You'll feel better."

"My car's down the street."

"In front of the Carlisle house," he said.

Sophie took a small bite of the sandwich, the bread soft, the cheese mild. She hadn't forgotten he was a police officer. Of course he'd keep track of her. Even if she hadn't already guessed who he was when she saw him at the ruin on the Beara Peninsula, she'd have figured out he was in law enforcement just by looking at him.

"I'll bet they don't tap you much for undercover work," she said. "You'd be pegged as a cop in a heartbeat."

He grinned at her. "Maybe I can turn the cop thing on and off. Come on. I'll walk you back to your car."

As they started down the wide sidewalk, Sophie noticed a woman moving toward them at a fast pace, then saw that it was Helen Carlisle. She had on the same red sweater she'd worn last night, this time over slim jeans and black boots that were obviously expensive but suited for a walking city such as Boston.

"The police just left," she said, not bothering with a greeting. "I was at the museum most of the morning — on my own. I didn't need Cliff to protect me. He's not — he wasn't a personal bodyguard. He evaluated our security and made recommendations, and he looked after the house, especially while Percy and I were away. He didn't follow either of us around."

"Mrs. Carlisle," Sophie said, "I'm sorry —"

"Helen. Please. For heaven's sake, 'Mrs. Carlisle' makes me feel old, and I'm not *that* much older than you." She smiled, taking any sting out of her words but, at the same time, clearly was on the verge of panic. "I was on my way back to the museum, but I saw you two and had my cab drop me off on the corner. The police said you found Cliff."

Scoop balled up his sandwich wrapper and tossed it into a trash can. "I can get you another cab."

"I've changed my mind. I don't want to go to the museum now. I'll head back home. I guess I don't know what to do with myself after this tragedy. Walk with me, won't you?"

"I'm parked just up the street from your

201

house," Sophie said. She'd taken a few more bites of her sandwich, already feeling steadier on her feet. She glanced at Scoop. "If you have to be somewhere —"

"Not a problem." His dark eyes held hers for an instant. "I'm right where I need to be."

They continued up the street toward the Carlisle house. Helen walked with her arms crossed on her chest, as if she were trying to hold in her emotions. Sophie could imagine what she was feeling — the doubts, the regrets, the fears. Could she have done anything to prevent Cliff Rafferty's death?

"Have you talked to Percy?" Sophie asked her. "Does he know what happened?"

Helen shook her head. "I haven't heard from him. The police want to talk to him, which I understand. Cliff worked for us." She gave Scoop a quick glance, then faced forward again as they came to an intersection. "They have to keep an open mind and consider all the possibilities, including homicide, but it looks as if it was a suicide, doesn't it?"

"One step at a time," Scoop said.

"Cliff had been preoccupied, enough for me to notice but not to be alarmed. I didn't know him that well. I assumed he was still adjusting to his retirement. Maybe it didn't agree with him."

They crossed the street and walked past large, elegant Back Bay houses, Scoop on the edge of the sidewalk, Sophie between him and Helen. "Did Cliff stay at your house last night?" he asked.

Helen shook her head. "He has a room here, but he went back to his place. As I said, he's not a bodyguard. He was working on a total security makeover for us. Alarm systems, computers, finances. Percy has been so casual about security. He can't imagine anyone would want to do him harm."

"I didn't realize Cliff was such an expert in security," Scoop said. "You aren't afraid to be in the house alone?"

"Of course not. I've only been married — a Carlisle, if you will — for a few months. I've worked all my life. I'm accustomed to being on my own." She lowered her arms from her chest, her sweater swinging open in the slight, pleasant breeze. "Percy liked Cliff. He said Cliff seemed to have no idea what to do after he retired. I think Percy just wanted to do a man who'd devoted his life to serving the people a good turn, as well as beef up security here. He was very upset after Jay Augustine's arrest, but he didn't want to overreact. Hiring Cliff seemed like a reasonable solution."

"Do you have friends in Boston?" Sophie asked.

"A few," Helen said. She lapsed into silence as they crossed a side street and came to her house on the corner. She stood at the iron fence. "I didn't realize how much I'd miss Percy. I understand he needs his space. He's brilliant, you know. He's just quieter and more cerebral than his father was. I think Percy was overshadowed by him, really. Did you ever meet Percy Sr., Sophie?"

"A few times."

Helen seemed distracted, exhausted. She motioned broadly at the mansion behind her. "This place is like a museum dedicated to him. I think it took marrying me for Percy to be able to go through the house top to bottom and at least try to make it his own, although we could end up selling it. He still isn't over his father's death. It's been three years, but everyone's different."

"You're worried about him," Sophie said

"Wouldn't you be?" Helen paused, the strain of the day evident, her skin very pale against her dark hair and the vibrant red of her sweater. "I don't know what effect Cliff's death will have on Percy."

"Are you concerned about your husband's

safety?" Scoop asked.

She seemed surprised. "No, should I be?"

Scoop shrugged without answering.

Helen abandoned the subject. "Won't you come inside? I can at least offer you a drink."

"That'd be great," Sophie said before Scoop could respond. She turned to him. "Don't let us keep you."

"I'm good," he said, his eyes lingering on her for a fraction longer than was necessary — just enough to communicate his lack of enthusiasm for her decision to accept Helen's invitation.

They took a brick walk flanked by formal hedges and thick ground cover, then went down an offshoot to a side entrance. Helen produced a single key from a sweater pocket. "I hate carrying around scads of keys on some massive key ring, but I probably should. I'm always losing them," she said cheerfully as she pushed open the door, faltering slightly as she added, "Cliff would tease me about it."

She led her guests down a hall, a thick Persian runner on the gleaming hardwood floor, its white walls decorated with a line of precisely spaced botanical prints of New England wildflowers — columbine, lady slipper, aster, trillium. They came to a cool kitchen with stark white cabinets and black granite counters.

Helen set her key on a round table with a large vase of autumn flowers in the center, and sighed. "It's ghastly, isn't it? This place. It's so cold. Beautiful and tasteful, of course — but it needs some warmth. A house needs to be lived in and loved, don't you think?"

"You're living here," Scoop said.

"I haven't put my stamp on it yet. It still very much feels like Percy Sr.'s house. I've sometimes wondered why the Carlisles didn't turn it into a museum when they had the chance. It'd be perfect." She peeled off her sweater and draped it over the back of a chair. "Well, things are changing. If we decide not to sell, once we finish renovations, we'll have a constant stream of friends, families and parties. And dogs. I'm determined to get a couple of dogs."

Sophie remained standing, Scoop right next to her.

Helen gave them a self-conscious smile. "I'm talking a mile a minute." She ran her fingertips over the edge of the table. "It's hard to believe Cliff sat right here last night. We talked about your visit before he went home. He figured it meant something. He was always on guard, always suspicious. It can't have been an easy way to live."

"Did he ever discuss his work as a police officer with you?" Sophie asked.

"Only in general terms. He couldn't imagine what it must have been like for Charlotte Augustine to discover she was married to a murderer. Cliff was divorced himself, estranged from his children — they're adults. They live in North Carolina, I believe. He hoped being retired would help him rebuild his relationship with them." With an abrupt burst of energy, Helen walked over to the refrigerator. "What can I get you? Soda, wine, beer?"

Scoop shook his head. "Nothing, thanks."

"Would having even a nonalcoholic drink violate police rules or something? Here, Sophie. You're not trained to find dead bodies — at least recently dead bodies. I imagine you've seen a few ancient bones in your day."

"Thanks, but we should go," Sophie said.

"Nonsense." Helen got down a glass from an open shelf and filled it with water from the tap, handing it to Sophie. "As you know, Cliff and Percy met when detectives had Percy stop by the Augustine showroom. They were going through the inventory. Apparently the Augustines didn't keep very good records. There was a lot of confusion.

Percy was able to identify a painting in storage that he'd traded to the Augustines for a sculpture he'd had his eye on."

"Who else was there?" Scoop asked.

"Besides Cliff? Several homicide and robbery detectives. I don't know their names." She shuddered as she handed Sophie a glass of water. "When I heard about Cliff's death, I'm ashamed to admit it, but I was angry with Percy. I didn't want to have to face this alone."

Sophie drank some of her water, then placed the glass in the sink. She noticed tears in the other woman's eyes. "You're newlyweds. It's natural to miss him, don't you think?"

"Yes, but now that the initial shock's worn off a bit, I'm glad he's not here."

"Still no idea where he is?" Scoop asked.

She shook her head. "Not really, no. I'll keep trying to reach him."

Sophie looked out the window over the sink at the Carlisles' enclosed courtyard, at least twice the size of the one she shared on Beacon Hill. She noticed potted trees, a border of autumn perennials, vines and benches, even a small wrought-iron table and chairs. She almost asked Helen Carlisle if she could sit out there for a few minutes, just to be alone and think, process what she'd just witnessed.

"Is anyone working on your renovations today?" Scoop asked.

"Not today, no," Helen said. "Next week. Are you sure you don't want anything to eat? I can make sandwiches. When Percy's here, we have a full-time cook and house-keeper, but I'm used to doing things for myself. He likes that about me. When we first met, I wasn't sure he would. He seems so old-fashioned, doesn't he?"

"We should let you get your bearings," Sophie said, pulling her gaze from the court-yard.

"I dealt with security in my work in New York," Helen said, almost to herself, "but I never worried about my personal safety — beyond the occasional can of pepper spray."

Sophie stopped in the doorway, aware that Scoop hadn't yet moved to follow her. Maybe he'd stay behind to talk to Helen Carlisle alone. "I'm truly sorry about what happened."

Helen picked up her sweater off the chair and clutched it in both hands. "The police said Cliff asked you to come by his apart-ment this morning. Can you tell me why?"

"He didn't say."

"He told me he'd help me go through this place. I was looking forward to digging through all these musty rooms with him. I don't have the baggage of being a blood Carlisle. Neither did Cliff." Tears were on her pale cheeks now. "I'm sorry. His death is a blow."

"I know it must be," Sophie said quietly.

"I'm glad we ran into each other." Obviously sinking emotionally, Helen slipped her sweater back on. "Maybe I'll go back to the museum after all. Thank you for distracting me at least a little while."

Sophie said goodbye and started down the hall, Scoop next to her. Helen didn't see them out. They descended the steps into the formal front yard, and Sophie gulped in the afternoon air, taking in the crush of cars out on the street, the feel of the sun on her face.

Scoop didn't say a word until they reached the Mini. Then he caught her by the shoulders and turned her to him. "You're all right?"

"Yes, why, do I look —"

"Because I'm going to yell at you. You're Professor Malone or Doctor Malone or Miss Malone. You're not Detective Malone. You got that? It's not just what you said in there. It's your body language. I had the same sense back in the ruin in Ireland."

"What sense?"

"That you've got a bit in your teeth and you're running."

He had a point, but she argued with him anyway. "I wouldn't have made it through graduate school without asking questions."

"Or without self-discipline. Adopt a little now."

She angled a look at him. "You done?"

"Yeah. Yeah, I'm done." He dropped his hands from her shoulders. "I'll watch you get in your car. Then you just head right back to Beacon Hill."

She dug out Taryn's keys. "Nothing like a Scoop Wisdom reality check. Do you need a ride anywhere?"

"No." He took a sharp breath, then added, "Thanks for the offer. Just go on about your day and forget all this."

"Oh, that'll be easy. I'll just head back to my apartment and arrange mums in the courtyard —"

"Sounds good."

"I was being sarcastic." She opened up the driver's door. "But maybe that *is* what I'll do. I could use a little normalcy right now, and it'll help me think."

"Where are you getting the mums?"

She wondered if he knew he was being annoying and was certain he did. "Maybe I'll steal some out of yards on Beacon Hill."

211

"Funny, Sophie."

"It's been a long day already. When will you be able to determine if Cliff Rafferty was murdered?"

"There are flower shops on Charles. Try there." Scoop headed down the sidewalk, away from the Carlisle house, but turned, facing her as he walked backward. "I like a mix of colors — reminds me of all the different shades of autumn leaves more than a solid color does."

"A gardener, are you?"

He pointed a thick finger at her. "Be where we can find you. At your apartment with the mums. Tutoring hockey players. Anywhere but near a police investigation."

"I was thinking about Morrigan's after the mums," she said, suspecting she was being annoying, too. "But I wouldn't want to be provocative again and have you catch me there with a Guinness."

"That wouldn't be provocative this time. That would be smart."

She got into the Mini and watched him turn back around and walk another few yards. He wasn't at all what she'd expected from Colm's descriptions and news accounts of his heroism, his work, his injuries. He was more self-contained, funnier, not nearly as cocky as she'd have imagined.

The man was a gardener, for heaven's sake.

But he was still a police detective — an intense, committed one at that — and she would be smart, she thought, to keep that in mind.

Nonetheless, she called to him, "What does Detective Acosta have against you?"

"Pick out a nice yellow mum for me," he said without so much as a glance back at her.

"Did he do something to come to the attention of internal affairs?"

Scoop didn't respond. Sophie wasn't surprised. Whether Acosta had or hadn't had a run-in with internal affairs, Scoop wasn't about to tell her — even if it was a matter of public record. He was a man who kept his own counsel. Not a talker, not a confider. It wasn't just training or part of his job description. It was the way he was.

He didn't change his mind and trot back to her and climb into the passenger seat. Sophie didn't know if she wanted him to or not.

She wondered how long she had before he heard from Tim's Brits and showed up at her door for more details.

Enough time to buy mums, even?

As she started the car, she wondered, too,

how close she'd been to ending up like Cliff Rafferty a year ago. If not hanged, just as dead.

13

Dublin, Ireland

Josie let Myles drive the last bit to Dublin. He was behind the wheel when they stopped in front of the Rush Hotel off St. Stephen's Green. She doubted she'd shut her eyes the entire hour he'd been driving, but it wasn't because she was afraid he'd run them into a ditch. She'd kept imagining Sophie Malone venturing out to a tiny island alone.

"I'm not very brave," she said as Myles turned off the engine.

He glanced at her, his eyes flinty in the late-day light. "Is that why you didn't want to drive in Dublin? It takes a brave heart."

"Are you never serious unless someone has a gun to your head? I'm initiating a heart-to-heart conversation."

"No, you're not. You're looking for sympathy, and I've none to offer. Besides, if you wanted to talk, you'd have waited until we were sitting in the pub with a couple of pints, not watching a doorman come to us."

"This is a five-star hotel. I'm not sure it has a pub. Our doorman is Lizzie's cousin Justin, by the way. He's the youngest of the lot. Can you see the family resemblance?"

"Not really, no."

"His hair's lighter, but the strong jaw, the determined walk — Lizzie has them, don't you think?"

Myles sighed. "What she has is Will Davenport's heart and soul."

"That she does. No question." Suddenly awkward at Myles's unexpected romantic insight, Josie unfastened her seat belt and tried to stretch the kink out of her lower back. She'd left several messages for Scoop Wisdom, but so far he hadn't returned her call. "I suppose you're right about this not being the moment for a heart-to-heart conversation, but you already know you're right, don't you, Myles?"

"Always, love. Always." He winked at her without smiling. "And you are very brave."

"Hardly. When I think about what you've —"

"Don't think about what I've been through. I don't."

She wanted to throttle him where he sat. The hours on the road and the mad traffic seemed not to have fazed him in the least.

216

No nightmares, no worries about being back close to her, no fretting about the past or the future. He looked no more or less drawn and tired than he had at the beginning of the trip.

"I have a thirteen-year-old son who wants to follow your footsteps straight into the SAS," she said tartly. "I suppose that qualifies as brave."

Myles jumped out of the car with a bounce to his step and greeted Justin Rush as if they were longtime friends. Josie had no illusions that being with her had put Myles in a lighthearted, sardonic mood. He grabbed his rucksack and trotted up the steps and through the brass-trimmed door into the hotel. However tired he was, he wouldn't let it get in the way of his mission, which, at the moment, was Sophie Malone.

As Josie climbed out of the car, Justin Rush retrieved her bag from the back. "Lizzie would like you to meet her in her room when you've got yourselves settled," he said. "Keira will be joining you, too."

"Lovely," Josie said.

Explaining that the hotel was quiet, Justin carried Josie's bag into the lobby, where a fire glowed in a marble fireplace. He slipped behind the elegant front desk. "I've jotted down Lizzie's room number for you. She's on the second floor. You're on the third. She booked you and Mr. Fletcher each a room. They're adjoining." He handed Josie the keys, adding, matter-of-factly, "There's a connecting door between them. I've given you that key, as well."

"Wonderful," Josie said briskly. "Thanks much, Justin. I'll take my bag from here. Do tell Lizzie we'll be down shortly, won't you?"

"Happy to," Justin said.

Mercifully, Myles had stayed out of the exchange. He silently followed Josie up the curving stairs off the lobby. Just thinking about hotel rooms and beds and baths and towels had her feeling all afire and on edge, but she quickly blamed her sleepless night and the interminable drive across Ireland.

As they came to their rooms, she handed Myles his set of keys. "Good job, love," he said. "I'll see you in Lizzie's room in a few."

"Taking a nap, Myles, or checking on Will and Simon?"

But he was already through the door, which automatically shut quietly behind him. Josie resisted pounding her fist on it and instead went into her own room, a charming and tasteful mix of modern and traditional furnishings. From what she'd learned in having known Lizzie Rush for a month, each of the boutique hotel's twenty-seven rooms was individually appointed, with an eye to the comfort of the guests.

Now that she was finally alone, Josie let down her guard and tried to diminish the tension in her back and shoulders with a few stretches while the tub filled. She added a dollop of the ginger-and-ginseng-scented bath oil that came with her room, stripped, left her clothes in a heap on the floor and sank into the steaming water, closing her eyes as the events of the day drifted away for a bit.

When she imagined Myles letting himself in through the connecting door, she bolted straight up out of the tub, toweled off and slipped into a soft, cuddly hotel bathrobe ready on a hook on the door.

By then, Scoop Wisdom was ringing her from Boston. She'd tried him several times on the drive from Dublin and expected to dive in and tell him about her conversation with Tim O'Donovan, but he had developments of his own. Josie sat on a chair in a window overlooking a darkening Dublin street and listened without interruption as the Boston detective related his unpleasant news — that he and Sophie Malone had found a man dead.

"Cliff Rafferty," Scoop said.

Josie frowned. "I'm not familiar with the name."

"He was a police officer. He had a peripheral role with the Augustine case until he retired a few weeks ago. He took a private security job with Percy and Helen Carlisle."

"Who're the Carlisles?"

"Wealthy couple from Boston — at least he is. He stopped to see Sophie in Kenmare her last night in Ireland. His wife had already left. She's back in Boston now. Her husband didn't return with her, but we don't know where he is. We'd like to find him."

"Do you suspect he's involved in this officer's death?"

"I'm not on the case."

That wasn't exactly an answer, but Josie assumed Scoop hadn't intended for it to be one. "Did he stay in Ireland? Is he here somewhere?"

"We don't know what he did after he saw Sophie in Kenmare. He travels a lot. He has a home in London and friends and favorite hotels all over the place." Scoop paused. "Where's your friend Myles Fletcher? He's there with you?"

"What makes you think he's here?"

"The lilt in your voice."

She clicked her tongue behind her teeth. "Cheeky bastard."

He laughed, which wasn't, Josie decided, bad to hear, but he was serious again when he went on. "Tell Fletcher to call me."

After Scoop disconnected, Josie gritted her teeth at her phone as if he were still there giving orders. He could be a decidedly annoying man. She used the house phone to ring Myles in his room. "Your new detective friend in Boston wants you to call him. He and our Sophie Malone just found a dead police officer."

"I've already told him all I know."

"You never tell anyone all you know," Josie said. "Ring him now. I'd prefer not to have him involve the guards. I like my room. The ginger-and-ginseng bath salts are particularly delightful."

"I'm getting images, love."

"Enjoy them, because that's all you'll get. Make the call, Myles. I don't want to spend the night in an Irish jail cell because you're too stubborn to meet Detective Wisdom halfway. He'll call the guards. You know bloody well he will."

Myles was silent a moment. "All right. I'll join you in Lizzie's room after I've had a chat with Wisdom. Unless, of course, you'd rather —"

221

"Lizzie's room in a few minutes is perfect."

She cradled the phone, feeling flushed and agitated. She glanced at the connecting door. What *would* she do if Myles came through it wearing nothing but a bathrobe and carrying a jar of bath salts?

"Dear heavens," she muttered at her wild imagination and quickly got dressed.

She took the stairs to the second floor. Lizzie opened the door to a small suite as elegant and quirky as the rest of the hotel. A table in front of the sofa was laid out with plates of fruit, cheese, brown bread and scones, with little dishes of jams and butter and a large pot of tea. Keira was there, too, both women casually dressed and clearly unaware of more violence in Boston. Josie filled them in with what she'd learned from Scoop Wisdom.

Neither Lizzie nor Keira knew the dead man, Cliff Rafferty.

"This has turned ugly fast, hasn't it?" Lizzie gathered up a deck of playing cards on the table, next to a graceful copper vase, and shuffled them idly, a long-standing habit. "Arabella Davenport wants to measure Keira and me for dresses in London. Given this latest news, I suppose that's what Will and Simon would have us do."

Will's younger sister was primarily a wedding dress designer, but Josie decided not to point that out; obviously Lizzie would know, and the state of her and Will's relationship was none of Josie's affair — not that she lacked for an opinion. She believed their whirlwind romance was true love at work and Will Davenport, so hard to read about so much else, had found his soul mate in Lizzie Rush.

Josie trusted herself to judge other people's love lives. With her own, she was clueless.

She plucked a perfectly chilled grape from the tray.

"Arabella sounds as happy and content as ever," Lizzie continued. "I'm sure it helps that she has no idea where Simon and Will are. Do you know, Josie?"

Josie nibbled on her grape, grateful that for once she could give a complete and honest answer to that particular question. "No."

"Would you tell us if you did?" Keira asked, skeptical.

Lizzie set the cards back on the table and plopped onto the soft cushions of the sofa. "Egad, Josie. You look terrible."

Apparently her bath hadn't helped as much as she'd hoped. "It's been a strange day." As she helped herself to a perfectly

223

browned scone, she remained on her feet and told her two friends about her conversations with Seamus Harrigan and then Tim O'Donovan in Kenmare. "During the entire drive across Ireland that afternoon, I couldn't stop thinking about Sophie being left for dead in a dark, dank cave on a remote island."

Keira rose, her pale hair pulled back, gleaming in the room's pleasant light. "There are obvious similarities between what happened to Sophie and my night in the ruin on the Beara, but there are differences, too. I heard whispers, and I was left there, trapped, but I didn't come across the blood smeared on the tree branches until the next morning, after I was already safe."

"Augustine left the blood for you — or whoever came looking for you — to find," Josie said. "It wasn't part of a grand plan. He happened onto a recently dead sheep in the pasture. He didn't kill the poor thing."

Keira pulled back a drape and stared out the window. "You said the bloody branches Sophie saw in the cave disappeared before the fisherman and the guards got there. Simon was with me when I found the sheep's blood. I had a witness. I had evidence to corroborate my story."

Not minding that she was the only one

eating, Josie added little mounds of clotted cream and raspberry jam to the side of her small plate. "Augustine hasn't explained himself. To my knowledge, he's hardly spoken a word since his arrest."

"We may never know how many people he's killed." Keira spoke with remarkable self-control, although her ordeal early that summer was clearly still a struggle for her. "I just want to live my life. Draw, paint, laugh, love. I don't want to think about killers anymore."

Lizzie, who had gone somewhat pale, nodded. "I don't, either."

"That's precisely what you both should do, then," Josie said. "You needn't be involved with whatever's happening now in Boston. Arabella Davenport awaits you in London with her measuring tape."

As Keira moved away from the window, she exhibited none of her usual positive spirit, the carefree wanderlust that Josie had seen in her even just a few weeks ago. Normally Keira was bubbling with creativity and enthusiasm. "I was never afraid in the ruin," she said. "I can't explain it, but I felt safe."

"The fairies," Josie said.

"The black dog was there, too," Lizzie interjected from her position on the sofa.

"Of course, for all we know, he's a shape-shifting fairy himself."

"Anything's possible." Keira settled her troubled gaze on Josie. "I can't not be involved, Josie. I have to do what I can."

Josie added fresh fruit to her plate and finally sat with it on a side chair that seemed to envelop her in its soft cushions. "Oh, my, Lizzie," she said, deliberately cheerful. "Did you choose this particular chair to remind people how tired they are?" But when Lizzie managed only a weak smile, Josie made up her mind. "I think it best that you two return to London first thing tomorrow. I'll make the arrangements. If you don't want to let Arabella measure you for dresses, you can all have tea or visit Buckingham Palace—"

"Or catch Taryn Malone on stage," Lizzie said, perking up.

Josie sighed. "That's not what I had in mind."

Lizzie didn't give up. "I'd love to see Arabella, but Keira and I can look into whether Percy Carlisle is in London."

"Lizzie," Josie said, "the Boston police want to talk to Percy in connection with the highly suspicious death of one of their own."

She nodded. "Exactly."

Keira, too, seemed to rally now that a plan

226

was in the works. "Maybe he's in London and just didn't tell his wife — not necessarily for nefarious reasons but because he's not used to being married."

"I can get us names of his friends and acquaintances there," Lizzie added.

The Rushes were themselves wealthy Bostonians, but even if they weren't, Josie had no doubt that Lizzie and Keira would manage to get the names. These were two very capable women — capable on multiple levels — but Josie wasn't keen on having to explain to her bosses in London, should Lizzie and Keira land themselves in trouble, why she'd given them free rein and even encouraged them.

There was also the prospect of explaining herself to Will and Simon, too.

"You've done your investigative bit these past few months," she said, "and you have no legal authority to start poking into this man's affairs."

"It's perfectly reasonable that I'd look him up," Keira said.

"How? You just said you don't know him."

"We're both from Boston," Keira said, "and we share an interest in art, history and archaeology. He's a natural to approach about the Boston-Cork folklore conference. I'm surprised I haven't thought of him before now."

Josie put far too much clotted cream on the last bit of her scone, but she didn't care. "That's utterly transparent. He'll know in a minute you have an ulterior motive."

Lizzie dropped her feet to the floor and reached for a piece of brown bread and a small plate. "So? We'll have found him." She dipped a knife into soft butter and smeared it on her bread. "That's the main thing, isn't it?"

"There's no danger, Josie," Keira said, the life returning to her eyes. "Even if this police officer in Boston was murdered and didn't commit suicide, his killer is there, not here."

Josie recognized defeat when it was upon her. "I'll have someone meet you in London."

"Who? Scotland Yard?" Definitely more animated now, Keira walked over to the small table and took the smallest triangle of cheese from the tray. "MI5 — MI6?"

Josie smiled. "Such an imagination."

She was spared further grilling by Myles's belated arrival. He was freshly showered, shaved and as sexy as she'd ever seen him. She told herself her heightened emotions were a result of the troubling news from Boston and how it might intersect with the Kenmare fisherman's tale of a cave, blood and lost Celtic gold — not, she thought, to the reemergence of one formerly dead military and intelligence officer in her life.

Well, not in her life. In her presence, at best. Myles wasn't a man who let himself be in anyone else's life. He preferred to stand apart. She'd known that about him even before the ill-fated firefight in Afghanistan.

She noticed his gray eyes were less red-rimmed than an hour ago, and he moved with his usual energy and purpose. He plucked two slices of brown bread from the tray, skipped a plate, jam and butter and sat next to Lizzie. "Sorry to interrupt your chat."

"We were discussing wedding dresses," Lizzie said with a wry smile.

"Terrifying. Put me back on the Maine coast with Norman Estabrook's thugs. You were quite the firecracker ally that day, Lizzie, love."

She scooted to the corner of the sofa with her knees tucked up under her chin, so that she was facing Myles. "I had no choice," she said.

"We always have a choice. Yours was to act. Your father taught you well."

She frowned. "It's him. In London. It's my father you're having meet us, isn't it,

Josie? He was just in Ireland for the first time since my mother's death. I haven't heard from him in a week or so, but I know he hasn't returned to Las Vegas."

Josie relished another bite of scone. "Let's chuck everything and open a tea shop on a tree-lined street in a little town on the Irish coast." She took a moment to consider the myriad complications that the mention of Harlan Rush presented. Widower, gambler, hotelier, veteran spy — and a man very devoted to Lizzie, his only child. "If your father is in London, Lizzie, perhaps he's there to help you site the very first Rush hotel in Great Britain."

"Not a chance," Lizzie said. "My dear father may be a vice president in the family business, but that doesn't mean he knows a thing about it. My uncle would never let him get involved in opening a hotel."

Josie ate some of her fruit, although she wanted another scone. "When I made that comment, I had no one specific in mind. I can't say I've ever met your father."

Myles eyed Lizzie with a measure of respect he reserved for very few. They'd bonded in the last hours of Abigail Browning's captivity, when Norman Estabrook and his thugs had holed up in the old Rush house on the Maine coast. Once Estabrook and most of his men were dead and Abigail and Lizzie were safe, Myles had jumped in a boat and disappeared. Will could have stopped him, but he hadn't.

Lizzie seemed to curl up into an even tighter ball. "You came back here voluntarily. Simon and Will couldn't order you. Even if they tried to, you'd only listen if you thought it was in the interest of your mission to do as they asked."

Myles popped a chunk of brown bread into his mouth. "I'm starving. There's a pub in this place, isn't there?"

"Lower level," Lizzie said. "You know I hate being ignored, don't you?"

He grinned. "You'll definitely keep Lord Will on his toes."

Keira shook her head. "You people," she said cheerfully. "If I could paint, I'd hole up here, but I can't." She returned to the window and looked out at the Dublin night again. "Maybe I'll turn into a painter of dreary, depressing scenes."

"That's not even possible," Josie said.

"I hope not." She let the drape fall back in place. "Lizzie, are you going to tell them about Justin?"

"Oh, right." Lizzie seemed to put aside trying to get more information from Myles. "My cousin Justin reminded me that Jeremiah — his older brother — had a fierce crush on Sophie Malone when she worked at our hotel in Boston. He was still in high school."

Josie resisted the crumbs on her plate. "Where is Jeremiah now?"

"He's working reception at the Whitcomb. I called him while I was waiting for you all to get here." Lizzie sat up, dropping her feet to the floor. "He helped me remember that Sophie got to know John March. The FBI director. It could mean nothing —"

Josie shook her head. "In my experience, the words 'John March' in a sentence never mean nothing."

"True," Lizzie said, undeterred. "Jeremiah and I both think there's more that we're just not remembering. Justin, too. It'll come to us."

They chatted a bit more, but Josie finally felt her fatigue and walked back up the stairs to her room. She thought Myles might head to the pub, but he was right behind her. She didn't get through her door before he had her in his arms. His mouth found hers, and a thousand responses flooded her at once — a stern reprimand, a knee to the groin, tears, another attempt at a heart-to-heart talk. He was physically stronger and an experienced combat soldier, but he was exhausted and obviously wasn't in a defensive mode. She was well trained herself and very much on her guard, but all her options fell away with the taste of him, the feel of his hands on her.

She kicked the door shut with her heel. It'd been a month since she'd learned he hadn't been dragged off and killed, wasn't a traitor. She'd had time to imagine this moment and how she'd respond — or, more to the point, wouldn't respond.

She pushed back all the warnings she'd given herself not to succumb to being near him again and do exactly what she was doing now. Kissing him back, aching for him.

"This kept me going so many times," he said, drawing her to him, every inch of him lean and rock-hard. He lifted her as if she were slim and small, which she was not, and she could feel his arousal against her. "Just thinking about loving you again got me through one dark night after another."

"Rubbish." Josie draped her arms around his neck and tilted back from their kiss. "You never think about the past or the future."

He grinned at her. "Except when it comes to you, love."

He kissed her again, and she was hot now, her mind spinning. She responded to him, deepening their kiss, letting go of everything but that heady combination of needs she always felt with him. It'd been two years since she'd had a man. But she wouldn't tell him. Never.

The thought rocked her to her core. She clutched his upper arms and pulled back from their kiss. "I mourned you, Myles. I didn't have the luxury of thinking this day would come."

He set her back on the floor. "I'll be mature and give you time to sort this out." He took a curl of her hair and tucked it behind her ear, as gentle a move as he'd ever made with her. "Just not too much time. You're decisive. You'll know."

"There's nothing to sort out. You were wrong for me two years ago. Now you're just more wrong." She adjusted her clothing and cleared her throat. "I know it's not that late, but it's been a long day in the car."

He winked at her. "Now it'll be a long night alone in our beds."

He went back out through the hall door, and before she could change her mind, Josie threw on the dead bolt and pulled a chair in front of the connecting door. If he tried to sneak in, at least she'd have fair warning and could dry her tears. In her thirteen years with British intelligence, not once had she let a colleague see her cry.

And that was what Myles Fletcher was. A colleague.

"Bastard," she said, picking up a pillow and flinging it to the floor.

What would she get if she trashed her five-star hotel room out of pure frustration? She could present Myles to hotel security. Lizzie Rush could intervene and explain. Having taken on armed thugs and a violent billionaire with Myles, she would understand why Josie had been driven to breaking windows and kicking the feathers out of pillows.

Instead she picked up the pillow and sat on the bed with her knees tucked up under her chin. She touched her lips with her fingertips and looked at the connecting door. "Damn you, Myles," she said in a hoarse whisper. "I love you as much as ever."

Which, of course, was why he'd kissed her. He knew she loved him. He'd always known — and if that *had* given him comfort during the past two years, wasn't it a good thing? As a professional, shouldn't she draw some satisfaction that their relationship had helped an agent on a difficult, dangerous mission — one he hadn't expected to survive?

Some, perhaps, but never mind the past. What about the future?

Not to mention the present. Josie dipped under the silken duvet, shivering at the feel of the cool sheets. It *would, indeed,* be long night alone in her bed.

14

Boston, Massachusetts

Scoop returned to his desk at BPD head-quarters in Roxbury for the first time since he'd been shredded by shrapnel. Everything was just as he'd left it. He'd turned over all his notes on the possible involvement of a member of the department with the thugs who'd kidnapped Abigail Browning. The firewall was up between him and the investigation. It had gone up the second the bomb went off.

There was nothing for him to do except avoid people he didn't want to talk to. Josie's report was raging in his head, but he had to pull himself together before he talked to anyone — especially Sophie. He returned to Charles Street, the temperature dropping fast, the early evening air cool, even chilly. For once Jeremiah Rush wasn't at the reception desk in the Whitcomb lobby. Scoop rode the elevator with a couple from Houston who were in town to see as many historic sites as they could fit in. The wife wanted to be sure to visit the Louisa May Alcott house in Concord. The husband wanted to visit Bunker Hill in Charlestown.

They looked at Scoop to settle the issue. He grinned. "I'd go to a Red Sox game."

"Do you work for the hotel?" the wife asked. "Our tub drain's slow."

The husband winced as if he wanted to crawl out of there, but Scoop just said, "I'll let the front desk know."

She blushed. "Thank you. I'm sorry. I thought —"

"Not a problem."

They looked relieved when he got off the elevator. His room had been serviced, even his toothbrush, razor and toothpaste set in a clean glass. He didn't know what to do with himself. He thought about having a drink at the bar. Calling O'Reilly to join him. Tracking down Abigail on her honeymoon. Before the bomb, the three of them would get together in the backyard or in one of their kitchens and talk about whatever was on their minds. Now everything was different. He, Abigail and Bob O'Reilly were stuck on the wrong side of the investigation.

He rubbed a palm over his head.

He could go up and fix the Houston couple's drain.

Scoop grabbed a zip-up sweatshirt and returned to the lobby, bypassing Morrigan's and heading back outside. He turned up Mt. Vernon Street, telling himself he was just getting some air, working off the last of his jet lag and the effects of his long day. The nagging questions about Cliff's role in the bomb blast. His death. The bizarre scene at his apartment.

Sophie's wide, blue eyes as she'd taken in the disturbing, bizarre skulls, glass beads, DVD, cast-iron pot — the bomb-making materials and the former police officer hanging in his dining room.

As he came to the top of Beacon Hill, Scoop gritted his teeth, but he already knew what he was going to do. He continued on to the Malone twins' apartment. The gate was unlocked, which was an issue for him. He didn't ring the bell, just descended the steps and walked through the archway back to a cute little courtyard.

Sophie was, in fact, arranging mums. She was on her knees, a half dozen mums in apple baskets in front of her. She moved a yellow one behind a dark maroon one and rolled back onto her heels. "There. Better."

She glanced up at Scoop. "What do you think?"

He nodded back toward the street. "I think you should keep your gate locked."

"That must have been one of the neighbors who share the courtyard. I'm in a batten-down-the-hatches mood myself."

"Smart. The mums look great. Perfect. Don't touch a thing."

She stood up and smiled at him. "You don't care, do you?"

"I like gardening when it involves something I can have for dinner."

"Ah. What have you been up to?"

"I just got mistaken for a plumber. Thought you'd be pleased. Not everyone looks at me and thinks 'cop.' "

She brushed loose potting soil off her hands. "Would you like to come inside?"

"I'm homeless. Sure."

She led him into the tiny apartment. The low ceilings would have him nuts in half a day, but that was affordable Beacon Hill. Unaffordable Beacon Hill came with higher ceilings. He noticed a laptop and papers by the fireplace, but otherwise, there was no indication Sophie had truly moved in.

"I know why you're here," she said.

That was good because he wasn't sure he knew.

She motioned to what passed for a kitchen. "Can I get you anything?"

"No, but help yourself."

She shook her head. "I haven't been able to eat a thing since that half of your sandwich. Have a seat."

He pulled out a chair at the table by the windows and sat down, but she stayed on her feet between him and the entry, watching him as if she were wondering if she'd lost her mind inviting him in. She'd twisted her hair up into some kind of knot that was coming apart, tangled strands of dark red falling into her face.

She walked over to the low sectional and stood in front of the fireplace. "It'll be easier if I start at the beginning." She took a moment to study him with those smart, bright blue eyes. "But you know my story already, don't you? Two Brits talked to a fisherman in Kenmare this morning. They're friends of yours, aren't they?"

"Not friends, exactly."

"They're reporting to you —"

"Sort of, yes. It doesn't matter, Sophie. I want to hear you tell me what happened."

"All right." She stared past him out the window, but he doubted she even saw the array of autumn flowers. "Last September, I explored a tiny, uninhabited island off the

Iveragh Peninsula as a break from writing my dissertation."

Scoop smiled at her. "Couldn't just go to the local pub?"

She seemed to relax a little. "I did some of my best writing in my local pub. My island trips were different. I'd get out on the water and in the air and not think about my page quotas, my arguments, my future. How many years it'd taken me to get to that point and how in debt I was, with no certainty I'd get the kind of job I wanted in the end."

"All that cheerful stuff," Scoop said.

"It all fell away on those trips. I was looking forward to finally getting my doctorate, but it was a transition. Going out to the island was just what I needed. A lark. No past, no future. Just the present." She turned back to the fireplace. "Tim had told me a story that'd been handed down by priests in a local village, about Celtic treasure hidden on an island. We figured out this could be the island described in the story. I never thought I'd find anything — neither did Tim. That wasn't the point."

"When was your first trip out there?"

"Late August. I went four or five times. Tim would drop me off and come back after a few hours. This last time was in late

September. I'd talked him into leaving me there overnight."

"Did it take a lot of talking?" Scoop asked.

She gave him a small smile. "As a matter of fact, yes. Tim thought I was completely daft. I was curious, I was having fun. I wanted to check out the center of the island. It's not difficult to get to — I just couldn't do it and get back to where Tim would pick me up in a few hours."

Scoop settled back in his chair. "Did you head there the minute you arrived on the island?"

She nodded. "I wasn't the least bit concerned about staying out there on my own. I happened on a small cave almost right in the middle of the island. I wasn't even sure at first it was a cave."

"It's not marked on a map?"

"No." Sophie sat on the edge of the sectional, as if she knew she might jump back up and run out of there at any moment. "It was a beautiful day. Clear, calm. By the time I discovered the cave it was getting late, but I figured I could camp there."

"No worries at that moment, then," Scoop said.

"None. I've investigated caves before. I set my pack on a ledge by the entrance and had a look inside. My flashlight hit on something. I got all excited. I was having fun, remember." She paused and stared down at her hands, her fingers splayed in front of her, and Scoop knew she was back in that cave a year ago. "I came upon what appeared to be a spun-bronze cauldron filled with pagan Celtic metalwork. Of course, I can't be sure what it was without further examination."

"You didn't get that chance."

"That's right." She raised her gaze from her hands, then pushed to her feet, clearly restless. "I was still examining the find when I heard a noise — what sounded like whispers. I turned off my flashlight and ducked a bit deeper into the cave until I could figure out what was going on."

"These whispers." Scoop kept his voice even, calm. "Describe them."

"I couldn't make out any words. It sounded as if whoever was out there was deliberately trying to scare me."

"You're sure someone was there."

"Yes, I'm sure. Whatever I heard wasn't the wind or the ocean."

Scoop glanced out the window, the late-day sun hitting the pretty courtyard. When Jay Augustine had come upon Keira Sullivan in the ruin on the Beara Peninsula, he had whispered her name before trapping her inside.

"What happened next?" he asked quietly.

Sophie came and sat down across from him. "I hid behind a boulder. I had a partial view of the entrance to the cave. There were . . ." She shut her eyes, inhaling through her nose. "I saw branches — branches of a hawthorn tree — placed in the shape of an X at the entrance to the cave."

"You could see that clearly?"

She opened her eyes again. "It was still daylight. I wasn't that far away."

"Any significance that it was a hawthorn tree?"

"Fairies are said to gather and dance under hawthorns. It's considered bad luck to cut one down."

"Ah."

"The branches had to have been brought in by boat. There are no trees — hawthorn or otherwise — on the island. It's mostly rock, with a few grassy spots." She shifted her gaze back to the courtyard, her blue eyes wide now. "The leaves of the branches had been soaked in what appeared to be blood."

"Oh, good," Scoop said.

She managed a smile. "You knew that was coming. Tim wouldn't have left that out of whatever he told your British friends." Her smile faded, her skin pale in the dim light. "Whoever placed those branches knew I was there. I half rolled, half crawled deeper into the cave. I remember searching in the dark, feeling with my hands, for a loose rock I could use to defend myself."

Scoop grimaced. "Whispers. Bloody branches. Hiding for your life in a cave. I have to tell you, sweetheart, that'd do it for me."

"It was rather terrifying, I have to say. I don't remember what happened next. I was hit on the head somehow."

"Where on the head?"

"Right here." She put her hand behind her right ear. "I could have banged into a jutting rock, or someone could have hit me. I was knocked out — I don't know for how long." She pointed to her wrist. "I wasn't wearing a watch. When I regained consciousness, it was pitch dark. I didn't move. I swear I didn't breathe."

"Were you afraid you'd been trapped in the cave?"

"Yes," she said, her voice almost inaudible. "I finally couldn't stand it and crept forward. I was dizzy, in pain, but when I felt the fresh air and heard the ocean . . ." She sat up straight, collecting herself. "At least I knew there hadn't been a cave-in while I

246

was unconscious. I wasn't trapped. The cauldron was gone. The branches were gone. I didn't hear more whispers . . ." She trailed off, as if she were back in that cave.

Scoop could understand why the Irish police hadn't done more to investigate.

"I was a mess," she said, almost matter-of-fact. "I figured my backpack was a lost cause. I'd heard it fall — or get shoved — off the ledge. I was left for dead, Scoop. I'm convinced of that."

"I have no reason to argue with you."

"I was hurt, dehydrated, shivering non-stop." Her voice was even, steady. "I had a concussion and mild hypothermia, but I was still coherent. I stayed in the cave, out of the wind. I knew Tim would come find me."

"Weren't you afraid he was responsible —"

"No, never. Not for one second."

She got up again, pulling clips out of her hair and shaking it loose, which was almost more than Scoop could stand watching. All that red. The freckles. The eyes. He let his gaze drift to her shape under her jeans and T-shirt, then stopped himself because he just wasn't going that far. At least not right then, anyway.

"Your fisherman friend found you?"

She nodded, more animated now. "I heard

him calling me. He was pretty frantic by then. I crawled out of the cave on my own, and Tim was standing on a ledge — he was scared to death, Scoop. He'd spotted my backpack. It looked as if it'd tipped over where I'd left it and fallen into a deep, wet crevice."

Scoop rose next to her. "Hell, Sophie."

"Tim gave me water and his jacket. He had a small first-aid kit with him and did what he could for my scrapes and bruises. I told him everything. It sounded crazy, there in the morning sun, with birds circling overhead, waves crashing on the rocks. Tim obviously thought I'd hit my head crawling in the cave and hallucinated or dreamed everything else, but he called the guards."

"There wasn't much they could do by the time they got out there," Scoop said.

"That's right. They didn't find a drop of blood, a footprint, a witness, evidence of another boat."

"Nothing to corroborate your story."

She shoved both hands through her hair again, coming up with more pins that she set on the table. "I'm sure that was the idea. If by some miracle I lived through the night, I'd have a crazy story to tell. If I didn't, I'd look as if I'd died of natural causes after a mishap."

Scoop brushed a few strands of her wild hair out of her eyes. "It took some effort and planning to get those bloody branches out to that island."

"They could have been part of a ritual, or just designed to scare me. I suppose there's a chance the guards missed a bit of forensic evidence, but the island's not a hospitable place for tracking the stray eyelash or blood spot. Whoever followed me out there was careful not to leave anything obvious behind." She gave him a challenging look. "A cop would know how to do that."

He let her comment slide. "When you heard about Keira Sullivan's experience on the Beara Peninsula, you thought of what happened to you on the island. You two have similar backgrounds — you're both from Boston, you know Colm Dermott, you're interested in old Irish stories, you're around the same age."

"I only learned the details about Keira's experience when I talked to Colm last week. I didn't want to sound any alarms without more information. If Jay Augustine was responsible for my ordeal on the island . . ." She paused, sinking back onto her chair at the table. "He's in jail. I figured I didn't have to worry about more violence."

"Then came this morning," Scoop said,

sitting across from her.

The fading daylight struck her eyes and made them seem darker, richer. "Your British friends have been in touch with the Irish authorities."

"We need to know what crimes Augustine committed. All of them."

"Including the theft and sale of illegal or stolen art and antiquities?"

Scoop was silent a moment. "Sophie —"

She sprang up without a word and headed for the door, charging out to the courtyard. He watched her from the window as she got down onto her knees and started rearranging the mums. He rose, feeling a pull of pain in his hip for the first time since that morning in the ruin. He went outside. The temperature had dropped fast, but Sophie didn't seem cold.

"The low ceilings got to me," she said without looking up. "I'll be okay in a second."

"What about the Carlisles? How much do they know about what happened last year?"

"Percy wasn't seeing Helen then, although I imagine they knew each other." Sophie's tone was unreadable. She stood up, almost bumping into Scoop. "He was in Killarney in early September. I'd already made a couple of day trips out to the island by then.

He came to see me. I was surprised, but I didn't think that much about it. When he stopped in Kenmare the other night, he said he'd heard I was chasing a story with an Irish fisherman. He was convinced I was modeling myself after his father, but that wasn't the case at all."

"Did you know his father?"

"Yes, but not well. I ran into him a few times at the Carlisle Museum when I was a student in Boston. He was an amateur archaeologist. He was quite the adventurer."

Scoop ran the toe of his shoe over a worn brick missing a corner. "What about this Irish fisherman?"

"I told you, I trust Tim. He had multiple opportunities to pitch me overboard or throw me off the ledge along with my backpack, but he didn't."

"Bringing you back alive kept him from answering even tougher questions."

"I realize I'm not a law enforcement officer who has to keep an open mind — which apparently means not trusting anyone — but I trust Tim. He's not working with Augustine or anyone else involved in black market antiquities."

"You two aren't a team?"

She gave him a cool look, no indication his question had irritated or surprised her.

"Ah. I see. Tim helps with transportation and local lore, and I identify authentic artifacts and find collectors willing to buy them and not ask questions."

Scoop shrugged. "Or you work together and create a compelling story, plant fakes and sell them to people who can't complain if they find out, since they obtained them illegally."

"None of the above," Sophie said without hesitation. "It's not logical for me to have called attention to myself with a made-up story about an Irish cave if I were a thief."

"I could make a case for it."

"A tortured argument at best. All these years working toward my Ph.D. and living hand-to-mouth and I'd chuck it for some crazy scheme? That doesn't even make sense."

He tilted his head back and eyed her. "Give me a D, would you, Professor Malone?"

She seemed to make an effort to smile but bent down suddenly, picked up a yellow mum by the edge of its basket and moved it behind a white one, then stood up again. "There. I like that better."

"I see no difference."

"The yellow works better in the background —"

"Sophie."

She sighed. "All right. Here's my take. One, the artifacts I saw in the cave are authentic and were stolen by someone who followed me to the island hoping I'd find something. Two, they were stolen by someone who, for whatever reason, *hoped or knew* I'd find these particular artifacts. Three, they are fakes planted by someone who wanted me to find them —"

"A ruse," Scoop said, finishing for her. "All the drama with the whispers and the blood helps."

"Except I've kept quiet about the incident, at the request of the Irish authorities — not that I needed their suggestion. I wouldn't want to encourage treasure hunters, or certainly to come across as one myself."

"That wouldn't look so good on your CV. You're sure you met Cliff Rafferty for the first time last night?"

The pain of that morning showed in her face. "As far as I know, yes. If I encountered him on the street when he was a police officer, I don't remember."

"When was the last time you were in Boston?"

"In the spring — well before the violence here started."

"Unless it started with you a year ago.

253

That's what you're worried about, isn't it?"

Sophie didn't answer. She walked past him to her apartment window and picked a dried leaf off the sill, desperately in need of scraping and a fresh coat of paint. "Summer's gone now."

"Do you miss Ireland already?"

"I love Boston, too." She crumpled up the leaf and let the bits fall to the brick courtyard. "It's a bad idea for you to be here, isn't it? Or are you on duty?"

"Technically I'm still on medical leave for getting blown into my compost bin."

She brushed her hands off and smiled at him. "You're a driven, hard-ass, career-oriented, cynical cop, aren't you, Scoop?"

He grinned. "I'm not cynical."

"You're good at detecting lies. Why?"

"It's my job. Nothing special. No lying women or lying family I'm getting back at or trying to understand."

"How long have you been in internal affairs?"

He noticed she looked cold now. She'd run out of the apartment without a jacket or sweater. "Two years," he said.

"What's next?"

"Getting fired if I'm not careful with you. It's not going over well, Sophie, this not telling me everything."

"I just told you —"

"It wasn't everything."

"I haven't lied to you, Scoop."

"Omitting pertinent information is equivalent to lying." He had lined up his questions. "What about your octogenarian art theft expert?"

He saw a flicker of surprise in her face. "Ah. Wendell Sharpe." With one foot, she straightened a ragged doormat. "Your British friends are enterprising if they've learned about him. He's such a gentleman, as well as brilliant. I went to see him in Dublin —"

"After you talked to Colm Dermott about Keira's experience," Scoop said.

"I asked him if Irish Celtic artifacts had turned up on the black market in the past year. I assumed the guards would know if they had and would have said something, but . . ." She gave the doormat one last shove with her foot. "It was a good opportunity to talk to an expert. He gave me a tutorial on his world. It was fascinating."

"I'll bet it was." Scoop could see her energy was flagging. "Your mums need water."

This time she did manage a smile. "I guess I can't pretend to be a gardener, can I?" But she wasn't ready to quit. "I've heard a bad cop's like an infection that spreads in ways you can't control or predict."

"I can't go there, Sophie."

She stepped up to her apartment door, its dark green paint almost black in the shadows. "I still don't believe Cliff Rafferty killed himself." She paused, one hand on the brass knob as she turned back to him. "I wouldn't be surprised if the autopsy shows he was unconscious or already dead when he was hanged. I have theories, just as you do."

Scoop was right behind her, a yellow mum brushing his leg, but he didn't move. "No freelancing, okay?"

"What about you, Scoop? Are you sure you're not blinded by your friendship with Bob O'Reilly and Abigail Browning — with other detectives in the department? You've been out of the country for a month. What if one of your fellow police officers is involved with Rafferty's death?"

"You speak your mind, don't you?"

"Most academics don't get far if they don't."

She pulled open the door and stalked back into her apartment. Scoop scratched the side of his mouth. He guessed she'd told him. He walked over to the door and raised his hand to knock, but she opened it up. "Anyone who can stay with you?" he asked.

"I'm not worried."

"You can stay at the Whitcomb for a few days. Let things settle down."

"I'll stay here."

He touched her hair. Craziness. "This morning was bad. I'm sorry you saw that."

"It wasn't your fault."

"Didn't say it was."

He raised his eyebrows.

She let out a breath. "Sorry. You're trying to help. I know that."

"You're smart, you're well educated and you tend to be stubborn in your views and theories. Am I right?" He winked at her. "You don't have to answer that. Tell me something about you that doesn't involve artifacts and blood-soaked branches."

"I listen to traditional Irish music, I light candles when I work and I do yoga." Her defensiveness eased, and he saw her smile reach her eyes this time. "I'm not very good at kicking butt."

He laughed. "And you don't do well in the sun."

"Are you unafraid?" she asked him quietly.

"I don't let fear get into the equation. I focus on what I have to do — which is what you did in that cave. You calculated the risks as best as you could and did what you had to do to survive." He lifted a hand to her. "I'm two minutes away. Call me anytime.

257

Don't hesitate."

She slipped outside, took his hand in hers and kissed him on the cheek, her lips soft, cool. "Thank you," she whispered. "Thank you for not letting me go alone this morning, and thank you for listening to my story."

"Sophie —"

But she'd already fled back inside and shut the door.

Scoop found Jeremiah Rush at his desk in the lobby, checking in a mother and teenage daughter on a Boston shopping trip. They regarded Scoop as if they expected him to fix their drain, too.

Once they were in the elevator, Jeremiah stood up in his expensive, wrinkle-free suit. "Is everything all right with your room, Detective?"

"I'm still willing to give Yarborough's sofa bed a try."

"You're welcome to stay here as long as you like."

"Your cousin alerted us to a bomb seconds before it went off. We owe you all, not the other way around."

"I didn't do anything. Did you see Lizzie in Ireland?"

"Briefly the night before I left."

"She and Lord Davenport . . ." Still on

his feet, Jeremiah reached down and tapped a few keys on his computer. "Everything happened so fast between them. Will strikes me as a man with a lot on his mind."

"That's one way of putting it. I don't know Lizzie well, but she strikes me as a woman who doesn't like being bored."

"No kidding," Jeremiah said with a touch of affectionate exasperation. "In fact, I talked to Lizzie a little while ago."

Scoop kept his expression neutral. "What did she have to say?"

"She was trying to remember . . ." He looked uncomfortable. "Sophie knew FBI Director March from her days working here."

"March, huh?"

"Lizzie asked me if I remembered anything else about their relationship, and I do — I don't know that it's significant, but Sophie's brother is an FBI agent. Damian Malone. He's in D.C."

"Is he close to March?"

"I don't know. I haven't seen him in a long time."

"How long?"

"Since early spring, maybe. Damian's not as — I don't know how to say this. Sophie's an archaeologist. Taryn's an actress. He's . . ."

259

"He's an FBI agent," Scoop said. "Explains it all."

Jeremiah didn't argue, and Scoop trotted downstairs to Morrigan's. Bob O'Reilly was at a table with a beer. "It's an O'Doul's," he said. "Nonalcoholic. I think of myself as being on the job right now, but you and I are in the same leaky boat, Scoop. We're supposed to stay a thousand miles from this thing."

Scoop sat across from him. "No way Cliff killed himself."

"Nope. No way."

"Think the bomb-making evidence was legit or planted?"

"I don't know. I'm getting information on the side but not all of it, seeing how it was our house that was bombed. If Cliff isn't our guy, someone wants him to be. If he is our guy —"

"Then if he was strung up, whoever did it wanted him exposed as the bomber but not talking to us."

"It's been a bad damn day," Bob said, watching Fiona, his nineteen-year-old harpist daughter, slim, blonde and blue-eyed, bound into the pub with her college musician friends, all of them with instrument cases slung over their shoulders. "Let's listen to a little Irish music, Scoop, while you tell me everything you know about our Dr. Malone."

15

Sophie watered the mums, using a hose everyone on the courtyard seemed to share. It belonged to Taryn's landlords, the outdoor faucet located under the stairs that led up to their main floor. The courtyard was cast in shadows, chilly and still, the autumn flowers a cheerful counter to the fading light — and her own mood, she thought, getting a dribble of the extra-cold water from the hose on her pant leg. She didn't care. She needed to cool off, relax and pull herself together after telling Scoop her story.

Had she really given him that little kiss on the cheek?

"Gad," she said, dragging the hose back under the stairs. "What were you thinking?"

She shut off the faucet and wound the hose into an ancient-looking pot. She knew exactly what she'd been thinking. Here was a solid, physical, intelligent man who wasn't as rigid and rules-bound as she'd expected

— who was self-controlled without being controlling.

And here was she, an archaeologist fresh from postdoctoral work in Ireland, a woman who'd taken him to a grisly scene of death and who now had told him about a horrible experience in her life — one that her own family didn't know about.

At least for now. How long before her brother dragged it out of her?

She ducked back under the stairs into the courtyard, the mums perking up after she'd practically drowned them with the hose. She went back inside, appreciating the warmth and coziness of the apartment, barely noticing the low ceilings. She washed her hands, unsnarled her hair and changed clothes.

In ten minutes, she was in front of the Whitcomb Hotel. She could have continued down Charles Street to a favorite restaurant, or taken a walk through Boston Common, but she entered the lobby, following a trio of young women who immediately veered down to Morrigan's.

Jeremiah Rush motioned for Sophie to join him by the marble fireplace, where he was stirring a low fire, more for atmosphere than heat. He replaced the screen in front of the flames and set the iron poker back in its rack. "I told on you."

263

"Told what on me and to whom?"

He grimaced. "I told Detective Wisdom that you have a brother who's an FBI agent."

"That's not a secret, Jeremiah. After this morning, he'd find out, anyway. No worries. Where is he now?"

"Up in his room." The flames glowed on his good-looking face. "Lieutenant O'Reilly is downstairs. Fiona's performing. That could be why he's here."

"Would you like me to sneak out the back?"

"Won't work. Sophie . . ."

She felt the heat of the fire. "What else, Jeremiah?"

He really looked tortured now. "Director March will be arriving here soon."

"Ah. Okay. Thanks for the heads-up."

She was tempted to leave, but did she want a bunch of FBI agents and Boston cops showing up at Taryn's apartment? Because that was what would happen. If John March wanted to talk to her, he'd find a way. She took the stairs down to Morrigan's. She noticed the women who'd entered the hotel with her were at the bar, laughing, enjoying the company of friends they'd obviously met there.

Bob O'Reilly rose from a square table

under the windows. "Dr. Malone," he said, pulling out a chair across from him and motioning to it with one hand. "Scoop'll be down in a minute. You and I can talk."

She took the hint and sat down. He returned to his side of the table. Fiona O'Reilly, her blonde hair curled and shining, was over by the stage with her friends. Sophie smiled. "I see your daughter's resemblance to you."

"Don't tell her that."

He was a homicide detective, she remembered. He had to have seen a lot in his years as a police officer, but that morning, a man he'd known — a colleague — had died, amid evidence that he'd planted a bomb at the home of three Boston detectives. It could have easily killed O'Reilly, his daughter, Scoop, even Abigail Browning, although the purpose of the bomb had been to aid in her kidnapping.

Sophie slumped in her chair. "I just felt a big wave of jet lag. All of a sudden it feels like it's the middle of the night."

"It is in Ireland. Wish you were there after today?"

"Being there wouldn't erase what I saw this morning." She looked away from O'Reilly. The musicians were chatting among themselves, more people had crowded together at the bar. She heard glasses clinking, a shriek of laughter. Finally she said, "I worked here as a student. I assume you know that. I'd see John March every once in a while. Not often. My older brother stopped by one day. He was in law school at the time."

"Now he's an FBI agent," Bob said.

"Jeremiah Rush told you, too?"

"Scoop. You should have known he'd find out. He's a bulldog."

"And he has his sources — in Ireland as well as here. By the way, Lizzie Rush will probably remember Damian."

"She's more of a pit bull than a bulldog."

Sophie smiled but said nothing. Lieutenant O'Reilly couldn't drop the subject of her brother fast enough to suit her.

He was watching his daughter as he continued. "Scoop doesn't let his heart get involved in his work. He keeps a tight rein on himself, but something about you has gotten to him."

That worked both ways, she thought. "We've only known each other a few days." Out of the corner of her eye, she noticed Fiona O'Reilly give her a wary look. Sophie wasn't offended. Scoop had saved Fiona's life. It stood to reason she'd be protective of him. "I wish I knew more."

"You know what happened to you in that cave."

"Yes, I do, and I've told the truth about my experience."

"I like this place," O'Reilly said, deceptively casual. "I never even stepped foot in here until a few weeks ago. Turns out my daughter and her friends had been playing here for a few months. John March has been coming here for thirty years. He knew Lizzie Rush's mother before she died. How'd you end up working here?"

She knew it wasn't an idle question. "I needed a job and I discovered the Whitcomb had an Irish pub."

"You were born in Ireland, right?"

"That's right. In Cork."

"Scoop's from the sticks. He always wanted to be a big-city cop. He's poised for rapid advancement in the department."

"You don't want me to get him into trouble."

"If he gets in trouble, it'll be his fault not yours." O'Reilly paused, listening as his daughter played a few warm-up notes on her small lap harp. "Fiona's in music school. She's taking violin and conducting class this semester. She's not as good at violin as she is the harp. She's all excited about our trip to Ireland this Christmas. I don't need more places for her to drag me to, but feel free to give her tips."

"You're not sure about me, are you, Detective?"

"These days I'm not sure about anyone."

FBI Director John March arrived with an entourage of agents, who stayed near the door. He was a tall, straight-backed man with iron-gray hair and a temperament to match. Scoop was right behind him. The two men joined Sophie and Bob O'Reilly at their square table, sitting across from each other, March to her right, Scoop to her left.

"Hello, Sophie," March said. "Long time."

"Director March. It's good to see you. It has been a long time."

"You're Dr. Malone now. Good for you." He pushed back in his chair, crossing one leg over the other, but not, she thought, even slightly off his guard. "Lizzie told me you were in town. She asked me if I remembered you. Of course I do. You were the bright student interested in Ireland and archaeology. I remember your twin sister, too. Taryn, the budding actress."

Sophie didn't flinch from his unrelenting gaze. "And my brother you encouraged to pursue a career with the FBI."

"Yes. I remember Damian, too."

She was very glad she hadn't ordered

alcohol. "Does he know —"

"That I came to Boston specifically to see you? No, not yet. I haven't been in touch with him. From all I've heard, he's a fine agent."

"I haven't told him about this morning," she said.

"I did," Scoop said, his bluntness a contrast to March's smooth tone. "I just got off the phone with him. We had a professional conversation, except for the part about him flying up here and kicking our asses if we let anything happen to you."

Sophie couldn't resist a smile. "Damian's protective of Taryn and me. He can't get over that we're not six anymore."

"Yep. He said you two gave him fits as little kids in Ireland."

She laughed suddenly. "We 'ruined his life.'"

March's dark eyes narrowed on her for longer than she found comfortable, but it was Bob O'Reilly who spoke. "Does your brother know Percy Carlisle?"

"I doubt it," Sophie said, the question taking her by surprise. "The Carlisles and the Malones live in two different worlds."

"You and the father, Percy Sr., shared an interest in archaeology," March said. "I don't recall from my time in Boston, Sophie.

269

Did any of his adventures take him to Ireland?"

She fought an urge to look away — to jump up and run. How far would she get if she did? With March, O'Reilly and Scoop within inches of her? With the FBI agents by the exits?

Not far, she thought, and answered March's question. "I know of one, yes."

Scoop eyed her. "There's more."

It wasn't a question or even a challenge to her. It was a statement of fact. Obviously he and the other two law enforcement officers at the table already had their answer. Sophie collected her thoughts as a waiter arrived with a tray of coffee. She hadn't ordered any, but didn't refuse when he put a mug in front of her.

"I have a feeling I know where you're going with this. Percy Sr. was never particularly drawn to Ireland. I know of only one excursion he took there. It was late in his life." She felt the heat rise from her ultra-hot coffee. "He had a bit of a misadventure."

"Anything like yours last September?" March asked quietly.

Of course Scoop would have filled March in. He'd probably written a report already for his superiors. Even as she'd told him her story, Sophie had warned herself not to

270

think they were having an intimate, private talk.

"No, Percy Sr.'s experience was quite different." Which, of course, March would know. She kept her tone even as she continued. "He was briefly arrested in Dublin for attempting to smuggle artifacts out of Ireland. It was a mix-up — a misunderstanding between his staff and Irish authorities. He was released almost immediately. He was furious, though, and fired his entire staff the minute he got back to Boston."

"You weren't on his staff?" Bob O'Reilly asked.

She shook her head. "I was working here. This was seven years ago. I was a student. I did research at the Carlisle Museum."

"There was a break-in at the museum not long after the firings," O'Reilly said. "The old man's office was trashed, and a painting disappeared — a Winslow Homer seascape from the Carlisles' private collection."

Sophie realized her heart was racing, as if she were under attack when she knew, in fact, she had nothing to hide from these men. Why hadn't she stayed in Kenmare, or grabbed her sleeping bag and gone hiking with her parents? She pulled herself out of her regrets — her fears — and grabbed the cream pitcher. "I suppose you all are watch-

271

ing your cholesterol. I will another day. Right now, I want real cream in my coffee. And I'm guessing where you're going with this. Cliff Rafferty was the first officer on the scene after the break-in, wasn't he?"

It was O'Reilly who answered. "Were you at the museum at the time?"

"No. The break-in occurred — or at least was discovered — late at night by a security guard." She dumped cream into her mug and set down the pitcher. "I was here washing dishes and mopping floors. I didn't find out anything until the next day."

"No one called you?" March asked. "The Carlisles, any of the fired staff?"

"No, and I thought nothing of it at the time — nor does it bother me now, in retrospect. I was just another student. I never heard there were any indications of Celtic rituals or any Celtic symbols at the scene. No blood," she added pointedly, her throat dry as she lifted her mug, "no skulls, broken weapons or torcs."

"Were you already specializing in Celtic archaeology?" Scoop asked.

"Yes, I was." She glanced at March, whose expression was impossible to read. "I remember you were here at Morrigan's when I came into work the night after the break-in. I'd been at the museum most of the day, in the library. I told you what happened and how shocked I was."

"I remember," March said. He leaned closer to her, less tense and confrontational. "I remember you said you didn't know much about nineteenth-century American painters."

She relaxed slightly. "I still don't."

"It bothered you. You like knowing things."

She smiled. "Are you suggesting I'm a bit of a know-it-all, Director March?"

"You're curious." He didn't smile back at her. "You have an investigative mind. You like to tackle a problem and take it to its conclusion."

Damn, she thought. She'd stepped right into that one. Damian knew John March better than she did and had warned her March was the master — not a man to be underestimated on any level. He'd been a street cop, a homicide detective, a lawyer and an FBI agent, and now he was the FBI director, with huge responsibilities on his shoulders.

"I stayed out of anything to do with the break-in," she said.

"Did you sympathize with the fired staff?" O'Reilly asked.

She faced him. "Of course, but I wasn't friends with any of them."

273

O'Reilly ran a thick finger along the handle of his coffee mug. "Did you think Percy Sr. was an SOB for what he did?"

"Sure. Who wouldn't?"

"His son," March said. "What did he think?"

"We didn't discuss it," Sophie said, raising her eyes to Scoop. "As I told Detective Wisdom, Percy and I weren't and aren't that close."

Scoop's expression was unreadable. "I checked the file. You weren't questioned by police."

"That's right," she said.

O'Reilly reached for the cream pitcher. "Hell, I'm game. It's been a bad day, and my doctor's not here." He poured the cream into his coffee but his cornflower-blue eyes were on Sophie. "Percy Sr. and Percy Jr. were both in Boston at the time of the break-in. The mother — Isabel Carlisle, Percy Sr.'s wife — had died the previous year. Cancer."

Sophie nodded. "I remember. It was a sad time."

O'Reilly set the pitcher back down. "The old man showed up at the museum right when Cliff pulled in. The son was in London at the time."

"Rafferty said he met Percy this summer

after Jay Augustine's arrest. . . ." She trailed off, recognizing that the law enforcement officers at the table would already have thought of that.

"Ripple effects, Lizzie calls them," March said. "How one thing can unexpectedly lead to and impact another. We have no idea it's coming, or how bad it'll be. You remind me of Shauna Morrigan, Lizzie's mother. She was fearless, and she had great instincts." He sighed grimly at the two Boston detectives. "Bad cops. Bombs. Ritualistic murder or whatever the hell it was. We can't have any of it."

"No, we can't," O'Reilly said, looking straight at Sophie.

March rose. "Good night, gentlemen." He nodded to Sophie. "Sophie, take care of yourself. I hope next time we see each other it's under better circumstances. Good luck with your career in archaeology." His dark eyes narrowed slightly on her. "Stay in touch."

Once he and his hulking agents started up the bottom of the stairs, O'Reilly blew out a heavy breath. "Damn. I love it when the FBI comes in and tells me my job. March was like that when he was on the force." He picked up his mug. "I'm taking two sips and then ordering a beer. In the meantime, Dr.

Malone, we have two choices where you're concerned. One, you're trouble. Two, you're not trouble. Which is it?"

"Life's not that black-and-white," she said.

"My life is."

His daughter and her friends were playing "O'Sullivan's March." The tune put Sophie back in Kenmare, in a cozy pub on a dark, rainy night, with Tim O'Donovan transfixing her with his tale of treasure, adventure, triumph and tragedy.

She pulled herself back to the present. "Does your niece know about Cliff Rafferty's death?" she asked O'Reilly.

He nodded. "Yeah. I told her."

"Did she know —"

"I talked to Keira this morning," he said, obviously not wanting to discuss his daughter. "She's in Ireland. I don't know if your FBI brother knows Simon Cahill. He's the man in Keira's life." The homicide detective's gaze bored into Sophie. "Simon's FBI. You know that, right?"

Her heart was racing again, but she tried to maintain an outward calm. "Yes, I do."

"Good. You look like you're going to slide under the table, Doc. Buy you a burger?"

"I think I'll just grab a few nuts and go."

"Sit a while, Sophie," Scoop said, touching her hand. "Have a Guinness and a bite

276

to eat. Talk to us."

She told herself to get up and get out of there, but the prospect of Taryn's quiet apartment suddenly was less appealing than staying here with the lively music, the crowd — even these two suspicious, intense police officers. Scoop and O'Reilly were on her side, she told herself, even if they believed she'd been holding back on them.

Damian would remind her that law enforcement officers always had their own agenda. Probably good advice, she thought, and decided to skip the Guinness and just take Bob O'Reilly up on his offer of a burger.

16

Dublin, Ireland

Keira and Lizzie departed for London after breakfast. Josie tried to slip out of the hotel by herself, but Myles, who both excelled at following people and had nothing else to do, caught up with her before the door had swung shut behind her.

He handed her a compact umbrella. "I thought you could use this."

"Listen to the weather forecast, did you?"

He pointed upward. "I looked at the sky."

She tightened the belt on her coat and tucked the umbrella under one arm. It was a bleak morning, gray, windy with brief outbreaks of showers that undoubtedly would turn to a steady rain as the day wore on. The sidewalk was already wet. Dubliners were getting on with their day, cars and buses speeding past, pedestrians rushing. A family — obviously tourists — on the corner unfurled a map that immediately folded in on itself in a wind gust.

Josie walked down the busy street, Myles ambling alongside her as if they were off for a romantic stroll. They headed in the general direction of Trinity College. Well before they reached the historic campus, Josie, following directions that Justin Rush had provided her, turned off onto a narrow side street, right into a wind gust that blew cold rain into her face. She didn't bother pulling up her hood, and the umbrella would be useless in the wind. Myles seemed equally unperturbed by the conditions.

They came to an unprepossessing brick building where Wendell Sharpe managed the Dublin office of Fine Art Recovery, a small, discreet company that specialized in providing expertise to private businesses and government agencies on the investigation and recovery of stolen art and cultural properties. His grandson had an office in the U.S. Josie didn't know in which city. Not Boston, she hoped.

Myles was so sexy she could hardly stand being near him. He seemed oblivious to the effect he was having on her — or was pretending to be. He could know and take secret delight in having starchy Josie Goodwin all aquiver and afire. Spending the night in an adjoining room had brought back memories of their time together before Afghanistan — and of the pain and anguish of the past two years. As she'd lain in her plush, five-star hotel bed, she'd envisioned him in the next room, an arm thrown over his forehead as he slept. For the past month, she'd alternated between relief that he was alive and anger that the bloody bastard had left her twisting in the wind — mourning him, hating him — for so many months.

How could he not have found a way to get word to her that he was alive? That he wasn't a traitor?

Will had taken Myles's reemergence into their world in stride, but Josie had made the incomparable mistake of having slept with him.

Having fallen in love with him.

She thrust the umbrella back to him. He dropped it into his jacket pocket. "You can stay out here while I speak with our Mr. Sharpe," she said crisply.

"As you wish."

She debated saying something else but didn't know what. His eyes were unreadable, the gloomy weather deepening their gray, their mystery and sexiness.

Either that or she needed more sunlight, Josie thought as she ran for the entrance to the small building. She'd lost her mind, obviously. Best simply to focus on her mission in Dublin. Scoop Wisdom had called late last night and filled her in on the latest developments in Boston.

Sharpe's offices were located on the third floor in an unexpectedly contemporary corner suite overlooking the street. He himself didn't look a minute over sixty. He was expecting her and rose from his cluttered desk to greet her. "Welcome, Mrs. Goodwin," he said, his accent a mix of Dublin and Boston. He was white-haired and lean, around her height, and wore a bow tie and plaid suspenders. "How is Lord Davenport?"

"Alive, last I checked."

He chuckled. "I was warned you can be irreverent. I haven't had the pleasure of meeting Will yet, of course, but I've done a bit of work with his father from time to time. The marquess is one of your great admirers."

"He's quite a character himself."

"I haven't spoken to him in several months. I hope he's well." Sharpe gestured to a small sofa. "Please, make yourself comfortable."

"I'm fine, thanks," Josie said. "I'm restless this morning."

"All right, then. What can I do for you,

281

Mrs. Goodwin? You want to talk to me about Sophie Malone. What's she up to?"

"She's returned to Boston. I believe she's trying to figure out whether something that happened to her last year was part of the violence this summer involving Will and his friends in Boston."

The old man sighed. "I've been following events there as best I can. Sophie's studied and worked with Colm Dermott, the Irish anthropologist —"

"Yes, I know," Josie said.

"She's a dedicated scholar. She's certainly no art thief, if that's what's on your mind."

Josie wasn't put off by his defensiveness. Everything she'd learned about Sophie Malone suggested she was a well-liked, capable, energetic woman whose positive attitude and sense of adventure were contagious. "How much do you know about what happened to Sophie last September off the Iveragh Peninsula?"

Sharpe returned to his desk. "Very little. She wouldn't go into specifics, but I know there was something. Tell me, won't you?"

Josie suspected that Wendell Sharpe was a man who invited the sort of soul-baring that one tended later to regret and not quite know how it had happened. He was an expert of unimpeachable discretion, keen intelligence and decades of experience. If she didn't give what she knew to him straight — if she hedged or played games — he would clam up or kick her out. Or both.

On the other hand, she saw no reason not to tell Sharpe about Sophie's cave experience. She was as complete and as thorough as she could be in her account, noting her various sources and omitting her own theories about Celtic archaeology, boats or remote Irish caves.

"There it is," she said when she'd finished. "All I know."

Sharpe settled back in his soft leather chair. Rain was falling steadily outside now, but Myles, fortunately, seemed to be staying put out on the street and had yet to appear. Finally Sharpe said, "None of what you told me contradicts what Sophie herself told me a week ago."

"Do you have any theories about this incident — what she saw, what actually happened on that island?"

"Now that you've fleshed out the details, I suppose I could come up with a host of theories, but I've found theorizing does little good. Following the evidence works best."

"There was no evidence."

"You know better, don't you, Mrs. Goodwin? There's always evidence."

"Does any of yours take you into the Boston Police Department?"

"I see. The bad-cop theory." He rose again and walked to a tall window. If Myles was down there, leaning against a post, staring up at the building, Sharpe gave no indication of noticing him. He kept his back to Josie as he continued. "There's been some evidence this serial killer in Boston — Jay Augustine — occasionally moved stolen works, and that he had assistance. He wasn't a major player. It's unclear if whoever helped him was an expert or an opportunist or even was deeply involved."

"But you believe Augustine didn't work alone. Whatever he was up to wasn't a solo operation."

The old man turned from the window. "What I'm telling you is barely a notch above speculation."

Josie showed him a photograph Scoop Wisdom had e-mailed her of the dead police officer in Boston, along with a curt explanation of the latest developments there. Justin Rush had printed it out for her before breakfast. "His name was Cliff Rafferty. He was recently retired."

"I'll check my files and see if his name comes up." He nodded to a dust-encrusted desktop computer at a separate station

along an exposed brick wall. "I keep extensive files."

"What did you tell Sophie?"

He smiled. "Theories."

"What about Percy Carlisle?"

"Which one?"

"Both."

Sharpe moved away from the window and
sat back at his desk. "I knew the senior
Carlisle, although not well. I've never met
the son."

"There was an incident seven years ago
involving the father —"

"Yes, a mistake on the part of his staff that
landed him in quite a pickle here in Ireland.
He was held briefly by Irish authorities on
suspicion of smuggling artifacts — late
Bronze Age pieces, as I recall. It was all a
terrible misunderstanding. He was released
almost immediately."

Unable to resist, Josie walked over to the
window and saw that Myles was, indeed,
leaning against a lamppost. He glanced up,
almost as if he'd sensed her presence. She
spun back to Wendell Sharpe. "Are you
satisfied Percy Carlisle Sr. was merely the
victim of a staff error?"

"I'm satisfied he didn't steal any valuable
art or cultural properties from Ireland.
Nothing more." Sharpe hesitated before

continuing. "The Winslow Homer painting that disappeared in the subsequent break-in in Boston is a source of considerable speculation among those of us in my field."

"One can imagine," Josie said. "Do you have any idea where the younger Carlisle might be right now? You can understand why we want to locate him."

"Indeed," Sharpe said, using a stub of a pencil to jot a few lines on an index card, which he handed to her. "His father sometimes stayed with an American couple here in Dublin. Their house is a few blocks from here, near Merrion Park. It's a shot in the dark, you understand. I wish I could be of more help."

Josie thanked him and left, taking the stairs slowly as she considered their conversation. She found Myles still leaning against a lamppost in the rain. He hadn't bothered with the umbrella. "I have an address for us to check out here in Dublin," she said. "We can walk."

Myles smiled. "Would you like to hold hands?"

"No," she said, suddenly irritated, and stalked ahead of him.

He caught up with her easily. They crossed into St. Stephen's Green, the rain stopping outright as they walked among the formal flower beds, bubbling fountains and statues of famous Dubliners and revolutionaries. Josie focused on the matter at hand. No lingering, she thought. No holding hands and enjoying the ambience of the historic green. As they crossed to the quiet residential streets of the Georgian district, she typed the address Wendell Sharpe had given her onto her BlackBerry. She had no desire to get lost on the streets of Dublin in the rain.

"I imagine the Boston police are looking into whether the dead police officer was in Ireland recently," she said, determined not to be distracted by hand-holding and such with Myles. "Our missing Percy Carlisle might have lied about when he and Officer Rafferty met."

"You're suggesting they could have met after the break-in at the Carlisle Museum seven years ago," Myles said.

"I'm not suggesting anything. I'm speculating."

Myles continued down the block in silence. Finally he said, "I suspect our Detective Wisdom was onto a connection between Boston thugs and a police officer before I arrived in Keira's cottage to tell him."

"You confirmed his worst suspicions. Whatever he had on this connection wasn't enough to stop his house from being bombed." Josie grimaced at the thought of Scoop Wisdom's frustration. "I know only too well, Myles, how that would eat at me."

They came to a classic eighteenth-century Georgian house and mounted steps to a bright yellow door, above it an elegant segmented fanlight. Josie bypassed the large brass knocker and pressed the more modern doorbell.

When no one came to the door, Myles stood up from the wrought-iron rail. "I suspect my breaking-and-entering skills aren't as rusty as yours."

Josie moved aside. "If the guards arrest us, you'll make the call to London."

She turned with her back to him, blocking any view of him from the street as best she could, but she didn't have a chance to regret her actions before he spoke. "We're in," he said calmly, without a hint of cockiness.

The interior of the house was cool and elegantly, if sparsely, furnished. They entered the first-floor drawing room, its tall ceilings and warm blue-and-cream décor a counter to the dreary weather. Staying together, they quickly and efficiently checked every room on every floor but found no missing American, no socks on the floor or shaving gear in the guestroom

— nothing to indicate Percy Carlisle was visiting and had simply popped out for a stroll.

"It's unsettling," Josie said as they returned to the front hall. "Suppose he is on some personal retreat as his wife says. I still don't understand why we can't find him. It's not as if we're searching for a trained military and intelligence officer out to stop a major terrorist attack."

Myles ignored her mild barb and stepped past her. "Look here."

Josie saw that he'd paused in front of a small framed painting by the door. It was one of Keira Sullivan's distinctive wildflower watercolors — a cluster of purple thistle. "Small world." She was aware of the emotion that just that simple painting elicited; it was one of Keira's gifts as an artist. "She has an amazing talent. I hope being around all of us doesn't suck the life out of it. She has painter's block —"

"She's worried about Simon. He'll be back."

"Then go off again," Josie said.

"Maybe. She'll get used to it."

"Easy for you to say. We should go. I swear I'm waiting for hounds to wake up and come after us."

Myles grinned at her. "Worried about getting caught, are you?"

She bristled. "No, I mean that literally about the hounds. One never knows. By the way, I can handle myself in the field quite well. I don't require your assistance or protection."

"You're glad to have me with you, though, in case the guards or dogs come after us."

"Of course. I can feed you to either or both and go scot-free myself."

He seemed amused, unworried about the guards, dogs or her. They headed back outside. Josie locked the door behind her and descended the steps, trying to appear to anyone who might pass by that she hadn't a worry in the world. She glanced back, half expecting hounds barking in all the windows.

She checked her BlackBerry and saw she had a text message from Lizzie and Keira. It wasn't Will's father or Lizzie's father who'd met them in London. It was Will and Simon themselves.

She smiled and relayed the news to Myles, who was obviously unsurprised. "Did you know they were back?" she demanded.

He shrugged and squinted up at the sky. "We're in for a bit of clearing, don't you think?"

"It won't last," she said, shoving her

BlackBerry back into her coat pocket. "I'm going to find a quiet banker."

"Didn't you marry a quiet banker?"

"I'm not going to encourage you by answering. Doesn't it feel as if we're caught inside a Celtic circle ourselves and can't find our way out?"

"I wouldn't know a bloody Celtic circle from a hula hoop." He took her hand into his as they crossed to St. Stephen's Green. "Let's enjoy our walk through the park."

"Myles —"

"Moments, love. Life is full of little moments."

17

Boston, Massachusetts

Sophie stretched out with her laptop on the sectional in front of the fireplace. She'd brought in a pot of burgundy mums and set it on the hearth. After a bad night of tossing and turning and obsessing on her chitchat with John March and the BPD detectives — not to mention kissing Scoop, which was *insane* — she had decided on a proactive morning. She'd started with a run on the Esplanade, then stocked up on groceries and dived into her work. For the next hour, she immersed herself in preparing a call for papers for her panel at the Boston-Cork conference.

Her iPhone rang, startling her. She saw it was Damian — no text message this time. She sat up straight. "Director March has paid you a visit?" she asked.

Silence on the other end. "No," her brother said, "he hasn't."

She winced. "I've been debating whether to warn you that he might turn up in your office. I couldn't decide if it would help to know in advance or if you'd rather be surprised. Plausible deniability and all that. Normally I'm not indecisive, but we're talking about the director of the FBI." She could feel herself digging a deeper hole for herself. "All in all, I think it's best I didn't warn you. You have nothing to hide."

"Sophie? What are you talking about?"

"Never mind. I was lost in my work . . ." She shut her laptop and focused on her conversation with her brother. "I can hang up, and you can call back and I'll start over."

"Forget it. I'm not worried about Director March. I'm worried about you, Sophie. You're there alone."

She immediately thought of Scoop but reminded herself she'd only known him a short time. Mentioning him certainly wouldn't reassure her brother. "You don't have to worry about me, Damian."

"You and Taryn worried me even before you were born. The day Mom announced she was having twins, I knew I was screwed."

Sophie smiled. "We had a happy childhood."

"Right. *You* did." But this was pure Damian. "Wendell Sharpe called me. He had

293

to rave about how brilliant you are first. Then he told me he'd just met with a British woman who's in touch with the BPD. She asked about you. I sent you to Sharpe not for a second thinking you'd get mixed up in criminal investigations. Bombs, murders, kidnappings. Damn, Sophie."

"I'm not involved in any of that."

"The cops you're hanging out with are, and you found a murdered police officer yesterday."

"I don't know that he was murdered. Do you?"

"Not officially."

She stood up and looked out at the brick courtyard, inviting and romantic in the midday autumn sun. She'd planned on lunch outside among her mums. "What else did Wendell Sharpe tell you?"

"Nothing you don't already know. Sophie . . ." Her brother hesitated, which was unusual for him. "Last September in Ireland?"

She couldn't go through it. Not again, not so soon. "Unusually dry and mild."

"Damn it, I'm trying to help —"

"I know you are, Damian," she said, her head clear now. She could see him in some FBI office, with his dark auburn hair, his good looks, his gun strapped to his side. He loved his work as much as she and Taryn loved theirs. "Maybe it's just as well you don't know all the details."

"You're my sister. I want to know." He sounded worried again, less combative. "I have some of the details. I can get a flight up there the minute you say so. If you have any information on where Percy Carlisle is, tell me or tell the police. Then back off. I don't like how this thing feels, Sophie. If we were talking about a major archaeological excavation, I'd listen to you."

Sophie sat at the table, in Scoop's chair from yesterday, when he'd patiently listened to her story. "The internal affairs detective who was hurt in the bomb blast has been on my heels. We ran into each other in Ireland."

Damian was silent a moment. "Cyrus Wisdom. Scoop."

"Do you know him?"

"Of him. He's top-notch. Just remember, Sophie. Cops tell you only what they want you to know, and they can lie. You can't lie to them, but that doesn't mean they can't lie to you."

"Do you know Scoop is lying to me, Damian?"

"That was a general statement. If I were you, I'd be very careful trusting anyone right now except Taryn, Mom, Dad and me."

She thanked him for calling — for his advice and concern — but he was back to being Damian and just grunted and disconnected. It was all Sophie could do not to throw her iPhone against the fireplace, not because of her brother but her situation. She'd felt safe when she'd headed to the Beara Peninsula to check out Keira's ruin, figuring if Jay Augustine was responsible for both their ordeals, at least he was in jail and no longer a danger. But what if Cliff Rafferty's death had nothing to do with either her or Keira, and the Celtic symbols in his apartment were just a diversion — a way to obfuscate and mislead?

To what end?

Sophie shut down her laptop and headed out to the courtyard. She smiled at her pots of mums, as if they were a symbol of happiness and normalcy. She could easily see Scoop taking up gardening. He was physical, results-oriented — he'd appreciate hoeing, weeding, harvesting.

She gave herself a mental shake and remembered her brother's cautionary words. Scoop was a detective recovering from a bomb exploding within yards of him, and yesterday morning she'd led him to the probable bomb-maker — who was dead.

What if the bomb-making materials had been planted on Cliff Rafferty's coffee table?

Whatever the case, did she really think Scoop had *gardening* on his mind?

Feeling considerably less jet-lagged than she had yesterday, Sophie was too restless for lunch and continued through the archway and up the steps to the street. Damian was right. She was accustomed to being contained and decisive in her world as an archaeologist, but she'd been off balance ever since she'd learned more details about Keira Sullivan's experience on the Beara Peninsula.

Avoiding Charles Street and the Whitcomb Hotel, she wound her way down to busy Beacon Street and crossed to the Boston Public Garden, a Victorian botanical oasis in the heart of the city. She immediately relaxed amid its enormous shade trees and well-kept lawns and flower beds. She noticed leaves just beginning to change color, tinted gold, orange and red, and walked past the shallow man-made pond where the foot-pedaled Swan Boats had entertained tourists and locals alike for more than a century. She could have spent the afternoon on a bench, or brought her laptop with her and worked on turning her dissertation into a book, as Colm Dermott was encouraging her to do.

Instead she crossed Boylston Street and continued toward Jay and Charlotte Augustine's showroom in the South End.

Scoop materialized on the next corner and fell in next to her. Sophie angled a look at him. "How long have you been following me?"

"Since the Swan Boats."

"I'm not good at spotting a tail. I guess I'd have to learn if I decide to be an FBI agent, huh?" Her breath caught at his grim intensity. "What's wrong?"

He stayed close to her as they crossed the street. "Jay Augustine died this morning in his jail cell, probably of a massive stroke."

"Then whatever secrets he had died with him. Had he been sick?"

"Not that anyone knew. He was one evil son of a bitch. I wouldn't be surprised if he willed his own death — made himself have a stroke so he could be with the devil he admired so much."

A crowd of office workers and shoppers swarmed past them. "Could he have suspected something was wrong with him and refused to tell anyone?"

"It doesn't matter now. He's done."

"Did Cliff Rafferty ever meet him, talk to him?"

Scoop shook his head. "Not that we know of. What's on your mind, Sophie?"

She nodded vaguely down the street. "I'm on my way to the Augustine showroom in the South End. I wonder if anyone's there to let me in."

"All right." Scoop was cool, hard to read. "We'll walk over there together. Someone will be there today."

Because of Augustine's death, she realized.

Scoop matched her pace. "Hell of a co-incidence after yesterday. Maybe Cliff had a word with the devil and they summoned old Jay home."

They came to a narrow building with an upscale health club on the first floor. Scoop opened a glass door to the small entry. The Augustine showroom — or former show-room, Sophie thought, since it was now closed — was on the third floor. They took a cramped elevator that barely fit the two of them. She was intensely aware of the brush of his arm against hers, the shape of his chest, his thick thighs.

Scoop smiled at her as if reading her mind. "Tight quarters."

The elevator clanked to a stop and opened into a reception area. Frank Acosta was there with a uniformed officer. "Figured you two would show up," he said, leaning against the edge of an empty rolltop oak desk. "I came by after I heard about Augustine. Bastard did us a favor by dropping dead on his jail cell floor. He was never going to talk."

"We'd like to take a look around," Scoop said.

Acosta dropped onto a chair at the desk. "Go right ahead. We're done here. Charlotte Augustine has an auction house lined up to sell off the inventory as soon as she's legally cleared to get rid of this place. It'll be easier now with her husband dead on his jail cell floor. Everything's packed up." He glanced at Sophie with half-closed eyes. "Take your time."

She started to thank him, but Scoop stepped in front of her and pushed open the door to an adjoining room, holding it for her. She entered a long, narrow storeroom with deep shelves on one wall. The floor and shelves were stacked with neatly labeled crates and boxes, only a few pieces not packed up and ready to be moved out.

Scoop followed her down a row of crates. She ran her fingertips over one that came up to her waist. "I'm telling you," she said. "Detective Acosta doesn't like you."

"He doesn't like internal affairs."

"Has he had run-ins with other internal affairs detectives or with you personally?"

"Sophie, I can't discuss —"

"Internal affairs deals with administrative issues that aren't necessarily criminal," she said, moving down the row. "Laziness, lying to superiors, sexual indiscretions, showing up drunk on the job. Any of those describe Detective Acosta? Did he cross a line that got him into trouble with his bosses but not the district attorney?"

Ignoring her questions, Scoop bent down for a closer look at a hip-high marble statue. "He's not wearing any clothes."

Sophie gave up but couldn't resist a smile. "You can be very stubborn. That statue is a high-quality copy of the Greek god Apollo, by the way. It's marked as such, so there's no deception."

He straightened. "I don't think I'd want Apollo here in my dining room."

She checked out more crates, noting labels and staying alert in case anything jumped out at her that could help her understand what "Celtic pieces" the worker claimed to have seen and were now nowhere to be found.

"Tell me what you see, Sophie," Scoop said, serious now.

"A lot of crates. It'd be helpful to find one labeled 'stolen Celtic artifacts,' wouldn't it?"

Acosta came up behind them. "I can let you into the climate-controlled room where the kid who used to work here said he saw them."

"That'd be great," Sophie said as he hit buttons on an alarm panel.

"You must have brought an ill wind back from Ireland," Acosta said, standing back from the door. "Cliff dies. Now Augustine dies, not that anyone will miss him."

Sophie felt Scoop stiffen next to her, but he made no comment as they entered the climate-controlled room. "How did Cliff Rafferty end up working security here?" she asked. "Did he request the assignment?"

"Take a look around, Dr. Malone," Acosta said, ignoring her question. "Tell us if you see anything."

"Maybe he stole the missing artifacts himself. If he had a buyer in the wings —"

Acosta didn't let her finish. "I'll wait outside."

He withdrew, and Sophie frowned at Scoop. "He doesn't like me, either. Do *you* know how Rafferty ended up working security here? Did he and Detective Acosta know each other when the break-in happened at the Carlisle Museum?"

"Probably." Scoop's dark eyes settled on her. "No freelancing, Sophie, remember?"

She smiled suddenly. "I ask a lot of questions. It's the nature of what I do."

"Same here. I understand, but you still need to watch yourself — for your own sake."

She moved deeper into the small, windowless room, taking note of more boxes and crates of canvases, statues, porcelain and metalwork on shelves and leaned up against the walls. "Are other pieces missing from the inventory, or just the Celtic artifacts the worker says he saw?"

"Just those."

She looked up at an ornate clock set on a top shelf, then stepped back to the middle of the room. "Anything Celtic is in high demand these days. It doesn't matter what era or country of origin. I don't see anything here that's obviously Celtic — Iron Age or otherwise — never mind resembles what I saw in the cave. I thought it might help to see what's here. I'm not sure it does."

They returned to the reception area. Sophie thanked Acosta.

"Yeah, no problem," he said, then grinned at her. "Don't you have a job?"

"As a matter of fact, I'm on my way to see about tutoring my hockey players."

"I'll meet you downstairs," Scoop said.

She took the stairs instead of the elevator. When she reached the street, she called Tim O'Donovan in Ireland. After a quick hello, she said, "When I met Percy Carlisle at the pub the other night, he had just come from Killarney National Park. Last year he was staying with friends there when he looked me up. I wonder if they might know where he is now."

"You don't expect me to know everyone in Killarney, now, do you?"

"No, of course not."

Maybe Percy was having an affair, Sophie thought, although she had no reason to think so and it struck her as ridiculous. He and Helen seemed happy together, with plans for the future. More likely, he was simply off enjoying himself — golfing, hiking, whatever — in an ultra-private setting and had no idea that his security guard was dead.

Sophie shook off her thoughts. "I was hoping maybe you or one of your friends had seen Percy with these friends from Killarney."

"Are they Irish?"

"I don't know. They'd be well off if they're Percy's friends."

"I'll see what I can do, Sophie," Tim said,

his tone neutral. "What are you up to?"

"Jay Augustine is dead — the serial killer."

"That's not a bad thing."

"Did you get the photo I e-mailed you of the police officer who died?"

"I did. I don't recognize him, either. I'll show him to the boys when I ask about the friends from Killarney. I'm no help. Sophie . . ."

She heard the worry in his voice and smiled into her phone. "We'll be back to dancing an Irish jig and drinking Guinness before long."

"Your new detective friend?"

"I don't know if he's much on dancing, but we can teach him."

Tim didn't sound very reassured before they disconnected.

Scoop caught up with her at an intersection. "Figured I'd give you a minute to finish your call. Family?"

"Tim O'Donovan."

"The fisherman and fiddle player." He stepped off the curb and flagged a passing cab. "Have fun with your hockey players."

"I doubt I'll actually start tutoring today. I'm just getting acquainted with everyone."

He opened the cab door for her. "Stay busy. Keep my number handy."

She nodded, thanking him as she climbed

in and sank against the seat. She was keyed up, and just as Scoop shut the door, she almost asked him to get in the cab with her — almost told him she didn't want to be alone. Instead she flashed him a quick smile. The man had enough on his mind without adding her to the equation.

Ten minutes later, the cab dropped her off at a squat, unattractive building near Boston University. The tutoring center was located on the first floor. She enjoyed working one-on-one with students, and she needed the income.

As she headed inside, Tim called her back. "None of the boys recognized your cop," he said, "but they have an idea of who Percy Carlisle's friends in Killarney might be. They're in Kenmare often."

"You have any names?"

"I do, indeed. David and Sarah Healy."

He gave her what details he had on the Healys, and after he hung up, Sophie dialed Scoop's number. "Are you back at work?" she asked him.

"Nope. I had this urge to make sure you got to your destination. I'm half a block behind you."

She turned around, and he waved to her from farther down the wide sidewalk. She laughed. "I'll have to take 'Spotting a Tail

101.' I'll wait for you —"

"Tell me now. I can hear in your voice that you have something for me."

What else, she wondered, could he hear in her voice? She shook off the thought. "I have the name and address of a couple in Killarney who are friends with Percy Carlisle. They might have an idea where he is." Sophie paused, watching Scoop make his way steadily toward her. "Maybe your British friends can check them out."

18

Killarney, Southwest Ireland

Josie had steeled herself for Myles to abandon her in Dublin, but not only did he accompany her to the airport, he boarded a small plane with her for the short flight to the west of Ireland. She'd arranged for a car when they arrived. He took the keys. She didn't object.

"I'll navigate," she said, reaching for her seat belt in the passenger seat.

It was very dark when they arrived at an attractive stone house just past a confusing roundabout near Killarney National Park. Lights shining in the first-floor windows suggested Percy Carlisle's friends, David and Sarah Healy, were at home.

Myles popped out of the car with no hint of the fatigue Josie had noticed when she'd first walked into Keira's cottage, and there he was. As they headed up the walk in a light rain, she fought a sudden sagging of

308

her own energy and spirit. "I'd love just to wander among the oaks and yews with nothing more pressing to do than find the next waterfall."

She expected a smart retort from Myles, but he brushed his fingers over the top of her hand. "We'll get there, you and I."

"Ever the optimist." She mounted the front steps to the house. "I wonder if we'll find Percy Carlisle sitting by the fire with a whiskey."

Myles didn't answer right away. She thought he might go soft on her again, but he rallied. "Let's find out, shall we?"

David Healy, an amiable middle-aged Irishman, greeted them at the door, obviously curious as Josie introduced herself and Myles as best she could. "A mutual friend told us we might find Percy Carlisle here. We thought we'd drop in and say hello."

"Sorry, you've missed him. He was here four or five nights ago. He stayed just the one night. He'd come straight from London. Helen wasn't with him. She'd already left for Boston — or maybe it was New York, then Boston. Percy and I took a long hike in Killarney National Park. My wife stayed behind. He left early that evening."

Myles leaned against a wet iron rail. "Did he say where he was going?"

"Kenmare. He planned to see an archaeologist he knows."

"And after Kenmare?" Josie asked.

Healy's expression by itself said he hadn't a clue. "He didn't say. He was quite preoccupied. He gets that way. He did say he wanted to go off on his own for a bit — I don't know more than that, I'm afraid. My wife, either."

The man was looking worried. Josie gave him a cheerful smile. "Well, we're terribly sorry to have missed him. Thank you for your help."

Healy started to shut the door but stopped. "There's nothing at all unusual in Percy wanting to be on his own. He's been like that for as long as I've known him, which has been for at least ten years. Percy's always appreciated his solitude. He says that's why he married so late. Helen understands."

"She wasn't upset, then, about him going off?" Josie asked.

"Not according to Percy."

Myles stood up from the rail. "Percy visited you last year around this time, as well, didn't he?"

Healy frowned. "Yes, for a few days. We played a bit of golf."

"Did he mention his archaeologist friend

310

then?" Josie asked.

"I don't recall, to be honest. Something's wrong, isn't it?"

"We hope not," she said, handing him a card. "My number and e-mail — please let us know if you hear from Percy, won't you?"

He promised he would, and Josie thanked him and retreated back down the walk. Myles stepped in front of her and opened the car door for her. "Do I look as if I'd have run straight into it?"

"I'm being chivalrous."

"Oh. I don't think I've ever had anyone be chivalrous. It's rather nice." She smiled as she got into the passenger seat. "You'll shut the door next?"

"I'll try not to get your foot."

She checked her BlackBerry. She had a message from Will. No news in London. He and Simon were checking into Percy Carlisle's friends, acquaintances and activities there, as well as taking another, closer look at Jay Augustine's travels in Great Britain and Ireland. Undoubtedly Lizzie and Keira were deeply involved, too. They all wanted to know who could have been on the tiny island with Sophie Malone last September.

Simon had suggested that Josie — Moneypenny, as he called her — work directly with the Irish guards, but to what end? She knew nothing they didn't.

She had a message, too, from Adrian, all about his day at school. It made her smile and wish to be back home. She glanced at Myles. But everything had changed, hadn't it? Would she even be allowed to tell her son that his idol hadn't vanished into thin air?

"Where to now?" Myles asked as he started the car.

Scoop Wisdom had reported earlier that Sophie Malone had offered the use of her cottage to his "British sources" in Ireland.

That would be Myles and me, Josie thought.

"Back to Kenmare," she said.

The interior of the Malone cottage was charming and quite chilly, and the moment Josie crossed the threshold, she knew she was lost. Myles eased an arm around her middle and kissed the top of her head. "Josie."

All his anguish and pain came out in that one gesture, that one whisper. She'd kept hers in a tight ball inside her, refusing to acknowledge her feelings much less let them leak out and destroy her. She couldn't hold it in any longer. "Myles . . . I missed you so much."

"I know, love. I'm sorry."

"No, don't," she said. "Don't be sorry."

In one motion, he caught her up into his arms as if she were a swooning fairy-tale princess and carried her upstairs, kicking open a door and laying her on a frighteningly cold bed. They hadn't lit a fire or turned on the heat.

"We'll warm right up," he said, kissing her.

Moonlight streamed through the window, striking his face. Josie held him fiercely and whispered how much she hated him, loved him, wanted him, and he let her get it all out before he kissed her again, taking his time. After that, she wasn't cold anymore. He lifted off her shirt, and she got his off, half expecting a different Myles underneath — new scars, new muscles. But she found that it didn't matter. She felt only the heat of his skin against hers.

They made love slowly at first, as if it were all so momentous and one wrong move would doom them to perdition, but when he was inside her, Josie grabbed him by the hips and pulled him deeper into her. He moaned, his mouth finding hers in the dark as he drove into her. There was nothing slow about their lovemaking after that.

Later, tucked under the duvet, holding on to him as she'd imagined alone in her bed night after night, Josie smiled. "I should have guessed this would happen when you opened the car door for me."

He laughed. "You did guess."

She laughed, too. "So I did."

19

When she arrived back on Beacon Hill, Sophie found the gate to the archway and courtyard unlocked and thought nothing of it as she shut it firmly behind her, locking it again. Her afternoon on her own had left her feeling more normal — determined, even, to back off from trying to find answers to last September herself. Cliff Rafferty and now Jay Augustine were dead. Percy Carlisle was still out of touch. She'd done what she could to figure out what was going on, and she'd told the police everything she knew.

The police included Scoop, she reminded herself. Whatever attraction she felt toward him didn't change the fact that he was a police officer, as well as a victim of the spiral of violence over the past summer.

The archway, which was unlit, felt cold and dank, reminding her of the cave. It was late afternoon and downright chilly, a sign of the short, frigid winter days ahead. She hadn't lived through a full-blown New England winter in several years. She decided she might as well look forward to a nor'easter, because one surely would blow through Boston before too long.

The courtyard was much darker than she'd expected. The wind or a cat, or maybe even a squirrel, had blown over one of her mums — a white one. She crouched down to right it and stopped, her hand in midair, convinced she'd heard a rustling sound. There was no wind now, not even the stirring of a breeze.

Sophie didn't breathe as she listened.

She heard a whisper in the shadows by the landlords' stairs and shot to her feet. The door to her sister's apartment was shut tight, no sign anyone had broken in.

She heard more whispers — or what sounded like whispers. *A neighbor? Music?*

A cat yowled, startling her. She jumped back, her heart pounding. She couldn't see the cat but thought the yowl had come from under the stairs. Had the cat been spooked by the whispers, too?

Enough, Sophie thought, and bolted back through the archway, digging out her iPhone and dialing Scoop's number as she headed through the gate and up the stairs to the street. She heard him pick up. "Are you near Beacon Hill?" she asked before he could speak.

"I'm at the Whitcomb. What's wrong?"

"I'm okay." She looked up and down the quiet street as she spoke but saw no one. "I heard something in the courtyard. Whispers. It could have been a cat —"

"Where are you now?"

"On the street."

"Is anyone with you?"

"No. I'm not worried. I just don't want to go back to the courtyard by myself."

"I'm on my way."

While she waited, Sophie peered down the steps through the open gate and archway, but she didn't see a neighbor, a cat, anything. She stood up straight and watched a young couple walk past her, holding hands. They exchanged a pleasant greeting, and as she watched them continue past her, she spotted Scoop making his way up the steep street, moving fast. She waved to him, wishing she could say with assurance the whispers were nothing, that no one had been out in the courtyard with her.

"It was quicker to walk," he said when he reached her, slipping an arm around her as if it didn't occur to him to do anything else.

"I could have mistaken —"

"Either way, I'm glad you called me." He winked at her. "Better safe than bonked on the head, right? I'll take a look."

"I'll go with you," she said. "Honestly, it could have been a cat."

"That'd be good. I like cats."

They went down the steps and through the archway back to the courtyard, quiet and still in the fading daylight. Scoop took a quick look around, but none of the neighbors that shared the courtyard had doors wide open or windows broken. No one was lurking behind a bench or under the stairs where Sophie had heard the cat.

"Any other exits besides through the archway?" Scoop asked.

"There's a skinny walk out to the street behind us. It has a locked gate. It's seldom used. I don't even have a key."

"Hide under the stairs, then scoot out the back while you head through the archway." He shrugged, contemplating the situation. "It could work. Let's take a look at your apartment."

The door was locked, not so much as a fresh scratch in the dark green paint. Scoop checked the windows. "Anything look different to you?"

"No, nothing. If I hadn't heard the whispers . . ." Sophie pulled her sweater tightly around her, cold now. "I'm on edge."

"Understandable," he said, glancing back at the pretty courtyard. "Did your sister give a key to anyone?"

"I don't think so. The friend who was here over the summer returned her key and said she didn't make a copy."

"Who else knows you're in Boston, staying here?"

"My family. A few friends, the tutoring center. Colm Dermott knows. He probably told Eileen Sullivan."

"The Carlisles," Scoop added.

"I imagine just about everyone in the Boston Police Department knows, too."

He plucked a wilted blossom off a yellow mum by the door. "It's a Harry Potter sort of place you've got here. Let's go inside and see if anyone paid you a visit while you were out."

As she dug out her keys, a black-and-white shorthaired cat leaped out from under the stairs and landed on all fours by a small wrought-iron bench. "Hey, there," Sophie said, gently, keeping any tension out of her voice. "I haven't seen you before. Where are you from?"

The cat arched its back and hissed, more out of fear, Sophie thought, than aggression. She hadn't seen the cat in her few days at the apartment. Scoop squatted down. "What's up, fella? Something spook you out here?"

An older woman came out of another apartment across the courtyard. "There you are," she said, gathering the cat up into her arms. "I've been looking all over for you."

Scoop stood up. "He's your cat?"

She nodded. "He never gets out. I was washing windows. I turned my back and he was gone. At first I thought he was hiding in the house. Something must have startled him for him to have jumped out the window."

"How long ago was this?" Scoop asked.

"Maybe ten minutes. I'm so glad he's all right." She nuzzled the cat, who was purring now, clearly calmer. But the woman stiffened as she glanced from Scoop to Sophie and back again. "Is something wrong?"

"It's okay," Scoop said. "Did you see or hear anything unusual out here in the court-yard?"

"No, nothing. I've been here all day, too." The cat wriggled in her arms. "I should get him back inside."

She returned to her apartment, and Sophie stuck her key in the lock. "Maybe it was just the cat," she said, pushing open the door.

"And maybe what startled you is what startled the cat."

They entered her apartment, which obviously hadn't been disturbed, but Scoop checked its entire four-hundred square feet, including the bedroom. Sophie had made the bed, put her clothes away, hadn't left out anything too personal — not that he'd care. He was looking for an intruder, not lace undies on the floor.

Not that she even *owned* lace underwear.

"I'll be fine here," she said when he returned to the main room. "I can use the dead bolt. Even if someone else has a key —"

"If someone wants to get in here, they can get in. A brick through the window would do it. Who needs a key?"

"I'm glad you're on our side," Sophie said dryly.

He shrugged his big shoulders. "I'm just saying."

They both were standing in the middle of the room as if they didn't quite know what to do with themselves now that the crisis — or whatever it was — had passed. "I'm sorry I got you up here."

"Did you hear whispers or didn't you?"

"I did."

"Did you think someone was hiding in the courtyard?"

She nodded, dropping onto a chair at the table.

"The gate was unlocked," he said. "You did the right thing, Sophie. Don't second-guess yourself. Maybe someone in the neighborhood's reported a burglary, saw someone suspicious —" He stopped. "You get what I'm saying, right?"

"I do. Thanks." She glanced out at the courtyard, dark now, cozy in the glow of lights from neighboring apartments. "Did you hear from your friends in Ireland?"

Scoop stood by the chair across from her but didn't sit down. "They located the Healys in Killarney. Percy wasn't there. He stayed with them the night before he met you in Kenmare. Just him. Helen was already on her way back here."

"It wasn't Percy who was just out there whispering in the courtyard, if that's what you're thinking. He's not . . ." Sophie hesitated, giving herself a moment to get her bearings before she said the wrong thing. "Percy's not the sort to sneak into a courtyard or follow someone to a remote island."

"Unlike his father?"

"His father could be impulsive and a little tyrannical at times, and he loved a good adventure. I didn't know him that well, as I've said, but I've never heard anything to suggest he was dishonest. If you're thinking there's some father-son rivalry at work here —"

"I'm not thinking anything," Scoop said, still not sitting down.

"I asked Wendell Sharpe if he thought Percy Sr. had arranged the break-in at the museum himself in order to steal the Winslow Homer painting — for the insurance. Wendell said no. The Carlisles have no money worries." Sophie rose suddenly, aware of Scoop's gaze on her — she felt as if she were hiding something when she wasn't. "Even if Percy Jr. feels he doesn't measure up to his father and has tried to find ways to prove himself, I don't believe he would frighten or hurt me."

"A month ago I wouldn't have believed a police officer would place a bomb on the back porch of another police officer — of anyone — but it looks as if that's exactly what happened. It's called keeping an open mind, Sophie. Don't rule anyone or anything out until you know for sure."

She knew he was right. She'd given herself the same lecture. "If Percy let himself be used, he'd be furious and embarrassed." She stared out the window, seeing her reflection. "If he did something stupid like get involved with a crooked art dealer who turned out to be a serial killer . . ." She didn't finish and smiled at Scoop. "Don't you just want to take a drive up to Vermont and go leaf-peeping?"

He came around the table next to her. "Enough's enough, Sophie. It's crazy to stay here alone with what's been going on. Jeremiah Rush has an old crush on you. I'll bet he'll give you a break on a room." Scoop brushed a few strands of hair out of her face. His hands were steady, warm. "The alternative is for me to stay here with you."

There was no separation of space in the tiny apartment and just one bed. The sofa that was too short for either of them.

Which he had to know.

"I shouldn't have left you up here last night," he said. "Did you even sleep?"

"Not much. I'm not fooled, by the way. You want to keep an eye on me."

"Ah-huh." He lowered his mouth to hers and kissed her lightly, then stood up straight and grinned at her. "For a number of reasons."

"You're going to regret that in about ten seconds."

He laughed. "I doubt it."

"I'll get my stuff."

She retreated to the bedroom and pulled out her backpack. She was happy not to argue, even if a five-star boutique hotel wasn't in her budget. But what was she doing? She'd just sworn off getting herself deeper into this mess, and here she was, about to head off with a Boston detective — a man obsessed, understandably so, with finding out why a fellow police officer had been found dead yesterday amid bomb-making materials and dark Celtic symbols.

Never mind head off with him. She'd just kissed him. Again.

And not for the last time, she thought, gritting her teeth as she threw clothes together, including some prettier tops that Taryn had left behind.

She went back out into the courtyard with Scoop. She slung her backpack over one shoulder and didn't even think to protest when he put a hand on her hip as they went back through the archway out to the street.

20

Without even trying, Scoop came up with a half-dozen reasons not to stay in the same hotel as Sophie, but he ignored them all as he stood with her in the elegant little lobby of the Whitcomb. Jeremiah Rush maintained a neutral expression behind his desk. "I have you on the third floor," he said, handing her a real key, not a flimsy key card. "You're down the hall from Detective Wisdom, as requested. Your room overlooks the back of the hotel, but I think you'll be pleased."

"I'm sure I will be, Jeremiah," she said, smiling. "Thanks. I won't cause any trouble, I promise."

"Right. That was what Lizzie said last month, and I had cops and spies all through the place." The younger Rush shook his head. "I want to enjoy life. I have a golden retriever, friends and a good job. I don't need to kick butt like Lizzie, and her dad —" He stopped himself as if he'd gone too far, then leaned toward Sophie and whispered, "Uncle Harlan threatened to bug the lobby if we all didn't behave."

Scoop grinned. "Good for him. What does he think of Will Davenport?"

Jeremiah stood up straight and gave a long-suffering laugh. "You don't think he'd tell me, do you? Enjoy your stay, Sophie. Let me know if there's anything I can do to make you more comfortable."

Scoop took the elevator up with her and walked with her down the hall to her room. He'd offered to carry her backpack a half-dozen times and finally had taken the hint that she was doing this herself and wasn't sure about any of it — the whispers, calling him, kissing him, now moving into the Whitcomb. As she unlocked the door to her room, he leaned against the wall and said, "You're thinking right now you never should have gone to check out Keira's ruin when you did."

"It's not really her ruin, is it? She'd be the first to say so, I imagine. It belongs to the farmer who owns the pasture."

"Not my point."

Which she obviously knew, but she held open the door and said, "After you," as if she accepted that he'd have to see inside for himself, make sure she would be safe there.

He went in, and she followed him and set her backpack on a rack, obviously used to being on her own, traveling. Feeling secure. She'd regained her composure, but her expression was still tight, tense, as she turned to him. "We'd have met on the plane," she said. "It would have been the same. Somehow, we'd be here right now even if I hadn't gone to the Beara when I did."

"Are we talking fairy dust?"

That brought a spark to her eyes, and she even managed a small laugh. "Maybe we are."

Scoop stood at the window, aware of the shortening days. Where would he be come winter? Not here, he thought. Not at a five-star Boston hotel. Back at the triple-decker? On Yarborough's sofa bed? He glanced at Sophie and wondered where she'd be, but pushed aside his questions. "Tell me the rest about the cave," he said quietly, seeing immediately that he'd caught her by surprise. "Never mind the objective facts. I want to hear about the subjective parts. Don't be a scholar. Be someone alone on a tiny uninhabited island off the Irish coast."

She unzipped her pack but didn't open it up. "Where will that get us?"

"I don't know. Maybe you'll remember

something you wouldn't otherwise." He turned from the window. "I want to hear from Sophie, not just Dr. Malone."

"Do I ever get to hear from Scoop, not just Detective Wisdom?"

"Maybe you are right now."

She glanced around her room, everything spotless, perfect. "The Whitcomb's a beautiful hotel, isn't it? Jeremiah's insisting on paying for the room, but we'll fight that one out later. It's decent of him."

"You remind him of the high school crush he had on you."

"Don't let him fool you. Jeremiah's as independent and driven as his brothers and cousin. When I worked at Morrigan's, I never imagined I'd stay here under these circumstances. . . ."

"The cave, Sophie."

"I was terrified," she said quickly, almost as if she'd been building up to this moment. "I questioned myself for going out there on my own in the first place."

"Why did you?"

"I wanted to do something adventurous — something that took me away from my day-to-day work and worries. I considered Tim's story about hidden Celtic treasure a mix of legend, myth and folklore, even if it arose from an actual event." She abandoned her backpack and went over to the window. "I was filled with doubts about my work. I'd been so focused on getting my doctorate that I didn't think about what would happen after that, and all of a sudden it was upon me."

"Think back. Put yourself in that cave that night." Scoop spoke softly, sat on the edge of the bed. "Try to remember."

"Do you think I haven't done that?"

"Yeah. I think you haven't done that. Not in the way I'm talking about."

"I don't want to," she said, more to herself than to him.

"I know you don't."

She glanced sideways at him. "The bomb? Did you make yourself —"

"Yes, I made myself go back there and relive every moment of what happened. I put myself back in the hours that led up to the blast and took myself right up to when I saw Bob O'Reilly sitting by my hospital bed, looking grim and pissed off. Only then could I step back and be objective about the experience itself."

"So it helped with the investigation?"

He shrugged and grinned. "Not really. I was badly injured, then shot up with morphine. I have gaps. I wish I could remember everything."

"Was Cliff Rafferty at your house before the bomb went off? Looking back, can you see that he was the one who planted it?"

"We're not talking about me right now."

She smiled. "When do we get to talk about you?"

"After you've told me about the cave and we've had a couple drinks."

She turned back to the window and gazed down at the alley behind the hotel. "I was having a great time," she said, her voice steady, calm. "It was a beautiful September day, and I loved exploring the island. I was careful not to disturb any nesting sites or fragile areas. I looked for seabirds, seals — the rare Kerry spotted slug."

"You can tell me about the rare Kerry spotted slug later."

She was so intent on her memories that she obviously didn't notice he wasn't serious. "I didn't expect to find one given the conditions on the island. I was also on the lookout for ancient sites — a hermit-monk hut, for instance — but I had no reason to believe I'd find one."

"Sophie," Scoop said, "could anyone else have already been on the island when you got there?"

"I don't see how but it's possible."

"Who else knew you planned to go out

331

there that day?"

She shook her head. "No one but Tim that I'm aware of. We didn't broadcast what we were doing to everyone in town, but we knew there was talk."

Scoop let that one go. "Someone could have seen the two of you go off in his boat and put two and two together."

She nodded. Obviously it was a scenario she'd considered herself. "Anyway, after Tim dropped me off, I watched him head back across the bay. I had binoculars. I saw other boats but none came toward the island. I had a bite to eat, then I went exploring. I heard birds calling but otherwise . . . I'm sure of it, Scoop. I was alone."

She paused, but he didn't move or speak. He let her get her mind back to that day on the island.

"I didn't hear a boat after Tim left. Whoever stole the artifacts and scared the hell out of me could have shut down the engine so that I wouldn't be alerted, or had a boat with a quiet engine, or rowed over from shore or another boat. It's not easy to drop someone off on the island. There's no dock, obviously. The shore's rocky, the waves and currents are tricky — you have to know what you're doing."

"Which your Irish fisherman friend does,"

Scoop said.

"Definitely. Fast-forward to when I first became aware I wasn't alone. It wasn't just a feeling. I'm not particularly psychic. I'd just entered the cave — it must have been five, at most ten, minutes later when I heard gravel or small stones crunching." She turned to him. "And whispers."

"Close your eyes. Put yourself there."

She did, but he could tell she wasn't there — the spell had been broken. She sighed and opened her eyes, gave him a quick smile. "I'm in an Irish pub with a Guinness and friends."

"Why would someone want to scare you?"

"I have no idea. To create a diversion, to mislead, to act out a fantasy. I suppose there are a dozen possibilities."

"What do the whispers and the blood-soaked branches tell you?"

"That we're dealing with a twisted son of a bitch —"

"Professionally this time. From what you know about ancient rituals."

"People can twist anything to justify and rationalize their own actions. Roman writers describe walking into sacred Celtic groves and discovering human flesh hanging from trees, branches smeared with human blood. Not that the Romans were all

333

sweetness and light. But there's ample evidence that the Celts practiced human sacrifice."

"To what end?"

"Tribal welfare, fertility — we know actually very little about Celtic religious beliefs. Druids would study for years — decades, even — but committed everything they learned to memory. It wasn't written down. In the early days of Christianity, Irish monks wrote down epic pagan tales. They're a blend of fancy, folklore, tradition, legend and mythology, not to mention adjusted here and there to serve the purposes of the church. That doesn't mean they don't provide important insight and information on the Celts of prehistory. Early Christians in Ireland incorporated pagan traditions instead of trying to stamp them out altogether. For instance, we'll find holy wells on the same site as pagan wells." Sophie moved from the window but remained on her feet. "There's so much more to learn."

Scoop could feel her passion for her field of study. "Whoever left that mess at Cliff's place could have their own interpretation of Celtic lore." He stood up. "Back to the cave, Sophie. You heard the whispers. You saw the branches."

She shut her eyes, then opened them

again, shaking her head. "It's just as I told you. I can't remember how I hit my head. I remember the terror I felt . . . scrambling deeper into the cave, knowing there was no way out but past whoever was at the entrance with the bloody branches. Then —" She stopped, her face pale, if not as pale as when he'd found her on Beacon Hill. She sighed. "Then I woke up in the pitch dark with a screaming headache."

Scoop walked over to her and took her hand as she rose. "What you went through is tough, Sophie."

She smoothed her fingertips over a scar on the back of his hand. "This from someone who survived a bomb blast."

"I wasn't alone. I had people right there with me."

"You almost bled to death. I just got banged on the head and a few scrapes and bruises, and I was cold."

"Your Irish fisherman might not have found you in time."

"And you could have had a piece of shrapnel hit an artery or a vital organ."

His throat caught. "I'll be downstairs in the bar. Let me buy you dinner and a drink." He smiled. "A couple of drinks."

He left her to regroup and shut the door quietly behind him. Downstairs in Morrigan's, Fiona O'Reilly was sipping a soda at a table under the windows, a glossy Ireland guidebook in front of her. He sat across from her. "How's school?"

"Intense. I'm practicing myself bloody."

"You love it, though, don't you?"

She beamed. "Every minute."

"Still excited about your trip to Ireland at Christmas?"

"Yep. I've got most of the details worked out, including where to have Christmas dinner. Not that there are many choices. Virtually every restaurant in Dublin is closed on Christmas Day. Then there's St. Stephen's Day the next day." She waved her long, slender harpist's fingers, the tips callused, the nails blunt. "It'll be so much fun."

"I hear Jeremiah Rush has a cute younger brother who works at their Dublin hotel."

She rolled her eyes, but her cheeks turned bright pink.

Scoop grinned. "You look just like your father when you make that face. It's the long-suffering O'Reilly face. Except he'd never blush."

"I'm not blushing. I'm just excited about Ireland. I'm counting down the days. We're having Christmas Eve tea at the Rush Hotel. Lizzie plans to join us." Fiona shut her guidebook, her cornflower-blue eyes — her father's eyes — wide and serious. "I keep reliving those first minutes after the bomb went off, with my Dad yelling and the smoke and the fire and all the blood. Scoop . . . I thought you were dead."

"I know, Fi."

"If you'd died saving me, how would I have gone on?"

"You'd have figured it out. I'm glad you didn't have to."

"My music helps," she said quietly. "Do you have anything that helps?"

"Helps what? I'm fine. I don't even remember bleeding all over you."

She rolled her eyes again. "You have a million scars. Don't tell me you never think about what happened."

"I think about it a lot, Fi, but I don't let it control me."

"Yeah. Yeah, that's what I do, too. The police officer you and Sophie Malone found dead . . ." She looked down at her guidebook again, rubbed her fingertips over the picturesque scene of a white-painted stone cottage on the cover. "Scoop."

She couldn't seem to go on. "Fi, think about Ireland and your music. Let us worry about the rest of it. If you don't —"

"I saw him."

Scoop went still. "What do you mean, you

saw him?"

"The day before the bomb went off." She cleared her throat, her gaze clear and steady when she lifted it to him again. "I saw Cliff Rafferty."

"Where?"

"Jamaica Plain. A few blocks from your house. He was in a car — he drove past me on my way from the subway to see my dad."

"You recognized him then — or only now, looking back?"

"Then," she said. "He'd stop by to see my dad every now and then, more often when I was little than lately. I recognized him but couldn't think of his name. I didn't remember I'd seen him until I heard he'd died. Do you think if I'd remembered sooner he'd still be alive?"

"No."

"You didn't even hesitate. How could you not hesitate? You don't *know*."

"I do know." He'd made her smile, and that was enough for now. "Rafferty turning up in the neighborhood doesn't make him guilty of planting the bomb. It's another piece of evidence and that's all it is. I'm just back from Ireland. Let me know if you want any suggestions."

"Oh, great. *Everyone* will have been to Ireland before I get there."

"You're nineteen. You've got time."

"Like you're so old." She slid to her feet, tucking her guidebook under one arm. "I need to get ready. My friends will be here any second."

Sophie arrived, obviously fresh out of the shower. Scoop introduced them. Fiona was gracious, but she gave him a knowing, if somewhat protective, smile as she ambled off to the end of the bar where her friends were gathering.

"She's very talented," Sophie said, taking Fiona's place at the small table. "She seems to be doing well. She's as tough as her father in her own way, isn't she?"

Scoop laughed, relieved to see the color back in Sophie's cheeks. "Bob's fine with her majoring in music. He doesn't want any Criminal Justice majors in the family. He knows it's not his call, but he's not shy about his opinions."

"You always wanted to be a police officer."

"My family couldn't keep me on the farm."

"Did they try?"

He shook his head. "No. We're a tight-knit group. We get along."

"Any archaeologists among them?"

He grinned. "Not one."

"When will Abigail Browning return from her honeymoon?"

"I don't know. Soon. Bob was already on her about all the drama in her life before she was kidnapped."

"Do you think she'll remain a detective?"

"Up to her."

"But she's a friend," Sophie said. "Her husband, Owen Garrison, was almost killed that day, too."

"It wasn't a great day, but we all survived. I suppose you could say we have the luxury of being frustrated because none of us spotted the bomb. We could all have blown up instead."

"But you're still frustrated. The bomb was placed where you wouldn't see it. Is Abigail fully recovered from her ordeal? Physically, I mean."

"She still had bruises when I saw her at her wedding, but they were healing. Norman Estabrook smacked her while he had her on the phone with her father, so March would hear her scream. Estabrook wanted to be John March's personal nemesis."

"Director March has suffered enough," Sophie said.

Abigail had said much the same thing about her father. At her wedding reception she'd told Scoop she wasn't convinced they'd ever know how the bomb had ended up under the grill. "This is a wedding, not a funeral, and thank God for that," Bob had said, pouring champagne.

Sophie interrupted Scoop's drifting thoughts. "Your lives had a nice routine, and this summer destroyed it. You all must feel isolated, at least to some degree."

Maybe so, Scoop thought. Their lives had changed this past summer. There was no going back to what they'd been before the bomb blast. He looked around at the bar, more people drifting in as Fiona and her friends laughed with each other, setting up for their two hours of Irish music.

Finally he smiled at Sophie. "Abigail and Owen are having a baby."

"That's wonderful."

"It is." He sat back. "Let's forget about bombs and blood-smeared branches for a while. Let's talk about what wine you want to drink with dinner." He leaned across the table. "Trust me or don't, Sophie, but it's time to decide."

"That's a two-way street."

"Nope. One-way."

She smiled. "I'll have the Malbec."

21

Scoop headed to Jamaica Plain after breakfast in the Whitcomb's elegant dining room with Sophie's bright blue eyes, freckles and sharp mind across from him. She planned to work on her laptop, in her room, then stop by the Boston-Cork conference offices and maybe drop in on academic friends in town.

He didn't tell her as much about his plans. She didn't seem annoyed, but she didn't seem happy, either.

As he parked in front of the triple-decker, he received the latest report from Ireland, this time from Myles Fletcher, not Josie Goodwin. "We don't have a bloody thing for you, mate," Fletcher said. "We're off to talk to the fisherman again. Percy Carlisle can't have vanished. We'll find him."

Scoop hung up and got out of his car. It was warm out on the street. He ducked under the yellow caution tape. Bob O'Reilly was on the front steps with a contractor, one of his friends from Southie, who saw Scoop, mumbled something about hero cops and left.

Bob nodded toward his departing friend. "He can't fit in the pool and cabana in the backyard."

"Funny, Bob," Scoop said.

"Yeah. I talked the city out of condemning the place. That might not have been smart. We could turn the lot into a community vegetable garden and pitch tents."

"At least the damage wasn't as bad as we originally thought."

"We?" Bob grinned. "You were on morphine. You should have seen the people trooping in and out of your hospital room. Who knew an internal affairs SOB could have so many friends?"

His entire family had come, too, Scoop remembered. He'd faked being passed out during one of their early visits, just to spare them from having to think of what to say. Later, when he was in better shape, they'd all had an easier time. They got along, but that didn't mean they were talkers.

Bob rubbed a big hand over the top of his head. "Fiona feels guilty, but she shouldn't. I never would have thought twice if I saw Cliff on Abigail's porch with a damn bomb in his hands, never mind passing through the neighborhood."

"Probably the bomb would have tipped you off he was up to no good."

"Who knows? I wasn't Cliff's biggest fan over the years, but I never figured him for blowing up this place — damn near killing my daughter. If I'd seen him with a bomb, I'd have assumed it was a dummy and he was doing a drill or some damn thing. When you're not suspicious, you're not suspicious."

Scoop shrugged. "Maybe I'm never not suspicious."

Bob let that one go without a response. "Acosta's here. He's in back. He's angry and frustrated, and he's looking to take it out on someone. He doesn't much like you on a good day, Scoop."

"So why's he here?"

"He figured out you were already looking into whether a member of the department was involved with some Boston muscle."

Scoop noticed that Bob hadn't asked a question. He made no comment himself.

"Acosta doesn't want to go down with Cliff," Bob said.

They headed out back where Acosta was checking out the burned-out first-floor porch as if he could make sense of why his

344

former partner might have wanted to plant a bomb there — for money, revenge, satisfaction? Was he being blackmailed? Was it part of some bizarre ritual he was into?

Bob pulled out white plastic chairs he'd hosed off, although they were still stained black from soot. "Have a seat, fellas. Let's talk. View's not that great right now, but look at that sky. Not a cloud in it. It's a perfect fall day."

Acosta wasn't in a friendly mood. "Cliff was murdered," he said, practically spitting the words at Bob and Scoop. "Homicide can be as tight-lipped as they want. Cliff wouldn't off himself by tying a rope around his own neck and hanging himself from a plant hook. He'd eat a bullet. He was a son of a bitch in a lot of ways, and he was lazy. He had his run-ins with internal affairs over the years. But someone hit him on the head, put a noose around his neck, tied the rope to a door, hoisted him up and let him hang to death."

Scoop sat on one of the chairs. "He'd have been deadweight."

"He was scrawny." Acosta stalked over to the edge of Scoop's garden and kicked at squash vines, for no apparent reason except frustration. "So far there are no witnesses who saw anyone or anything unusual in the neighborhood. Could have been someone familiar."

"Ex-wife?" Scoop asked.

"She'd have shot him," Bob said, dropping heavily into a chair. "She wouldn't go to all the trouble of hanging him. I'm not officially on the case, but cause of death was asphyxia. I can tell you that much. He was hit on the head — the blow was hard enough that it might have killed him eventually by itself."

"Why go to the trouble to hang him?"

"Probably some kind of ritual significance, given the rest of the scene," Bob said, watching Acosta. "Whoever killed Cliff didn't go to a lot of trouble to make it look like a suicide."

Acosta picked up a half-rotten tomato and threw it against the compost bin, constructed of slats and chicken wire. "I'm not fooled, Lieutenant. You're only telling me this so you can watch my reaction." He picked up another tomato and splattered it against the compost bin, too. "We have nothing."

Bob shook his head. "We have a lot. We just can't make sense of it yet."

"Now Augustine's dead. If he knew anything . . ." Acosta bit off a sigh. "It wouldn't have mattered. He'd never tell us."

"If you're chewing on anything, Frank, you know you need to tell us." Bob's tone was patient, but his gaze was narrowed intently on the robbery detective. "Otherwise go home."

"Go to hell," Acosta said tonelessly.

Bob ignored him and addressed Scoop. "Where's your archaeologist today?"

But there was something in Bob's voice, and Scoop turned in his cheap chair and saw Sophie coming down the walk, her hair pulled back as neatly as he'd ever seen it. She had on a pumpkin-colored sweater and slim jeans, and his heart skipped a couple of beats. He figured Bob and maybe even Acosta noticed, but whatever. This was how it was going to be until the fairy spell wore off or he just accepted that he was in love.

He glanced over at Bob. "You invited her?"

"She's Irish," he said with a shrug, as if that explained everything. "I thought she could sweep the bad fairies out of the corners of the house before we renovate."

"You want her to see where the bomb went off."

He got up. "Maybe it'll help jog our memories."

Sophie gave them a strained smile. "Hello, Detectives."

Acosta moved away from the compost bin,

looking irritated and out of place, as if he'd beamed himself into the middle of the wrong meeting. He didn't say a word to Sophie as she gazed up at the burned-out back of the house. "It must have been an awful day."

"It started better than it ended, that's for damn sure," Bob said.

She pointed to Scoop's trampled, overgrown garden. "The compost bin was the only possible place to take cover." Her blue eyes leveled on him. "How did you think of it?"

"I didn't," he said. "I reacted."

"You relied on your instincts and training." Spots of color appeared high in her cheeks. "And your fear for Fiona."

"For myself, too. Hell if I wanted to get blown up."

Acosta muttered under his breath, then shifted to Scoop and Bob. "I have to go."

Sophie watched him retreat back up the walk and out to the street before she spoke again. "He blames me for his friend's death."

"Why do you say that?" Bob asked.

"Because he does." She stepped into the remains of Scoop's vegetable garden. "No pumpkins?"

"Butternut squash," Scoop said, following

her to the edge of the garden. "I don't eat pumpkins."

"I love squash. I'm a terrible cook. I don't mind cleaning, though." She took a long step over knee-high weeds to the compost bin. "Is the compost in here still okay?"

"Should be. I can pick out any shrapnel that ended up in it."

Bob walked around to the other side of the bin, behind Sophie. "Would an archaeologist be interested in an ancient compost bin?"

She laughed, relaxing some. "We deal with the material remains of a culture. Compost would be decomposed."

"Not the shrapnel," Bob said. With a broad sweep of one arm, he took in the entire yard. "Imagine keeping everything just as it is and then making sense of this backyard a thousand years from now."

"It would be a challenge," Sophie said.

"Aren't archaeologists part scientist and part historian?"

Scoop didn't know where Bob was going — maybe nowhere — but she didn't seem to mind. "Archaeologists are archaeologists," she said with a light smile. "There are many areas of specialization. Mine is visual arts. We often work with other experts — geologists, botanists, philologists — who can help interpret various discoveries."

"Did you have a good grasp of the geology of the island you ventured to a year ago?"

"Yes, as a matter of fact, I did. It's not that difficult."

"Rock," Bob said with a smile.

"I knew there could be a cave on the island. In fact, I was hoping there'd be."

"Perfect hiding spot for your treasure."

"It's not my treasure," she said, matter-of-fact. She squinted up at the boarded-up windows and charred wood of the triple-decker. "Lizzie Rush managed to warn you right before the bomb went off. It must have been horrible, knowing your daughter was down here."

"Yep. Horrible."

"The bomb and Abigail Browning's kidnapping were orchestrated by Norman Estabrook. He and most of his men were killed when Lizzie, Will Davenport and Simon Cahill rescued Abigail in southern Maine. One was killed here in Boston, wasn't he?"

Fletcher's doing, Scoop thought. It wasn't Bob's favorite subject. The senior detective settled back on his heels and said, "Estabrook hired local muscle."

Sophie glanced back at him. "Cliff Rafferty?"

"He was a police officer then," Bob said, his tone neutral.

"He was a police officer when he set the bomb —"

"That's right, he was."

"Detective Browning survived her ordeal." Sophie seemed to jerk herself out of whatever dark thoughts she was thinking. "That's the main thing, isn't it?"

Bob nodded. "Yeah. That's the main thing. She did what she could to help with her rescue, but she kept those bastards from killing her. Did you run into Will Davenport when he was in Ireland this summer?"

She shook her head. "No. I don't think Tim did, either." She grimaced again at the fire damage. "You can trace some of the bomb-making materials found at Officer Rafferty's apartment, can't you? You can figure out if the evidence on his coffee table matches up with any evidence here, check his receipts, talk with his friends —"

"We can do all that," Bob said with no hint of sarcasm.

"I can only imagine how difficult this situation must be for you and everyone in the police department. Given what's happened, I gather you're taking another look at what he was up to at the Augustine showroom in the last days as a police officer — and whether he had anything to do with the break-in at the Carlisle Museum seven years ago. The Winslow Homer painting that disappeared that day has never been recovered."

"Cliff wasn't that smart," Bob said.

"Augustine was," Sophie said, but she abruptly squared her shoulders and smiled at the two men. "I've taken up enough of your time. You know how to reach me if you have more questions. I have nothing to hide."

Bob walked across the yard with her. "Any more stray cats at your apartment?"

His question obviously caught her by surprise. Scoop had called Bob last night, after he'd talked himself out of following Sophie up to her room. He'd had a drink, listened to Fiona and her friends for a little while, then went up to his own room and got Bob's take on the whispers in the courtyard — which was straightforward enough. He'd said next time tell Sophie to call 911.

"I haven't been back there yet," she said calmly. "I didn't make up what I heard —"

"Not saying you did. Be good, Sophie."

She glanced at Scoop, said nothing more and left. As she disappeared out of sight, Bob glared at Scoop. "You're going to stay on her, right?"

He was already on his way.

Scoop tried Sophie's number but she didn't answer. He checked the Whitcomb first. Before he could even pose a question, Jeremiah Rush jumped up from behind his desk. "Sophie said to tell you she's gone back up to her sister's apartment."

"Did she check out of the hotel?"

"She wanted to but I told her she could let me know for sure later." Jeremiah frowned. "Is everything all right?"

"No worries. Anything from your cousin?"

"She's in London with Will, Keira Sullivan and Simon Cahill. That's all I know."

"Do me a favor. Call me if you hear from any of them or if Sophie comes back here. If you need me for any reason, don't hesitate. Call. Got that?"

"I do, yes."

Scoop dialed Sophie again as he headed up Beacon Hill but she still didn't answer.

The gate was locked this time. She buzzed him in.

She had books and photographs on the Celts spread out on the table. He noticed a color photograph of a miniature boat in gold, complete with tiny oars, and another of a half-dozen ornate gold torcs. She'd let her hair down, the dark red framing her face, bringing out the blue in her eyes. "I left most of my research materials in Ireland. My parents can ship me anything I need when they get back from their hike."

Scoop looked up from the photos. "You're here but you're not here. Part of you wants to be back in Ireland."

"I'll adjust," she said tightly.

"It'd help to go a few days without a crisis." Scoop flipped through more color photographs of Celtic art. "Tell me about shape-shifting."

"Have you ever wanted to turn yourself into a bird or a dog?"

"When I was nine, maybe."

"Think of it. Being able to metamorphose into a bird would give a man or woman — or even a god — an enormous advantage. A bird can fly into an enemy camp. It can see things a human wouldn't otherwise see. Never mind the practical advantages, shape-shifting plays a symbolic role. A beautiful queen becomes a hag. A young girl becomes a swan. A hero becomes a hawk. As I've mentioned, the Celts didn't have firm lines between this world and the other world — between the living and the dead, between gods and men. Think of shape-shifting in that context."

"You're just scratching the surface, aren't you?"

She smiled faintly. "It's difficult to talk about 'the Celts.' There are many stories of shape-shifting in Irish mythology. The goddess Maeve is said to have shape-shifted into a hag and a raven, terrorizing and horrifying her enemies. Why are you asking about shape-shifting?"

"I don't know. Your big black dog in Ireland, maybe." He changed the subject. "You said the elder Percy Carlisle was an adventurer, but his son isn't. Was there tension between them?"

"I've told you, I didn't know them that well."

"But you heard rumors. You worked at an upscale Beacon Hill pub, you did research at their museum, you were majoring in the field that most interested the father."

"I was a student. I wasn't on their radar, and I didn't have a lot of time for rumors. If Percy felt inadequate — if his father made him feel inadequate — I wasn't that aware of it."

" 'That' aware."

She smiled. "Okay, so I was a little aware, but Percy's a grown man now with his own interests and accomplishments. He's married. His father's gone. If you're suggesting he engineered the cave last summer as some way to prove himself —" She stopped, shaking her head. "I don't believe it."

"Helen doesn't seem to mind that he's a bit of a wimp."

"I don't think of him as a wimp, and I know you said that just to see my reaction."

"Never fantasized about Prince Charming Percy Carlisle sweeping you off to his castle in Back Bay?"

"No."

Scoop almost asked her about fantasizing about a scarred, weight-lifting cop, but he resisted.

She gathered up her materials into both arms and dumped them on the floor in front of the fireplace. "I've been wondering if I missed it somehow and Percy Sr. did explore that island on one of his adventures. But I don't see how. Tim O'Donovan would have known. He and his family have been fishing off the southwest coast of Ireland for decades."

"Going out there was all your idea?"

She nodded.

"What about the break-in at the museum? How did that affect your relationship with the Carlisles?"

"I had nothing to do with it, and it was a long time ago —"

"Not that long."

She sighed. "Both Carlisles were uncomfortable around me after that."

"Did they ever consider you a suspect?"

"No, and neither did the police." Her voice was calm. "There were rumors — never mind. Rumors don't matter now."

"Maybe they do."

"Police officers dig into people's most private areas, don't they?"

"Just doing a job. What rumors?"

"That Percy Sr. was in on the break-in."

"Motive?"

"He could sell the Homer to a discreet, rich friend and collect insurance on it at the same time. There were rumors he needed cash, but I don't believe that so much — I don't believe he was involved at all, but if he had been, it would be because he liked the risk and he was getting back at someone. He was very . . ." She paused, obviously searching for the right word. "He could be very rigid and unforgiving."

"What was his wife like?"

"Quiet, cerebral. The museum was her creation."

"Married to it and her work there. So we had the near disaster and scandal over the smuggling in Ireland and the firings, the break-in and the heist in Boston. Now you're an expert in the field Percy Sr. thought of himself as an expert in. You know all this stuff, and Percy Jr. knows you know."

"That's why I was surprised when he looked me up a year ago."

"And your brain didn't go *ding-ding-ding* after the island experience?"

"No."

"Did you tell the Irish police about Percy?"

"It didn't even occur to me. I can't even say he was still in Ireland at the time. I doubt it."

"Not the type to chase after you to a remote, rockbound island?"

"Definitely not the type."

"Why did he come see you in Kenmare? Go through that conversation with me again."

She debated, then nodded. "Have a seat."

He listened without interruption while she talked. He wasn't a lot of things, but he was a damn good listener. And he liked hearing her talk. She was curious, analytical and interested as well as interesting — and it didn't take long for him to figure out that she hadn't been waiting for Percy Carlisle to sweep her off her feet. Or any man, for that matter. Sophie Malone, Ph.D., was very much her own person.

She'd just finished when she got a text message. She glanced at her iPhone, then smiled, her blue eyes sparking with obvious pleasure. "Taryn's here," she said as her fingers flew, texting her back. "You get to meet my twin sister. She's right outside."

Sophie leaped up and buzzed her in, and thirty seconds later, Taryn Malone was surveying Scoop with eyes as blue and incisive as her sister's. But she spoke directly to Sophie. "I'm only blowing in here to say hello, then I'm on my way to New York. I'll be there for two days. Then it's back to London. How are you? And who is this?"

"This is the detective I told you about," Sophie said, and made the introductions.

Taryn beamed a smile at him. "So good to meet you, Detective Wisdom."

"I'll go for a walk and let you two visit," he said, looking at Sophie. "Then I'm coming back."

22

Taryn gulped in a breath after Scoop left. Sophie held up a hand before her sister could say a word. "I know. What am I doing? I should take Damian's advice and go back to Ireland and dig in the dirt."

"No argument from me," Taryn said, stretching out on the sectional. "I didn't let Damian know I was coming here. I knew he'd tell me not to. Sophie, are you in trouble with the police?"

She shook her head. "I can't be. I've told them everything and I haven't done anything wrong."

"Please don't stay here alone."

"I'm not. I'm staying at the Whitcomb."

"Good. Unless — wait. Is this detective staying there, too?"

"For now."

Taryn moaned as if she were in pain. "I suppose there isn't a Malone born who does things the easy way. All right, then. If you're not in trouble with the cops — if they don't suspect you of wrongdoing — then let them help."

"Cliff Rafferty was a police officer, Taryn. Scoop's a detective. He can't turn that off even for half a second."

"Why would you want him to? Never mind. Scratch that. Dumb question now that I've seen him." She rose suddenly, a bundle of nervous energy. "Look, I'd stay if I could, but I have this crazy thing called a living to make. You could come to New York with me."

"Thanks, but I can't. I have commitments here."

"I know. I understand." Taryn dashed into the bedroom, yanked open the closet and pulled out a pair of black heels, tucking them under one arm as she returned to the living room. "I didn't think I'd need these. I hope I don't break an ankle. Oh, Sophie. You'll stay safe, won't you? You and I are so different and yet so similar. Do you miss Ireland?"

"Yes, but I'll go back. Taryn —"

"Don't go there," she said, as if she were reading her sister's mind. "I won't ask Tim to give up his life, and he won't ask me to give up mine."

Sophie leaned against the door jamb.

"What would you say if he did ask?"

"He and I are both hopeless romantics. That's what attracted me to him in the first place, but I have to be practical."

"Tim's a romantic?"

Taryn blushed and quickly led the way back out to the street. She had asked her cab to wait. It was just like her to make a separate stop in Boston for something she could easily pick up in New York, but that wasn't, Sophie knew, really why her sister was there. "Damian's worried," Taryn said in a half whisper. "*I'm* worried. I want to trust this detective, but what do you know about him? What if he's playing everyone? What if *he's* actually the one who planted the bomb?"

"He was almost killed —"

"Yeah, but he wasn't killed, and what a way to fool everyone. You must trust him or you wouldn't be alone with him." Taryn straightened abruptly, her hand on the open cab door. "Sophie! Are you falling for him? No, don't answer. It's the adrenaline. You bonded during a crisis."

"It started on the Beara Peninsula," Sophie admitted.

"Ah. Fairies, then. He's a total stud, I know — I have eyes — but . . ." Taryn didn't finish. "Just be careful, okay?"

"I will. Thanks for stopping by. Have fun in New York."

"Yes." She smiled, betraying a rare hint of uncertainty. "I'm not sure it's what I want."

"Maybe going there will help you figure that out."

"I can't afford to be a romantic about making a living . . ." Taryn brushed off her uncertainty. "Listen to me. You're dealing with a real crisis. I'm just in angst mode."

"I'm here anytime. You know that. If you want to talk about acting and a certain Irish fisherman —"

"Oh, stop. You saw that awful beard. Tim O'Donovan's *not* the man for me."

Sophie laughed. "He can quote Yeats by heart."

"So can Damian, and can you imagine ending up with him?"

That made them both laugh, just as Scoop returned, easing toward the gate back to the courtyard. Taryn glared at him. "Be good to my sister," she said, and quickly ducked into the cab, shut the door and waved goodbye.

Sophie half expected Scoop to question her about her sister's visit, but he just walked with her back through the archway to her apartment, letting her go in first. "I bought a few things at the grocery that I should use up," she said. "I warned you that

I'm not a great cook, but I feel like putting a meal together. I don't do a bad spaghetti sauce and salad. I mean, who does? I have all the ingredients. I hate to see them go to waste."

He pulled off his jacket. "I'll help."

"Thanks, but just having you here . . . someone to talk to . . . makes a difference." She pulled open the refrigerator. "I spent long hours alone when I was working on my dissertation."

"What's it about?"

"Gad. You don't want to hear *that*."

He smiled at her. "Give me the short version."

She talked as she cooked. He stood next to her at the counter, chopping an onion, garlic, a carrot on a thick wooden board. It was a tiny kitchen with the refrigerator, sink and stove all on one wall and not much counter space, but surprisingly efficient and bigger, Sophie thought, than the kitchen had been in her apartment in Cork.

Once she finished describing her dissertation, Scoop asked about her time in Ireland. "I loved it," she said, watching steam rise from her pot of water for the spaghetti. "I worked hard and was always scrambling to keep the wolf from the door, but I met so many great people there."

364

"How long do you think you'll stay here?"

"My sister's apartment? I don't know. What about you — when can you get back into your triple-decker?"

"It'll be a few months. Depends on whether we decide to make improvements or just focus on repairs. Abigail won't be back, but we'll cross that bridge when we get to it. I'll figure something out in the meantime. I can't stay at the Whitcomb much longer." He grinned at her. "I'll be disappointed when I don't find chocolates on my pillow."

"You live alone, though?"

"I have two cats but no live-in girlfriend, no ex-wives, no kids."

She laid dried spaghetti in boiling water, aware of Scoop inches away by the sink. "Cliff Rafferty said you were quite the ladies' man."

"I'm never sure what something like that means."

She liked his response, she decided. It wasn't defensive, but it wasn't a total dodge, either — and he hadn't just pushed her off and told her his love life was none of her damn business. She stood back from the stove while the spaghetti cooked. "Tell me about your cats."

"They're stray Russian blues I rescued

two years ago." He got a colander down from a hook. "I was working a case — I'd just started in internal affairs. I nailed a cop for hiring prostitutes on the job. I set up a stakeout, and here were these scrawny little kittens mewing in an alley."

"Do you have a soft heart, Cyrus Wisdom?"

He laughed, setting the colander in the sink. "It would be a serious mistake for anyone to think that. I took the cats home figuring I'd give them to a friend, but I ended up keeping them. They adopted me more than I adopted them. Bob's two younger daughters have been taking care of them."

Her throat tightened with unexpected emotion. "You've had a terrible time, Scoop. You're so strong and so focused on the present — at least you come across that way — that it's easy to forget what you've gone through. Do you want to retire from the Boston Police Department after you put in your twenty or thirty years?"

"You're thinking about Cliff," he said.

"I want to know about you."

"The job's a good one."

"Not everything is as it appears to be with you, is it?"

His dark eyes narrowed on her. "If you're

a thief and you're lying to me —"

"If you're a bad cop and you're lying to me . . ."

She grabbed potholders and poured the spaghetti into the colander, steam from the hot water rising in her face, probably turned her skin red. She set the empty pot back on the stove. The sauce was simmering. The salad was made. Why did she feel so out of her element?

"I'm not a bad cop," Scoop said, "and I'm not lying to you."

He caught her in his arms, and Sophie placed her hands on his waist. He was muscular, sexy. Even through his shirt, she could feel the ragged edges of the scars from the bomb. "Scoop . . ." Rarely at a loss for words, she couldn't think of what to say. "I'm glad I met you, and I'm glad I met you the way I did."

"Covered in mud, with a big black dog at your side. Think he's a shape-shifter?"

She smiled. "Right now anything feels possible."

His mouth found hers, and this time it wasn't a light kiss. He drew her against him, lifting her off her feet as they deepened their kiss. "Sophie, Sophie," he said, lowering his hands to her hips, lifting her higher. He smiled, setting her back down. "Ah, Sophie.

I do like saying your name."

"The sauce is about to boil over."

He winked at her. "So it is."

Taryn called later that evening, when Sophie was back in her room at the Whitcomb, her laptop out on her bed as she went over study skills sheets for her tutoring students. "I'm in New York," Taryn said. "I feel guilty for leaving you alone. Damian's threatening to fly up there as soon as he can get away. Do you want me to call Mom and Dad and get them to Boston?"

"No, let them enjoy their hike. And Damian should focus on his job. I'm fine."

"Where is Scoop Wisdom right now?"

"About ten yards from me."

"Sophie!"

She smiled. "He's not stalking me. He's in the next room at the Whitcomb."

"I guess that's good. If there's anything I can do, call me. Don't hesitate. I can figure out London."

"What about Tim O'Donovan?"

Her sister gave a small laugh. "I can't figure him out at all."

23

Kenmare, Southwest Ireland

Josie stood on a stone bridge above a waterfall that tumbled over black rocks, forming whitecaps and filling the air with its soothing rhythmic sound. She'd gone on ahead while Myles showered and dressed back at the Malone house. He'd catch up with her. They'd both needed a moment to themselves before they got too deep into the day. She wasn't confused, but she was unsure of the way forward. The past was falling away, no longer tearing at her.

Myles was alive. He'd come back from the dead.

He acted as if he'd never gone, but that was Myles. The reasons he could carry on as if nothing had happened were the same reasons he'd taken on his difficult mission in the first place — the same reasons he'd survived. He was resilient. He learned from the past and planned for the future, but he lived in the moment.

She saw him coming toward her, ambling as if he were just another tourist off for a wander in the Irish hills. When he reached her, he leaned over the stone wall. "You'd hit your head on a rock if you tried to dive in there," Josie said.

"I was thinking we could spend the day fly-fishing."

She gave a mock shudder. "I'd rather take on blood-smeared branches. I tell people Will's fishing in Scotland when he doesn't want to answer questions."

"It's not questions I'm avoiding. I actually do want to go fly-fishing."

"How long has it been since you've taken time just to be yourself, Myles?"

"I'm myself now."

"I meant —"

"I know what you meant." He wasn't being abrupt, but he'd made it clear he wasn't going there, either. "You're the boss. Where to from here?"

"We need to find Percy Carlisle. I suggest we start with Tim O'Donovan."

"All right, then."

They continued on foot toward the village and walked out to the pier, but O'Donovan was already off on his boat for the day. Josie debated hiring a boat herself and chasing after him, but she hadn't a clue where to start — and she didn't particularly care for boats. Myles suggested they return to the Malone house. Not bloody likely, Josie thought. With the dreary weather, they'd be tempted to light a fire and spend the day being utterly useless, which she suspected was Myles's aim.

Instead she decided they ought to head to a quiet pub, sit by the fire and review all they knew. Myles didn't object, and as they walked to the village, she texted Seamus Harrigan to join them at his convenience. In the meantime, maybe they'd get lucky and Percy Carlisle would wander in, or someone who knew him. They had his photo and both she and Myles had committed his face to memory.

"This could end badly," Josie said.

Myles slung an arm over her shoulder and gave her a good squeeze. "We'll do all we can to make sure it doesn't."

24

Boston, Massachusetts

Sophie woke up far too early and had coffee with Jeremiah Rush in the lobby of the Whitcomb. "Do you sleep under your desk with your golden retriever? I swear you're here all the time."

"Now there's a thought. Get a dog's view of the family business." He grinned at her, clearly no longer the high school kid she'd known when she worked there. "All's well this morning, Sophie?"

"I hope so."

"Where's your detective?"

"*My* detective, Jeremiah?"

"Sparks, Sophie. Sparks."

"I think something weird happened in the Irish ruin where we met. I'm — I can't explain it."

"You're crazy about him."

She sighed. It seemed so soon. So fast. Maybe that was partly because everything

372

else in her life was slow. She'd been in school forever. Her dissertation had taken forever to write. Even archaeology was by its nature painstaking, breakthroughs seldom happening fast or suddenly — certainly not as fast and suddenly as Scoop's entrance into her life. He'd been on the Beara Peninsula for two weeks before they'd run into each other. She'd been in Kenmare most of that time. Maybe being in such close proximity had had an effect.

She smiled at Jeremiah. "Tell me about what's going on with you these days."

They chatted a few minutes, Jeremiah making her laugh with tales of his family and hotel life. Finally Sophie refilled her coffee, grabbed a muffin and asked him if he'd let Scoop know she was going to the Carlisle Museum. "It's a beautiful day," she said, heading for the exit. "Tell him I'm walking."

"You don't think he has you under surveillance?"

"Thanks, Jeremiah, that's just what I needed on my mind."

"Hey, we're a full-service hotel."

Charles Street was quiet, the morning air crisp and bright. In no hurry, Sophie turned onto Beacon Street and meandered through the narrow downtown streets with her coffee and muffin, reconnecting with being back in Boston. It was a great walking city, and she loved to walk. She continued past Government Center and on to the waterfront, where the Carlisle Museum was located in a low, renovated brick building on its own wharf. By the time she got there, the main offices were open, although the museum itself wouldn't open until ten. A stone walkway took her through a garden of herbs, wild asters and coneflowers to the administrative entrance.

The receptionist, a young woman with spiky jet-black hair, was new since Sophie had done research at the museum. She recognized Sophie's name. "I'm majoring in art history," she said. "Your article on Irish Iron Age art was assigned reading in one of my classes. Helen Carlisle said you might come by now that you're back from Ireland."

"Is she here?" Sophie asked.

"Not yet. I'd love to go to Ireland some day. I want to see the Book of Kells in person."

"I hope you can. My family has a home in Ireland — I won't stay away too long — but it's good to be back in Boston, too." Sophie motioned toward the corridor behind the receptionist's desk. "I'd like to take a look around —"

"Sure. Let me know if you need anything. There aren't many people here yet."

Sophie headed down the wide hall, welcoming the natural light and simplicity of the building's design. From the beginning, the Carlisles had seen the museum as placing equal emphasis on education, research and exhibits. She'd told Scoop the truth about the break-in seven years ago, but if there was some tidbit she hadn't remembered that could help find Percy or explain what had happened to Cliff Rafferty, maybe being back here would help.

She heard a rushing sound — like a wide-open faucet — and paused at the open door to a conference suite. The table wasn't set up for a meeting, nor had anyone dropped off materials, a briefcase, a coat. She remembered the suite had an office, a small kitchen and a full bathroom. Isabel Carlisle had seen to every detail of the conversion of the building, from the exhibit halls to the comfort of the administrative offices.

Sophie entered the main room and crossed over to a hall that led to the kitchen, wondering if someone she knew might be back there cleaning up. It had to be running water she heard.

The kitchen was dark — no sign of anyone there.

The bathroom was farther down the hall. Not wanting to disturb anyone taking a shower before work, she started to turn back to the conference room, but stopped abruptly, noticing the bathroom door was open, water was streaming over the threshold into the hall.

Sophie edged down the hall. Had a toilet or sink stopped up?

Trying to stay clear of the water on the floor, she peeked into the bathroom. Directly ahead of her was a white porcelain pedestal, but the faucet wasn't on and the basin was dry.

Out of the corner of her eye, she saw a man's foot — a black running shoe — and immediately yelled for help, hoping a security guard or the receptionist would hear her. She stepped into the bathroom, the tile floor slippery, more water pouring through the doorway, flooding the bathroom and hall.

A man was shoved headfirst into the overflowing bathtub, his legs askew, hanging over the edge onto the floor. He wasn't struggling. He wasn't moving at all.

If he was still alive, he had to get out of the water fast, or he'd drown. She ran to the tub. The man was dressed in tan slacks and a light blue shirt. She couldn't see his face, but he had dark hair. She didn't see any signs of injury, but she had no choice. She had to move him. She had to get him out of the water.

Grabbing him by the belt, she pulled him up a little, then got her arms around his middle. He was heavy, deadweight. She pushed her feet against the wall, bracing herself as best she could on the wet floor, and lifted him up and out of the tub. Momentum carried her backward, with him on top of her as she went down on her side into the cold water on the floor.

He was moving . . .

No, he was being lifted off her.

"Sophie." Scoop's voice. "You okay?"

She sat up, nodding, breathing hard. "He was in the tub —"

"Yeah."

It was Frank Acosta. His skin was pasty and bluish in color, waterlogged. Scoop laid his fellow police officer flat on the floor, checked his airway, his breathing. "Hell, Frank, don't make me have to do CPR on you."

Acosta coughed and vomited water, rolling onto his side.

Sophie rose, quickly shut off the faucet. A

torc, fashioned out of gold wire, just like the one at Cliff Rafferty's apartment, was broken in half and set on the edge of the tub, along with a clump of vines — ivy — smeared with what appeared to be blood. "Scoop."

"I see them."

Acosta got up onto his knees, groaning, spitting into the pooled water.

"Can you talk, Frank?" Scoop asked.

"Yeah. Yeah, I'm okay."

"You need to get checked out."

He held up a hand in protest. "No. I'm okay."

Scoop didn't relent. "Were you hit on the head? Drugged?"

"I don't know." He sat on the tile floor in the water and sank back against the tub, wincing, coughing some more. He put a hand up to the right side of his neck. "Head hurts."

Scoop took a look. "You've got some swelling."

"Yeah. I remember now." He breathed in, steadier. "Whew."

"What happened?"

"I called you. You were already on your way here. I was closer and got here first. I walked into the conference room and saw a light down the hall and came in to investi-

378

gate and — *bam.*" He wiped his mouth with the back of his hand, which was visibly trembling. "Next thing I'm soaking wet, choking to death and looking at your ugly face."

"You came alone?" Scoop asked.

"Yeah. No one knows I'm here except you. I'm not on duty until later."

Scoop put a hand out to him. "You'll get hypothermia sitting in that cold water —"

"I can get up on my own."

Acosta started to his feet, slipped and fell back against the tub with a moan. He was shivering, drenched, water dripping out of his hair down his face.

Scoop sighed. "Screw this."

He took Acosta by the upper arm, hauled him up with one quick motion and in two strides had him out in the hall. Shivering now herself, Sophie grabbed a bath towel off a hook and followed them to the kitchen, where Scoop sat Acosta on the dry floor. He was ashen. She flipped on a light switch and handed him the towel.

His hands were shaking uncontrollably and he was still clearly weak, but he dried off his face and managed to glare up at her. "Why are you here?"

Scoop, his eyes on Acosta, answered. "She walked over from the hotel first thing this morning. She's why I came. I just didn't tell you that when you called. She's the one who pulled you out of the water. Did you see anyone when you arrived?"

"Just the receptionist."

"I must have arrived after he did," Sophie said. "I took my time. I've only seen the receptionist, too."

"Doesn't answer my question," Acosta said, clutching the towel. "Where's your friend Percy? Do you two have something going? We only have your word Cliff looked you up on Beacon Hill the other morning."

Meaning, she thought, no witnesses. She walked over to the stainless-steel sink and pulled open a drawer, got out dish towels and did her best to dry herself off. She was aware of the two men — the two police officers — watching her.

She pointed toward the conference room with her towel. "I can wait out there —"

"You could have killed Cliff yourself," Acosta interjected, not letting up. "All that ritualistic crap. That could have been you. Kill him, go back to Beacon Hill, make up that whole bit about him coming to find you. You know you've got Scoop wrapped around your little finger."

"I'm going now," Sophie said, heading for the door.

Scoop shook his head. "Stay with me. Whoever tried to kill Frank could still be out there. He can't have been in the water long or he'd be dead."

Acosta cast the towel aside and staggered to his feet, his skin, if possible, turning even grayer. "Check out your archaeologist, Wisdom." He coughed, gritted his teeth visibly as he seemed to fight off pain and nausea. "She's the one with axes to grind. We don't know what happened with her and Cliff. No one does. It's just her word."

"Take it easy, Frank. You probably have a concussion. You've had a bad scare —"

"A bad scare? I damn near *drowned.* This woman's the expert. If she's obsessed with Celtic whatever — art, religion, history, bones, I don't know — she could have her own game. What if she set this up — sold fake Celtic jewelry, or found the real thing and wants to keep it for herself? What if she's blackmailing Percy Carlisle to get him to buy them or get someone else to buy them?"

Scoop hadn't interrupted Acosta's rant. "You need to take it easy, Frank."

Acosta ignored him. "Your Dr. Malone could have thrown Percy Carlisle off some damn Irish cliff before she flew back to Boston."

"The Irish are looking for him," Scoop said. "We can talk about all this after the paramedics have checked you over."

"What if your archaeologist was behind the break-in here seven years ago? She's smart as hell. She could have orchestrated the mess with the old man in Ireland, then broken in here so that we'd all look to some disgruntled employee. Maybe the son suspected her but couldn't prove it. Maybe he went to Ireland to confront her."

"You're speculating," Scoop said.

"Brainstorming. There's a difference." Acosta's dark eyes — bloodshot, red-rimmed, accusatory — were riveted on Scoop. "I'm not emotionally involved."

"You are emotionally involved." Scoop's voice was calm. "Cliff was your friend."

"Friend? Cliff didn't have friends. He was a lazy, cynical SOB who blamed his problems on everyone else."

"Was he involved with the thugs Estabrook hired?"

"How the hell would I know?"

Museum security and two uniformed BPD officers arrived. Acosta shook off their help, then stumbled. They caught him as he fainted.

Scoop touched Sophie's elbow. "You okay?"

382

She nodded. He walked with her back to the conference room. Paramedics and the homicide detectives investigating Cliff Rafferty's death arrived next.

Bob O'Reilly was right behind them. "Damn," he said, glaring at Scoop, then at Sophie. "You two again."

By the time she finished with the BPD, Sophie was dry enough to head over to the main part of the museum. She'd loved wandering through the different collections as a student and welcomed being among the familiar paintings, sculptures and artifacts. The homicide detectives had been thorough and professional, but she had no illusions. They grilled her not just about how and why she'd come to the museum this morning, what she'd seen, what she'd done, but about everything — her life from meeting the Carlisles as a student to sitting in the conference room answering their questions.

Scoop hadn't stayed with her. She wasn't sure he would have been allowed to, and he had his own questions to answer. The police and museum security had shut down the museum and searched it for possible assailants, witnesses and evidence.

Sophie was staring blankly at a trio of

Early Medieval Irish silver chalices behind a glass case when Scoop found her. "They're beautiful, aren't they?" Her voice was hoarse, but she continued. "You can see the Celtic motifs. The spirals, the knots. The museum doesn't have a lot of Irish works — these are on loan from a private collector."

"You don't have to be here."

She looked up from the chalices and saw that his gaze was on her, nothing about him easy to read — easy on any level. "I didn't wait for you this morning because I wanted to come here alone. It was a beautiful morning for a walk. It never occurred to me I'd find . . ." She didn't finish. "Security's obviously not as tight in the administrative offices as out here in the exhibits."

He touched a hand to her upper arm. "I can take you back to the hotel."

She nodded but moved over to a series of small, dark paintings. "If Percy's in Boston — if he's into dark pagan rituals, twisting them for his own purposes, and all this is his doing . . ." She shook her head. "I can't imagine. Helen would be devastated. Everyone here would be. When Detective Acosta was 'brainstorming,' all I could think about was how many possible explanations there are to what's happened. Percy could be hiding and afraid — he could think he's being framed for something he didn't do. He could have been working with Rafferty or Augustine."

"That's why you have to leave the investigation to the police. They'll follow the evidence wherever it takes them."

She turned from the paintings. "Was it blood on the torc and the ivy?"

"Yes."

"At least it wasn't Detective Acosta's blood." She glanced at Scoop. "There's much, much more to the Celts than human sacrifice."

Scoop almost smiled. "Feeling a little defensive about them?"

"I just don't want to paint too incomplete a picture."

"Makes sense a killer's not going to pick happy Celtic symbols and whatnot to latch on to, right? What a Celt who's been dead for a couple thousand years would think about what's going on here doesn't matter. I want whoever tried to drown Acosta." Scoop's expression, although still grim, softened somewhat. "You did all right in there, Sophie."

"Detective Acosta wouldn't have been here at all if I hadn't —"

"Don't go there. It won't get you any-where."

Probably it wouldn't, Sophie thought. The police would talk to Jeremiah Rush, if they hadn't already, and find out if he'd told anyone else where she was headed. She hugged her arms to herself, suddenly cold again. "You all are taking another look at the incident with Percy Sr. in Ireland and the break-in here, aren't you?"

"We're taking care of it, Detective Malone."

She attempted a smile. "I think I like the sound of Agent Malone better, although my brother would find a way to keep me out of the FBI academy."

"What about Professor Malone?"

"That has an even better ring to it."

Helen Carlisle swept into the room, alone, wearing a long, lightweight coat as if she'd just walked in from the street. Her dark hair was pulled back neatly, her red lipstick standing out against her pale skin. "The director of the museum called me as soon as he could, and I came right away. Thank heavens no one was seriously hurt."

"Where were you?" Scoop asked.

"The house. Alone. The housekeeper might have seen me if you'd like me to provide an alibi." When he didn't respond, she turned to Sophie. "Did someone offer you something to drink? Would you like to sit down?"

"Walking around in here helps."

"Of course. It's a fantastic museum. It needs updating, but the trustees are working on a long-term plan . . ." Helen faltered, tears rising in her big eyes. "I'm trying to put up a brave face, but I feel so vulnerable. I keep thinking the phone will ring, or the door will open, and Percy will be there." She spun around and faced Scoop. "I don't believe my husband is involved in whatever's going on, Detective Wisdom. Not for one second."

"We just want to find him, Mrs. Carlisle," Scoop said.

She nodded, tightening her coat around her. "I'm thinking about going to New York for a few days. I just want to be on my own — away from all this. I had a moment of panic about security, but if I were a target, I'd be dead now. It seems to me police officers are more vulnerable than I am. It's frightening, but whatever's going on doesn't really involve me." She added coolly, "Or my husband."

Scoop buttoned up his own jacket. "Then you're not worried about him?"

"I wouldn't think twice about where he is

if not for Cliff's death and now this with Detective Acosta."

"Did your husband ever mention the break-in here?"

"No, why should he have? You're grasping now, aren't you, Detective? I have to go. I'm meeting the director. I never . . ." She shuddered, a glamorous, beautiful woman caught in the middle of a violent drama. "This isn't what I signed on for. I don't know if I'm up to it."

She didn't wait for a response as she swept back out of the gallery.

Sophie felt her energy flagging. "I have to stop at the tutoring center . . . and I promised a friend at BU I'd come by at the same time. I'm teaching a class there next semester." She reined in her thoughts and focused on Scoop. "What about you? Are you okay?"

"Yeah, sure."

"Hauling Detective Acosta around didn't tear open any of your injuries?"

He shook his head. "All set."

She smiled. "Would you tell me if you were about to double over in pain right now?"

It was clearly not what he'd expected her to say, and he smiled back at her. "Probably not."

"Are you kicking yourself because you

didn't connect the dots and figure out sooner Cliff Rafferty was the police link to those local thugs?"

"That's still an open investigation. Whatever happens, you have your victories and your defeats in this job." He shrugged. "You hope the defeats don't get anyone killed."

"If they do, you'd rather it be yourself who's hurt than someone else?"

He didn't answer. "Come on. I have my car. I'll drop you off."

"I don't mind walking."

Scoop put his arm over her shoulders. "I can't wait to see you on that Irish panel, arguing with your colleagues about some point of ancient history. Is Celtic archaeology controversial?"

"It can be."

He laughed softly. "That's my point. Academics." He let his arm fall to her waist and held her close. "You just saved a man's life. The day could have gotten off to a worse start."

"I guess that's one way to look at it."

He tilted his head back. "What's on your mind, Sophie?"

She lifted his hand and touched her fingertips to a jagged scar on his wrist. "The bomb did this to you. It burned your house. Cliff Rafferty was hanged. Now Frank

Acosta was nearly drowned. Our perpetrator seems to be obsessed with Celtic rituals, appropriating bits and pieces of Celtic lore from a variety of sources, jumbling them up to suit his or her needs. Some scholars believe that burning, hanging and drowning represent fire, earth and water — fundamental elements associated with specific Celtic deities. The god Esus with earth, Taranis with fire, Teutates with water."

"So you don't think the choice of the tub was a coincidence?"

"It might have been quick thinking, since whoever is responsible couldn't have known Detective Acosta would be here this morning. I'm not suggesting there's a coherent strategy or recreation of any particular set of sacrificial rites at work."

"Jay Augustine wasn't a scholar of the devil and evil," Scoop said. "He just latched on to what suited his purposes."

"To kill." Sophie could feel the blood draining from her face. "In 1984, the corpse of a young Celt was discovered in a bog in England. It was extremely well preserved because of the anaerobic conditions. He'd met a terribly violent death. He'd been hit on the head several times — hard enough that he'd have died soon after. But that's not what killed him."

"Was he burned, hanged or drowned?"

"Garroted, basically. The cord used was still around his neck two thousand years later. A stick had been tucked into the back of it to add to the force of the strangulation. It actually broke his neck."

"Charming."

"That wasn't the end of it. Then his throat was cut and his body deposited in the bog. He could have been a willing victim, sacrificing his life for the welfare of the tribe, victory in battle — we don't know. Whatever the purpose of his death, he'd have felt no pain after the initial blow."

Scoop grimaced. "And here I thought you just dug up pretty jewelry buried for hundreds of years. Come on. Let's go see your hockey players."

"I think I will take you up on the offer of a ride over to the tutoring center."

He slipped an arm around her. "I thought you might."

25

After he dropped off Sophie with her hockey players, Scoop parked at the Whitcomb, changed clothes and walked up Beacon Street to the bow-front, early-nineteenth-century Garrison house. He'd gone back to the conference room after she'd left and checked in with Bob O'Reilly. They'd agreed to meet here, in the first-floor drawing room. It was used for meetings, parties and, on occasion, a practice room for Fiona and her friends. The offices of the foundation named in honor of Owen Garrison's sister were located on the second and third floors. Dorothy Garrison's drowning death off the coast of Maine at fourteen was connected, indirectly, to the death of Christopher Browning, Abigail's first husband, eight years ago — four days into their honeymoon.

Lizzie Rush had a point about ripple effects, Scoop thought.

The Rushes would have put Bob up at any of their hotels, too, but he was staying here, in his niece's attic apartment.

Bright autumn sunshine streamed through the tall windows that looked across busy Beacon Street to the Common, crawling with tourists, shoppers, kids and dogs. The gold-domed Massachusetts State House was a few doors up the street.

Bob cut his gaze over to Scoop. "You have your head screwed on straight with this Sophie Malone?"

Scoop shrugged. "More or less."

"She's not one of these women who come and go in your life. Whatever's going on with you two isn't the same."

"It doesn't matter. I can do my job."

"You're not on the case," Bob said. "I'm not, either. That prick Yarborough threatened to report me when I showed up at the museum this morning."

"You'd have done the same."

"Yeah, probably."

That was the end of that. Scoop noticed Fiona O'Reilly waiting for traffic on the other side of Beacon, some kind of instrument case slung over one shoulder. "As far as we can tell, Percy Carlisle hasn't boarded a flight to the U.S. since Sophie saw him in Ireland."

"Maybe he sprouted wings," Bob said. "The way things are going, nothing would surprise me. Anyone wanting to fry, hang or drown us has had multiple opportunities."

"That's just a theory."

"I know, I know." He nodded out the window. "Here comes Fiona with her violin. She's not getting any better on that thing. Either that or I just don't like violin music."

"We can go talk somewhere else."

"Nah." He continued to stare out the window as Fiona, blonde hair flying, ran across the street. "We've all turned into shit magnets, Scoop. I thought it was Abigail. Widowed, kidnapped, John March's only daughter. It's not just her. It's you and me, too."

"It's not always the enemies you know that get you," Scoop said. "Sometimes it's ones you don't know."

"Most of the time. Talk to me, Scoop. Talk to Abigail and me."

"She's here?"

He nodded. "She and Owen got back late last night."

Owen Garrison entered the drawing room at the same time that Fiona came through the front door, smiling easily, as if she had nothing on her mind but a few hours of practicing in a quiet, pretty setting. She set her violin down and grabbed tall, angular Owen in a big hug. He looked over the top of her head at Bob and Scoop. "Abigail's upstairs. I'll stay down here with Fi."

Scoop led the way. He could feel a pull of pain in his hip now. He hadn't noticed any pain when he'd half carried Acosta down the hall. Worse had been hearing the running water, hearing Sophie yell for help — not knowing what was going on, if he'd get to her in time. He hadn't told her that.

He hadn't told her that he'd fallen in love with her. It was just that simple. Love at first sight. Him. Who'd have thought it?

He came to the attic landing and entered the small apartment. Abigail was on her feet. "Scoop," she said, hugging him. "I've missed you."

He laughed. "Yeah, right, let me go tell Owen —"

She grinned at him, a spark in her dark eyes — her father's eyes. "You know what I mean. Well, you look better than when I saw you at the wedding."

Bob grinned. "He reminds me of Herman Munster." He nodded toward Abigail as he addressed Scoop. "Looks pretty good, doesn't she? Being rich and married agrees with her. You'd never know she was kidnapped and nearly killed a month ago."

Abigail rolled her eyes. "At least you didn't make a pregnancy joke. The first one who does, I shoot."

"I'll consider that fair warning," Scoop said.

He pulled out a chair at the small table where Keira used to draw and paint. Bob hadn't done much to the place. He sat at the table, too. Pads and pencils were stacked to one side. Scoop felt a tug of emotion. He, Abigail and Bob had bought the triple-decker together because they'd all needed a place to live and were looking at the same time, and it'd been a way to pool their resources in Boston's expensive real estate market. As different as they were — in temperament, background, likes and dislikes — they'd become friends. When one would be chewing on a problem, they'd get out the pads and pens and a six-pack and brain-storm.

The past year had turned their lives upside down and changed them forever.

Abigail sat between the two men. Her baby was due in six months. Talk about big changes, Scoop thought.

"Did your father ever mention Sophie Malone to you?" he asked.

"No, but that wouldn't be unusual. He's always tried to keep a firewall between his job and his family. It hasn't worked very well, though, has it?" Abigail was quiet a moment. "Strange how things work out sometimes."

"I don't think this was strange," Scoop said.

"Destined?"

He shook his head. "Deliberate. What happened at the Carlisle Museum seven years ago and on that island a year ago and what happened here in Boston this past summer are all of a piece."

Bob distributed the pads and pencils. "We can take our time," he said. "Fiona will be practicing that damn violin for at least a couple hours. You can save me from having to go down there."

Abigail seemed comfortable to be back in her role as a detective. "All right," she said. "Let's see what we've got."

26

Kenmare, Southwest Ireland

Josie was yawning when Tim O'Donovan arrived in the pub in which she and Myles had situated themselves for most of the day, with breaks for walks back to the pier and disturbing calls from Boston. Another violent attack on a police officer. She and Myles both had felt stunningly useless. Seamus Harrigan had met with them briefly, essentially to tell them to stay out of the investigation. By dark, even Myles had seemed ready to give up and return to Dublin. He could look dead tired — he could *be* dead tired — but would never let his fatigue, or anything else, for that matter, interfere with his performance. It wasn't just training. It was the way the man was hardwired.

O'Donovan wasn't performing that night but had popped in for a Guinness. He looked as if he had, indeed, spent the day at

sea. "I thought you'd gone back to London,"
he said, pulling up a low stool to their table.

"It's been a decidedly frustrating day,"
Josie said. "Do you mind if I come straight
to the point? We'd like you to go over the
time line of Sophie's adventure with us in
more detail. For instance, how did she find
the cave on this visit to the island but not
on the earlier visits?"

"It's at the center of the island. She hadn't
got that far before."

"So she stumbles on this cave, and here's
a Celtic treasure, right at her feet?" Josie
raised her eyebrows skeptically. "Even if no
one but one priest every generation knows
this story of yours, don't you think someone
in the past thousand or so years would have
stumbled on this cauldron by now?"

"Stranger things have happened. Celtic
hoards have been found in lakes, streams
and rivers right where they were offered to
the gods hundreds and hundreds of years
ago. Farmers have come across Celtic
treasure plowing their fields. Why in 1894
and not 1794?"

Myles tipped back in his chair. "Others
could have known what you and Sophie
were up to."

O'Donovan shrugged. "We didn't go out
of our way to tell anyone, but we weren't

secretive, either."

"Were you always the one to take Sophie on her expeditions?" Josie asked.

"She tried to go on her own once and almost drowned. She's not good with boats. Everything else." His expression was warm as he added, "She and her sister both."

"Carlisle could be a killer," Josie said crisply, "or he could have hired a killer, or he could be a victim or a potential victim. We need to know what he knows. The guards are looking for him."

"So I've heard."

Josie bit back her frustration. "Tell us all you can about Sophie, won't you? Did you ever get the feeling there was anything between her and Percy? Animosity, love, friendship? Anything at all? Was she jealous of the woman he ended up marrying? Was Sophie broke and looking to Percy for money — did she ask him for a loan, a job, a recommendation?"

"You fired off all those questions at once deliberately, didn't you?" O'Donovan was obviously no one's fool. "Here's my answer to you. I trust Sophie. She's the best. She loves her work, and she's honest."

"What about her relationships in Ireland?" Josie asked.

"Men, you mean? She saw a few academics from time to time, but nothing ever worked out."

"You two?"

His eyes were unchanged. "Friends."

"What about her family? They have a house here —"

"Friends, also."

"Ah." Josie saw the look in his eyes. "What about you and Taryn, the sister —"

"You're going too far now."

"Indeed," she said.

Myles stood up. Obviously he'd heard enough. "We want to see the island for ourselves. Can you take us?"

"Tomorrow. Bring a warm jacket, and fair warning — it'll be choppy."

"Splendid," Josie muttered without enthusiasm.

The Irishman headed to the bar and joined a group of men — other fishermen from the looks of them — who'd just come in. Josie debated interrogating them, too, but Myles slung an arm around her and grinned. "Looks as if we'll be bouncing in waves tomorrow."

"I hate boats."

"We'll be fine."

She shuddered at the prospect. "You're sure we won't turn over?"

"Positive."

"Liar. You spent time on Norman Estabrook's luxurious yacht, not on what Tim O'Donovan calls a boat."

"You don't trust me, love?"

"I don't know you well enough anymore to know whether or not to trust you. Despite last night, I remain wary."

She felt hot suddenly, thinking about their lovemaking. She wasn't embarrassed so much as mystified. They'd behaved as if they were completely and utterly in love, muttering sweet things, holding each other in the dark. It'd been a long time for both of them. Perhaps they'd simply needed to make love and be done with it in order to get on with their lives.

She was aware of Myles watching her and felt quite confident his thoughts weren't remotely similar to hers. She dismissed last night and nodded to O'Donovan, who was serious, not laughing as he sat with a pint. "You know our new Irish friend is reporting everything back to Sophie, don't you?"

"Of course he is."

27

Boston, Massachusetts

Sophie locked the door to her hotel room and flopped onto her bed, lying against the pillows and staring at the moldings along the edge of the ceiling. She had met her hockey-player students. By no means was every player on the team in need of tutoring, but she looked forward to working with them. One had guessed she'd had an eventful morning and another had heard that she'd found Cliff Rafferty; they all agreed that should she need them for anything, she had only to say the word. They'd be there.

As she walked back to Charles Street, she'd heard from Tim and had reassured him that telling the Brits everything wasn't just fine but also smart. She wished he could be left out of the investigation entirely, but it was too late for that.

Meanwhile, her brother was again threatening to come up to Boston. Sophie sat up on the bed cross-legged, texting him to ask if there was anything he could do on his end to help find Percy Carlisle.

Damian's answer was immediate: Stay out of it.

She texted him back: Helen came back early. To NYC. Maybe he's in NYC?

This time he called instead of texting her. "I thought you were tutoring."

"I was. It was just a meet-and-greet. The guys are great. They can see through BS a lot quicker than I can. I always see nuances and shades of gray, complications and pitfalls. Sometimes I want to live in a black-and-white, win-lose world."

"Yeah. I know the feeling, Sophie. We could be Taryn, raked over the coals if she sneezes on stage. Get yourself some hockey tickets and go enjoy yourself. Line up those job interviews. Stay focused on what's good for you."

"Who are you advising — me or yourself?"

He laughed. "Both of us."

"Damian, based on your experience and what you might know but can't tell me — which I don't assume is very much — do you believe Percy is alive?"

"I hope so, Sophie. This morning had to be rough on you."

"I did what anyone else would have done.

If Percy's involved —"

"It's not your problem. You can come here to D.C. Just head to the airport right now and get on a plane. I have an extra room."

"You let that dog of yours sleep on the bed, don't you?"

"It's not a question of 'let,' " he said. "Take care of yourself."

After they disconnected, Sophie headed down to Morrigan's. Fiona O'Reilly had arrived with several friends, her father on a stool at the bar, watching his daughter as if he couldn't quite shake the notion that something else might happen to her — that she wasn't safe and never would be again.

Sophie climbed onto a stool next to him. O'Reilly sighed at her. "Your parents are smart. Go hiking and leave the kids on their own."

"We're adults. Taryn, Damian and me. We're not teenagers, and we weren't almost killed in a bomb blast."

"This morning —"

"I was never in danger."

"You didn't know who was in the tub. Could have been someone faking being drowned, waiting for you to rush in and save him. He could have nailed you, and we'd have been drawing a chalk line around your body instead of talking to you about human

405

sacrifice."

She ordered a Guinness. "What a way to think."

"I'm just saying. And trust me — your folks remember when you and your brother and sister were drooling little babies." He looked toward the stairs, and Sophie turned and saw Scoop heading into the bar. When she turned back to O'Reilly, he shook his head. "I don't know what happened to him in Ireland. He's still mean as hell, but he likes you."

"Lieutenant . . ."

He didn't back off. "He likes you a lot."

"You've all had a difficult few months."

"Yes, we have," the senior detective said as he stood up. He greeted Scoop. "I'm not staying. Time to pack up the lace from Keira's windows. My sister says she'll take them. I'm in the attic for the long haul. Keira called. She and Simon are renting a loft in Owen's new building on the water-front. I guess Simon's getting assigned to Boston. Great, huh, Scoop? Another FBI agent to breathe down our necks."

He thumped up the stairs.

Scoop grinned. "That's Bob in a good mood." He took his friend's place at the bar. "How are you, Sophie? How's the job hunt?"

"All my years of school and I'd make a better living pouring Guinness. It'd be a great job —"

"But it's not what you're trained to do."

"It's tough out there even for the best."

"My sources tell me you are the best and you have great prospects. In fact, you yourself said you have a decent chance at a tenure-track position here in Boston."

"I'm crying in my beer?"

"Just a little. It's understandable given the past couple days. Being back here after so much time in Ireland would be enough of a transition by itself."

"You're very understanding, Cyrus Wisdom."

His eyebrows went up. "That's a first from anyone."

"You're not afraid you're losing your edge, are you?"

"Nope."

"Good, because I've seen you in action three times now, and I wouldn't want to run into you if I had ill intentions in mind."

He laughed softly. " 'Ill intentions.' You crack me up, Dr. Malone. I'm just glad we got to Acosta before he drowned. He's not grateful. He still says he was just about to haul himself out of the water when we barged in."

"If that helps him get through this, then fine. I don't need credit. Except for whatever he ran afoul of you for, he's a good detective?"

"Not my judgment to make."

Which was all the answer she needed. "I wonder when Rafferty knew that he wasn't going to be a captain or the police commissioner or make detective."

"He would always say he didn't want to. He just wanted to get his full pension."

"And work as a security guard for the Carlisles? Do you believe that?"

"I think he wanted to retire in the sun."

"He faced that moment we all do when we decide to take action to turn the dream into reality. Work with the right people, put yourself out there, go for it, know that you might have to face rejection and disappointment and betrayal."

"Are we talking about Cliff or you?"

She suddenly was overwhelmed with emotion. "I'm going upstairs."

She moved fast, taking the stairs two at a time. She avoided even a glance at Jeremiah Rush in the lobby and was grateful she was alone on the elevator. Once she was in her room, she splashed cold water on her face and fought back tears.

There was a knock on the door. "Sophie

— it's Scoop. You okay in there?"

She opened the door, forcing herself to smile. "Sorry. Come in. I've noticed I get walloped with jet lag right about this time of the evening. It's better every day."

"Not that the quiet homecoming you've had helps."

She held up a hand. "Don't talk. Let me explain." She led him into the room, the door shutting quietly behind him. She paced on the soft rug. "I've worked hard, and I've done well — no question. I'm grateful. It wasn't an easy path."

"There are no easy paths."

"I've encountered jealousy, envy, criticism, disappointment and broken promises along the way. Who hasn't? You do your best and in the end . . ." She turned back to him. "In the end you can't base your happiness on whether you achieved all your dreams. You enjoy the journey. You let go of the disappointments and betrayals."

"You weren't just on a lark last year."

She smiled. "Always the detective." Her smile faded. "I faced a dark night of the soul. Tell me, Scoop, isn't that what you were doing in Ireland?"

"It felt like I was facing a thousand dark nights of the soul."

Her breath caught. He wasn't a talkative,

409

introspective man, but his words brought home just what he'd experienced only a few weeks ago. "You've been to hell and back, haven't you?"

"The key word is back." He brushed his knuckles along her jaw and eased his hand around the back of her neck, threading his fingers into her hair. "I can't think of anywhere I'd rather be right now, and if I had to go through hell to get here — well, then it was worth it."

He lowered his mouth to hers, slowly, as if giving her time to tell him to go back down to the bar and have a drink. She didn't. "You're why I knew I had to see the ruin on the Beara," she whispered. "I was pulled there. I knew I had to go. There was a rainbow that morning after we met. Scoop . . ."

"I can do a lot of things, sweetheart, but rainbows are above my pay grade."

She didn't have a chance to laugh before he kissed her, softly, tenderly, even as he lifted her into his arms and she could feel the tension in his muscles. She'd seen how he'd handled Acosta. She wasn't worried about him hurting himself with her. Clearly he wasn't, either. Their kiss deepened, and she wrapped her legs around his waist, sinking into him. He was aroused, hard against her. She could feel herself melting into him, hot and liquid.

He carried her to the bed and pulled back the covers. Her iPhone went flying. He laid her on her back. "I'm not very good with little buttons," he said, eyeing her blouse. "Either I rip it off or you —"

"It's an old top I found in Taryn's apartment."

He had it off in seconds, and then he took his time, touching her through the silky fabric of her bra, easing her pants over her hips with great care as he trailed kisses, his tongue, along her throat, then lower, tasting, lingering, sweetly torturing. She wasn't even aware he'd dispensed with her pants until she felt the sheets cool under her bare skin, his touch between her legs. She reached for him, traced his hardness with her fingertips. He thrust against her hand, a promise of what was to come.

"Scoop . . . I haven't . . ." She wasn't sure how to get the words out. "It's been a long time."

"Good," he whispered, easing his fingers into her, where she was hot, ready. "I'll be gentle."

She smiled. "Not too gentle."

She tore at his shirt, but he didn't budge, just moved his fingers deeper, probing, his

411

thumb circling, until she cried out and gave herself up to the sensations coursing through her. He kissed her, his tongue matching the erotic rhythm of his fingers. With his free hand, he caught her nipple between his fingertips.

"I can't last," she said between kisses.

"Then don't."

"I want to feel you inside me."

"You will," he said, driving his fingers in faster, even deeper. "Trust me, Sophie, you will."

She was gone, rocking against him, letting the waves take her. He wasted no time. He got his clothes off in short order, and he came to her, easing on top of her. She ran her palms along his hips, up his back, feeling the strong muscles, the ripples of scars. Just the touch of him against her sent a bolt of urgency through her. He must have felt it, or was past his limits. He entered her, careful at first, but she was more than ready.

In seconds, they were in unison, fused, responding, giving — knowing where and when to touch, to move — and when she came this time, it was with him, together.

Later, she propped herself up on one elbow and looked at him in the fading light. "You're an amazing man, Cyrus Wisdom, but I think it was my mud-encrusted wellies that caught your eye in Ireland."

"Must have been," he said, laughing as he took her back in his arms.

28

Sophie walked over to the Boston-Cork
folklore conference offices after a pleasant
breakfast with Scoop. They'd agreed not to
discuss anything to do with the police
investigations. They had no trouble finding
subjects of mutual interest. Afterward, she
e-mailed Wendell Sharpe and asked him
about the Carlisle Museum and anyone
Percy Sr. fired who was still in the art world
— who could, she thought but didn't say,
want revenge.

He replied immediately: Everyone fired
checks out.

She found Eileen Sullivan back in Colm
Dermott's office, staring out at the Charles
River. "I've been thinking about taking up
rowing," she said, then shifted to Sophie. "I
heard about Frank Acosta, Sophie. Even my
brother's shaken by what's happened. I
can't talk to him about it, but I believe Cliff
planted that bomb. I've been thinking a lot

about him. He was filled with entitlement and envy."

"That's a difficult place to be."

"Yes, it is. He was retiring. His wife had left him. His children didn't like being around him. He was bitter and alone." Eileen turned from the window and seemed to shake off her melancholy. "Keira and Simon will be back in Boston soon. They want to stay here. Make a home together. She thought I rejected her when I adopted a religious life. I didn't — but I hadn't chosen that life for all the right reasons."

"What kind of life do you want now?"

She smiled, a spark in her eyes now. "The one I have. I'm looking forward to going back to Ireland at Christmas with Keira and my brother and nieces. I'll go again in April for the Cork part of the conference."

"I hope all your lives will be back to normal by then." Sophie withdrew a sheet of paper from her bag and handed it to Eileen. "I brought a draft of what I want to do with the panel. I e-mailed it to Colm already."

They returned to her office and discussed the conference for a few minutes, Sophie impressed with Eileen Sullivan's knowledge and enthusiasm for her work and the topics they'd cover. She was open-minded and kind, and if she was still haunted by her encounter with a serial killer, she'd found a way to cope.

"When Keira and Simon are back," she said, "we'll have to get you together with them."

"I'd love that," Sophie said, the older woman's optimism infectious.

Tim called her on her way back down the stairs to the street. "I'm on the pier. The Brits will be here in seconds, but I wanted to tell you first. The photo you sent me of this police officer who was hanged? I just showed it to an old fisherman I know. I didn't think of it before now. He remembers seeing him."

"Last year?"

"Oh, yes. He has a great memory for faces. I don't, but I'm sure I never met him."

"Where did this fisherman see him?"

"He was on the pier asking about hiring a boat. He specifically asked about me."

"And he's sure it was Cliff Rafferty?"

"He's sure, Sophie. The Brits and the guards can check the dates Rafferty was here and see if it was the same time you had your misadventure."

"He told me he'd been to Ireland," Sophie said half to herself. "He could have been anticipating someone would remember him,

416

or look into whether he'd been to Ireland if he came under suspicion. Was anyone with him?"

"Not that my friend saw."

Sophie became aware of Frank Acosta behind her on the wide sidewalk. He eased in alongside her just as she hung up with Tim. "That Cliff," Acosta said, shaking his head. "He never could get out of his own damn way."

"You seem to be in good shape today."

"I woke up with a hell of a headache, but, yeah, I'm fine. Relax, Doc. I'm on your side." Acosta gave her a relaxed, sexy grin. "Sophie security."

She slowed her pace, unsettled at having him there with her. "I have a feeling you're on your own side."

"Which is the same as being on your side."

"Don't you have a partner?"

"Day off. I'm recuperating. It's a beautiful autumn morning." He touched her elbow. "Let's just keep walking."

"Is that an order from a police officer?"

"Nah. We're meeting your pal Scoop at the Carlisle house. I'll keep you company while we wait."

Scoop would have told her if he wanted her to meet him anywhere. "What about Helen Carlisle? Is she —"

"She's waiting for us."

Sophie slowed her pace. Her iPhone dinged, announcing a text message. It was from Damian. She saw Don't go near Helen Carlisle before Acosta took her phone. He glanced at the screen. "You don't want your FBI agent brother to worry, do you, Sophie?"

"What are you doing?"

"I'm lousy with these things. Let's see." He typed onto the screen. "N-o p-r-o-b-l-e-m. There. That'll do it. Let me hit Send and we're done." He smiled at her and tucked the iPhone into his pocket. "There. All set."

"What else did Damian say?"

"Nothing." Acosta tightened his grip on her elbow. "Come on. Helen's waiting."

"You saw my brother's warning. He's an FBI agent." Sophie's step faltered. "Detective Acosta, if Helen Carlisle isn't —"

"I didn't kill Cliff. He was a lazy son of a bitch, but we were partners." Acosta glared down at Sophie. "Helen didn't kill him, either."

"You're a dirty cop."

He laughed. "Time for a shower. I just saved your brother from a lot of fretting over nothing. Helen's not what either of you thinks." He edged in very close to her.

"Don't make me throw you in handcuffs. I thought it was you and Percy. I thought you two went after Cliff because he figured out you'd hooked up with Augustine over the missing artifacts."

"Where's Percy now?"

"Hiding. He's a chicken at heart."

"Then who killed Cliff? Who do you think hit you on the head yesterday and tried to drown you? Not me, I hope. I saved your life —"

"You could have known Scoop was coming. Maybe Percy hired someone to get rid of me. He's rich." Acosta glanced down at Sophie. "Relax, Sophie. I haven't ruled you out entirely but I don't think you were a part of it."

"I wasn't," she said. "Neither was Percy. Be smart, Detective. If Helen —"

"Enough, Doc. Let's go meet Scoop and talk to Helen. I want you to see you're wrong."

Half shoving her, half dragging her, he took her to the side entrance of the Carlisle house. "For all I know," he said, "Cliff killed himself and homicide's putting out misinformation. Maybe he committed suicide after all. He was an experienced cop. He knew how to create a suspicious crime scene. He knew Scoop was onto him for the bomb and I was onto him for the missing artifacts."

"Did you know he'd responded to the break-in at the museum seven years ago?"

"I do now."

"He and Augustine —"

Acosta didn't let her finish. "Cliff was caught and he went out the way he wanted to go out."

"He was murdered. Did you kill him yourself?" Sophie shook her head. "No. You didn't. He was scared. He knew he was in over his head."

The door to the side entrance was unlocked, slightly ajar. Acosta pushed it open. "Sorry I got rough with you. Let's go inside and figure this out."

"You're in over your head, too, Detective, and you're scared. We need to get out of here."

He shoved her into the hall. His eyes were half closed, his jaw set stubbornly, as if he knew he had to ward off anything she said that didn't agree with his version of events. "You're smart and resourceful, Dr. Malone. You're just not that experienced."

"That was you in my courtyard."

"Yep. It was me. If you'd spotted me, I'd have said I was checking out your place because of Cliff and the missing artifacts. I

420

needed to know what you were up to."

"Did you get inside my apartment?"

"You showed up first."

"You deliberately scared the hell out of me."

"If you'd caught me, I'd have said I wanted to see how you reacted. If you thought I was your partner in crime or if you'd made up the whole thing and knew you were caught. I bought just enough time to get out of there."

"You're saying you'd have talked your way out of it."

"I'm a cop. You're an expert and a witness."

"It's Helen, Detective Acosta. Rafferty figured out she's out of control and isn't going to stop." Sophie took in a breath, remembering Helen swooping out of her house in her bright-red sweater. She pictured the scene at Cliff Rafferty's apartment, in the bathroom at the museum. "She's a shape-shifter. She's transforming herself into some kind of a warrior queen. Listen to me. Whatever your dealings with her, you must understand — she's going to kill you."

Acosta didn't listen. Sophie turned to get out of there, but he grabbed her by the elbow and shoved her down the hall. "You'll see you're wrong."

"Cliff couldn't control Helen's violence," Sophie said, hoping she could get through to him. "He must have wanted to talk to me about the pieces from the cave — what she could want with them. He knew he was in big trouble the minute Jay Augustine was arrested. He asked you for the security job at the showroom to cover his trail."

"It's been a hell of a week," Acosta said.

"When did you know Rafferty stole the missing artifacts?" But he didn't answer, just yanked on her arm and shoved her into the kitchen. Her momentum took her into the counter. She winced in pain, stood up straight. "Did Rafferty plant the bomb or did you?"

He was staring past her, his face ashen. "My mistake wasn't violence or money."

Sophie followed his gaze to three skulls — just like the ones she'd seen at Rafferty's apartment — tacked to the courtyard door.

The branch of an oak tree was propped up against the woodwork, its dark green leaves dripping with what appeared to be blood.

The garden door opened, and Helen Carlisle stood there in a flowing, bright red cape. She wore a red wig, and she had a gun pointed at the two people in her kitchen.

"No," Sophie whispered next to the stunned detective. "Your mistake was Helen."

29

Off the Iveragh Peninsula, Southwest Ireland
The ride out to the island was horrifyingly bumpy. Tim O'Donovan had made a point of telling Josie that Sophie had never vomited on her trips out there. She was an archaeologist. Josie was a professional intelligence officer. Time to buck up. But she had never liked boats. Myles, of course, was now best friends with the fisherman, neither of whom seemed even to notice the waves, the salt spray or her seasickness.

Josie managed not to vomit. She did, however, slip on the wet rock and go down on her butt. Myles grinned down at her and offered her a hand. "I've my pride," she said, and bounced back to her feet. "I'm a Londoner. I don't do bloody rocks in the middle of the bloody ocean."

She went on in that vein for some time. The day was only slightly overcast, the light soft, the view to the Iveragh Peninsula with its breathtaking sweep of rugged mountains, the highest peaks in Ireland. The island itself was a bald mass of rock with grassy bits.

"In the old days," Tim said, "monasteries were built along the Irish coast."

"Yes, Seamus Harrigan's been trying to talk me into touring the old monastery on Skellig Michael. I understand it's very difficult to get to — even worse than here — and quite inhospitable."

The Irishman glanced down at her as if she were completely weak-kneed. "The monastery was in operation for over six hundred years."

"I can hold my own in difficult conditions, but if I had another choice, I can tell you that I wouldn't live on barren rock on a remote island. Do you suppose the artifacts Sophie saw in the cave were from Skellig Michael? I understand she believes they're pagan in origin, but if they're gold and of historic and cultural value — well, I suppose it doesn't matter."

Tim shrugged his big shoulders. "Anything's possible."

Myles pointed toward the center of the island. "Is that the way to the cave?"

"That's it. Sophie was careful not to disturb any breeding ground for birds and sea life."

"We'll do the same," Josie said, "and tread carefully."

They followed O'Donovan up and then down again over the gray, bleak rock. Occasionally Josie would look out at the view of the coastline and water and fight off an urge to chuck everything, phone Will in London and tell him she and Myles were going off to hike the Kerry Way and stay in quaint Irish bed-and-breakfasts and have picnics.

Except, of course, Myles was riveted to his adopted mission of finding Percy Carlisle.

In her own way, so was she, Josie thought, feeling less wobbly now that she was on firm ground again. She had a terrible feeling about Carlisle.

Tim stopped atop a ledge and pointed down to a rock formation. "Sophie's cave is there."

Josie stood next to him, refocusing on why they were on this inhospitable hunk of rock. "I could come out here every day for a thousand years and not notice it," she said.

Tim grunted next to her. "Sophie knows what to look for."

Myles jumped down to the mouth of the cave. Josie sighed and edged down to him. She wasn't as put off by tight, dark places as she was by boats. She tightened her jacket — she'd borrowed a waterproof one from the Malones — and crawled in for a peek. He followed her, and she imagined him and Will investigating caves in Afghanistan for weapons caches, terrorist plans. She did her part from a warm office in London.

"This is a lark for you," she said, letting her eyes adjust to the dim light just inside the cave, "much as it was for Sophie Malone."

"It's not a lark if she saw what she claims."

They crouched down amid the damp rock. "It's not a pleasant spot to spend the night, is it?" Josie shuddered. "I might have made up blood-soaked branches and whispers myself, and I've been through all sorts of training. Sophie's an archaeologist with a great deal of experience in the field, but still."

"This place gives me the bloody willies."

That did cut to the chase, Josie thought.

Myles turned to Tim, who had climbed down and stood at the cave's entrance two yards from them. "Where did Sophie plan to camp?"

"There's a spot of decent ground near where we landed. She had a tent, food, water — she was prepared and not at all worried."

Josie peered into the dark at the back of the cave. "Tell me, Tim," she said, "if you had gold treasure you wanted to keep out of the hands of the Vikings or whomever, would you hide it on this island?"

"If I knew about the cave," he said.

"Do you think it was a ghost or fairies?" Myles asked.

"Ireland's full of folklore."

It wasn't a direct answer, but Myles let it go.

"An archaeologist wouldn't necessarily think of this place in the same way that we do," Josie said. "To me, it's desolate, remote and inhospitable. To Sophie —"

"It's fascinating," Tim said.

They heard a sound deeper inside the cave.

A moan.

Josie glanced at Myles but saw that he'd heard it, too. At the mouth of the cave, Tim O'Donovan was silent.

Someone was back there in the dark.

30

Boston, Massachusetts

Scoop spoke briefly with Eileen Sullivan at the Boston-Cork conference offices, then walked back down to the street. He left Sophie another voice mail. "Call me as soon as you can."

He dropped his phone in his jacket pocket. He had it on Ring and Vibrate. No way would he miss her if she called him back. He'd been trying to reach her for the past twenty minutes. She'd left the conference offices fifteen minutes ago.

He'd joined forces with Bob and Abigail and pried information on the investigation out of Tom Yarborough, probably Yarborough's first tweak of protocol since he'd told his mother no at two. Cliff Rafferty had almost certainly built and planted the bomb. His trail was relatively easy to follow once they had C4 sitting on his coffee table. They knew what questions to ask. They'd found more materials in his garage and traced them to their source.

The bastard had assembled the bomb, walked into the yard of fellow officers and placed it under a gas grill, ensuring added explosive power when it went off.

"He used our trust against us," Abigail had said.

"We never saw him," Scoop had said. "None of us did. He sneaked in back with his damn bomb because he knew we'd ask questions if we saw him. It could have been anyone."

But it wasn't. It was a cop. Someone they knew.

And he'd been murdered.

Scoop walked down the street to the Carlisle house. Josie Goodwin and Myles Fletcher were checking Sophie's island, but they hadn't reported back yet. They'd be out there now, maybe even in the cave itself.

His phone rang and vibrated in his jacket. He had it out in seconds, but it wasn't Sophie. Instead it was Damian Malone, her FBI-agent brother. "Helen Carlisle took a flight from London to Boston the same day you and Sophie got back," Damian said. "She arrived a couple hours after you did. I'm checking, but I'll bet she was in Ireland

when her husband met Sophie in Kenmare."

"Then she didn't come from New York.
She told us a bald-faced lie. Why?"

"Good question. Is she on the skids with
Percy? Does she suspect he was involved
with moving stolen art with Jay Augustine?"
Damian sounded focused — and worried.
"And where's my sister? She texted me a
little while ago that there was no problem.
It was an odd message."

"I'll find her," Scoop said.

He headed into the formal front yard of
the Carlisle house and turned up the walk
to the side door. It was partially open. He
entered the elegant house, dialing Bob
O'Reilly.

"I was about to call you," Bob said. "Yarborough's on his way. He wants to talk to
Helen Carlisle about a few lies she told."

"About when she left her husband in Ireland?"

"We checked the auction house where she
worked. She turned up in June of last year.
Before that she was at a smaller auction
house — a totally different woman. Quiet,
timid. Not at all glamorous." Bob paused.
"Scoop, Helen Carlisle isn't who she says
she is."

He entered the kitchen and saw skulls and

blood-dripping branches. "Yeah, Bob," Scoop said, tightening his grip on the phone, "I can see that."

31

Helen Carlisle had transformed the large, elegant courtyard into her own notion of a sacred wood. Sophie stood next to Acosta by a potting bench. The blood dripping from the branches was definitely real. Helen had taken it from several "rodents" she'd killed, their carcasses hanging from the branches of a potted oak sapling.

In the middle of the courtyard was a giant cast-iron cauldron set on a grate over an open fire. Sophie could feel the blistering heat of the flames.

Helen kept her gun — one of Cliff Rafferty's, she'd explained — pointed at her prisoners.

Her future victims, Sophie thought. "Were you here earlier today?" she asked Acosta.

He nodded, transfixed by the frightening image Helen presented with her red wig and cape pinned at the shoulder with a gold brooch of distinctive Celtic design. His skin was gray, pasty. "I deluded myself." He slurred his words slightly, his voice barely audible. "She tried to kill me yesterday. I see that now."

"Listen to me." Sophie knew she had to pull him out of his shock and self-pity if they were to survive. "Did Helen give you anything? Tea, a glass of water —"

"Tea."

"She's drugged you. She thinks she's some kind of warrior queen or goddess. She thinks she's drawing power from you. You're a police officer. A warrior. A lover. A threat. She has wild ideas but she's not insane. She knows exactly what she's doing and what she wants."

Helen sniffed. "What are you saying, Sophie? I told Jay Augustine that you had a knack for adventure and archaeology. I told him that you had a gift and it was just a matter of time before you discovered something of value and interest. I was right." She didn't lower her weapon a fraction of an inch. "When Percy told me about you and your Irish fisherman . . . I knew."

"Rafferty and Augustine played you."

"Oh, they tried. Certainly. Cliff was an opportunist. Jay was a killer — I didn't know at first. Now I see he was sent to me as a sign that it was time I took action."

434

"You transformed yourself," Sophie said, wishing somehow she could get Helen to move closer to the flames, catch her cape on fire — fall against the bubbling cauldron.

"Jay and Cliff thought I was a mousy know-nothing who dusted artwork in one of New York's lesser auction houses. And I was, until I became the woman Percy Carlisle fell in love with." Her beautiful eyes leveled on Sophie. "I sought him out because of you."

"Because of my expertise in Celtic archaeology."

"Jay was amused by my transformation. Cliff didn't even know until after Ireland." Her tone was superior — she was enjoying telling her story. "After he and Jay did what I wanted."

Sophie kept her tone steady, unafraid. "They followed me to the island."

"Can you imagine?" Helen smiled, but she didn't lower her gun. "Percy told me about your research in Ireland and your family home in Kenmare. Everything. Cliff was stupid and lazy in many ways, but he saw you go off with your Irish fisherman. He had binoculars. He was able to follow you and figure out where you were going."

"He got lucky. If he'd followed me the first five trips out to the island, he'd have come back empty-handed."

"It wasn't luck. Those pieces were meant to find their way to me. Jay wasn't tuned in to anything except opportunities for himself, and look what it got him? He died alone in a jail cell."

"Did you know that would happen, too?"

"Yes, as a matter of fact, I did."

Acosta sank onto a bench. "Get the hell out of here," he whispered to Sophie. "Save yourself. I knew she was out of control but not this. Damn."

"If we can keep her talking —"

"No, don't. Don't, Sophie. Get out of here."

Helen glanced at him with disdain. "He'll fall asleep. He won't die from what I gave him."

"How did you kill Cliff?"

"I waited for him to get back from whining to you. I hit him on the head hard enough to knock him out. Then I hanged him. It was all planned. He had to be sacrificed. I wanted what power he had left in him."

"You'd fantasized about doing just that to someone."

"I don't fantasize." She came closer to Acosta as he fought to stay conscious. "I found myself when I delved into the study of true ancient pagan Celtic ways. I have a special insight because of my past. That's one thing that mouse I used to be gave me."

"There's nothing authentic about what you've done, Helen, or what you're doing now. It's pure, self-indulgent violence. It won't get you what you want."

"It will, Sophie."

"You think you're a destructress — that you'll gain power by creating chaos. You've intentionally adopted these beliefs to justify and rationalize your violence. Your understanding of early pagan Celtic rites and rituals is limited, as well as warped."

"*Don't you dare* tell me what I know and don't know. Jay and Cliff underestimated me. They hid the treasure from the cave — *my* treasure — from me. They never thought I'd be the buyer. Then when I married Percy . . ." She stood up straighter, taller. "When I became Mrs. Percy Carlisle, Jay understood."

"Then he went after Keira —"

"And he was arrested for murder while my treasure was sitting in his vault."

"You seduced Detective Acosta. You got Cliff to make sure he was assigned to security at the showroom." Sophie's throat was dry, but she was focused on this woman. Helen was lost in her own reality. There was

437

no reasoning with her. There was only delaying her. "He brought you the treasure."

"That's right. The cauldron you found is a source of rejuvenation and abundance," Helen said, the flames glowing in her eyes. "I will use it to consolidate my power. I have no doubts, Sophie. I have absolute certainty. Look at me. Look at what I've done. I'm a Carlisle."

"You want to be here," Sophie said softly. "You belong in this beautiful house. You love this life, Helen."

"That's right. I will give up nothing."

"If you go through with this, you'll give up Percy."

"He is going through his own transformation. He will understand. He's under my control."

Acosta passed out, sinking onto the brick courtyard.

He might have been one of her butchered squirrels for the look she gave him. "For a long time, I was weak and powerless. No one noticed me. Then I changed. Now look at me. I'm Helen Carlisle. I'm Mrs. Percy Carlisle. I'm desired by warriors like Frank Acosta."

"Cliff Rafferty wanted my opinion on what you were up to, didn't he? He was going to confess —"

"I'm the one who found his bomb-making materials and laid them out for his police friends." She kept her gun pointed at Sophie. "You could join me. Think of what you could become, Sophie."

"Not in a million years. What about Percy, Helen? What have you done with your husband?"

32

Off the Iveragh Peninsula, Southwest Ireland
Josie recognized Percy Carlisle, unshaven, filthy, one hand cuffed to a bolt drilled into the rock wall of the cave. He'd been left with blankets, water, minimal food and modest portable toilet facilities — just enough for basic subsistence, an ordeal for anyone, never mind a man accustomed to the creature comforts as he was. But he was alive.

Traumatized and exhausted, the poor man couldn't speak. His graying hair was matted to his skull, his skin pasty beneath the mud. Together, Josie and Myles got him out of the cave.

Tim O'Donovan had called the guards. He looked shaken, stunned by this development. Josie welcomed the stiff, cold, wet wind as she sat atop a boulder. "It wasn't you who left him here, was it, Tim?"

He seemed to take no offense at her question. "No, and it wasn't Sophie, either."

Myles saw to Carlisle, checking his vital signs, talking quietly with him. Finally Carlisle rallied a bit. "I came out here to make my peace."

"How did you know about the island, Percy?" Josie asked gently.

"Helen. Helen told me this was the island Sophie had explored. I remembered . . ." He paused, talking difficult for him. "I'd told Helen about what I'd heard — that Sophie was chasing a story with an Irish fisherman. I was so afraid we both had been used by Jay Augustine."

"Go on, mate," Myles said.

"I came out here at dawn. A woman was already on the island." Percy's voice was distant, hoarse. "She wore a red cape and she had long red hair. I didn't get a good look at her face, but it wasn't Sophie."

"No, it was your wife," Josie said bluntly. Of course, she thought. Helen Carlisle hadn't gone straight back to the U.S. after all.

But she could see Percy had figured that out. "I married first and then asked questions. I was stupid because such a woman took an interest in me."

Josie had it on the tip of her tongue to tell him that everyone made mistakes in love, but that was absurd. Not everyone was left handcuffed to a cave on an uninhabited island off the coast of Ireland.

His wife wanted Carlisle money and power.

"She's a shape-shifter," Percy said. "Helen. I don't even know if that's her real name."

33

Sophie was talking about magical cauldrons when Scoop entered the courtyard, staying out of sight. "You could use this cauldron for such good," she said in a gentle, professorial tone. "It could rejuvenate this house. It could replenish your energy and power. You deserve to live a life of plenty after all you've endured."

She stood next to a large cast-iron pot on a fire, herb-scented steam rising from the boiling water. Scoop had a good view of her from the edge of a trellis covered in ivy. He had his weapon drawn. Josie had texted him that she, Fletcher and Tim O'Donovan had found Percy Carlisle alive on the island.

"I am using the cauldron for good," Helen Carlisle said, just out of his sight behind a potted tree. "Sacrifices must be made. You of all people must know that, Sophie. The gods demand it. *I* demand it."

"Your cauldron, Helen? Those baubles you're wearing? Total fakes. That's no Tara brooch on your cloak. Not even close. All the pieces in your sacred wood here are garbage. Trust me. I'm the expert. I know."

"You're lying," Helen said, cool but clearly annoyed, agitated.

"I know you're not stupid or crazy. You believe what you're doing will get you what you want and deserve. You know exactly what will happen if the police catch you."

She gave a throaty laugh. "Oh, that's good, Sophie. Let me remind you that it's a police officer passed out at my feet. It's a police officer I'm going to sacrifice."

"You tried and failed to kill him yesterday."

Acosta, Scoop thought, edging closer to the cauldron. He could hear the water boiling. Acosta was out of sight, probably by the potted oak with the woman who was about to kill him. Sophie was obviously trying to save him, just as she had yesterday, this time by distracting his would-be killer. She touched her hair, one finger pointing very slightly in Scoop's direction. It was enough. She knew he was there.

"Yesterday wasn't a failure," Helen said. "It was an opportunity."

"Fire, earth, water. I get that. He surprised

you at the museum. What were you doing, drawing your own blood? Butchering a squirrel?"

"You think you're so smart, Sophie, don't you?"

"Come out and let me show you why your artifacts are fakes and you're a phony."

"Frank's ready now," Helen said. "I don't want him to feel pain. I used a drug this time, but I know how to exhaust him in other ways. We'd have sex out here in the garden when Percy was away. We'd meet in the museum — right down the hall from where he almost died yesterday. He couldn't get over my energy, my passion. You've never had that experience with a man, have you, Sophie?"

Sophie didn't rise to the bait. "Did Cliff know?"

Helen snorted. "Oh, please. He wanted me, too. He thought about having me every waking moment. You wouldn't know, of course. You've never had a man completely intoxicated with you."

"Who will you have after you've sacrificed Detective Acosta?"

"Whoever I want. I'll draw strength from Frank after he is dead. He's asleep for now." She paused, adding casually, "He'll wake up when I get him into the cauldron. You'll help me, Sophie. You have no choice."

The branches on the oak moved, and Scoop saw a flash of red — Helen, with a 9 mm pistol leveled at Sophie.

"Drop the gun," Scoop said, his weapon pointed at her.

She turned her pistol to him, and he fired.

Acosta was a mess when he came to. "Helen set up a slow death for me. She was going to roast me over a spit."

"Worse," Sophie said, pacing in front of the cauldron. She left it at that.

Scoop was more blunt and added the details she'd given him. "Helen was going to boil you, eat the meat off your bones and then drink the water."

Acosta grimaced but said nothing. Scoop sat next to him on the brick courtyard. He'd secured the scene. They weren't touching anything. The water was still bubbling in the pot a few yards away.

Without looking at either Scoop or Sophie, Acosta continued. "So here I am, looking into this bastard Augustine's business to see if he'd been into trafficking of stolen art in addition to killing people, when I run into Cliff. I get him assigned to work security at the showroom. He'd had a lousy career and his wife had left him and I figured I'd do him a good turn. He played me. It never occurred to me he was doing a little cash business with Augustine on the side. Then Helen shows up and I'm done. Head over heels. Gone."

"Did you know Rafferty was involved with the thugs who kidnapped Abigail?"

"Not in time to do anything about it. I didn't figure it out until too late. Augustine had hired them to do some work for him. That's how Estabrook hooked up with them. Cliff let his failures eat at him. He couldn't let go. All it took was those guys putting cash in his hands to place a bomb at your house."

"Any of us could have been killed. Fiona O'Reilly was an innocent teenager."

"Norman Estabrook paid a lot of money to those guys. Cliff was about cash and an island life. Me . . ." He glanced toward the potted oak trees. Sophie had explained that oaks were a sacred tree. "I was about Helen. Once she was in my life there was nothing else but her."

Scoop figured now wasn't the time to tell Acosta what a damn fool he'd been. "Following Sophie out to the island was Augustine's idea, after Helen told him about the rumors Sophie was investigating a story Tim O'Donovan had told her."

"Augustine loved scaring the hell out of her. Cliff said it was his first real clue that Augustine wasn't just an occasional thief."

"They left Sophie for dead, Frank."

Acosta cut his eyes to Sophie but addressed Scoop as he spoke. "She didn't die. She's an archaeologist. She's used to digs, rough conditions. She had the fisherman coming back for her. She got through the night."

"Rafferty told you all this?" Scoop asked.

"The afternoon before Helen killed him. I didn't see it coming. I was figuring out what to do when I heard he was dead."

"She believed Rafferty and Augustine appropriated and misused her rituals, but she was inspired to act on her violent impulses after realizing what Augustine was." Sophie was very pale now. "More of Lizzie Rush's ripple effects."

Acosta looked up at Scoop. "You should have let Helen turn me into a stew."

"When did she come into your life?"

"July. After she and Percy were married. I was under her spell. She sucked me dry. She used me."

Scoop was unsympathetic. "You knew the merry-go-round would stop one day."

"I figured I'd be in a penthouse with Helen when it did." He looked ragged, exhausted. "Warrior queen. Hell."

Bob O'Reilly and Tom Yarborough, a straight-back, fair-haired homicide detective, arrived. Abigail Browning was a split second behind them. Scoop no longer had any question about whether she was giving up the job — she was in full-blown detective mode.

Scoop knew he and Sophie had a long night ahead of them. He slipped his hand into hers. "So, Dr. Malone, what was your backup plan if I didn't show up with guns blazing?"

A touch of color returned to her cheeks. It wasn't much, but it was a start. She squeezed his hand. "I was going to take one of her blood-soaked branches and knock her on her ass with it."

"Whoa." Scoop grinned at her. "You might end up as Agent Malone yet."

But her face was pale again. "Scoop . . ."

"It'll take time, Sophie. For both of us."

34

Beara Peninsula, Southwest Ireland

Josie entered the little pub in Keira's village on the Beara Peninsula and ordered herself a Midleton, because, after all, no one had chained her to a remote island cave or tried to burn, drown or hang her. A peat fire glowed in the fireplace. A dog slept on the hearth. A hurling match was on the television. Local farmers, fishermen and laborers had gathered at tables by the window, teasing each other with the familiarity of men who'd known they'd live their entire lives in their quiet village hugging the rocky southwest Irish coast.

Not far away, people who'd lived on these shores more than a thousand years ago had fashioned a bronze cauldron, gold brooches and torcs, glass bangles and beads. Someone — they'd never know who — had slipped them into an island cave. They would be returned to the Irish. They were a national treasure. Josie supposed she might see them for herself one day, but, she had to admit, she was in no hurry.

"I'll be back in London tomorrow," she told Eddie O'Shea, the barman. "I'll enjoy my Irish whiskey tonight."

"You're ready to be home."

She smiled. "So I am."

Will and Lizzie were there. Apparently her father was in town, too. Josie looked forward to meeting the legendary Harlan Rush. Simon and Keira had already returned to Boston. Of course, she was painting again. Josie had never had a doubt that she would, and soon.

After explaining what they'd been up to in Ireland to the guards and delivering Percy Carlisle to them, she and Myles had three days together at Keira's little cottage up the lane. Josie sipped her Midleton, savoring the memories. He could have told her where he was going — she had the proper security clearances — but he hadn't.

"Ah, Eddie, she could always drink me under the table, this one could."

It was his voice, but she blamed the whiskey and the cold, dark Irish night. She couldn't possibly have conjured up Myles Fletcher onto the bar stool next to her. Maybe he'd never come to her that late-

September morning in Kenmare a week ago. Maybe she'd conjured him up then, too, and she'd searched for Percy Carlisle with an illusion and made love to a perfect figment of her imagination.

"I'll have a pint of Guinness."

Josie put down her drink and looked at the man next to her. "You look and sound just like someone I know," she told him.

He touched the rim of her glass and peered at the amber liquid. "Just how much whiskey have you had, love?"

"Not enough."

He smiled at her, his gray eyes crinkling in that way that was pure Myles Fletcher. There was no use pretending. He was there.

"If you leave me again," she said, "I'll smother you with a pillow."

"Ah, there you have it," Eddie O'Shea said, setting a pint in front of Myles. "She could do it, too."

"If you're smothering me with a pillow, love, it means you're in bed with me. I'd die a happy man."

Eddie roared with laughter, and Josie felt her cheeks warm with a blush, probably her first since she'd turned thirteen.

Myles drank some of his Guinness, but his eyes were serious now. "I'm ready for a desk, Josie."

452

She snorted. "The hell you are."

"Your boy needs a man in his life. His dad's fine, but he spends more time with you. You're too soft on him."

Josie rolled her eyes.

"He'll be a fine big brother one day. It'll be good for him, having a tot or two running after him."

That brought her up short. "Myles." Damn if she didn't have tears in her eyes. "You just wandered off again a few days ago."

"I had to know that I could do this," he said. "Now I do."

"I've always known you could."

"That's what kept me going," he whispered, brushing a finger over a tear on her cheek. "For two years, Josie, I counted on your certainty. And I knew I had your love."

"All right, then." She sniffled, collecting herself. "Shall we take our drinks by the fire and sit a while?"

He eased onto his feet. "I'll carry your drink, love." He winked at her. "In case you swoon. Wouldn't want you to spill your whiskey."

She glanced back at the barman. "Keep the number for the guards handy, Eddie. I might kill him right here in your pub."

Eddie grinned at them both. Myles set

their drinks on a small table by the fire. Josie sat close to him and took his hand into hers. All was well in her world. Not simple, she thought, but well.

35

Sophie climbed onto a rock outcropping with a three-hundred-and-sixty-degree view of the ocean. Just across the water, the jagged ridges of the Iveragh Peninsula were outlined against a stunning clear blue sky. Tim had dropped her off and was waiting just offshore in his boat.

Scoop was already there. Her life had changed, she thought. It had changed the moment Tim O'Donovan had told her his story about hidden Celtic treasure, a haunted island and priests who'd held their secret close, and she'd gone exploring.

A lark, a break from work, a way to face her fears about the future — whatever had driven her here had led her to a man she loved with all her heart and soul.

He sat on a boulder as if he didn't have a fear in the world. But she knew that wasn't true, and it was good. "Hey, Sophie," he said. "I knew it would involve an adventure to find you."

"Did Tim bring you out here?"

"Nope. I'm not coming between you two."

She frowned and thought a moment. She'd flown to Ireland two days ago to join her worried family in Kenmare and reassure them. Damian, her FBI agent rake of a brother, had met her there.

That was it. "Damian," she said. "My brother got you out here."

"Maybe it was the fairies."

She laughed. "Anything is possible." But she looked down toward the entrance to the cave. "Percy is recovering in London. He's putting his house in Boston on the market. He'll continue to serve on the museum board of trustees, but I doubt he'll ever live in Boston again."

"Have you seen him?"

She shook her head. "He would hate it that I feel bad for him. He's always assumed that I've thought he doesn't measure up to his father, but that's just his own sense of inadequacy coming through. It's unfair to make that sort of comparison. In his case, it also proved dangerous."

"Helen resented her own failings and inadequacies, at least as she perceived them."

"Why wasn't I one of Jay Augustine's victims?"

"You were."

"He didn't kill me."

"Cliff Rafferty was with him, for one thing. For another, Augustine latched on to the narrative of a mother and daughter when he heard the story about the stone angel. That's what he did. He latched on to narratives. He was obsessed with an old murder in Boston — with the devil and evil."

"What I found was pagan Celtic."

"Which he wanted purely for profit. Scaring you and leaving you for dead were a bonus."

"He was already a killer then."

"As far as we can tell, he hadn't killed anyone in several years. He needed the narrative."

"He didn't know Tim's story. He only had what Helen told him to go on. Percy was terrified he'd done something terrible, but he couldn't put the pieces together. He didn't know that Helen had chosen to embrace a way of thinking, believing and living. She romanticized and twisted bits and pieces of what she knew of Celtic history, culture and traditions — interpreted the past to rationalize her own identity and desires."

"Good analysis, Agent Malone."

She smiled suddenly. "John March and Wendell Sharpe have asked me to consult from time to time on art recovery cases."

"You can still be a professor."

"Most certainly. I have a real shot at that tenure-track position in Boston I told you about. Then there's the Boston-Cork conference in April. My hockey players."

Scoop winked at her. "Life is good."

"My brother tells me you have a new job."

"Yeah. It's what happens when you get blown up. They promote you."

"You're a man of courage and integrity, Scoop, but you're also very kind. And sexy."

"I'm not making love to you out here on these rocks."

She laughed. "My family can't wait to meet you. Taryn's taking a break from acting. Tim swept her up from the table last night in the pub and danced with her. That was it. I think she wants a different life. She's going to stay in Kenmare and see what happens."

"Keira and Simon are inviting you to their wedding. They're working out the details to get married when they're here at Christmas. Will and Lizzie will be next. Who knows with those two? They could get married in

Dublin, Boston, Las Vegas, London, Scotland. My guess is it'll be the old Rush place on the Maine coast."

"New lives getting started."

He stared out at the rugged mountains across the sparkling bay. "Bob and I figured out what to do with the triple-decker. We're busting up into the attic and adding stairs. My brothers and some of his friends from Southie are taking a look. We'll each have two floors."

"That's a lot of room."

He looked at her. "Yeah, it is. It'll have shiny new floors and white walls. Office space. Lots of light. It's close to Logan to go back and forth to Ireland."

"You like it here," she said.

"I do, but I was thinking of you."

"Scoop."

"Tim O'Donovan figures we should have an Ireland honeymoon after the Cork end of the April conference."

"He does, does he?"

"I love you, Sophie. I want to marry you."

"When did you decide this?"

"The day we met in an Irish ruin."

She smiled. "I knew it then, too. It was love at first sight." She leaned against him, felt his lips brush the top of her head. "I love you, Scoop."

A gust of wind blew in from the west, but she wasn't cold, and she realized the only whispers she heard now were those of the ocean waves.

ACKNOWLEDGMENTS

One of the great pleasures of writing *The Whisper* has been the opportunity it's given me to explore Ireland in so many different ways — through trips, books, Internet sites, music, art and friends. While in Kenmare last September, I was introduced to a thick, gorgeous book that I couldn't resist and highly recommend: *The Iveragh Peninsula: A Cultural Atlas of the Ring of Kerry*, edited by John Crowley and John Sheehan. I also read numerous books on Irish history, archaeology and the Celts, including *The Celts*, by T.G.E. Powell; *The World of the Celts*, by Simon James; *Pagan Celtic Ireland: The Enigma of the Irish Iron Age*, by Barry Raftery; *Celtic Art*, by Ruth and Vincent Megaw. My deepest appreciation goes to these scholars and their work.

Many thanks to my cousin Gregory Harrell for his insights into the work of an Internal

Affairs detective, and to my daughter, Kate Jewell, a doctoral student in history, for her help and expertise. My husband and I rushed back from Ireland to welcome her and Conor's firstborn, who decided to arrive a bit early. That very morning Joe and I had hiked a gorgeous trail on the Beara Peninsula, not far from where baby Leo's paternal great-great-grandfather was born.

Finally, a special thank you to Margaret Marbury and Adam Wilson at MIRA Books, and to Jodi Reamer at Writers House for all you do.

ABOUT THE AUTHOR

Carla Neggers is the *New York Times* bestselling author of many novels, including *The Mist, The Angel, The Widow, Cold Pursuit,* and *Cold River.* She lives with her family in New England.